THE
UNION

ALSO BY LEAH VERNON

Unashamed: Musings of a Fat, Black Muslim

THE
UNION

LEAH VERNON

Published by 47North, Seattle

www.apub.com

Amazon, the Amazon logo, and 47North are trademarks of Amazon.com, Inc., or its affiliates.

ISBN-13: 9781662500350 (paperback)
ISBN-13: 9781662500367 (digital)

Cover design by Mike Heath
Cover Image Credit: © Mark Nazh / Shutterstock

Printed in the United States of America

THE
UNION

Chapter One
SAIGE

When the automated blowing noise started from the fat clear tube hanging over the sink, my toes curled in anticipation. A soft chilled bundle fell into my palms. The morning's electrolyte-enhanced sustenance for us workers. I drank eagerly; chocolate-flavored liquid flowed down my tongue, my throat, trickled from the corners of my mouth. Before I knew it, the last few drops were gone. The pack flattened.

I resisted the urge to heave it across the room. Knowing yet another strike would form against me once they calculated the missing container. Every little thing was accounted for there.

This same dance occurred every day for Lower Residents, who resided in the overcrowded projects of the Subdivisions. Cube 771 was my personal hellhole within the Union of Civilization. It mirrored every other stale cube: four white walls with low white ceilings. An oval-shaped slumber pod in a corner. And an opening next to the can with six nude government-issued bodysuits. One for each day of required labor.

After giving the pack one more hopeful squeeze to see if just maybe anything else was left inside, I placed the empty debris under the tube. The sensor vacuumed it right from my hand. Where it all went or came from, no one knew. My stomach rumbled. Unsatisfied. I thought I'd be used to it by then. The hunger. Word on the streets was that the government was slowly lessening the rations, bit by bit, starving us before the illness took us all out for good.

I was hungry. Always. And not just for sustenance.

I'd overstayed my welcome. That was why it was time for me to go. Right over that barrier we'd built. I wouldn't last much longer as a half-breed slave to the Union anyway.

But until I could figure out a plan to escape, I was forced to work as a custodian at the Academy. A pretentious campus where all the region's future leaders were prepped to rule unjustly over those who hadn't been born rich in melanin.

I possessed some but was unlucky enough to be on the lighter end. Ma's genes were too strong. I wasn't pink or cream colored like the others, but being half–Upper Resident wasn't enough for the Union to render me anything other than a class Impure. There were three classes of Lower Residents: Domestic, Chattel, and Impure. All workers. Color determined everything: the paler you were, the worse you got it.

Existing as an Impure meant being at the bottom of the food chain. Every time I stepped outside of my cube, I was constantly reminded of how people like me weren't accepted in this world. I was reminded of how being of two worlds, merely existing, had afforded Ma only death. And for me, suffering.

As I entered the busy streets, programs began to play on holoscreen billboards, on the side of brick buildings, and on uneven pavement. The same recording played too often. Head Gardner's face and upper body were constantly plastered in my world. I could never forget her, even if I tried, after what she'd done.

"Attention, Lower Residents: Salutations. Security status is in the yellow zone due to increased amounts of rebellion activity. Please report any suspicious actions to your nearest watchmen hive. Your cooperation is greatly appreciated. And as always, long live the Union of

Civilization." Head Gardner balled her fist and held it in the air. The Union's signature salute.

Head Gardner was the Union's hero, their protector. To me, she was enemy number one.

And Ma's murderer.

Throughout every single day, I was reminded of Head Gardner giving orders to have Ma executed for hiding me, for having had a part in creating me. I used to think it would've been better if Ma had just tossed me over the side of the nearest bridgeway after I was born, like most of the other parents had who'd been burdened with Impure children. At least then she'd still be alive. Besides, I had no place in the region anyway. Never had. Never would.

I was a threat to them. All Impures were. We were too close to the Elites, the purest of blood, the ruling class above the Upper Residents, and they couldn't have that.

I arrived at the hovertram station, where workers loaded onto escalators; armed watchmen were stationed at every corner of the raised platform. Discussions that had begun on the ground level had stopped and were replaced by the hovertram's propeller blades slicing the air. *Swish. Swish. Swish. Swish.*

We were packed on the platform like microshrimp, moving forward little by little on the backs of each other's heels. I was almost to the hovertram's sliding entrance when a worker's body rammed into the back of mine. Over my shoulder, I scowled; I didn't like being touched. Especially by anyone with a dick. Watchmen were on the hunt for any minute disturbance. They were terrorists in official military gear.

Not wanting to bring attention to myself, I let it go.

The worker bumped me again, but this time he staggered, grabbed my arm, then fell to his knees. His head was parallel to the ground, and one hand concealed the lower part of his face. He wheezed, and with every exhale came a high-pitched whistle.

"Help," he exhaled.

3

"Lemme go," I grunted, barely opening my mouth.

Watchmen began shoving bodies to clear a path as workers rushed toward the entrance of the hovertram. I tried to move with the crowd, too, but the man's grip was strong. A tug-of-war ensued.

Faster than anything I'd ever seen, a ring cleared around us as if a bubble had formed. The man's shoulders shuddered as he forced his mouth to remain shut, muffling coughs. His skin and lips were chalky, under his eyes were shadows of bluish green, and his palm was hot and sticky. He looked up at me with great terror. Something I knew all too well.

A watchman shoved me while another jerked the man backward. He twisted about like a worm. The worker's fingers slipped, scraping the arm of my bodysuit and leaving welts on my wrist.

"I am not"—he gagged on coughs—"infected."

Tired of the ruckus, the watchmen injected a substance into his neck, and the struggle just stopped. They dragged his limp body away by the back of his bodysuit as if he were last evening's rubbish.

People bumped into me as I watched it all unfold. Tears weren't shed for him. No outrage. No one questioned the commotion. We didn't have the luxury of questions or choice. Life just went on as the doors on the hovertram dinged and then closed on another day in the Subdivisions.

❖ ❖ ❖

The hovertram was a series of attached bullet-shaped holds that floated over a double-railed track that led into the city's Square. Watchmen were posted everywhere, even inside the compartments. I'd noticed their increased presence as of late.

I stood in the back of the hovertram and pressed myself against the window. No seats. Just body to body. The Union didn't think we deserved even the simplest of conveniences. We moved so fast through the sky that the shiny steel structures—built by slave labor—whizzed by, becoming blurred shapes. I closed my eyes. For just a moment, I wasn't there. I was somewhere else. I was with Ma again in some imaginary safe place that could never exist.

Pleasant memories were a hot commodity these days.

When I heard the ding again, I watched a herd of workers spill through the sliding-glass doors of the hovertram. As for me, I was forced back into a dream-covered nightmare that was called the Square.

Upper Residents lounged underneath large umbrellas, sipped artisanal red teas at cafés, and chatted away on wristcoms. A suburban city much cleaner and grander than the Subdivisions. They laid out blankets for picnics on the greenest grass I'd ever seen, underneath bountiful trees, so vivid that it looked like an oil canvas in one of those ancient texts. A place where every walkway led to an open park, where joggers met up at the circular fountain and stretched their calves on benches while spliced canines with feline features caught electric boomerangs in midair. The Union loved cooking up new things in their labs. Half of the animals were experiments since most of the original species had died off with climate change.

The winters were treacherous, but the summers were very hot, humid. The atmosphere had never been the same since the industrial eras of the mid-2500s that had jacked up the glaciers and aided in global warming. The Union was supposedly still working on a global weather reset. They'd put into our heads that in order for that to happen, we'd need to have fewer people using valuable resources on Earth.

Upper Residents were the only ones who had temp regulators built inside their bodysuits; apparently, they needed them more for a full day of shopping storefronts and stuffing their faces. Many of us workers had died from heat exhaustion and freezing temperatures in the mines and on the Farmlands. Tech that could save lives or make one's life a little more bearable was only allocated to Upper Residents. Here, we were expendable. If we died, we died. On to the next.

Upper and Lower Residents blended together, seemingly in harmony. If you were visiting the Square and knew nothing about our way of life, you wouldn't have believed that anything was grim. The Union had done well at domesticating us like livestock. A quick glance at our daily commutes would have yielded no alarm. Nude bodysuits mixed in with the other colors, so diverse to the eye. But I knew the truth, the affliction beneath the trained expressions painted on the pale faces.

And there was nothing enticing about lies.

❖   ❖   ❖

Six days out of the week, we workers headed straight to the Academy's entrance lab to undergo the check-in process. Twenty-two of us between the ages of nine and nineteen stood in two straight lines facing a bulky steel door. We were to stand still and quiet until it opened. Until they were ready for us.

"Psst, Winnie," a male worker whispered.

He stood opposite her. Winnie was in front of me with her hands unnaturally straight at her sides. All I could see was the back of her head.

"It's a go," he spoke, barely moving his lips. I kept my gaze forward as he did. Who knew who was watching, looking for the smallest deviation.

She shook her head once, shivering slightly.

He said harshly, under his breath, "You got this."

I rolled my eyes. I had heard faint whispers of the rebellion spreading. How a few custodians in the Academy were planning something big. How stupid was he? Plotting right before clock-in wasn't the best strategy. In my peripheral vision, I could see the surveillance camera perched in the corner of the ceiling. A green dot pulsed steadily.

Winnie's voice shook. "I don't think I—"

"It's hidden inside the refectory's freezer unit. We've got Jamil and Oya. You got Avi."

Oya. Jamil. Avi? Avi! Damn it. Ratch me.

Two Elites. And the General's daughter. What did he mean by *got*? What had they planned on doing to them? Whatever it was, it wasn't going to end well.

The rebels wanted to make a statement. The rebellion was getting traction, but each time a group popped up, the Union came down harder and harder. Wiping out anyone in their way. And making it harsher for the rest of us, who didn't want anything to do with the fight. If they were going to go through with whatever silly plan they had mapped, I might get dragged in and go down with them. I wasn't a snitch, but now we were all guilty.

I had myself to think about.

The door finally unlocked. We moved as one into a tight space, a glorified storage room that included rows of elevated chairs. Unlike the rest of the facility, it was gray and crowded with old machinery piled on pushcarts with sharp metal edges. Counters held misshapen tubes and robotic limbs. Wires, thick and skinny, meandered on the ground, trailed along the walls, and hung from the ceiling.

Each of us settled in our assigned positions with our hands behind our backs, awaiting the Administrator's arrival.

The worker who had spoken to Winnie stood across from me, staring over my head. He had deep eye sockets and almost nonexistent lips. His auburn hair, cut unevenly, fell flat against his forehead. All the workers present were as fair as milk.

Seconds before the Administrator arrived, Winnie hacked into her hand. She grimaced at the fleshy cherry blob in her palm and quickly concealed it once she realized that a physician had noticed and had begun typing on his holopad.

Heavy boots clapped. If I hadn't already known that it was the Administrator, I would have imagined it were a stallion's massive hooves striking the ground. We were not allowed to glance in her direction until she said *at ease*. She was heavyset, about three hundred pounds, and the tallest Upper Resident female I had ever seen. Perhaps she was mixed, like me—except part giant, part human. She had a coveted body type in the region: the curvier, the bigger, the better. A well-fed body meant that one had the funds for proper nourishment, enough for overnourishment.

Her thighs rubbed together when she walked; her bodysuit fabric probably created enough friction to start a territory fire. Her skin was an even russet color. She slathered cocoa butter on herself while ordering us around: *Clean this, clean that, you are moving too slow.* As long as you stayed out of her way and did exactly what she ordered, then you were safe. I was good at staying under the radar despite being the only Impure.

She stepped in front of me and moved in uncomfortably close. I imagined her biting a chunk out of me. The thought quickly dissolved. I had never actually seen an Upper Resident partake in cannibalism, but who knew what the so-called civilized race was capable of?

"An ugly combination." She shuddered. "What in the galaxy were they thinking when they mixed bloodlines?"

She flounced away as physicians began strapping workers into their seats. One brought in a new girl, a little girl that I'd never seen before, as the chairs tilted us backward at an angle. As he strapped her in, I couldn't help but compare her whitish hair and bushy black brows to someone that I used to know. Her arms and legs were narrow, and they could have easily slipped out of the restraints. Must've been her first day on the job. I hope she learned quickly for her own sake.

A worker beside her asked the girl's name. "Eve," she said simply and laid her head back.

"The process of truth," the Administrator said, clapping once.

The process of truth was the period when machines scanned the invisible barcodes located in our irises. If the scan yielded no pain, then you knew that you hadn't committed any prior work violations. If you had, you were then electrocuted through the base of your skull, and you hoped that you would never, ever do whatever you had done again.

There was always at least one worker thrashing against the straps placed across our foreheads, chests, wrists, and ankles. That day, it was Winnie, and her day only got worse from there. When her shrieks became too unbearable for the Administrator, she ordered a physician to force quieting solution down Winnie's throat.

Silence.

"I absolutely despise these means of punishment. I truly do, indeed. Such a shame." Her lips puckered. "But for the rest of you, that is an example to never, ever be late for an important assignment. I allot more than enough time to get all of your duties completed. Now, on to the next step."

A physician with neatly sectioned locs that skimmed the tops of her shoulders parked a hovercart in the middle of the row. Physicians swarmed it like flies. They slapped on latex gloves, then began separating silver pills into individual tiny plastic cups. Mandatory supplements, they said. According to reports issued by the Health Department, Lower Residents were more likely to carry and spread infections. So, in order for us to stay safe and healthy for the region, we must take them. The pills always looked the same, but each dose had different effects. A few of them made us feel oddly euphoric. Some gave us diarrhea. Others had no effect at all. I had no clue what was in any of them. We weren't allowed to ask. Either way, there was no rejecting a dose. You either took it willingly or had your mouth pried open and were forced to swallow. This particular one was to dissolve underneath the tongue; it felt cool as it entered my stream. I was just glad that it hadn't made me nauseous or itchy like last week's doses.

"Now to the last step of our morning process: watching our beloved leader." The Administrator clasped her hands together. "General Jore."

A holoscreen played the same clip that we had seen over and over and over. I had memorized every word, every scene, every flash of light and transition, but still I didn't believe the lies, the propaganda they force-fed us.

A photo of the General and his family in the Citadel's Great Room, perched on a long deep purple couch, glided across the display. He wore a black-and-silver armored bodysuit. Next to him was his wife, dressed in a black velvet bodysuit lined in sparkly silver. Beside these Elite parents were their daughters. Jade and Avi.

Avi. Winnie's target.

Honestly, it wouldn't be a crime to rid the world of people like them. No one was innocent in this system, and especially not the Elites. Workers stared blankly at the screens while I resisted the urge to hock a fat wad while the General made a statement about the UC thriving, the UC all-powerful, the mighty UC, and more riffraff bullshit.

I held in a yawn.

The clip finally ended. The chairs lifted back into position, and our restraints were withdrawn, but we weren't done until we repeated the slogan.

Each physician was stationed between workers to make sure we said it loudly and with vigor. Not enough enthusiasm would mean electrocution the following day. We placed our right hands over the left sides of our chests. The Administrator mouthed, "Honor the Union of Civilization, which has offered us a place within their kingdom. We owe to this entity our lives and our souls, and we shall forever be indebted to their mercy. Long live the Union of Civilization."

We balled our fists and shot them into the air.

Chapter Two
AVI

I had planned for the day to be a normal one like all the others. Wake up in the lap of luxury, hold my breath while at the Academy until I could no longer take the scrutiny. I often found asylum in the lavatory, the only time I had silence and solitude. After all had transpired, I would return to my compound with a handful of watchmen guarding my every movement, only to get examined by family, staff until I'd slip away into my chambers for a restless slumber, and then do it all again, day after day, for the remaining years until I was crowned succeeding Head General, and then ultimately die.

That was what I had to look forward to. What every Elite had to look forward to.

But that particular day, there was something much more in store for me. Something that'd change my path completely.

Watchmen met Jade and me at the Citadel per usual. Three stood by the grand entrance and the other two at each door of an official armored hovervehicle.

"Morning salutations," the watchman offered like a machine. I couldn't tell if he was a droid or not.

I smiled gingerly, just as Mother constantly encouraged. Outside appearances meant everything to her. "Morning salutations."

Jade scoffed and double tapped the wireless bud in her ear as she slipped in the back seat, her long face hidden behind a straight bang that went past her thick eyebrows. She was the female version of Father: hardheaded and straight to business. Not one moment for small talk. Unlike me, she didn't care much about what people thought of her. That was one thing that I wished I possessed.

Her skin was a deep fawn color due to her getting dark pigment inoculations from the appearance-tech surgeons. She had been born much lighter in tone despite Mother choosing the darkest setting for skin options during her conception period. Every few months, she got her skin darkened because a pupil had once teased her about being mistaken for an Impure. Jade had never let that go. So she overcompensated for her light skin by being extra revolutionary.

I sank into the smooth leather as the door lowered, then sealed itself shut. I stayed close to the tinted window, and Jade remained near hers. We were always on different planes even though we were only a little bit over a year apart in age.

As the engines roared, holoscreens flickered to life. Father encouraged us to stay abreast of current Southern Region news.

It appeared that every segment they aired had been about the looming rebellion by the Lower Residents. And their clandestine Impure ringleader, Mama Seeya. How she was beginning to use darker-skinned and passing Impures to infiltrate government operations.

That morning, the news reported seventeen Impures had been successfully detained, including Mama Seeya's closest henchman, who Head Gardner had been tracking for months. They'd been found guilty of an attempted attack on one of the Health Department's main research facilities. I struggled to comprehend why the rebels were trying to destroy an organization that was created to keep everyone healthy.

The station played several clips of rebels in masks breaking laboratory equipment and slinging handmade grenades into workstations. They were rowdy and appeared hyper, perhaps even high out of their senses. I had been doing quite a bit of research for my project at the Academy, and drugs seemed to be the root of the staggering Lower Resident crime rates and aggressions. If we had stronger initiatives in place to get drugs out of the Subdivisions, then I just knew we'd win half the battle.

Head Gardner's press conference began. She had been in the media lately, displaying her usual snide and powerful persona. I didn't necessarily agree with her legislations around capital punishment, but my sister hung from her every word. Jade popped out her earbud to listen closely as Head Gardner stood at the podium. She was short and thick and very agile, a natural beauty, her long black hair in four simple cornrows cascading over her shoulders. Before she was promoted to the head of the Lower Resident Crime Prevention Division, she had been Bilcress Gardner of Gardner Subdivision. They governed the detention facilities and all the surrounding lands. Her family was one of the four Elite lines that kept the Southern Region afloat, in command.

"Let's begin," she ordered.

Only five of the seventeen criminals were present. All were on their knees with their arms secured behind their backs. She nodded to the watchmen to pull off their hoods. The crowd gasped. The camera zoomed in, slowly panning across each rebel. Their faces were covered in purple, red, and black bruises. Fresh blood still seeped from their wounds, and many of their eyes were swollen shut.

A female reporter raised a finger. "How were you able to identify the suspects if their faces were covered by masks?"

Head Gardner always had a certain expression, one that reminded me of a person who took pleasure in knowing secrets about you that could end your entire career.

"Firstly," she began, "they are no longer suspects. They have confessed to their crimes. Next."

Another person inquired, "And what about the others? Weren't there seventeen suspects total?"

She blew air through her nose forcefully. "They died trying to fight back or flee. Next."

"What about Mama Seeya? Any leads on her whereabouts?"

"This operation has been one of our most successful to date. We are the closest we've ever been to apprehending this—Impure terrorist. We are working diligently to pass the Impure Cleansing Act but have come across unpatriotic sympathizers who have never been in the field. Never witnessed how dangerous and deadly Impures are. They are irredeemable. Beyond saving. It is us or them. And we will use whatever tactics necessary to extract the exact location of the Impure who is feeding a lost-cause rebellion against not only Elites but everyday Upper Residents. I have the utmost faith that she will be taken into custody sooner rather than later, and this irritation of a rebellion will be snuffed out as fast as it began."

A journalist raised a holopad above his head. "What else do we know about this extremist, other than her being an Impure who's empowered many to fight back?"

Head Gardner ripped the tiny microphone from her chest. "No further questions."

A roar erupted as cameras flashed and hands shot into the air.

The prisoners' hoods were replaced, and they were ushered out of the conference room. The Union didn't believe in housing convicted criminals for long periods of time, reluctant to spend precious resources on people who couldn't be rehabilitated. Criminals had a week, maybe two, on the death queue, and afterward their executions by lethal injections were set and televised. No questions asked. I believed that the laws didn't have to be that way and that it was time for reform.

The reporter ended her segment with "We are certain that Head Gardner and the adjoining governments have everything under control . . . and we are not afraid of these terrorists."

I was starting to believe that it was just the opposite.

Jade gave an exaggerated sigh. "Those honks are nothing but inbreds. They don't belong here. Never have. Father should just get rid of them. Exterminate them like the cockroaches they are. The region deserves to be pure again. If I were General, that would be top priority."

"That's exactly why you'll never be General," I said, without looking at her.

Hatred festered within her. I knew it by the things she said, but I also saw something deeper. She was my kin, and despite the constant animosity between us, I knew her. My kin. My blood. Jade hated Lower Residents so much, and I didn't get why. I didn't hate them; I just didn't understand them. Why were they so bent on destroying us like they had thousands of years ago, before the Revolt? The reason for the insurgency was because of how my ancestors had been treated. How oppressive the old systems had been. No one who looked like me could ever get ahead. The Europes had made sure of that. My ancestor had led them all to a new world order where my people could finally thrive. In a war, there was always a losing side, but Father assured me—assured his people—that their basic needs were being provided for by the Union. Of course, they weren't living like us, but they got what they needed. That was more than I could say for what the Lower Residents had provided us with when the lands, the power had belonged to them. That was the way the structure worked. Who was I to question it? Who were they to go against it? We all just had to follow the rules until it was my turn to make things better.

Jade chuckled. "You don't even have the conviction to say it to my face."

I turned my eyes to meet hers. "You will never be General."

"Don't be so sure of that," she said matter-of-factly.

She was like a snake; the more I resisted, the tighter she'd constrict.

Her voice took a sinister tone. "Do you think because you're the eldest that you'll just be handed the highest position in the region?"

"I applaud your ambition. It'll surely take you far, but there's nothing you can do," I told her. "You can't stop the crowning ceremony. Everything is set."

She crossed her arms over her chest and laughed. "My ambition, you say?"

"Let it go. This will only consume you." I placed my hand on hers.

She jerked away. "If the eldest heir doesn't meet the leadership requirements, an election can and will take place." She'd been reading the political bylaws. "Ask Father. Just as he procured the position from his eldest sister, then so can I. I may be younger, but I have surpassed you in every way. You're not living up to your full potential despite Father shelling out for the region's best educators and trainers. It's disappointing how you just can't seem to catch on."

The hovervehicle landed. The door unsealed itself. The same watchmen stood guard outside.

"You don't have the heart to rule." I turned my back to her. "You're as cold as a droid and would throw the region into chaos."

Jade flew from the back seat and grabbed my wrists, pinning me against the frame. "There will come a day when I will be the one to wipe that self-righteous smirk off your face, and you and your honks will bow to me."

"Let. Me. Go," I hissed. I tried to pull away, but she was too strong.

Her grip tightened. "I'd rather be devoid of a heart than be a helpless weakling like you."

❖ ❖ ❖

I couldn't remember stumbling into the lavatory, because I was too shaken, too hyperfocused on holding in the sobs until I could reach my quiet place. I slipped into the lavatory, grateful that it was empty, and hid inside a stall. Red welts formed on my wrists. The more I stared at the marks, the more I despised Jade. I wasn't the smartest or the most outgoing, but I was kind, and that was what the region needed. Kindness. Our region was in disarray because we'd lost ourselves to power. Power wasn't what I was after, and that was the difference between Jade and me. I feared that she wasn't going to stop until she was voted General.

I wanted change.

I won't lie. Oftentimes, doubt crept in. I thought about attempting to leave. Disappearing to a place where no one could ever find me. Yes, a stupid idea, I knew it, but I wasn't sure I could keep living a life with people constantly relying on me to improve their situations and make things abundant and safe. I was often tempted to give the title to Jade and succumb to her self-imposed greatness.

The main door slid open. Someone was inside. I quickly wiped my tears and tried fanning away the redness in my eyes. A cleaning cart rolled in. I could hear a custodian disinfecting the stall beside me. Soon after, the door opened again, and in came a group of chattering pupils. I placed my ear to the cold divider. They all giggled, but from one came muffled cries. One of the pupils told someone to shut their mouth. I wasn't sure who they were bullying this time, but it wasn't an uncommon occurrence. I looped my arms through my slimpack and mustered the courage to exit the stall. I kept my head down and waved on the faucet. Liquid soap bubbles squirted into my palm.

"Get in there," one of the girls ordered as several feet scuffled about.

I worked the lather between each of my fingers, all the way up to my bruised wrists. The welts stung.

"Somebody, help me," a small voice echoed.

"I said to shut your mouth, honk!"

Over my shoulder, three female pupils in light-green bodysuits forced a custodian with long black hair to kneel. The ringleader was

Blair, Head Gardner's niece. She struck the worker in the face. "I said get in."

The milk-pale custodian noticed my presence. Her eyes were swollen. A red mark formed on her cheek. I quickly looked away. Scrubbing my palms too hard, too fast. Debating my next move. The best thing for me to do was to leave. Just not get involved. I wasn't a hero. I couldn't even protect myself from Jade.

"Please, help. Help me."

I glanced at Blair. She wore the same smug look as her aunt. It must've run in the family. She stared through me. Like I was transparent. Like she dared me to question her. The anger in my breast intensified. Just like Jade's had, the arrogance dripped from her pores.

"No one's going to help you, little honk," she told the custodian but looked directly at me.

"What have I done?" The custodian tried leaving, but the pupils were relentless and yanked her right back.

"You know exactly what your kind has done. And continues to do."

I turned away once more and rinsed the remaining soap from my fingers. In the corner, holding a suction machine, was another worker. An Impure I'd seen before. Saige. She was so quiet, so still that she almost blended in with the tile. I found myself unable to move as my extremities dripped water onto the floor. Her eyes were three different colors, brown mostly but with light-green and orange specks.

The pupils stuffed the worker's head into the bowl and flushed repeatedly, calling her a terrorist and a cockroach. As the worker gagged, the Impure continued disinfecting as if it were just any other ordinary day. I stood, frozen. Staring at the red welts on my wrists. Listening to the water swirl and swish as she choked, as they laughed.

We'd all seen that broadcast about the terrorists, but how did Blair and her friends know if the one they harassed now was one of them? They didn't. Just like Jade had attacked me, they now attacked her. Courage presented itself inside of me. Or perhaps it was rage.

Whatever it was, it all came flooding out of the gates, and I could no longer control it. Within the stall were lumps of the custodian's hair on the floor. I yanked one of the girls back by her collar and shoved both Blair and another against the walls; then I proceeded to pull the custodian's body from the silver bowl. Wet waves of the remaining hairs were pasted to her face, and her eyes were shut tight as she gasped for air. I tried to help her to her feet, but she kept slipping in the puddles.

The girls began to close in on me. The stall started to feel much tinier than it had before. The battered worker zoomed past, scrambling out the door. I backed away until I couldn't go any farther, cramped against the wall.

Blair grabbed my hair. "Rumor has it you were a honk lover. Didn't know it was true."

Saige and I locked eyes. I sensed pity before she, too, exited the lavatory, leaving me with the pack.

"You think just because you're going to become General that it means something?" Blair asked. "Remember my family is right there with yours. We make decisions, too, little Princess."

The next thing I knew, her friends locked both of my arms, and Blair grabbed a handful of my braided halo and pulled back. I screamed as hairs ripped from the roots. They forced me to my knees. I faced the bowl as the liquid thrashed.

"You are a sympathizer, so as far as I'm concerned, you *are* one of them too." Blair thrust my face into the water.

❖   ❖   ❖

The pupils only ceased their attack because an academy-wide notification alerted students that our modules were set to begin. They left me in a soaking heap. I couldn't stop crying and scrubbing my face raw with the harsh hand soap. I looked like a farmland worker on their worst of days.

When I finally exited the lavatory, the corridor was thankfully empty, devoid of light- and dark-green bodysuits. Apprehension covered me like a fog I couldn't escape. I was used to walking in a straight procession behind a group of other pupils, matching their strides like part of a herd. I still walked that line near the wall, though, vulnerable and regimented.

I had never had a chance to actually see what the Academy was like outside a session without my peers. The sun beamed through the circular panels in the ceiling, creating a light-and-dark effect along the polished floorboards. The walls held holographic prints of past and current pupils who had achieved exemplary scores or who successfully became integral leaders of the region. Each one echoed the exact image of the other: eyes fixed to the edge of the camera, trying to appear as regal as possible with outstretched necks and smirks. A Union flag, half-blue and half-red, was proudly stationed behind each pupil. The white lines and stars had been removed long ago. Father explained that those signs symbolized the division of the states and old powers that had fallen.

I held a gulp in as I punched in the code to the session. The door snapped open before the last two digits were entered.

Phoenix leaned on the edge of the opening, cloaked in a dark-green bodysuit. "Someone's in trouble," he sang.

His grin reminded me of a hyena's, and it didn't help that he always looked as though he wanted to devour me whole. His neck was long and wide; his expansive shoulders touched east and west. He sported a low Mohawk dyed a deep indigo, and the sides were short with wave designs rippling to the back. Every girl I knew was obsessed with him. Except me.

Our fathers were comrades; they had fought side by side in wars and had created an enhanced system for the Union. Commander Chi was like my second father.

"Has session already begun?" I hoped the galaxy was on my side for once.

"Yeah," he said. "If you were a prefect like me, then you'd never have to rush to session again."

He reveled in the fact that he was a prefect and never forgot to remind anyone who would listen.

"Excuse me," I said, moving to the side.

I bumped into his chest. "Relax, Princess. What's the rush? You're already late."

He leaned in. I leaned back and got a whiff of his dense cologne. It attacked the air around the both of us and threatened to render me unconscious.

"You know, you're very attractive when you're unsure."

"Pardon?" I sputtered.

Phoenix scratched the patch of hair on his chin. "You must not know . . ." His lungs contracted as he gave an exaggerated exhale.

"Kn—know what?" I asked, against intuition.

"We have a big surprise planned for you at the crowning ceremony."

"We?"

"See you later, Princess." He bowed as he drifted backward.

That word. Princess. I despised that too.

I stumbled into the session, still disoriented from Phoenix's games and his fumes. I'd never forgotten that smell. Even in his absence, I couldn't get away. I wanted to stick my head out of a window and just breathe, but none of the sessions had the option of fresh air. Instead we had a cold white room with workstations. Artificial lights from inverted sockets glowed. Bulbs shone like neon clouds against pasty plaster walls. Hints of gray metal with reflecting lenses rotated slowly over the ninety-nine other pupils and me. Below the surveillance cameras, an array of tans, chestnuts, mahoganies, and every skin tone in between lay against green bodysuits.

Pupils occupied stations surrounded by three touch panels. Mirror images from the screens flickered on monitor glasses. Pupils listened to instructions through wireless buds. I passed three rows, periodically bumping into firmly planted boots and bent knees.

Pupils rolled their eyes and scoffed until I made it to my assigned seat. Blair must've already gotten to them.

I put the slim frames on. They were clear and lightweight and used not only to record test responses but also to observe blink speeds, eye movement, and other patterns. There were rumors that the equipment had the ability to translate thoughts as well. I didn't want to believe that the instructors would intrude upon our memories, our ideas, but we were always instructed to clear our minds before any session.

On the center screen was Professor Mecca. On the side panels, video modules loaded.

"Pupil 881," she said in a clear voice. "Please confirm."

"Pupil 881 confirmed," I said.

She touched keys on her panel. An animated ticking clock appeared on the right side. It blinked red. "You are twelve minutes late for your social politics module."

"Affirmative," I responded.

"Valid excuse?" Her head tilted in annoyance.

I dropped my gaze. "I . . . I don't have one."

"Begin your module." Her face disappeared.

The module contained a lecture about the events that had led to the Revolt almost a thousand years ago. How the Union of Civilization came to power. Every Upper Resident was taught in depth about our history, starting at a young age at the Academy. The stories of our ancestors, the pride, our weaknesses, and the yearning to never go back to what we had been before kept us on top.

The world was in shambles when a global virus spread. The economy was weakened. Many immigrants left the Old States and migrated back to their original homes. All that was left was global warming, greedy Europes, and displaced Blacks and sporadic Indigenous communities.

High-level Europes had been warned about the effects of capitalism. Draining our planet. Killing and conniving for personal gain. Their gain. But they didn't listen.

My ancestors mobilized. Waged strategic wars. Overtook the government, the high-ranking and high-powered Europes. They even took out the sympathizers. The ones who thought Europes could be rehabilitated. We destroyed them from within as they had done to the rest of the world. The Elites built the Border, Browns took the northern part of the former United States, and Blacks took the South, uniting every remaining state under one power.

Back on the module, the Union of Civilization's flag danced in the wind as Father stood on a high pedestal, facing thousands of stationed watchmen. As one, they placed their hands over the left sides of their chests, then pumped their fists high, a sign of respect. A massive hovercopter rose behind him as the Union's heroic ballad played.

"For centuries, Europes were the strongest power the world had ever seen," said the professor. "Pupils, what tactics did they use to gain and maintain power?"

Every pupil raised their hand. Professor Mecca called on one boy named Jamil.

"They introduced diseases to the natives. Genocide."

"Correct," she said with a look of approval.

More palms reached toward the ceiling. Fingers wiggled like tentacles in anticipation of being chosen. She scanned the room and called on Fatwa.

"They stripped Africans of their belief systems and cultures, then introduced their own false religions to the slaves in order to control them."

Professor Mecca nodded and pointed to Blair.

"They separated families through auctions, where they were ogled at and inspected like cattle. The separation was especially effective at demolishing the slaves' familial foundation."

"All good answers, and with that said, we will segue into the discussion," the professor said.

A group of Lower Residents, their hair ranging from flat blond to curly bright red, was shown on the screen. Their eyes matched some of the colors in the rainbow. Their skins were the colors of alabaster, cream, and sand. Each wore a nude bodysuit that blended in with their hues.

"These are present-day Europe descendants. The very individuals that live in your dwellings, grow your crops, and serve your meals. Take a good look at them." She paused before starting again. "Almost a thousand years ago, we destroyed the old systems that were put in place for people rich in melanin to fail. Three generations is not that long ago, pupils. The great ancestor of General Jore led the Revolt at the end of the thirtieth century. Taking out the billionaires. The capitalists. The high-powered and the unattainable Europes that held ninety-seven percent of the wealth. They were never going to let it go, never planned on sharing the wealth, as they say, so they had to be exterminated. Sometimes, you have to be just as treacherous, even more so to win the game."

On the next slide was a black-and-white photo of a dark-skinned woman wearing a bonnet and a primitive housemaid's dress. Right below her a pale-skinned baby suckled on her breast. The pain in her eyes was indescribable. I couldn't imagine being forced to nourish my oppressor just so that their offspring could then, in turn, oppress mine.

Next, we were shown the backs of the slaves after being whipped bloody. The deep and thick vine-like gashes in their smooth skin made my stomach churn.

The last photograph was of a man's charred remains that hung from a branch that filled each screen. Even though the photo was old, one could still see the smoke winding into the sky. Europe men and women and their children surrounded the corpse. My ancestor. A few of them even grinned as if it were nothing but another day at the park.

"All of those horrible, heinous acts that they did to the natives, Africans, and even to their own could and will happen again," the professor said.

Pupils gasped. Jamil raised his hand. "How can it happen again? Doesn't the Union have them under control?"

"Have you not watched the broadcasts?" Professor Mecca's voice deepened. "The human mind is an interesting phenomenon. You can rewire and condition it however you please, but there's always a chance that a spark will ignite. And when that spark ignites, it soon becomes a blaze. Uncontrollable and wild. Right now, the Lower Residents have found their spark. We see it every day, do we not? The rebels. Their so-called revolution. This is not the end. It is only the beginning."

Blair looked around the room. "I know that I'm not speaking for myself when I say that we need to get rid of them. Every single one. It's them or us."

The session broke into collective agreements.

"Settle down now, pupils. We will talk about that soon enough. Right now, we will cover the term evaluations. Each of you was to choose an issue of the past, present, or future and create a government-based regulation. Some very interesting topics have been submitted. I'd like to hear what you've formulated," she said. "Jade, you've been working on research on the initial decline. I'd like for you to share your findings."

"My legislation is one that many of you have already been introduced to by the honorable Elites of Gardner City regarding Lower Resident population reduction." Jade sat up straighter. "I'd like to give you a bit of history first. In the beginning, one percent of Europes controlled the world's natural resources and capital. They successfully enslaved many by psychological reconditioning. Spreading ideologies of hate, capitalism, population control, and segregation by means of subliminal messaging through media and the obsolete internet. Their operation became so successful that it destroyed communities from the inside out.

"Our people stopped reading, disengaged from reality, and immersed themselves in music that degraded our skin color and promoted crime and ignorance. We were a watered-down and lost race, becoming the bottom feeders of the human chain.

"The gap between the poor and the privileged became unprecedented. Black and Brown people were murdered in cold blood by officers of the law. We were starved. Denied simple necessities such as safe neighborhoods or quality education. Access to health care and medicine dwindled. Pharmaceutical companies inflated prices of meds by four hundred and fifty-six percent. Money for the indigent had been drained. The government saw no use for us after they'd stripped us of our wealth, resources, and cultures. And it was all legal under the political parties. As mortality rates grew, the majority grew tired and unruly. They collaborated like never before, placing differences aside for one cause. To take down the autocratic government.

"I believe that it is never too early to start to get involved, to start revolutionary acts. All of us in this room are being prepped to take over high positions, and that is not a responsibility I take lightly. It is our duty to carry on what our forefathers have created. It is our duty to uphold our morals, our power for the generations to come. We cannot succeed with Europes and Impures running amok. They must be taken care of."

"Gratitude, Jade." Professor Mecca nodded in her direction. "In order to destroy or control, one must know the mechanics of their opponent, their motivations. What drives them to reach a specific goal. You must understand their psychological makeup. What are some of the Europes' stimuli?"

"Currency."

"Natural resources."

"Land."

"All good answers." She continued, "The issue that we are facing is with Lower Resident sympathizers. They believe that we can coexist. Equally. History has proven otherwise, yet there are people that will compare what we have done to what the Europes have done, but that is simply not the case."

I flinched when she called my name.

"Avi." She crossed her arms over her chest. "Why don't you share with the session your project?"

She didn't seem as enthused as she was about Jade's, but I was bound to come across naysayers like her, so it was practice.

"I'm working on an equality doctrine," I murmured.

She squinted. "Speak up so everyone can hear."

I planted my feet squarely on the ground and filled my chest with stale air. The room was so quiet that I could've sworn I heard my own fear boiling. "I'm working on an equality doctrine. One that will combat the Union's complications with race relations."

Pupils began to snicker, whispers traveling around the room.

"Silence," Professor Mecca growled. "Continue."

My voice shook. "I—I believe that we should tackle the drug peddling and high crime rates with better incentives within the Lower Resident communities. I don't have a full plan yet, but I'm researching different methods. Of course, there are no guarantees that it will work immediately, but it's a start. A new beginning for us all."

"She *is* a honk lover," a boy whispered to another pupil.

Jamil said, "After all they've done, you want to *help* them?"

Professor Mecca's face was devoid of emotion, but the muscles around her lips were taut. "Are you saying that the regulations that are currently in place are erroneous?"

I frowned. "I wouldn't necessarily use that word, but—"

She slammed her palm on the desk. The boom echoed through my earbud. "How dare you insinuate that our forefathers made an error?

That your own father, your grandmother, and her mother, and the rest of the cabinet are wrong in their decisions over this region?"

"Professor, I—"

"Another word and I will have you expelled," she warned. "That kind of talk is considered treason, Elite Jore."

Moments passed, and she began typing aggressively. On my screen, a message icon appeared. Inside was a citation: miscellaneous offense / session disruption.

"I challenge any one of you to dispute our methods," she screamed through the monitors.

Pupils looked at each other, but no one spoke. If a pupil had shared the same sentiments as I had, they surely wouldn't have spoken up about it after her outburst. I was shaken but not surprised by her anger.

"Surely we are nothing like them. We are not equal. Our genetic makeup has been tested, and the region's top scientists and physicians have proven the differences. We are mentally stable and intuitive. Everything that Europes have ever had, they stole from us!"

The professor breathed in hard through her nostrils and out forcefully through her mouth. "All Lower Residents were meant to be eradicated once the takeover was successful. Our people were disgusted by their crimes against humanity. Unfortunately, the United States had been destroyed: buildings were burned, bridges demolished, crops ruined. An executive order was made to maintain a small percentage of Lower Residents to work and rebuild. After an appointed time, the remaining were to be eliminated."

Old footage appeared of the aftermath of the Revolt. People had been slaughtered. Half-blistered faces with blackened teeth and bloated bodies floated in murky waters. Flies buzzed around the carcasses. I choked trying to hold back the burn that rose in my throat. I blinked rapidly as the professor's face materialized on my screen again. Perhaps her glasses had alerted her to an abnormality in my response data.

"Complete the examination in its entirety," she said. "Do you accept these terms?"

The hotness in my throat still wouldn't go away. I predicted my nutrition erupting like blood from a severed vein, liquid lumps splattering on the perfect, uncontaminated granite. Something inside my stomach wanted out. I wasn't sure how much more I could take without cracking completely open.

"Affirmative," I mumbled.

A translucent keyboard appeared below the screen. With shaky fingers, I was able to input my answers. My underarms prickled like tiny people were poking forks in my skin. My bodysuit felt way too restrictive. I could've sworn I was sweating, but I couldn't check or scratch. The Academy was watching all the time, like some malevolent deity. I had to maintain composure, show no signs of distress. Certain traits were associated with weakness. I was a future leader, and if I couldn't compose myself for an examination, I never would under duress.

I'd been through the testing process numerous times, but I still floundered. All the questions turned into a cluster of jumbled and indistinct symbols.

The clock winked red, a five-minute warning.

On question seventy, everything went dark. The answer blanks were gone, and so was my chance for an acceptable percentage. I tore the glasses off and massaged my eyes.

A notification rang, and doors slid open. I joined the line. We moved through the corridors in unison. I made it to my next destination on time and uniformly, like a watchman.

Chapter Three
SAIGE

·

My daily duties consisted of sanitizing the Academy, wherever it was needed, and sometimes the Archives. I was particularly interested in the physical books in the ancient section because Lower Residents could never access texts through the Net without an alert, followed by the usual severe punishment. I swept the duster across each binding, one by one. I had become familiar with these titles. I was one of the few Lower Residents who could read.

On the Outskirts, Mama Seeya had educated me, taught me how to survive, when Ma was taken away from me. I was lucky to have semiescaped from the complete reconditioning of Lower Resident adolescents. Syllables were strange and forbidden signs to most of them. To me, they meant freedom. Knowledge was better than a full stomach. And my key to escape.

I had been free once. Just for a little while until I—*we*—were recaptured. And I planned on being free again.

Every day since, I had dedicated myself to figuring out how to pay my debts, buy my freedom, and never turn back. I even resorted to dealing Glitter and dancing for an underground drug lord named Silver to speed up the process. When my debts were paid, he'd release me, give me the information I needed to flee the region. I didn't have much longer to peddle the remaining goods. I understood criminals and never placed my trust in men, so I knew there was a chance that he was just stringing me along. I needed a backup plan. So I snuck and read texts, looking for that very information he held over my head.

Thousands of days might have seemed like enough time to commit to the cause, but in reality, I had only moments to research before a pupil came trudging along, a surveillance camera panned to the left, or I was beckoned to another monotonous custodial task by the archivist.

No helpful information had turned up yet about any gaps in the Border that led out into the Northern Region, the one no one seemed to know much about. I was starting to think a real way out was a myth.

Back to the task at hand. Farther along the shelf, I noticed a text that I hadn't seen before. I had already taken a chance reading right before afternoon nourishment. Could I spare another few minutes? I had been doing it for so long, and besides, pupils hardly ever visited the ancient-book sections. Data in bindings was obsolete.

How was I supposed to know that I'd get caught?

Placed within a sea of others in gold print was a hardback titled *Maps and Sectors*. Someone had to have requested it. I had to read it. Time was running out. The archivist was a creature of habit. She was preoccupied with her usual duties. I looked to the right, then to the left, and at the monitor at the end of the row. A green light. A disturbance-free area. I dusted the shelf once more. My heart banged against my chest as I anticipated learning the information that I needed.

I placed my index finger on the edge of the book and tipped it over, made it look like an accident. The pages flapped to the ground like a bird shot from the sky. I flinched as it thudded near the tip of my work boot. Had anyone else heard? Risky, yes, but it'd bought me precious time. Seconds felt like hours. I got down, and my fingers scrambled through the index. *The Border, the Border*, I searched, moving down the list of areas located within the Southern Region, which covered the lower half of the old United States.

I hadn't even gotten a chance to locate the map before a flash of light nearly blinded me. Everything became still. The duster was still in my hand, so I swept it over the pages to create some sort of half-assed alibi. I rose from the ground and returned the text to its original spot.

Avi stood in front of me. She had a slender frame like a prepubescent male. Her silky skin was the same color as toffee, and her irises, black as her pupils, contrasted sharply against the whites of her eyes. Her stance was rigid and straight in an emerald bodysuit. Deep dimples met in the creases of her cheeks despite the lack of a smile. A disheveled braided halo sat on top of her head like a tiara.

Workers were taught to never speak first, so I lowered my gaze.

Her wristcom's light flared again, but this time at close range. Black dots floated in my vision. She had to be gathering more evidence against me. That way there would be no dispute of my guilt during an inevitable one-sided sentencing. Head Gardner would be pleased.

Avi reached out and lifted my jaw. I wanted to pull away, but instead, I looked down at her. She was a few inches shorter than me. The tepidness she had displayed before vanished. Her supple expression hardened—mostly in her forehead—as she studied me like some sort of specimen. Her head tilted as her fingers trailed across my cheek, then slowly slipped away.

"I saw you earlier," she said. "In the lavatory."

I nodded indifferently. I thought I'd be much more afraid of being discovered, but I wouldn't give someone like her the satisfaction of seeing me sweat.

"Hmm." She sounded disappointed. "I apologize that you had to witness such atrocities."

Silence.

"Speak freely," she commanded.

"I've seen worse."

An uncomfortable pause, then she said, "I've read about your kind. Very rare in the region. A mixture of the two. A unique combination."

The comment was much warmer than the one the Administrator had given during check-in.

"May I?" She lifted her wrist and took another still before I could respond. "It's a hobby of mine to capture candids of interesting things that I see. I don't see a lot of interesting things."

A notification appeared on her wristcom. A summons back to session. Avi sighed and slid the text from the shelf. Proof of my disobedience. "What were you reading?"

"I can't read." I might have said that too quickly to be believable.

She circled me with intent, glossing over the pages, then slammed the book shut. "It seems as though you are questioning my intelligence. I can tell if someone is reading. And you were, in fact, reading."

Avi handed the book to me, but I wouldn't take it. I couldn't talk my way out of it. It was over. I couldn't even get a word out—the stutters got caught in my throat as I imagined all the ways that I'd be punished. They'd take my eyes or maybe my tongue or just execute me altogether for the violation. Reading was top of the violation list, and I had crossed the damned line. I noticed the cameras panning as my temperature rose, my stomach tossed around acid. The archivist narrowed her eyes over the rim of her spectacles at the disturbance as Avi relentlessly tried forcing the book into my arms.

"Elite Jore, do you need assistance?" The archivist stepped from behind her booth.

"I'm fine." Avi's brows creased.

Why was she doing this? Was she trying to make up for her people's wrongdoings? It was a little too late for that.

It was like she read my mind. "We aren't all the same, you know. Some of us are different. Or at least trying to be."

Without thinking, I blurted out, "You are *all* the same."

Her eyes drooped a bit on the sides and became glossy. I could tell that that comment had cut her deeply.

"I probably deserved that," she said, backing away.

The archivist's piercing scream cut through the rows.

Avi whipped around and covered her mouth.

Winnie appeared. Gun in hand. Deranged but with a fierceness I'd never seen from her before. She pointed the barrel at the archivist.

"On your knees," Winnie ordered, wiping quiet tears from her cheek.

The woman pleaded, but a second later a beam of light went through her forehead. Her body dropped. Then Winnie made her way over to us. Gun pointed.

The surveillance camera zoomed in—two workers sandwiching an Elite.

Its light went from green to red. Sirens.

Winnie had seemed out of it before, but the blaring woke her. She jabbed Avi with the barrel. "Make them turn it off."

Avi stepped back, bumping into the bookshelf. "I—I can't."

"These sounds are hurting inside my head." Winnie pounded her temple.

I tried moving back too. This wasn't my fight.

"Get over there," she ordered us. The muscle above her upper lip jumped.

I didn't remember us raising our hands, but they stayed exactly where they were. Winnie alternated between sobs and mumbling. She placed the barrel between Avi's eyes this time.

"Please don't," Avi said.

"Please don't what?" Winnie enunciated every syllable. "I am dying because of you. You are killing us. Have killed us! If I could torture you before this, I would."

If she killed Avi, then I was surely next—by her hands or the Union's.

"You will never get out of this alive," I explained. "You won't get away with offing an Elite. Killing one isn't going to be enough to stop the system. You know that, right?"

"We aren't killing just one. We're taking all of them out. Like they did us. It's the only way to salvation, redemption. My duty. To God." She pointed the gun back at me, hacking phlegm just like the others. "I'm as good as dead anyway, but at least I can rid the world of people like her."

It was over for Winnie, but there was still a chance for me to redeem myself in some way. Maybe if I could talk her down, then Avi would put the whole reading situation behind her. Saving her life might mean something. It didn't make sense for both of us to get taken out of the game. Winnie had chosen her path.

There had to be audio somewhere around, so I put on an entire show. I reached out to Winnie carefully. "This isn't the way. She's just a girl like us. It's not her fault that she was born an Elite. Give me the gun before you get us all in trouble."

She put the gun to Avi's forehead again but spoke to me. "If you aren't with us, then you are against us. And you're next, traitor."

I lunged, shoving the gun to the side. She shot wildly into the shelves. Lasers ricocheted off the book spines and through wooden panels. One went into the ceiling as we tussled for control. She elbowed me in the chin, and I headbutted her until she stumbled and fell to her knees.

Her teeth were covered in red as she spat out a blob of blood.

I was able to rip the gun from her grip. I moved in closer and kept it trained on her.

"Just do it already!" She put the gun to her own face as I held on to it. "You and I both know what they're going to do to me. I'm dead anyway. Kill me, and then kill her before they come. I am begging you, sister. It's the only—"

A laser swiftly whizzed through the air and traveled right through her skull. Part of her head exploded. Then I felt the sting of that same laser pierce the upper part of my arm. Her matter dripped from my face, then her body thudded to the ground. Watchmen swarmed the row, guns drawn.

Neon-colored dots covered my torso like thorns on a cactus. The gun slid from my grip.

Gloved hands grabbed my arms and neck, yanking me every which way. Watchmen restrained me while physicians tended to

Avi. Guns stayed on Winnie's mangled corpse as if it'd return from death.

One of the watchmen drove his fist into my diaphragm. From behind, another pulled my hair until I straightened. Every word was shouted. "You think you can target the innocent?"

Before I could let them know that I was one of the innocents, he struck me across the face with the back of his hand. My head dangled. Red dripped from my mouth and onto the man's boot, *clip, clop*, like deliberate raindrops. Was it my blood or Winnie's?

I collapsed, and even then, I was kicked until I curled into a ball.

"Stop," Avi screeched.

The beating paused. The tinge of hatred in the watchman's voice disappeared as he addressed her. "This worker attempted to kill you."

They lifted me, pulling my arms so hard that I thought they'd rip right from the sockets.

"She saved me."

He shook his head. "Nothing to worry about, Elite Jore. A thorough investigation will ensue. You are safe. In the meantime, she will be in the Administrator's custody."

❖ ❖ ❖

As watchmen dragged me along the corridors, my chest stung with every inhale, every exhale. Hell, it even hurt to hold my breath. Those military boots to the chest must've done the trick.

We came upon a tall door with bold black letters: THE ADMINISTRATOR. A lens zoomed in on the watchman's eye, and the door slid open. I had never been inside her office, nor had I ever wanted to. I was thrust inside.

I had always imagined her space to be dim, off-putting, but it was the opposite with high ceilings and rectangular windows that overlooked the Quarter. Above a clear desk was a red crystal chandelier. Jazz played softly in the background. The room smelled like cocoa butter and jasmine.

The Administrator's mouth was stiff as she played the surveillance video of Winnie moments before she'd entered the Archives and blown away the archivist. The Administrator's shoulders slumped, and for a moment, I thought she'd begin sobbing. "What do you know about worker number 9934?"

"I don't know her at all, Administrator."

She clasped her hands over her massive chest. "You conspired to carry out this assassination. Terrorism!"

I shook my head. "I have not—"

"You all had planned on murdering—" She bit into her knuckle. "We have never had such a radical threat at this facility in all the decades since the inception of this great, great union. Ever! The General has entrusted me with the lives of thousands of pupils. So how is it that a group of cockroaches steals weaponry and inflicts havoc upon our peaceful society?"

"I didn't steal any weapons."

"Why should I believe you?" she hollered. "You think you are cleverer than us. Yes? I know that you people have had it out for us ever since the beginning of time. Any opportunity that arose for you to destroy us, you would take it."

"Administrator, I—I'm appreciative of the Union." I couldn't even look at her straight as I lied through my teeth.

"You plotted and you murdered. That's exactly what you did." She glared. "I should gut you right where you sit."

"I thought murder was something that the Union celebrated," I said.

The Administrator howled. If her eyes had been lasers, I'd have been full of holes. "You assassins killed innocent people!"

I couldn't believe it. The rebels had actually done it.

"I know exactly what happened," she said. "You had our beloved Elites right where you wanted them, you notified your partners, and then they were to . . ." She made a slicing motion at her throat.

I shook my head. "Ask the pupil—"

She stormed from her chair and hovered over me. I hadn't known she could move so fast. "You don't tell me how to run an investigation, you honk half-breed. Lives have been lost. The damage incomprehensible."

The Administrator tore away and peered through the window over the city. "You have made such a mess for me, my staff. News of this breach will travel far and wide, casting doubt on my ability to run a tight ship."

"Administrator, I had nothing to do—"

"Enough of the games." She sashayed to her seat and gestured to the watchmen. "I want the Academy on lockdown until further instruction. Take every single worker that was on shift today and execute them at once. I have a mess to clean up."

❖　❖　❖

A thick, rough hood was flung over my head and my arms cuffed tightly behind my back. They gagged me too. I was thrown into a hold in some kind of large hovertranscraft with several other workers. I wasn't sure how many, but I could hear bodies being tossed in beside me, moaning and crying through their muzzles. My vision was blackened. I sat cross legged as the craft lifted into the sky and zoomed to our execution. Droplets rolled along my face—I wasn't sure if they were tears or sweat. I hoped they weren't tears. I was better than that.

The craft landed with a soft thump. Anytime I heard a movement, my heart beat faster against my chest. Each time, I thought that was it, but no one ever came to retrieve us. So there we sat for hours on end as the temperature rose. Maybe that was our execution, death by asphyxiation.

A pair of restraints clinked against the metal. The muffled moans stopped as we all listened a little harder. Small footsteps carefully walked across the hold. One, two, three, four, five. Then the sound stopped.

"Shhh," a voice hushed.

What the hell was going on?

The strides started again. One, two, three. Dainty hands grabbed the base of my hood and lifted it over my head. My eyes bulged from the sockets and then focused on Eve's face. She removed my mouth restraint, placed her finger to her lips, then pointed at a man with a greasy-looking beard sitting beside me.

"Name?" his voice was barely audible.

"Saige."

"Joe," the man replied. "I have a plan."

I scoffed. "We aren't getting out."

"Lower your voice." His voice intensified, then got quieter again. "I made an oath to Eve's father on her first day on duty that I'd keep her away from harm. We do not have an option."

I laid my chin on my chest and exhaled, wondering if I had any fight left in me. The girl watched me harder with those blue eyes.

"They are waiting for something. If they weren't, they would've executed us already," Joe whispered. "You in?"

I nodded. What did I have to lose?

"Good," he said. "The rest of you nod if you are ready to fight."

The other hooded heads nodded, able to hear but not speak.

Eve replaced my mouth guard and carefully slipped me back into darkness.

Joe said, "I don't know what's waiting for us out there, but we've got to get out of these restraints. Someone, anyone will have to create a disturbance. They are prideful people. Get under their skin. Eve can pickpocket."

We were banking on a little girl's pickpocketing skills.

"She can get us the keywand. After that, every person for themselves."

We were as good as dead.

❖ ❖ ❖

Chaos ensued as watchmen began banging on the sides of the craft. They barked and howled like wild dogs before bursting into the hold and grabbing any limb they could.

"It's judgment day," one of them announced.

My breathing intensified as I inhaled my own stale breath. The thick fabric of the hood kept getting caught in my mouth, in my nostrils. I was hyperventilating as I was shoved along by a heavy-handed watchman. I was going to suffocate myself if I didn't get a grip. I never thought I'd be so afraid to die. Or maybe I was afraid of the unknown of surviving. If I survived. I had prided myself on being one step ahead, memorizing the steps before the steps came, and now I was just floating. There were only two options, yet the path was a blur. I could have death or freedom. Either way, I came to the conclusion that I didn't want to go out like this.

"Move forward, mutt," a watchman ordered, shoving me forward.

He snatched the sack off, and I knew exactly where we were. Subdivision Eighteen. Far away from the Square. Remote. A shoddy part of the city where the Union had given up on trying to regulate because the crime was just so rampant. We were in a place where people went but never returned. I should've known they wouldn't want to get their own backyards dirty with our blood.

He ripped the muzzle off, jammed my face into the wires of a metal fence, and searched me.

"Piss off," I said through gritted teeth.

He snorted. "Now, you wouldn't have anything on you that I need to know about, would you?" He checked the front of my body too slowly, sliding his fingers along my chest. I could feel his hot breath on my neck.

His hands glided over my breasts as he pushed in closer from behind. I pinched my eyes tight to keep the tears in. I was stronger than that.

His hands traveled along my torso, then grabbed my hips and shoved them back into a bulge.

"Hunt," another watchman called out. His nameplate read Broderick.

"What?" Hunt flipped me around. "Just making sure that the prisoners are weapon-free."

"We have strict orders," he reminded him.

Hunt dug his fingers into my curls and took a whiff.

I wanted to hurt him. Badly.

Reaching farther toward my scalp, he removed beads of Glitter from my hiding spots. In between the wild curls were cornrows where I'd smuggle the beads, then return them to the vials once I was in the clear. On any other day, I would've been scared shitless, but I had already been sentenced to death for a crime I hadn't committed, so what was another offense added to the list?

"What do we have here?" he said, examining the drugs. "I knew you looked familiar. You must be one of Silver's girls, yeah?"

"I am no one's girl."

"This says otherwise." Hunt dangled the Glitter in my face. "You're just a trick. A warm body like the rest."

"You don't know anything about me."

"That's what all the orphan drug dealers say."

His hands came at me again.

"If you touch me—" I hissed.

"You'll do what exactly?"

I gathered as much saliva as I could and spat in his face. "Ratch you."

Hunt's fist connected with my stomach. Before I collapsed, he gripped my cheeks. "Look into the light. Don't blink."

My eyes widened as the blue beam of the Identitech scanned my irises. I'd only ever seen watchmen use it before executions. Maybe it was to keep track of their murders.

"Take her to the others," Broderick said. "It's time."

Dozens of workers were rounded like cattle and forced onto their knees into staggered execution lines. There were people there that I hadn't even seen before. They were probably assigned to different wings of the Academy. Although there were workers of all ages, a lot of them looked younger than me. And most of them probably weren't involved in the rebellion. Just innocent kids in the wrong place at the wrong time.

Pebbles dug into the skin of my kneecaps as I clawed at the restraints. Watchmen stalked along the rows, scanning more workers in.

A voice at the end of Broderick's wristcom gave the confirmation. "It's clear."

The man next to Joe got up from his knees and stood with his chest out. Two other workers followed suit. Watchmen used the butts of their weapons to make them get back on their knees.

More workers stood taller. Joe looked to Eve and nodded once.

The plan was in motion.

Hunt got tired of beating the first man and removed his gag. "Tell them to stop resisting."

The bloodied man spat out a tooth. "The brotherhood will prevail."

Hunt grabbed the man's collar and flung him about like a wet rag. "What'd you say?"

"God is in control. The brotherhood will prevail."

"There is no brotherhood among you honks," Hunt said. "Fuckin' morons."

The man's neck extended. "God. Is. In. Control."

Hunt began mercilessly beating the man's head. Blood coated his fist as he delivered blow after blow. Workers turned away as he bashed. Watchmen piled in, trying to subdue the others who wouldn't get back on their knees, becoming a heap of legs and fists. I watched Eve closely. Wondering when she was going to slip from her restraints again and grab the keywand, but instead she pinched her eyes tight, until they became red, and the keywand slinked from Hunt's pocket and straight into her palm.

I blinked the sweat from my eyes, so much that they stung. What the hell had just happened?

"Get back in line." Broderick fired a shot into a female worker's leg. "That's an order."

The watchmen gained control as Eve passed the keywand to the person kneeling beside her.

Broderick got on one knee and wiped his forehead, smearing red right above his brow. "Lower Residents are not allowed to congregate for reasons other than work-related activities and authorized leisure time, so this brotherhood is an illegal gathering, yes?"

Every worker nodded vigorously.

"I'm glad you all agree," he continued, holstering his weapon and drawing a knife. "And most importantly, there is no God. Why? Because the Union said so. And you of all creatures should know that by now. That no one—up there—is going to deliver you. Save you. There's only down here. In our domain. We are the judges. The executioners."

Broderick lifted the man's swollen face to meet his knife. "I want you to look into my perfect Black face and to comprehend every word that flows from my mouth. There is no one on this planet who is going to save you. Not now, not ever. And right now, frankly, I am your God."

He grabbed the back of the man's head and slowly jammed the knife into his throat, twisting. The man choked as Broderick carefully laid him back down to drown.

He wiped the blade clean on the man's bodysuit as the worker gargled red liquid. "I am the giver and taker of life, as you can see."

Broderick turned his attention to Eve, pointing at her with the tip of the knife. "Grab her."

Hunt grabbed her by the hair. Joe slid on his knees toward her, but Broderick pulled out his gun. "Uh-uh. Stay."

Joe pleaded with snuffles.

"You've all been sentenced to death for partaking in the assassination of Elites, so without further ado." Broderick nodded. The watchman started at the farthest end of the line and shot a worker in the head. *Thud.* I kept my eye on the worker next to Joe, who was trying to release himself. Another bang. A body dropped. The watchman's boots slid over the gravel to the next. Then the next.

Come on, come on, come on. My hands trembled against the metal. *Bang.* Again.

Finally, Joe was able to get the keywand from the worker beside him and unlocked himself.

Bang. Thud. Another. He handed it to a woman beside him, who then unlocked her cuffs and then passed the keywand to me. My fingers fumbled. Trying to make the apparatus wave over the lock was almost impossible to do without seeing where the release bar was. The lock finally clicked, and the cuffs released. I lost count of how many more bodies dropped. *Thud. Thud.* Hunt shouted as Broderick unloaded his weapon.

Joe lunged at Hunt, who still hung tightly on to Eve.

Eve bit the watchman in the finger. His blood trickled from her top lip. Joe tussled with him for control of the gun. Stray shots were fired in the air as they fought. Joe struck him in the face. Hunt fell backward. Joe gained control of the watchman's weapon and fired a shot into his leg.

All I heard were my own ragged breaths as adrenaline pulsed through my veins. Joe shot at the remaining watchmen and was able to retrieve more weapons for the workers who hadn't fled. Outnumbered, the remaining watchmen, except Hunt, retreated. Others were too injured to flee, while a few still shot back at workers from behind dumpsters. Bodies both Black and pale lay in mangled heaps everywhere. I nestled the hook of the restraint in my fist and charged Hunt when he was wrestling with another worker.

I used the sharp latch of the shackle to slice his perfect face. It glided along his brow to his chin, ripping his dark flesh to expose pink and red. The shrieks that came from him didn't sound human.

Eve stayed in my peripheral vision as anarchy erupted around her. Never once did she cry or scream or run for cover. She just stood there, looking like what I'd have imagined an angel to look like, a very small angel with dirt and red smudged on her face. Unfortunately, like the Union, I didn't believe in angels. Ma had, though. She said they protected you. Like some sort of guardian. I always wondered where my guardian was, I had never felt protected by anyone or anything—except violence.

Hunt pulled out a knife. One last sad attempt. "Y—you can't hurt me."

"How so?" I humored him.

"I already scanned you in the Identitech."

"So?"

"If I don't bring your corpse in, they'll come after you." He wiped red tears from his good eye. "You won't last twenty-four hours, mutt."

"Look away, sweetheart," I heard Joe say to Eve.

He put a laser blast through Hunt's ear from several feet away. He then finished off each watchman that lay on the ground. He wiped the hilt of the weapon, then tossed it aside. "Thank you," he said to me.

"You two should get out of here."

I patted Hunt's corpse down to retrieve what he'd stolen, but the beads of Glitter were crushed. I grunted. "Fuck!"

A small hand touched mine, and I almost leaped out of my skin; I didn't like being touched.

Eve jerked back and stared at her scuffed black work boots. "Gratitude."

I sucked my teeth. I didn't know how to respond, so I just nodded. I wasn't a hero. I was just trying to get out alive. I was an opportunist. Not a savior.

And now I was something else, too: wanted.

Chapter Four
AVI

I was transported via a hoverstretcher down long twisting corridors while watchmen shouted at pupils to clear a path. Back and forth I swayed into more queasiness as they cut corners as if I were on my last breath. Although my head throbbed, I knew my injuries weren't fatal. But I was the General's daughter, so everything was exaggerated when it came to my safety and well-being.

Physicians in crisp white bodysuits gently transferred me onto an examination table that seemed as tall as a hilltop. I lay on my back with my palms faced down as they poked and tugged and disturbed my limbs. They scanned me with different mechanisms from crown to toe, asking me questions that I couldn't really comprehend or answer. My tongue was inoperative, or maybe it was my mind that was dysfunctional. I chalked it all up to being in shock.

The full diagnostic was finally complete.

I wanted to move from that hard, uncomfortable spot after they all retreated to their workstations, but I was unable to move. It was like I was stuck inside of my own body, my own head, as I tried to make sense of what had occurred. Each scrambled thought always returned to the cold metal of the worker's gun against my forehead. And the sound that was made when the laser went through her skull. The same sound it would've made if it had gone through mine.

The Administrator hovered over me with a sympathetic look on her face. She grabbed my shoulders and lifted me to a sitting position. My body ached. She then took a seat on a stool, where her thighs hung from the sides.

"Why in the galaxy are you crying?"

"My eyes water when I am exhausted." I wiped my tears with my thumb, surprised that they were even there to begin with. I wondered if she knew I was lying.

"This is a safe space."

False. I couldn't tell her anything without it being carved into my file for eternity.

"There, there." She forced my head into her pillow-like breasts. "We will get through this together and punish these terrorists for the mayhem they've caused. They are being taken care of as we speak."

Her attempt at consoling me had no effect.

"We've requested extra watchmen to escort not only you and your sister but every Elite pupil safely back to their dwellings after this terrifying ordeal. The General's camp has been notified of this attack, and in the meantime, we will need you to fill out an official document with your testimony. We must bring justice to Oya, Jamil, and the archivist."

My heart stopped. "Wh-what happened to Oya and Jamil?"

"Oh, dear. I thought you knew." Her lips pressed together, creating a long line. "Jamil has been injured, and Oya did not survive her wounds. We've never had any such travesty happen at this establishment, and we are doing everything in our power to right this wrong."

"I don't understand . . . any of this. She's gone." I began hyperventilating. I knew Oya. Her family were Elites like ours.

She placed her hand on my shoulder. "Avi, I know this is a lot to take in, but I really need your help. Do you think you can do that for me?"

I wiped the slobber from my chin. "I can help."

"This is great." She laid a holopad in my lap, then placed her heavy hand on top of it. "I need you to let the records know that the Academy has been very good to you, that you feel safe here, and that I, the Administrator, have followed exact protocol in order to minimize casualties."

"Pardon?" I sniffled.

"Be very specific about the events that occurred. We wouldn't want to make the court's job any harder by placing doubt in their minds about our decision to execute without trial."

"Forgive my ignorance, Administrator," I said. "Execute without trial?"

"Elite Jore, please recount what occurred in the Archives," she said, ignoring my question. "I shall give you a few moments to complete your report."

It took everything in me to not smash the holopad into dust. She was trying to cover herself, using me as insurance, but I had other plans. It didn't take long to type the account that she so desperately wanted. I found all the appropriate contacts within the government and sent an official affidavit to them all, including the Administrator.

She returned, leaving her once-sympathetic demeanor on the other side of the door.

"What is this?" She swiped the document from left to right, then up and down. Her expression stone. "Where is the rest of the report?"

"That's all there is."

She read it aloud. "'Innocent,' 'Saved by an Impure,' 'Witnessed watchmen brutality'? Elite Jore, I'll have you know that this is a legal and binding document that will be read by the highest judicial divisions. You have accused a branch of the law of callousness and prejudice."

"You've asked me to document the specifics, and I have," I said simply. "It's the truth."

She poked out her chin. "Is it?"

I huffed, trying to hold in my frustration, my grief. I had just witnessed a worker die. Oya was no longer with us. I had almost died, and she continued to push and pry.

"Are you sure that this"—she tossed the holopad beside me—"has nothing to do with the equality doctrine you've been working on? Your educator has recently brought it to my attention, and with all due respect, we're frankly concerned."

"Why would—of course not." My brows crinkled. "I'm telling the truth."

"You have the power to punish the person who took Oya's life, and you sit and still bat for these—these others," she said nastily, so close to my face that I could smell what she'd eaten. "They don't belong here, and you and I both know it. Stop fighting the system that we built, that your father built. Tell them that you are still in shock, delirious, and change your account this instant."

I cared about Oya's death, and I wanted to find the real culprit, but not by blaming the innocent. Not Saige.

I shook my head. "I apologize, but I can't do that."

"Very well, then." The Administrator turned her back. "You are dismissed."

Chapter Five
SAIGE

After the escape from execution, Joe and Eve went their separate way—wherever that was. I didn't ask, nor had I cared all that much. For one, I was suspicious of the way she'd gotten hold of the watchman's keywand. I was delirious from heat exhaustion and being beaten, and I wasn't sure what I had seen, or if it was even real at all. Maybe they'd been training kids in sleight of hand, or perhaps some new magnet tech had been invented that they'd gotten their hands on. The girl had also reminded me of someone I used to know, someone I used to care about. A person who was lost.

Either way, I was free—kinda—and all I knew for certain was that we'd left piles of watchmen behind. The Union was going to track down every person involved and make them pay publicly. I had been scanned into the system and was already as good as dead if I didn't figure out a way to leave the region soon. I couldn't go back to my cube. That was the first place they'd search. All dealers had safenooks located in different sections within the Subdivisions just in case shit went left. Some were dusty makeshift shacks located in moldy basements, and others were hidden shelters between buildings.

I looked left and right, then slipped through an opening in a fence and walked along the alleyway. I lifted the rotted wooden board and lowered myself into the shelter. Rusted cans, misshapen candles, and a moist-looking blanket were scattered on the ground. The space reeked of old piss, and mice scurried along the planks inside the walls. I thought about what it'd be like to just lie there in the filth and waste away inside that decaying hut, allowing them their final win. Another Impure crossed off the list . . .

Afraid of using any modern tech communication devices that the Union could utilize to track my calls, I took an outdated device that dealers used to stay under the radar to ring Silver. Of course, he wasn't available, but I heard him yelling in the background as his main man, Tony B., told me exactly how much I'd screwed up and what I'd have to do to recoup the losses.

"Ask Silver if we can make a new deal? I'll do whatever."

There was a long pause before Tony B. returned to the receiver. "You transport half a kilo this time."

"There's no way I can push that much Glitter through the subs, man," I pleaded.

"Not our problem."

"All right, all right . . . I—I need a cover."

"The package is on the way. Get it to the Underground in an hour or no deal."

Click. I smashed the phone against the counter.

❖   ❖   ❖

I awoke to rhythmic thumps banging on the shoddy door. A code. I cracked it open and stuck out my arm. I was passed a slimpack. Inside were the vials of Glitter and the promised curly red wig, bodysuit, tube of cream-colored molding, and new face tech rod to conceal my identity.

I lit the barely there wicks of melted candles and placed them on the rotted counter. I used my sleeve to clean the dust from the tiny mirror protruding from the wall. Parting my hair into sections, I started braiding the vials into each cornrow. The wig would go on top, hiding the drugs and my wild tresses. I had to look as little like me as possible.

I squeezed the tube of white molding, and a trail of it snaked along my fingertips. I began building a face. A pale one. One that matched the rest of the slaves in the region. Each stroke was creamy and cold, and the smells of clay and turpentine became stronger as I added layer upon layer. My eyes watered as the chemical did its work. My honey-colored skin itched something bad but faded along with my freak identity.

Whiteface was necessary and the only way to avoid capture, especially now that I was a fugitive. I used the wand to cement my new face in place.

I looked a little like Ma.

❖　❖　❖

Outside, graffiti stained the rock-and-mortar barriers that made up the street buildings and cubes. The sayings were scrawled in acid green. *Zombieland*, *Death is near*, and *God can't love us*.

The sun had just descended. Thick gray clouds formed near the skyline as the wind picked up. Empty vials rolled among scattered debris along a crumbled walkway. I was forced to take the path to get to the Underground Apex, to Silver.

The rain wasn't going to hold off. Red tresses flapped against my cheeks as I wove between workers. They passed one another staring straight ahead.

A humming rumbled from high above. The clank of thrusters. An armored hovervehicle lowered from the thick of the clouds, casting an unnatural azure-tinged shadow over us. A watchmen hive. The hatch opened; bulky men rappelled from shiny wires and landed with huge thuds.

Raindrops splattered the filthy concrete. My anxiety intensified as I sped up, only to be slowed down by a checkpoint. The crowd inched through. Random searches began, and turning back wasn't an option. Silver needed his shipment, and I needed my freedom.

Water and sweat mixed as they rolled along my face. With each bead, an amount of new face left with it, creating shadows of tiger-like stripes. I kept my head down and stayed on the heels of a tall, broad-shouldered woman. A watchman grabbed her so suddenly that I stumbled into his partner. "Watch it!" He seized my arm and searched me with narrowed eyes. His face was brown like pure cocoa. He tossed me back into the funneled crowd.

My heart thumped. Rain poured harder. My wig was drenched and heavy. I had to get out of there before the watchmen noticed the transformation.

Along the path, Disposables, old and no longer physically profitable to the Union, were crouched on wooden crates. They were beggars. A glance into a grim future of a Lower Resident.

A hunchbacked Disposable with yellowed eyes and a molded table-cloth around her shoulders grabbed my bag with a death grip. She was going to break the slimpack, spilling Silver's remaining product that I couldn't fit into my braids.

"Let go."

"Spare nutrition?"

With the other hand, she grazed my melting face, and white creamy residue colored her papery knuckles. "Ugh, mutt."

She ripped off the wig, exposing my braids. "Impure! Impure! I get the reward!"

A pause, then everyone started to flee. I felt watchmen's eyes burn holes through my back as I tussled with the woman. I had drawn the line at assaulting the elderly, but I punched her in the mouth, and immediately she released me, sliding from her crate, mumbling obscenities.

I locked eyes with a watchman. He drew his weapon. "Halt!"

I flew. Bodies became tangled. Shots echoed. I pushed forward until I was trapped in a sea of torsos. Several workers had been hit. Anyone who had fallen got trampled. Every time a succession of shots was fired, there was more clawing and shoving as people dodged lasers. I fought harder, as hard as I could, but everyone was so close together. Men tried to squish past, my braids were pulled, my face mushed against someone's shoulder blade. At a standstill, I couldn't even think about my next move because no movement existed. We were just stupid fish packed tightly in a can.

Instead of glancing forward and backward toward nothing but disorder, I tilted my head up, to the rumbling purple sky for answers. The rain pelted my eyelashes. The only real part of my face left. There was a calm silence in a loud place before I took a deep breath.

In my peripheral vision, I saw a girl grab her friend. Together, they cut diagonally through the mass. I stood on the tips of my toes to get a better look over the horde. I was never going to make it moving with the pack. Behind me, watchmen relentlessly picked people off one by one.

They were coming.

One of the watchmen pointed. "Right there!"

I ducked, wove, and crawled as I followed the girls, in the hope that they had a legitimate escape route. The second girl's legs wiggled through a crack in the foundation of a residential building before disappearing. I had no clue what was inside or how I'd eventually exit, but what other choice was there? I got on my stomach and slithered inside the darkness.

"Spread out. I want that Impure found!" the watchman shouted as I scooted my body farther into the bumpy crevice, scraping my shins and forearms in the process.

The fissure reeked of dung and fungus. I slipped out of my slimpack and pulled out a flashlight. When the light clicked, the girls gasped, shielding their eyes.

"Don't hurt us." The smallest one put her hand out. "We don't have any nutrition."

"Just show me how to get out of here," I said.

"I can do that." The taller girl began to inch into an even tighter passageway. I cursed under my breath.

After wiggling through winding tunnels, we came upon another crevice like the one we'd slipped into. I ducked underneath a crusted metal pipe and lifted myself from the hole. The girls dusted themselves off, then darted away.

I was safe. For now. But I still had to get to Silver in less than ten minutes with his package.

❖   ❖   ❖

A tired man rested on a stoop. The lower part of his face looked like it had been smashed in. He'd probably been beaten by watchmen back in his day. He yawned wide. No teeth. Only his eyes moved in my direction.

I adjusted my slimpack and said the password. "Daffodil green."

He used the rail to lift himself to his feet. His joints popped and cracked as if he'd been sitting in that same spot for days. He limped over and unlocked the door. I walked down the curved hall and knocked on cube 119. From the other side, it sounded like things were being shuffled across the floor and pushed against the walls.

"Daffodil green," I repeated quietly through the crack.

The door unsealed. Inside was dim and empty like my cube, seemingly normal to nosy watchmen, but I knew it wasn't. I followed the owner to a section of loose floor panels. He lifted one, motioning for me to quickly go inside. I pulled out the flashlight and ventured deeper.

Earth had been fashioned into a steep misshapen stairway. The tunnel was so dark that it threatened to take over the narrow beam of light. The shadows whispered on my skin, causing the fine hairs to stand erect. Water dribbled down the sides of rough walls, and the ground felt coarse and grainy beneath my soles. It was uncomfortably humid, and the smell of sulfur and wet dirt permeated the air. The journey was long and unpleasant. No matter how fast I walked, it still felt like an eternity to the end.

Distant sounds of upbeat music and raucous laughter filtered back to me as a smear of light shone ahead. It became brighter and brighter until I was in the middle of the crowded Row. The passage was filled with ice cream shops, stolen-tech merchants, dance bars, and tattoo parlors. You named it, someone down there could get it.

Suppliers and pimps ran the Underground. The unofficial Generals. That was what most visitors came for: along with the drugs, you got to be someone that you could never be aboveground. Working girls trailed their employers like armies. A well-known pimp named Augustus came through with his gaggle of ducks. An oily-looking man grabbed a girl's forearm. Augustus gave the man a onceover, nodded to the girl, then kept the parade moving through the crowd. That was how easily an assignment was made. Some strange man—or woman—just plucked you from a group like a grape from a stem.

The man licked her neck, leaving a trail of slime. Her body was youthful, but her face not so much. Layers of foundation covered her skin in an attempt to hide the discoloration. Underneath that bright-pink wig was probably stringy and overprocessed hair. Cheaper-paying clients didn't care what the girls looked like or what they were on; it was all they could afford. They just wanted a warm, able body.

Laced Glitter sucked every nutrient from the body. You could tell how long someone had been on it by the deep brown spots on their gums and on their teeth. I had stories for days about how girls would overdose on top of clients and in powder rooms, jerking about, having full-blown seizures.

Bearded workers huddled in a circle shooting dice, crumpled currency flailing above their heads, as a dealer shouted and pointed to the winner. Coal miners with darkened fingertips and tar-smudged faces had come straight from their job assignments to get high. Their eyes swirled as they lay dazed in some alcove. It was their only relief from being class Chattel workers, and I didn't blame them.

The funny thing was that Glitter wasn't only for working girls, but Elites used too. Theirs was just a purer form. That was one thing we did have in common. Addiction.

I entered the Vixen from the back entrance.

"Whoa." The bouncer pointed at my face. "Who'd ya make angry?"

"Long story." I didn't have the will to relay all the beatings I'd gotten that day.

Inside the Vixen was hazy. It'd get much darker once the girls got onstage and every corner of the place was occupied by sludge bags. Silver's men were everywhere, on the stage buffing the pole, on ladders stringing fat disco balls from the crackled ceiling, and at the bar preparing for a full house.

Although the place was tacky, my favorite part was a mural on a concrete wall overlooking the club. It was an image of a brown-skinned girl with flowing green hair. She held a bright world over her head. The details were crazy. I couldn't believe someone, a worker no less, had created it. I thought the Union had stripped them of all imagination.

Dancers had to check in with Silver before they were allowed into the powder room. He wanted to inspect us. We'd strip down so he could make sure we didn't have any sores or visible bruises on our bodies. At least that was what he told us. I thought he just got off on touching adolescents. During the inspection, he'd point a mini flasher in our mouths like some freak physician.

"Jus' checkin' fa rotten teeth and sores. Anythin' that'd disgust or othawise make a customah spen' less mullah," he'd say.

Disease was rampant, and who knew who was spreading what down there.

I took a seat in a dingy velvet booth that the patrons probably jerked off in. The same one that dealers, thieves, and even watchmen occupied to witness the grimy glam of underage dancers.

Drake, a dancer I knew, took the seat across from me.

"Love the new look."

She admired her long, elaborate nails up close. "I'd call it beat-the-fuck-outta-ya chic. It's all the rage, I heard."

I grunted, holding a chuckle in. She had always had a sense of humor.

We were cordial. Her station was right next to mine. She was a natural ginger; both sides of her head were shaved, but the middle was full of individual locs. Her eyes were warm and her cheeks devoid of freckles. I didn't get along with the other girls, but the two of us had similarities. We both had our secrets—she had an Adam's apple, and I was wanted. Again. We'd both agreed early on to mind our own damned business but to always look out for one another.

Silver's guards guzzled moonshine that had probably been concocted in lavatory bowls. They spoke without caution about the rebellion. Every time a minor revolt occurred, the Union would stamp out the flame under their polished leather boots. The largest rebellion had happened in the Outskirts—the one I was involved in seven years ago, where we'd been captured.

A worker with stubble on his chin gulped his brew. "There have been rebel wars before. What makes this one any different?"

"I tell ya why," a man wearing a discolored fedora exclaimed as if the boy had disrespected him. "They don't have respect for Gawd, the Lord above." He pointed over the rim.

"God?" The boy sniffed. "I don't believe. If there was one, he'd never let this happen . . ."

"Ahh!" the man growled, spilling some of his drink. "Tha's what they want ya ta believe, with their big strong walls separatin' the regions and flyin' cars . . . and anotha thing about that border that my forefathas built: it's not as perfec' as ya think." He took a swig.

The young one leaned in. "What are you yappin' about?"

"What I'm sayin' is that the Border ain't as solid like they say."

"Hey, you slippin' bad Glitter into this man's drinks?" the boy asked the bartender as he slapped the old man on the back. "Don't talk too loud. Might have some of those guards round recordin'."

The old man swiped the air. "I don' care. What else could they do ta me? Hell, I prolly won't live ta see them get what they deserve anyhow. But we gotta weapon dis time. A weapon from Gawd himself. Name's Liyo. He'll be ya savior."

I almost choked on my own spit when I heard that name.

Drake's legs uncrossed as she leaned forward. "You all right? Looks like something just spooked ya. You kinda look worse than you did before, if that's even possible."

"Never been better," I said.

My body tensed as I pictured a young boy with white hair, black eyebrows, and eyes the color of the sea.

Drake swept her hair over her shoulder, eyeing me too hard. "Have you heard about the 'savior' the streets are talking about?"

There had to be hundreds of Liyos. Maybe. "I haven't heard anything." He couldn't be talking about the one I used to know.

"Hmm," she noised. "Do you remember that superhero—I think his name was Electro-Man."

The one who'd been forced to his knees and made to watch his parents be executed. "I remember." The Liyo I'd tried to forget. The Liyo I'd thought was dead.

Drake got even closer. "They're saying there is a worker like him. Who can move things without touching them. Like a superhuman." She scooted back in her seat. "Can you believe that?"

Eve. She'd taken that watchman's keywand.

"It's wild how those physicians experimented on all those people in order to subdue their minds but ended up creating a weapon." She laughed. "Well, that is, if what they say is true, right?"

"Right." I nodded.

The bartender pointed a remote at an old boxy television set perched above the liquor bottles. He tucked a discolored towel into his apron and shushed everyone.

In the first clip, they showed a grainy photo of Mama Seeya in an undisclosed location. I jumped from my seat and moved closer to hear the broadcast.

"There's wide speculation that a radical Impure, whose street name is Mama Seeya, is leading the Lower Resident rebellion. And is suspected in connection with the terrorist attack on the Academy early this morning."

I hadn't seen her face since the Union had gassed our compound in the Outskirts. I hadn't known that she'd gotten out alive. Adults and children were executed alike. The only ones that made it out were Liyo and me. Just before they came, Mama Seeya had told us that the both of us had to be the ones to end it all. That we had to stick together no matter what. What she said replayed over and over again in my head as I saw her face, but I had already lost that drive to continue what she'd started a long time ago.

Somehow Liyo and I had been able to escape. We'd made it to the Square, but the toxins in the gas had done something to our systems, and we were both delirious. Seeing things that weren't there. I couldn't go any farther even though he'd dragged me as far as he could. I passed out at some point, and when I woke up concealed under brush, he was gone. I just knew the Union had gotten to him, and it was all my fault that I wasn't strong enough to stay awake. Fight the toxins or figure out how to flush them from my system. Mama Seeya had taught us all that just in case of an attack, but when the time came, I forgot about everything. Because I failed, I was alone again.

The broadcast cut to Head Gardner. A press conference. A grieving Elite family behind her. Clutching a photo of their dead Elite daughter displayed on a holopad.

Head Gardner put on her best sorrowful face as she addressed the nation. "Today, we regret to inform the nation of the cold-blooded murders of Oya Kazi and the beloved archivist, Safi Aqil. Two other Elites, Elite Avi Jore and Elite Jamil Bankole, have also been targeted but remain in stable condition."

"Is the murderer still on the loose?" a journalist inquired.

"At this time, we haven't apprehended all the suspects but guarantee that the Union's advanced crime task force will tear apart this region, starting from the top to beneath the surface, in search of the assailants responsible for these atrocities."

"Who are they?"

"Any leads?"

"Footage?"

They definitely had footage. Why hadn't they released it yet? Maybe they wanted to keep the details of the attack on the down low so they wouldn't seem incompetent, unable to protect their own. Perhaps they just wanted to quietly snuff us out without the usual theatrics. People were starting to notice the increase of violence, more rebel activity. They were gradually losing control.

My stomach dropped when the broadcast showed footage of Joe tied down. Both eyes swollen shut. His front teeth yanked from his gums as they questioned him, beat him in between. They knew what we'd done to those watchmen. They were going to draw out his torture and that of whoever else they'd captured. Where was Eve? Was she being tortured too?

Head Gardner stared straight into the camera, her gaze stabbing through the broadcast and right into me. "Details of the assassination are becoming clear as we are currently investigating a promising lead. The General has signed a temporary order to detain all Impures until further notice. And anyone, Lower or Upper Resident, who can lead us to who we are searching for will be rewarded handsomely."

The broadcast ended. The rest of the Vixen's patrons craned their necks to stare at me.

I had to go over that border. Tonight. And Silver was going to help me do it.

Tony B. cut the tension and led me into Silver's dungeon—office. I tossed the slimpack at the foot of his rickety desk.

"Good girl," he said, examining each vial to see if they were all intact.

I knew the drill and began unzipping my bodysuit. Silver owned the Vixen, and just like the Union, he also owned me.

"Late," he said, mini flasher in hand. "An' look at ya face!"

"Get it over with." I rolled my eyes and allowed him to do his touching thing with his clammy palms.

He stuck a stick in my mouth and flattened my tongue. "So ya ain't gonna tell me how ya damaged mah goods?"

I shivered in disgust. "Got into it with some watchmen."

His beady eyes got bigger as he took a step back. "Ya musta won."

When he finished the inspection, I slid my arms back into my bodysuit. "Something like that."

I sat back in a wobbly chair across from him, waiting for the information he'd promised, but his attention was on a glass room above his space for high-end clients who enjoyed the voyeurism element. They got their rocks off that way, and so could he and anyone else in the viewing stands. A nasty win-win. His fingers grazed his crotch.

"Heard it wa' a price on ya mutts' heads," he said, adjusting in his seat. "Ya jus' became a liability. Fa me. Fa my folks."

"I did what you asked. You owe me." I held back tears, and not because I wanted to cry but because I wanted to suffocate him to death.

His attention went back to the voyeur room, where an older man sat among three of Silver's girls. They were dressed like baby dolls: frilly white socks, poufy minidresses, and colorful belly shirts. A girl missing a shoe sat halfway sprawled across the man's chest. His hand squeezed her upper thigh. Her face, like everyone else's, was in a catatonic state. Their eyes sparkled like diamonds.

"How much Glitter did you feed them this time?"

His dry voice was obnoxious. "Nah, why would ya ask me that for? Ya know da game. I'm a bi'nessman. I give 'em what dey—"

"You're a sicko drug lord," I interrupted. "Nothing more, nothing less. Now where's my shit!"

Silver chuckled and rested his hands behind his head as if he were pleased with the title. "A drug lerd."

"I held up my end." I leaned over his desk. "I need a way out."

"Liddle gurl." Silver was tall and built and could probably fling me across the room with ease. "Ya come into ma office and disrepec' me in fron' of ma clients?"

"The deal was that you'd release me on my nineteenth birthday." I sat back down. "Look, I don't have a lot of time. They are—"

"After ya? I know." He said, "I got eyes, ma dear."

"I got you the stuff. I brought it to you."

"Ya did. Ha! Didn't thank ya could push dat much." He pulled out an envelope. I grabbed for it, but he pulled it back. "Aht, aht! Not yet. Dis is everythin' ya need. Amma nice guy, so amma release ya after tonight. Den ya free. Deal?"

"Deal."

"Ya headlinin'," Silver said, sliding my escape pack in a drawer and locking it. "Cova those bruises and get purdy for ya fans."

Tony B. finally escorted me to the powder room, where dancers crowded to get a glimpse of themselves in foggy mirrors. On hooks pasted on discolored walls were sequined bras and overplucked feather boas. Half-naked girls who smelled of scented talcum powder squeezed past one another to get a chance to occupy a metal-framed stool.

I'd turned to entertaining not because I wanted to but because I had to. Dancers were attracted to the glamorous life of the underground world. They never went hungry down there, and some became local celebrities. A chance to be something more than a slave worker. I never wanted the imaginary fame. I was there because I was indebted to Silver.

After I got separated from Liyo, I stayed on the streets, slept in stairways and halls inside of cubes. The scraps I'd found were stolen when I'd rest my eyes. Watchmen were crawling everywhere. One day, I got into a fight with a man who tried stealing my nutrient pack. I hadn't remembered the last time I'd eaten, and I wasn't going down without a brawl. He overpowered me and left me on the ground. I thought I'd die right there.

"Here." A hand with a nutrient pack lingered over me.

I sat up and grabbed it, emptying it until the last drop.

"Name's Drake."

I couldn't speak.

"I've been watching you." She smiled. "I can take you to a place where there's plenty more of that."

Drake introduced me to Silver. He'd forged official work papers for me to be a custodian at the Academy. They painfully installed a barcode in my irises. He made it appear as though I'd always been a member of the workforce and not an undocumented Impure from the Outskirts.

The contract stated that I would work for him until I turned nineteen. That was seven years of serving drinks and cleaning puke from stalls and making sure oil bottles and Glitter vials were filled. I picked up a little weight, filling out around my hips. Someone suggested that I'd be more profitable onstage. He offered to rescind the last agreement. The new one would put me front and center.

Patrons often called me exotic. There weren't too many Impures running around. Dancing wasn't that bad. Well, the actual dancing part wasn't. Sticky men trying to grab at your hips or lift your top or demand tricks was unbearable. I wasn't a girl who turned tricks for pocket change.

Silver asked what my stage name was. The Union had been making decisions for me up until that point, killing my people and almost killing me. I'd never had the opportunity to make an actual choice before.

I chose the name Lioness. Mama Seeya used to call me that during trainings. On my very first night, we made hills of money, and I became a hot commodity.

I emptied the contents of my makeup bag onto the counter one last time. I covered the black-and-blue marks with heavy foundation. Brushed sparkly metallic makeup on my cheeks and lids.

My last dance before I left for good.

"Welcome to the stage the one and only Lionessssssss."

Applause. I stuck a bare foot out to tease, then tore open the curtains. I didn't wear fancy strappy heels. I performed free of restrictions. The stage lights blinded me, so I bowed my head and listened to my breaths. I needed to get into the zone after everything that had happened, that would happen.

As the lights grew dim, I began to see it all. Every seat was occupied, more men than women. Even the standing section was full. Smiling eyes and smiling mouths shone with anticipation and money. In the front row were off-duty watchmen without their bulky suits, unsuccessfully trying to blend in. I scanned each one of their brown faces. Each expression dripped with superiority even though they risked it all to illegally be at the Vixen.

Music started. The tempo began real slow, creeping beneath seats and between customers' legs, coursing through their skins. I closed my eyes and swayed from side to side, caressing my hips through the sheer material of my bodysuit.

Whistling came from the back as the volume rose and the tempo sped. I became part of the texture of the instruments, hypnotized by the ripple of the octaves. My body was live art. A fine specimen, delicate and smooth, more satisfying when consumed slowly. I was nothing they said I was. I thought none of their universal thoughts. I was not a machine or a computer. I was not a Lower Resident or an Impure. I was flesh. I was human. I was a heart that pumped to the beats of the music around me.

As the song came to an end, sweat ran down my back and my neck remained outstretched and my face turned to the sky—the fissured ceiling. My arms were spread as if I were a baby bird in first flight with somewhere to go. A purpose.

The crowd cheered and threw money like confetti. Dollar signs floated around me.

I bowed. When I came back up, I noticed something—someone—cutting through the crowd. All I could see was his profile. Liyo? I stumbled but played it off by falling into an encore bow. I stayed down for some time, opening and closing my eyes. Was I imagining him?

I came upright, searching the crowd, but he wasn't there, which worried me even more. I checked every person's face at least twice. Again. The music played, and the lights dazzled across my body, which meant it was time for me to dance. I couldn't make myself move, though. I had seen him. I just knew it. Patrons looked at one another in confusion, and someone hollered to start.

Silver's voice screeched over the intercom, telling me to move or it was my ass.

I was the headliner. They wanted a show. I began to sway a little just to shut the crooked man up.

The anxiety of being on the run was causing me to think crazy, see things, people that weren't there. I knelt on the side of the stage, grabbed a shot of Fire from a random man's tray, and tossed it back. The crowd cheered. I stood once more, feeling the liquid burn my throat. I twirled on the pole. More money flowed.

I was on my fourth or fifth trick when I saw him again. This time, I was sure.

The pole suddenly became slippery, or maybe my hands became weak. I lost my grip and fell. The crowd gasped. I lay there, seeing floaters as the room spun. Tony B. climbed onstage and hauled me to the back. Silver quickly announced that Drake would be taking over. Tony B. peeled my eyelids back. I slapped his hand away.

"What kind of drugs you on?"

"None, you ape." I massaged the spot on my head that I'd fallen on.

Tony B. pulled an open hand back, but Silver caught him before he could strike.

"Stupid girl," Silver spat.

"Can I go now?" I mumbled.

"Ya leave when I say ya leave," Silver said. "You got a persona' dance reques'. And I swear befo' Gawd that ye betta not mess dis one up. Now git!"

I threw all my stuff into my slimpack, preparing for my last assignment before I left. If he tried to keep me any longer, I was going to tear through the entire place.

I freshened up and made my way to the lap room Silver had mentioned. It used to be a utility unit; Silver's business was expanding, so he'd added drywall around a generator and offered the area for private tricks. I slipped inside the dimly lit space covered in waxy brown paisley wallpaper. Music was set on medium. I shed my robe and then danced toward the man, rolling my body, tossing my hair. I couldn't see his face, though.

Private dances were five songs. After that, I was free to go. The sooner I began, the faster I'd be done.

I got on my knees and grabbed his inner thighs. He stiffened at the touch, then grabbed my hands.

"I don't bite," I said. "Relax, Daddy."

"Your name?" His face was still concealed.

"Lioness," I said. "Why don't you let go so I can do my job?"

He squeezed tighter. "Your real name?"

"Look, you creep, why don't you let me do what you paid for? No funny stuff. Or it can get real ugly, real quick."

When he released, I slithered along his body until I saw his face. Before I could back away, he caught my shoulders.

"I thought—I didn't—Liyo?"

It *was* him. Right in front of me. Much bigger than I'd remembered, healthier. He wasn't the same little boy I'd known back in the Outskirts. I'd thought he was dead all this time. I'd blamed myself for it. Now, he was there in the flesh like nothing had ever happened.

"What are you doing, Saige?"

I sat on my knees, trying to cover myself with my arms as best I could. I didn't want him to see me like this. I wasn't the shameful type, but this was different. We were different.

I had trained myself to keep it all bottled up. Never show emotions. Weakness was what emotions were. When I really wanted to tell him how lost I was without him. How much I missed his stupid face. How he kept me human when I thought everything was lost.

Instead, I asked, "Why'd you come here?"

That wounded him, I could tell. "For you."

Why had it taken him so long to find me? Why had he left me in the first place? I needed him. Seven years. His answer wasn't good enough.

"I saw your face on some leaked footage on the Cyberscape," he explained. "I had to see for myself. I've been trying to track you, but you've been under the radar."

"Well, here I am. Alive and well. Now what?" I fumbled through my slimpack, looking for a bodysuit.

His dark brows raised as he listened to the music. "I paid for five songs, and I have four remaining."

I zipped the front of the suit while facing him. "What do you want?"

"I want to know what happened. I want to know why you're doing"—he picked up the Glitter vial—"this."

"And *this*," I said, snatching the vial from his hand, "is none of your business or concern. You have some guts walking in here. I thought you were dead, Liyo. Dead. But I see you just up and left me."

"Left you? I could never leave you. Never." His voice cracked. "Look, I don't know what happened that day, but when I came to, you weren't there. I looked for you. I couldn't even sleep knowing you were out there. I checked every ditch, every nook. For as long as I could. *You* are my business now and forever."

Tears started streaming. He was breaking my shell again. I couldn't allow that. I was about to leave him again. And I wasn't carrying a broken heart with me. Not again. I'd already mourned him.

"Saige, you're a fighter, that same warrior girl that I grew up with. Who used to beat my ass in sparring. Remember that? Where's that girl?" He laughed. "What would Mama Seeya say if she saw you on that stage? For what, money?"

"You think I'm doing this because I want to?" I sniffled. "I'm doing this to escape! For freedom. You have no clue what it's like to be an Impure just trying to get by."

"You're right, I don't know what that's like." He smoothed his hair back. "But what I do know is that there is no freedom for us while the Union is still in power."

"That isn't my fight." I smiled through the pain.

"What have they done to you?"

He didn't want to know.

"You're so—so . . ."

"Different?" I began stuffing my things back into my bag.

69

"You know what they're doing to us out there." His eyes watered as he pointed hard.

I shrugged and pulled the strap over my chest. "What they've always done."

"Our people are ill, deteriorating from those so-called supplements they are forcing us to take. They won't stop, Saige. These are the final stages for them until they've wiped us clean. Like we've never existed. Come with me—with us, brethren, side by side. We cannot allow the Union to commit genocide for the sins of our fathers."

"Us?" I laughed. "I don't plan on fighting them. I've made it this far without anyone, and that's what I'm going to continue to do. We won't win this."

"Am I not your brother?" I could see the hurt in his face when I didn't answer.

"Silver offered me an escape through the Border. I'm taking it."

He snorted. "You and me are supposed to do this together. Mama Seeya wanted—"

"Where is she now? Where?" I yelled. "And why doesn't anyone ever ask what it is that I want?"

He was stupid to believe that he could lead an army of rebels against the Union. His parents failed. Mama failed.

"If you cared about me, then you'd come with me," I said.

"I'd go anywhere with you."

"But?"

"I won't give up on you. But I also can't give up on them."

I shook my head in disbelief. "You have a lot of nerve coming here, trying to recruit me for some lost-cause army." I poked him in the chest. "It doesn't matter, because you'll be a ghost soon, just like the rest. Nothing you do will stop what the government has planned. So just let it go. Okay?"

Shouts came from the other side of the door. Heavy thumps and bangs. Fights were common enough that I recognized the sound of a person being thrown against a wall. Liyo twisted the knob slowly and peeked out.

"What do you see?" I whispered.

He slammed the door fast. Locked it and began sliding the couch to create a barricade. "There are watchmen. Everywhere."

Fucking scum. Silver ratted me out. "They're here for me," I admitted.

A watchman announced from down the hall, "Where's the Impure?"

No one spoke at first.

A gunshot went off. A body hit the floor.

"I won't ask again," he roared. "Where's the Impure?"

A familiar voice rose from the silence. Silver said, "Check the lap rooms."

I'd kill him if I ever saw him again.

Too many sets of boots scuffled toward us.

Liyo gently squeezed my hand, bringing me back to reality. I hadn't even remembered him grabbing it. "We need to get as much as we can in front of that door."

We tossed tables and boxes on top of the couch, then stepped back when watchmen started to bang and twist the knob.

"Someone's in here," one said.

We packed ourselves into the generator closet.

"There's no way out." I slid down the wall.

He lowered himself to my level. "We will get out of here. I promise. Just stay with me."

I smiled. A real smile. I had forgotten how genuine concern from another human felt. "You're helping me after I said—"

His face softened. "Nothing you can ever say will change what I feel about you."

"They don't want you, Liyo," I said. "They want me. Just leave me."

The door splintered as the watchmen smashed into it over and over again.

"There's a generator here. There's got to be tunnels that lead into the heating ducts." He began feeling along the walls.

From the ground, I looked above us. "There." I pointed to a vent wide enough for us to fit into. Liyo removed the rusted cover and hoisted me first. My weight caused the rickety ventilation tube to creak with every movement.

Watchmen tore past our barrier. Liyo was agile for his size. He leaped up in one bound, pulling himself into the tube.

A voice from below echoed, "Up there!"

The watchmen fired multiple shots. Lasers pinged all around us as we scrambled through tight spaces filled with webs and droppings and who knew what else. Finally, the sounds of shots grew distant.

We lay belly down in the vents for some time, quietly waiting for things to smooth over. For the watchmen to get tired and leave. Try again the next day. But by that time, I'd be gone, so far away, on the other side. Maybe Liyo would change his mind by then and join me. Those thoughts kept me sane. How sweet freedom would be. Perhaps they were far-fetched pipe dreams, but the little hope I had left was the only thread holding me together.

More time passed, and no one came for us. No one crawled through the vents shooting lasers from either side.

I whispered, "Liyo, you awake?"

"It's kind of hard to rest in a two-by-two-foot space, don't you think?" He squeezed my ankle playfully.

I felt myself slowly becoming that little girl back in the Outskirts again. It was embarrassing, but I allowed the feeling for just a moment.

"We should start moving." There was an opening not too far ahead. "There."

I thrust out the vent's shield that separated us from the Row, but when I poked my head out to survey the scene, I was immediately met with a barrage of laser beams. I ducked back inside. Out of breath. Out of chances. Cornered.

72

"Surrender or you will be met with deadly force," a watchman warned through a megaphone. "You are surrounded."

I banged the back of my head against the tube. "Fuck!"

"Let's go back," Liyo said.

"We can't go back." I couldn't look him in the eye because of the tight space. "I messed up this time. Real bad."

"Saige, I—"

"Let. Me. Go." Sweat burned my eyes. "Don't come out until this is all over. Do you promise?"

He kicked the wall out of frustration. He knew deep down that one of us dead was better than both of us dead. Liyo had tried. We both had, but I couldn't bear the thought of him being tortured because of me. Besides, what did I have to live for anyway? How naive I was to think that I'd just escape the Union's clutches. This world wasn't built on fairness or justice. It was a fucking game that I'd lost at every turn. They had eyes and ears everywhere. Knew everything. They were always one step ahead.

He squeezed my ankle again, but this time it was much tighter. He didn't want to let go. We were like magnets.

I slowly crawled away from him, forward into the light.

I poked my hands through the vent. "I'm coming out."

There Liyo stayed. In that shaft. His head buried in his forearm.

"Turn around with your back facing us and move slowly," a watchman ordered.

I hadn't even taken two steps before a watchman shot me with a charged dart. Blue electrical currents bounced around my head and torso. Liyo's mouth widened in anguish. Every muscle, every bone in my body locked in place. I collapsed. Watchmen closed in. One stuck me in the neck with a baton. My jaw clamped as they turned the volts up higher and higher, my teeth grinding together until I bit my tongue and tasted metal. My vision blurred, and intense burning followed. My heart felt like it would explode behind my ribs.

Chapter Six
AVI

"Great universe!" Father's face materialized on my wristcom. "Avi?"

"I—I'm fine, Father."

A record number of watchmen had escorted Jade and me to the hovervehicle. A string of polished black-and-chrome vehicles moved in sync as we glided over the Academy.

I sensed the relief sweep over him. "I was in the field on the outer banks. A rebel cluster appeared on the radar just as the attack on the Academy ensued. This is no mere coincidence."

It definitely wasn't a coincidence, but there was nothing I was able to say that would lessen whatever happened next.

"I'm aware of the threat and have taken additional precautions to ensure your and Jade's safe return to the Citadel. Stay inside your quarters until you are both briefed."

"Affirmative," Jade and I said in unison.

"I promise that this will never happen again."

Before he cut communication, Jade spoke up. "Father, will Avi's crowning ceremony still commence this evening?"

I began, "I hardly think—"

"It's just that for the entire Southern Region, this ceremony is tradition. It would be a shame to cancel on account of these brutish rebels. That's probably what they wanted. To disrupt it all. What message are we sending to the region, to our people, if we allowed them to prevent such a majestic occasion?"

Thick lines appeared in Father's forehead as he weighed the pros and cons. He finished with a sigh. "Very well, then, the ceremony will continue as intended."

Jade's ear-to-ear grin oozed with disdain, which fed my irritation. I closed my eyes and laid my head back. A sickness still gurgled in my stomach.

"Isn't he just dreamy?"

My neck cranked mechanically. "Pardon?"

"There's only one Phoenix, Princess." Jade hissed the last word.

I hated being called Princess, and she knew it.

She eyed me in contempt, starting from the tops of my boots and ending at my face. "Out of all the girls with curves and dark skin and personality, he chooses you. What a pity indeed."

The tension between us was thick and suffocating like smog. Jade knew how to twist every knob. Play every move to get me to come out of character. She fed off my derision. I often wondered why she hated me so—was it jealousy? Other than the title of next General, I had nothing that she needed to be envious of. She could've still had a fruitful career in the government without being General. But she was the obsessive type. She wasn't going to stop until I was out of the way.

"Did you know that I was the one who told Mother that he was at the top of your guest list?"

"You—" My lids were peeled back so far that I couldn't even blink. Suddenly it was like his cologne was all around me again. "Window. Down. Please."

Chunks of whatever remained from this morning's nourishment erupted. I always had such a weak stomach.

❖　❖　❖

When Jade and I arrived at the Citadel, neither Father nor Mother were present, which I was thankful for. It would be difficult to get away from them once they returned. Father would dwell on the threats and bore us with regulation speeches about punishment and laws. As for Mother, when she got over the fact that I had almost died, she'd begin to obsess about every detail of the crowning ceremony, just like before. What I needed, wanted most, were time and space. Unfortunately, space was something I'd never be allowed, and time was limited.

I strolled along the path as soon as we disembarked, heading away from the Citadel.

"Elite Jore," a watchman called out.

I ignored him. Jade grabbed my arm. "Where do you think you're going?"

"Don't touch me." I glared, pulling myself away.

She folded her arms. "Father didn't authorize your leave from the Citadel." She tried so hard to sound official.

Watchmen stood on both sides of Jade as I stepped into the edge of the forest. They came closer, but I held my palm up. "Halt! That is an order."

They looked at Jade, waiting for an override.

From the path emerged Instructor Skylar. "No worries, I will take it from here."

Jade snarled, then tore away in the other direction.

I wanted to run up to him and jump in his arms like I had when I was younger, but I was a woman now, and that type of embrace wasn't becoming of an Elite, especially since he'd be under my authority soon.

I held out a firm hand instead.

He took it and shook. "So official now." He chuckled.

I couldn't hold in my giggles. It was a humorous attempt at being an adult.

I usually visited Instructor Skylar's greenhouse after academic sessions. He lived in the wilderness between the Farmlands and the Citadel, surrounded by the thickest and tallest trees, in an outdated wooden ranch left to him by his father. It was quaint and unspectacular compared to the other cabinet members' dwellings in our city. I always wondered why he opted to live outside of the realm of our high-tech world, secluded.

He had started his career early and worked his way through the ranks. Due to his accomplishments in the field, Father had appointed him head of the Watchmen Academy. He also became the older brother I'd never had. I could tell him anything without it getting back to Father. He understood me, and for that I respected him.

"Care for a stroll, Elite Jore?" He bowed ridiculously.

The Citadel's land spanned for hundreds of miles in each direction, our own thriving capital. We owned the Farmlands, which supplied the region's Upper Residents with fresh produce, grains, legumes, and dairy. Our Citadel was surrounded by lush forests and waterfalls. We even had an artificial beach. I had everything I thought I could ever want.

My memories of the property were wholesome, but lately, the climate had been changing. The world seemed much more tense, complex. I was also maturing; I didn't see things quite the same way anymore.

We strolled quietly along the winding paths as squirrels hopped from branch to branch and robobees floated along. I felt a sense of normalcy that I hardly ever got to experience.

We finally made it to his life-size terrarium. Despite his home being modest, the structure was massive, with three levels. Every plant, liana, and flower imaginable was inside. He had a section of cacti, and in another were vines that twisted their way over a bench and along the wall. It overlooked a large bed of color-coordinated pansies in purple, lavender, and dark pink. It was my favorite place to sit and think or lie and look up at the stars. And it was quiet; the only sound came from wild birds flapping in the fountain.

"I assume it's been one of those days?" He rested a tray of porcelain cups and a steaming teapot on the table. It was strange seeing an Upper Resident serving nourishments. "Sugar?"

"Yes, please." He dropped two lumps in and stirred purposefully.

His eyes were the most beautiful part of him. They were black, smoky, like he wore kohl, but it was just the natural thickness of his lashes. I was jealous mostly that he was beautiful without even trying, but he was just as rugged as he was put together. He had a short Mohawk, with shooting star patterns shaped on one side of his head.

I sipped the black tea, allowing the bitter liquid to warm my weary insides.

He placed his hand on top of mine. "What's going through your mind?"

All of a sudden, my hands began to shake. Tea dripped over the sides. Instructor Skylar quickly guided my cup back to its saucer.

No one had cared enough to inquire about my feelings. I tried to capture the sadness, hold on to it tight, but it only made the urge to cry stronger. I made my way into his arms, sobbed, hiding my face in the process, hiding the shame. He kissed the top of my head.

"Why is all of this happening?" I sniffled. I knew the answer, but I wanted someone to reassure me.

Instructor Skylar sat me back upright and then handed me a hand-kerchief. "There are many reasons that I can think of."

I dabbed my nose. "Tell me what to do."

"Avi, it's not about you." He explained, "They're angry because they want to be free. They want the same rights as Upper Residents. Actually, they want to take over entirely. Haven't you seen the broadcasts?"

"Affirmative. I watch them. Father's requirement," I said. "But there is no way that Lower Residents would ever have the same liberties as us. It's not how our system was designed."

"And that's why they're quite angry, fed up with how the system is run and by who's running it."

"Then we are back to square one," I said slowly.

Instructor Skylar chuckled.

"They want me and the others dead to make a statement," I admitted.

"Bingo. They want to show how much of a threat they are by assassinating the offspring of the most powerful people in the region," he explained. "The rebels will be taken care of soon enough, and peace will be restored once again. You will lead, and your children will lead, and so on and so forth. Just one totalitarian government."

My tea had become less appetizing. "An Impure girl saved my life."

"An Impure girl?" he said thoughtfully, as if he were recalling a distant memory.

"She disarmed the worker. She used skills like the ones you taught Jade and me. Isn't it peculiar that a worker would know such techniques?"

Instructor Skylar remained silent.

"Have I said something wrong?"

"Of course not. I was just . . . thinking." He came back to reality. "She'll be executed then."

"What kind of justice is that if truth doesn't prevail?"

"You know how this all ends, Avi," he said matter-of-factly. "The truth doesn't matter to the Administrator and definitely not to Head Gardner. They're out for blood these days. What's truth if you already have a preconceived notion of reality? The truth is that they don't want Impures here anymore. They don't want any workers here. They want a pure race to reign in the region. That's how we've built all of this. It's how we thrive. It's how you get to survive."

"And you are satisfied with this way?"

"It isn't about satisfaction or right or wrong or black or white. It's about power. It's always been that way, and that's the way it will always be."

"I can't allow—"

"Do you trust me?"

I nodded.

He placed his palm on his chest. "Then trust me when I tell you that there's absolutely *nothing* you can do. The Impure will die one way or another."

He wiped the tears from my cheeks.

"We can't live in the past, nor can we alter it. You have a grand ceremony to look forward to this evening. You should be basking in the beauty of this moment."

I yearned for my moral compass to be turned off that simply. "I'm just supposed to live with an executed worker on my conscience?"

"What other options are there?" He gathered the teacups, placed them back on the tray.

"I can request that Father grant her leniency."

"You could, but I wouldn't get my hopes up." He carried the tray into the galley. "I will meet you out front. Don't be long. We have a briefing."

He left me alone to be consumed by my own thoughts and fears of the future. I was at a standstill. I couldn't hide away in the greenhouse forever. My legs felt heavy as I hoisted myself from the bench. I took deep breaths. It was time to face actuality.

Something heavy toppled over in the distance.

Workers maintained the greenhouse, but it was usually cleared out by the evening.

"Instructor Skylar?" I called, not loud enough.

A light shone into the shadows from the potting chamber. I crawled beneath the window and carefully lifted myself on the ledge.

The worker had a long torso; the fabric of his bodysuit was stretched over his back and shoulders. His waist went in at just the right angle, planted on firm legs. He tucked white hair behind his ear.

There was a worn-out shelf in the corner with gardening equipment and small tools.

I held in a gasp when things started to move. By themselves. The boy intently worked at the counter. One wooden block, two blocks— no, four blocks—a lug nut, a hammer, metal nails, and a steel cup flew off the shelves and toward him like he was a magnetic force. They floated in orbit.

I took photos with my wristcom.

His fingers swayed like a conductor's, and chunks of timber bounced around. He grabbed a pair of garden scissors. The rest of the floating items glided across the space and neatly placed themselves back in their original spots.

He snipped the roots of a plant with oddly shaped leaves, then stuffed the clippings into a sack.

"What do you think you're doing?" I made my presence known from the entry.

The worker tried to conceal the sack behind his thigh.

I approached. "What do you have, worker?"

He was larger than me, but I was still his superior. I reached around him and took hold of the sack. I sifted through and found nothing but a mixture of plant parts and dirt.

"State your name?"

He hesitated. I sensed defiance.

"Your name, worker." My voice rose.

"Liyo."

"Have you been given authorization from Instructor Skylar to be here after work hours?"

"I'm gathering herbs," he replied.

"That's not what I asked."

"Someone I know is very sick." He came forward.

I moved back, stumbling into the edge of the doorframe. "Then take them to the Health Department."

Liyo scoffed. "Why in the galaxy would I do that when they're the ones making her sick in the first place?"

"What are you t—"

"Avi?" It was Instructor Skylar.

I turned my head for just a moment. Liyo snatched the sack from my clutch and zoomed out of the side exit.

❖ ❖ ❖

Instructor Skylar and I arrived at the Citadel and entered the Great Room. Seated at the massive round table were Father, Commander Chi, Jade, Mother, representatives of the two other Elite families, and every cabinet member except for Head Gardner, all ready to be briefed.

In our society, the hierarchy began with the General and flowed down to the four Elite families. The cabinet members followed, and then came everyone else.

My ancestor had fought and sacrificed for her bloodline to be deemed the purest, the top for future generations. The Jore name carried weight.

Mother peeled herself from her seat and embraced me like never before. She pressed my face into her shoulder and caressed my untidy braid. She laid moist kisses all over my cheeks and forehead. Usually, I would've protested, but I understood her excitement and her pain. She took my hand and sat me down next to her.

"You're not leaving my sight," she whispered.

I groaned inwardly.

Father tapped his gloved pointer fingers together. "As most of you are aware, I've called this emergency briefing because there was an assassination of our very blood at the Academy today."

The table erupted in outrage. Father paused, stroking his coarse beard. "Those fiends took innocent lives today. They have made a grave, grave mistake." He slammed his fist on the table, causing a boom. "Lightning will now storm upon their entire race."

Everyone began stomping and howling and throwing fists in the air.

"These rebels"—he chuckled through his words—"believe that they have the upper hand. They want to send us a message. They are telling us that they are united!"

Commander Chi shook his head fiercely. "Never that. Never."

Father said, "Oh, yes. They want us to fear them. Cower down. Give up all that we have sacrificed, died to preserve."

"No fear," Jade shouted.

He rose, his chest puffed proudly. "I will die a million deaths before I ever allow them to destroy what we've built. Things are about to change in the region, for the betterment of humankind. We will not allow Oya's death, the archivist's death to be in vain. They've chosen a battle, and now we'll give them war."

The entire table erupted. Glasses were knocked over and chairs tossed back. Workers replaced the soiled cups with new ones and started pouring fresh drinks.

"My comrades, my family." Father raised his glass toward me. "This evening, we celebrate life and hope as Avi evolves into adulthood. As she transitions into the position of the next succeeding Head General."

Cups clinked, and wine splattered the shiny wooden table.

He smiled that winning smile. "So let the celebrations begin."

❖   ❖   ❖

After the briefing, Mother tried leading me away.

"I need to speak with Father first." I pulled myself from her grasp. "It's dire."

"I shall go with you, then."

"No." I blocked her from going any farther. "Privately, Mother."

"Very well, then," she said. "The team is waiting for you."

"I'll be there shortly."

"The final fitting is at a quarter past," she nagged.

"Mother, I will be there," I promised.

My irises were scanned at Father's door. The entry pad turned green, and I was allowed access. I stepped forward with my hands clasped in front and cleared my throat, alerting him to my presence.

"Avi." His chair groaned as he leaned back. He faced the window, gazing reflectively at the waterfall.

"I'm a bit nervous about this evening," I confessed. "I'm unsure if I'm the right one for this grand duty."

"Nervousness is a good indication," he said. "It means you're passionate. That you care."

I rolled my eyes. "You make everything sound so easy, Father."

He motioned for me to take a seat. "I have been in many battles, confrontations with men and creatures from here on Earth to the stars. I have defeated them all. Do you know how?"

I shook my head.

There was a twinkle in his eyes. "I could read them. I knew their next decision before they did. It may have been strategy, statistics. Others call it intuition. Luck. The point is that I ask, What are they most likely to do based on whether their last decision or move was effective? The odds, my daughter. What are the odds of proposed outcomes? These are the things you must ask yourself. This world," he said, motioning to his mind, "can be the most wondrous place, or it can be the most wicked and vile. The key to ease is knowing, feeling your way around, and believing in yourself."

I took a deep breath with the intention of responding, telling him how I felt, but no words came out. I was afraid of him—what he'd think of me.

He sensed anxiety. I wasn't the best at hiding my emotions. "Go on," he urged.

"I agree with you, your thoughts on intuition. I've been listening to mine more as of late, and I've come to the conclusion that I need to help someone who's been falsely accused of a crime."

He ran his hand through his short, curly hair. "The Impure girl."

"You are aware?"

"I'm aware of more than you know." He turned away.

"Father?"

"There is no in between, Avi. It doesn't exist. Every decision leads to an outcome. We must look at the larger picture, the bigger result. Move beyond selfishness, and sacrifice for the greater good."

Father's lectures always put my troubles into perspective, but this time it just felt different. Like the mask had been slipped from over my eyes. He pulled me into an unexpected embrace. His beard tickled my forehead, and suddenly, I was his little girl again. His voice became much smoother. "I want you to know that I'm not your enemy, your family is not your enemy, and you must accept our failures and successes together, as we accept yours. In the end, we will be the only ones you can trust, who understand you." He brought my face forward and laid his warm lips on my cheek.

I pulled away. "How is it just that she is punished for a crime she didn't commit? There's no concrete evidence that implies her involvement. The Administrator just assumed it was all of the workers instead of launching a thorough investigation."

He swatted the air. "I've seen the footage, Avi. What you witnessed was her trying to go back on a plot that they'd been planning for months. She got scared. I don't believe this whole hero tale."

"It's not a tale. It's the truth," I said. "For me, I am begging you to make them investigate this with objectivity."

"I believe you have some sort of soft spot for this worker and that sometimes the mind can contextualize what it wants, how it wants."

Awkwardness covered me. It was like being near a stranger. I shouldn't have felt that way, but I couldn't help it. How could he turn his back on the law? Every worker had the right to a hearing.

"If what you say is true, then show me proof," I told him.

"Certainly. Holoscreen on," he commanded.

Father turned the volume to the highest level. The vibrations of bustling pupils, their footsteps, their conversations invaded every corner of his room. The Academy's surveillance units were so sensitive that we could hear Oya's exhales as the camera zoomed in and singled her out. She strolled along the courtyard with the other pupils, a reader clutched to her chest, softly humming a Marco Grant tune. The announcement rang, signaling pupils that the next session was set to begin. Immediately, I was catapulted back to that moment with Saige when I'd found her reading. I felt bad for keeping that information from Father, but he didn't need any more ammunition.

My intestines clenched at the thought of what would happen next.

Right there beyond the bushes were two workers—one male and one female. Without words, they plotted. I watched with dry eyes as the female bumped into Oya, knocking her reader from her arms. "Oh, so sorry, ma'am," the girl said.

It all happened within moments. The other pupils had cleared the area, returning to their next session. Oya went to collect her busted reader. The male grabbed her from behind. Oya's screams echoed, shaking every fiber in my body.

"No, no, no," I whispered, getting closer to the screen, but I couldn't turn away.

The man held Oya's forehead back, exposing her neck. The girl took out a blade. Oya pleaded and pleaded.

"For the Brotherhood," the girl said. And with no hesitation, she slit her throat.

Oya dropped to her knees. Eyes bulging from her head. The gurgles. Choking on her own gore. She tried to crawl as far as she could as she applied pressure to her wound, but the blood just kept leaking.

The man placed his boot on Oya's back and put his weight on her until she accepted her own demise. As blood pooled around her head, he turned to the camera. "The rebels are coming."

Then both of the workers shot themselves in the head.

The screen blacked out.

I shut my eyes so tight that I could only see purple and orange spots floating. A shudder swept over me that I would never be able to shed.

Father motioned to the display. "This is why I fight. Why my people fight. Risking their lives for the safety and betterment of the Union. How many more pupils have to die? I have to look into Oya's mother's face at her transition ceremony and assure her that I will do whatever is in my power to protect her remaining offspring and that this will never happen again."

"So we respond to murders with more killings?" My mouth felt as dry as cacti.

"You've seen what these rebels are capable of, what they are doing at this very moment. We are in a war. This Citadel that I've built to protect you will only last so long. How long do you think it is before they figure out a way to infiltrate our home?"

"Sometimes people are wicked, Father, but not all of them are."

He sat back. "Then you're much more naive than I thought."

That comment hit me like a jab.

"You have yet to show me proof of Saige's involvement."

"She's a criminal. She slaughtered multiple watchmen, then escaped. We can predict one's actions through patterns. They will do it again and again until someone corrects their behavior."

"And your first instinct is to correct those patterns by using death as punishment." I looked straight at him then.

"I am the judge." His voice rose. "And so will you be one day. And on that day, you will see how everything isn't as simple as you believe it is. But until then, my decision stands. Do you understand?"

"Affirmative, General."

Chapter Seven
SAIGE

I knew it was a dream. Because the edges were blurry and I knew Ma was dead. I could've stopped it if I wanted. Woken myself up. Jolted myself back into the nasty reality. But I wanted to see her again, even if it was only temporary, because I was starting to forget what she'd looked like. Sounded like.

Mama had just finished telling me about my father. She kissed the puzzle-piece-shaped birthmark on the base of my thumb and told me that he had the same one on his.

Like most dreams, nothing happened gradually. It was all bits here and loose ends there. Just sound bites of memories.

The next thing I knew, a flock of watchmen burst into our hideout. Lasers were pointed in our direction, crossing over one another in the light of the moon like loose crochet patterns. Her body trembled as she shielded me.

I stayed glued to the wall like a bug, but arms came from every which way, grabbing my limbs and yanking her hair, tugging the both of us forward. Screams turned into gagging coughs as they choked her. A silver needle glistened in the low light and stabbed me in the neck. I fell asleep . . . a layered nightmare.

When I woke up, I was curled into a ball like a feline on the frozen floor of a white cell, hair pasted to my forehead, my head in Ma's lap. I saw see-through clouds with every exhale.

"Ma." My teeth chattered. "Where are we?"

She stroked my cheek. "What's your best memory?"

That was easy. "The ones with me and you. Together."

"That's good to know that you enjoy me as much as I enjoy you," she said. "Saige, my beautiful baby girl. My prize."

"My soul. My heart," we said the rest in unison.

She stiffened at the sound of footsteps. Watchmen were coming.

"Ma?" I said, clutching her.

"Saige, listen to me. If anything happens, I want you to find Mama Seeya. Promise me you'll do what we practiced. Promise me?"

They unlatched the cell's door and found us crammed into a corner.

"Let's go," a watchman ordered Ma.

I pounded him with my little fists. He shoved me so hard that I flew back; the wind was knocked out of me. If only I were stronger, I thought. Before they snatched her through the exit, she mouthed, "Keep the promise."

A holoscreen appeared from a ball of static. The young woman on the display had big eyes that never seemed to blink. A red triangle was embroidered below the left shoulder of her white bodysuit. She told me her name. Head Gardner. I'd never forget it. She told me that Ma had been charged with violations. Because of me. No one like me should have been conceived. My existence was against everything the Union stood for.

It was the first time I heard the word *Impure*.

She input data on a translucent keypad. A picture of Ma's mug shot was projected into the corner of the screen alongside Head Gardner's profile. Then the display zoomed in on Head Gardner's face. "Impure child, is this your birth mother?"

I thought about lying, but I wasn't sure which answers would make them let Ma go. "Affirmative." I spoke unsurely.

She was satisfied. "Impure child, who is your birth father?"

"I'm not sure," I whispered, rubbing my birthmark.

"Speak up!" Head Gardner snapped.

"I don't know."

"I do not believe you," she said mockingly. "I believe your mother told you to lie, made you promise not to tell. Is this correct? Has the inmate coerced you?"

I peeled dead skin from around my nail bed. "What does 'coerce' mean?"

Head Gardner smirked and began typing once more.

Half of the screen changed over to Ma again, but this time she was in a metal chair with her hands, chest, and ankles confined. Watchmen posted behind her with guns cradled like babies.

"Impure child, if you do not answer my questions truthfully, I will have to execute your mother. Do you understand?"

Nothing I said was going to help. I had to take measures into my own hands. I began to scrape and bang on the padded exit door.

"Who is your birth father?" Head Gardner's voice boomed. It seemed to vibrate from every direction.

"I don't know," I cried, banging more violently.

"Shock her."

Electricity crackled from the cement below. Thin, crooked white-and-blue lines popped around like grasshoppers. My soles burned as surges sliced through me. I collapsed. Slobber dribbled from my mouth. The only thing I was able to do was watch Head Gardner set her sights on Ma.

She read Ma her rights. "Inmate, you will have one last chance to divulge to us whom you have had relations with. If you confess, the Union will give you leniency, for we are merciful, but if you do not comply, the punishment is death."

A countdown started.

Ma spoke. "The world will always be free to those who seek it."

The physician began the procedure. They stuck a needle with a cloudy serum into her. Mama dry heaved almost immediately. Red discolored her teeth. Oozed from her nose, the corners of her eyes, her ears. The gurgling sounded like thousands of bubbles being blown at once. She shook and shook through the restraints.

I screamed so loud and squeezed my ears until they burned.

Men dressed in white entered, held me down, and stuck me again.

I was dead.

Or at least I wanted to be.

I had jumped through time, it seemed like. But really, I had just awoken.

❖   ❖   ❖

An agonizing shriek reverberated against my eardrums, and I was blinded by bright lights. Blurred figures grabbed me. More bodies rushed into the cell, barking orders. I was disoriented, but then adrenaline quickly kicked in, and I managed to catch one of them in the face with my elbow. The shape grunted. I kicked another in the stomach. That was when they took my legs out.

An outline of a woman's face got close. I opened and closed my eyes, but no change. She lingered for a split second and then punched me in the nose. Every hand that held me had let go. I lay flat on my chest. The taste of cool metal ran down the inside of my cheek and onto my tongue. I spat wine-colored splotches.

The insistent inspector pulled my hair from behind. "Keep fighting, Impure, and I'll see to it that I personally knock every one of those pretty little teeth out." She threw my head forward. "Undress her."

They tore my bodysuit, unraveling me like a piece of candy. I lay there like a fuel-barren vessel. A woman choked, covering her nose. "She's soiled herself."

Another clicked her tongue. "A pig has more decency."

They tossed me onto a wet surface with a steel drain in the middle. A screen hovered above me.

"Prisoner number 7612, you will call me Head Gardner," she said from inside the screen. "Rise."

I scooted to the wall and used it to stand on shaky legs. The bot stayed over me, shining a thick beam of light directly in my face.

"I am the direct overseer—"

"I know"—my breaths were ragged—"who you are."

"Excellent." Head Gardner sounded flattered. "Because I know exactly who you are. And I've been waiting for you for such a long time."

"You have?" I wiped my nose with my thumb.

"Like mother, like daughter. Gene inheritance is an amazing phenomenon."

"Spare me the science lesson."

Her upper lip jumped. "I am the overseer of this detention facility in Gardner City. You have been charged with two counts of political assassination, two counts of attempted murder of an Upper Resident, and pending murder and aggravated assaults on watchmen. In addition, you have been charged with rebel affiliations, categorized under treason. You will receive a penalty of a publicized execution in approximately seven days. How do you plead?"

"Bite me," I managed to say after slipping.

She continued. "You are now in the decontamination process. Workers carry all sorts of foul disease. We take pride in keeping a germ-free facility. Most have described the process as . . . uncomfortable."

The hovering bot's screen darkened. The monitors removed themselves from the acrylic cage, and the sliding doors shut. Above, below, and from the sides, tiny hoses sprouted from the panels. I retreated backward against the wall. My feet stuck to the ground like magnets. My hands and arms locked in place like invisible chains were attached to them. I was spread out like a human X.

Each spout started spraying blue liquid. The streams squirted like spindly darts. The first pelt was a beesting. I cowered, shutting my eyes. Another hit my thigh, then another at my back, one at my thigh. The stings turned into small drills. My head dangled when I lost count of the stabbings, but it had to be dozens. My hands went limp as the burning sensation became an uncomfortable norm with no end in sight.

At first, I wanted to kill them all.

But by the end, I wanted them to kill me.

Chapter Eight
AVI

After the meeting with Father went askew, I had to deal with Mother. She pulled me along the corridors like a rag doll, rambling about a little bit of everything. I mostly remained silent, but every so often I'd reply with an "Oh, Mother!" so as not to appear too disconnected.

"Aren't you just excited about this evening?" she asked.

"Oh, Mother!"

She stopped abruptly right in front of the dressing quarter. "Avi." She threw her hands up.

"Hmm?"

Her brows were unusually high on her forehead. "I didn't think I had to bore you with the history, the importance of a crowning ceremony."

I knew very well the spectacle that was an Elite ceremony. I'd attended many, and on each occasion an Elite family would go above and beyond to outdo the previous families' festivities. It was an unspoken competition. All Elites had them once their child neared their eighteenth revolution around the sun. Grandmother had done it; Father had done it. Now it was my turn. I've dreaded the day since my standard birthdays were extra ostentatious, against my will, of course.

"We have a grand evening ahead of us. I know you are nervous and have had a terrifying day to say the least, but I need you here, with us. We've put a lot into the wardrobe, the entertainment, the guest list. The entire region will either be here or livestreaming the broadcast."

"Oh," I managed to say.

"Come, my very stubborn firstborn." Mother pulled me along. "I had Pea draw you a lemongrass and jojoba oil bath before we get started. Your favorite."

"Gratitude," I said.

The door slid open, revealing a transformed dressing quarter filled with racks upon racks of fluffy dresses, structured bodysuits, and tulle fabrics. A team of three odd-looking individuals stood next to Pea, my personal worker. Mother had clearly wanted to make a statement this time around, firing the old wardrobe team she'd used in the previous years.

She meant business.

There stood a tall mahogany man wearing all black with a stiff turtleneck that covered his mouth. His eyes were lined thickly with kohl. The second was much shorter, with a black bob with hot-pink bangs and shoulder feathers. The last was a bald woman with skin so smooth and dark like a black panther's coat. When the trio noticed our presence, they all began speaking over one another, offering different opinions on colors and textures. All the while, Turtleneck measured my waist, Pink Bangs pulled at my hair, and Smooth pinched my chin.

I felt like a cadaver being picked at by vultures.

Mother swatted them away. "Now, now. Before we begin, why don't you introduce yourselves?"

"Name's Parade," Turtleneck said through the solid fabric. "And I'll be your wardrobe stylist."

"Onyx." Smooth winked. "Makeup."

"Jal." Pink Bangs broke into a pirouette. "Hairstylist extraordinaire to the region's stars."

They all waited anxiously for me to respond, but I could only stare at their interesting garb choices. Were they going to make me into a rainbow pixie too?

"Madam." Pea stepped forward. "Your bath awaits."

"Nice to meet you all. Very, very excited to work with you." I tore past the squad and straight into the next room.

"Gratitude," I told Pea. "I was in dire need."

Her thin lips arched into a smile. "Glad to be of service, madam."

The bathing unit was steamy, moist. My favorite scents were subtle. Floating chandelier orbs created a mood. The walls, ceiling, and floor were transparent. I could see out into the forest and the waterfalls and the night skyline with specks of stars and the illumination of a full moon. We were in a life-size snow globe.

Pea unzipped my bodysuit and led me down the marble steps into the water. She gently laid my head back and began taking my braid down. I closed my eyes and slid deeper into the warmth.

Every once in a while, Pea coughed into her sleeve. I turned my body to face hers.

"Apologies, madam."

"Pea, you know you can be honest with me." I rested my chin on my knuckles.

"Of course."

"Are you ill?"

She shook her head. "Of course not, madam. I take all of my supplements."

I eyed her. Pea was always fast in her movements, but I sensed unease.

"I'm as healthy as a first-year watchman." She giggled.

"Do you know anything about an illness spreading among the workers?" Was what Liyo had said true? The girl in the library? I needed to hear it from Pea. She'd never lie to me.

She held a wrap as if it were going to leap from her grasp. "The Health Department notified workers of a low-grade virus making its way around. We are to immediately report to the department if we come in contact with any sickly workers."

She sounded like a paid endorsement.

When I stepped out, she wrapped the shawl around my body.

"Did they say how the virus is spread? Where it came from?" I pressed further.

"No, madam."

"Interesting," I said. "Someone told me that it was being deliberately released."

"Can't always believe what the streets say, madam," Pea replied.

We stared at one another until we heard a knock.

"The team is waiting." Mother again.

I wanted to hide, wait until the remainder of the evening was over. Pea patted my face dry.

I grabbed her hand. "I can't."

"Madam?"

"I can't do it. This isn't me. These are Father's plans. And Mother's. I don't want anything to do with this."

"Listen to me." Pea held my shoulders. "Cold feet, is all. You can do this."

"But . . ."

Her light eyes pierced mine. "Not going isn't an option. You know that, right? We all have a position to play."

I wanted to scream, but instead I mumbled, "I know." I leaned on her small frame as we headed toward the door together.

Fate awaited.

❖　❖　❖

Pea watched the team prep me from afar. Her face beamed with anticipation, and her short body stretched tall so she could peek over the frantic hands invading my figure. I wished that I could've had the same emotional response or at least something akin to excitement like she had, but no matter how hard I tried, I couldn't bring myself to care. All I wanted was to fast-forward time so it could all be over.

My hands and feet soaked in vats as Jal tugged at my roots. Onyx placed a tingly rejuvenating mud mask on my face. Parade leaped like a gazelle from rack to rack, showcasing and explaining every detail of each piece. They poked, prodded, painted, stripped, tightened, and scrubbed every part of me. I became an ornamental feast. Soon to be gobbled entirely.

I'd been subjected to rigorousness since before I could retain memories. Long days filled with activities and assignments until it was time to enter the slumber pod. Since I was the General's daughter, people assumed that I lived a life of independence, but they had no idea. It was something I was only able to dream about. And the more I visualized freedom, the more afraid I became. I probably couldn't function properly without the excessive scrutiny and supervision perched overhead: analyzing, documenting, and checking for abnormal behavior. Sometimes I wondered if I was even human. Weren't we supposed to feel something? Shouldn't I have been content?

"Open your eyes," Pea whispered. I hadn't known they were so tightly closed. "You look like a true General."

In the mirror, the reflection looking back was very beautiful, poised, and regal.

But it wasn't me.

"What do you think?" Jal asked, his bright-purple eyes staring back at me.

"Lovely."

"And the face?" Onyx squeezed into view in the mirror.

I gave a fake laugh. "Delightful."

Parade burst into the space next. "Okay, okay, okay. Time for ward-robe." He popped his tongue. "Just you wait. You are about to be mes-merized, glamorized, and beautified. You are going to be so dreg when I finish with you."

Pea followed close behind, apparently as excited as Parade. I'd never seen her like that before. I'd never seen any worker experience enjoy-ment. They weren't allowed access to the glitz of being an Elite. Their entire life was work. We made them work.

And I was ungrateful.

All I had done was mope and wish for a better life when workers had it so much worse. I observed peculiar punishments and televised executions, but like the rest of the Upper Residents, I hadn't accepted it as reality. It was our way of life, Father told us, and that had been enough justification for me.

❖   ❖   ❖

Parade put me in a bodysuit made of dark-red rose petals and a crown made of green thorns. It itched a great deal. For my grand entrance, I was positioned on the stage crouched inside a large rose and instructed to "blossom" through the enormous petals when the music began. Then I was to pose for the cameras. I did as instructed despite feeling utterly ridiculous. The crowd gasped at the artistic display and cheered as if something really important had just happened. The best part of that ensemble was when they removed it.

The second costume was a bright-yellow dress, billowy at the bot-tom. I liked that one until they stuffed me into a corset encrusted with crystals and pearls and hoisted me into the air like a chandelier. The theme: I was a sun deity floating in from the east and right into the middle of the crowd. The plan was to gracefully wave my arms and legs, then land into a fourth-position ballet pose. I'd rehearsed, but I'd never taken into account all those people. Watching me like some sort of otherworldly spectacle. I'd lost count of the moves, the transition now too late, and I ended up flipping around like a drunken puppet and backstroking through the air.

The last outfit of the evening was a ball gown that took up four place settings. Every time I tried to walk through the crowd, the dress would knock someone or something over. I told Mother that I wasn't happy. Her reply was that the photographers and broadcast crews were getting marvelous footage. There had to be at least a hundred reporters from every part of the Southern Region wanting to get a glimpse of the next succeeding General.

I hated stuffy soirées. The same wealthy Upper Residents munched on hors d'oeuvres, and adolescents vied for attention by flaunting the most elaborate jewelry money could buy. Music played, not that upbeat kind where you could really move like in the Square, but a royal kind with symphonies and opera singers. Desert music was what I called it.

I had a special seat made of the finest white velvet and adorned in white gold that I remained in or near. Patrons stood in a line wrapped around the entire ballroom to offer me gifts and wise words about maturing and ruling and being an upstanding lady. I was given every gift imaginable: necklaces, bags of gold, diamonds, rubies, crystals, and fine embroidered fabrics from faraway lands. Pea was in charge of sorting it all and ensuring it got safely to the vault. I'd never even been inside the vault before, but I knew it held tons of riches accumulated from every ceremony I'd ever had.

Hundreds upon hundreds of guests enjoyed the bizarre animatronics, the fire dancers, and the laserworks display. I had insisted that it was all too much, but Mother had informed me that it was never enough and that I should smile more.

I tried to hide my pout as more people kissed the back of my hand, embraced me, and tried to hold conversations that I wasn't interested in. I must've said *gratitude* a billion times that night. Bored and fighting to stay aware, I noticed one of the workers holding a tray of cocoa desserts. The same white-haired thief I'd seen in Instructor Skylar's greenhouse.

I hoisted myself up. Pea tugged at my dress. "Madam, please have a seat."

"It's him," I said without thinking.

Pea grabbed my arm, following my gaze. "How do you know him?"

"It doesn't matter." I frowned. "Fetch him."

"Madam, that's not a good idea right now," she pleaded. "You have guests waiting to speak to you."

I lifted the immense dress and darted into the gathering, Pea close behind. "Madam!"

"Leave me, Pea."

People gasped and yelped as I shoved them out of my path, causing them to spill their drinks and fall into bystanders. I was almost to him when Phoenix stepped in, blocking me.

"Avi?" He bowed and kissed my hand. "What a surprise—I was just thinking about your exquisiteness."

Liyo turned, close behind Phoenix. We stared at one another for what seemed like eons. I thought I saw a flash of electricity shift in his eyes, but I wasn't sure. I smiled nervously, stood on the tips of my toes, and wiggled my fingers in the air. Immediately, I figured that was the stupidest of gestures. His face didn't waver from that of a content worker's expression. He didn't smile or return the wave. He only read-justed the silver tray perched on his shoulder and ducked into a flood of colorfully draped bodies.

Phoenix peered over his shoulder. "Looks like you've just lost a friend."

I bit my lip in embarrassment. "How are you enjoying the festivities?"

"Better now that you've graced me with your presence."

I chuckled nervously, considering an escape, when Pea took my hand. "Madam, you must come back."

"Of course," I said quickly.

"We will speak again, Princess." He waved me away.

"Just a word of advice: don't get too comfortable with that worker." Pea linked arms with me. "He works on the Farmlands. He's class Chattel. He's only here because we needed the extra hands for this evening."

I stopped midstride. "You do know him?"

"I know every worker brought into the Citadel." She pulled me along. "People are watching. Promise that you won't ever do that again."

Mother reached out and smiled delicately. "Avi, come."

The ballroom got quiet as the Union's ballad played, and people moved aside, clearing a path to the magnificent dining table. The doors parted. Father emerged, wearing a dark-gray bodysuit with all the technological trimmings: some parts of his stomach, thighs, and upper arms were smooth, while others resembled a lizard's skin. It had been specially fitted by the region's best tailors to mold to his muscular physique. He wore his better than most.

Elites and Upper Residents cheered and offered the official salute. Father shook hands on his way down, waved, smiled. Mother blew him a kiss and clapped proudly. One day, I hoped to have the love that they had for one another.

He took a seat in the middle of the table and Mother next to him, while I was sandwiched between Phoenix and Jade. The rest of the guests got settled and awaited his word.

Father raised his hand as his voice echoed. "Bring the feast!"

It seemed like every worker from the region emerged carrying polished trays. Their faces remained neutral like their outer coverings, a skill learned in training, to not feel but to do. It was a sore sentiment that I felt every time they served me. They placed plates in front of the guests carefully and lifted the silver lids: lamb smothered in gravy, potatoes covered in sweet butter and seasonings, and grilled vegetables. They worked swiftly. As soon as the covers were off, someone else poured drinks, and another added silverware. Their actions were mechanic. Even when they stopped moving and perched behind us, waiting for an order, they still appeared unnatural. Forced.

"Wine, madam?"

I looked over my shoulder to ask what type of wine was being served, and here was Liyo holding a goblet.

"Wine?"

"Sure," I said, breathless.

"I have red, but we also have white." He showed me the options.

"Red," I managed to get out. "Please."

He poured carefully but confidently, and as he handed me the glass, he grazed my skin ever so slightly. A jolt of energy tingled, engulfing my entire left side. "Enjoy, madam."

Liyo had vanished, but I was stuck, staring at the golden cup. It was as if the ballroom had emptied, and I was the only one present.

The electricity.

"Avi." Phoenix took my hand.

I snapped back, jerking my hand away and resting it in my lap. "Apologies. I have much on my mind at the moment."

He said, "I'm just so excited for you to hear the announcement."

I shifted in my seat and glanced at Jade, who was clearly eavesdropping. I was sure she knew the details of this announcement. She smirked, looking down on everyone. On me.

Dessert was served: chocolate mousse with vanilla and raspberry sauce, topped with graham cracker crumbs. My favorite seemed less appetizing than usual.

"This is my second request," Jade complained.

The worker was sorrowful and stumbled to the kitchen. When she returned, her cheeks had ballooned like something was expanding in her jaw. When she set the glass down beside Jade, she began choking. Blood dribbled down her chin. She tried to cover her mouth, but it was too late.

Jade screamed at the sight. "Get her away from me!"

Guests stirred. Father flicked his hand. A watchman grabbed the girl and led her away as another worker came in and scrambled to sanitize the areas around Jade.

Father frowned and placed his thumb on his temple.

"Repulsive." Jade checked her bodysuit for any signs of the worker's sickness. "I cannot wait until the droids are here."

Not long ago droid prototypes had been integrated into Upper Residents' dwellings. They were supposed to replace workers because they used fewer resources and were less likely to rebel. They seemed efficient, but they scared people with their glowing eyes and cold titanium figures. They also weren't able to carry out complex commands, so they had been recalled until further notice. I knew the Union was working on the newer, improved models.

Commander Chi whispered something in Father's ear, then returned to his seat.

"We welcome you all to the Citadel to join in this momentous occasion," Father announced, "to celebrate our daughter, Avi Anais Jore, who will become the next General of the Southern Region."

Everyone applauded.

"But we also have another announcement." He lifted his glass to Phoenix.

I fiddled with the stem of my glass.

"I have always admired your father, and I have heard much about your accomplishments during our travels." Father patted Commander Chi on the shoulder with one strong hit. "Your son is truly a top achiever."

Phoenix sat even straighter, soaking in all the glory.

"Thank you, sir, General, sir," Phoenix said in a forced deep voice with his cup raised. "I'm honored that you think so highly of me. It's a great honor to be in your presence. If I can be a small percentage of the men you and my father are, I will have fulfilled my life's purpose."

Father touched his chest in appreciation. "I cherish both my daughters and my wife. They mean the universe to me. Avi is my eldest, and she will soon bear the weight of the world, the galaxy, and future generations to come. Avi is still transitioning into a true leader, and I can't wait for the day when she truly becomes who she is meant to be."

Jade held her breath, and I searched Mother's expression for answers.

"It's been decided that on Avi's nineteenth revolution around the sun, she and Phoenix will unite."

My hand jerked, causing the glass to tumble to its side, spilling its burgundy liquid as it rolled slowly across the marble tabletop.

Several holocams flew in front of me to capture my reaction, as a worker soaked the mess I'd made with a cloth. *You should smile more—it's polite.* Mother's voice. But I couldn't even muster politeness. I brought my palms up to my chest.

Jade clapped so fast that her hands became vibrations. "Oh joy, a matrimonial union. I must find a dress. What color should I wear? Cobalt? Or maybe lavender?"

Father lifted his goblet higher, rotating to me. "Phoenix will be an asset to you and the family. He will shape you into the woman and leader you are capable of being. Let us toast to this future union." Clinks of glasses ricocheted, and I spiraled.

I couldn't look at Father. I couldn't look at anyone. I knew that an arranged marriage was imminent for Elites my age, but I hadn't known that he'd expedited the process. My heart burst into grains of sand, then further ground into dust as it floated away. The chatter continued as the lights dimmed. Performers with neon beams attached to their tutus twirled and executed perfect pirouettes for the grand finale of my life officially being over.

I guzzled three glasses of wine during the show as if I hadn't drunk liquid in days.

People took my puffy eyes as a sign of joyous tears and hugged me harder in passing. Phoenix managed to move closer as the cameraman flashed lights in our faces. I stood in the middle of the one-sided interview as he spoke. But then someone directed a question at me.

"Elite Jore, do you have any comments about the bloodshed at the Academy earlier?"

The images. The laser shot. Saige. It all came flooding back. I felt sick.

"Pea, Pea! Take me back to my quarters," I said.

As we cut through the mob, Head Gardner grabbed and embraced me. I hadn't even known she was there. I stiffened. Unfamiliar with her affection.

"Congratulations, Avi." She beamed.

"Leaving the party so soon?" Blair, her niece, appeared behind us. "It's just getting started."

"I've become ill," I said simply. "Is there something I can do for you?"

"Not at all. Blair and I just wanted to wish you the best."

"Well, enjoy the festivities." I turned on my heels, preparing to walk away.

"Oh! How could I forget? That Impure girl. The one from the Academy. She's confessed to her crimes and has been detained. You won't have to worry about her any longer. Rest well, Princess." Head Gardner waved.

When Pea and I made it out of the dining hall, I ran to a nearby planter. Acid and all the wine I had consumed made their exit.

Chapter Nine
SAIGE

I awoke in a cold sweat. The moistness stuck to the back of a loose brown jumpsuit. It felt like someone heavy was sitting on my chest. Where the hell was I? Over the left side of my breast was an embroidered inmate number: 7612. No name.

I sat up on an uneven, lumpy mattress.

Outside our lockup was a beehive of other cells. We were on the highest level.

A head fell from the top bunk above me. I frowned at the upside-down face.

"Pretty," the inmate said, before disappearing back over the top.

She jumped from the bed, landing on bare, dirty feet. She nibbled on the ends of her hair. Her nails were chewed to nubs, and she had multiple scratches on her face, old scars mixed with new.

"I used to be a gymnast . . . for the grand festivals." Her nose twitched like a rabbit's before she fell into a full-on bow as if she were reliving the moments. "What's your name?"

I glared, hoping her stay in the cell would be short. I didn't want to talk. "Saige."

"Like the plant? I like sage." She scratched her chin with her pinky, then pulled the embroidered inmate number away from her chest. "2901. That's what they call me."

I called her Two.

Two was very peculiar, very annoying for the most part. She sat at the end of my bunk and just stared. I lunged in her direction to scare her away, but she just stared some more.

"Is there something you want?"

She shook her head, her cheeks flushed. "You look like my—my sister."

"Lower Residents are only allowed one child." I was beginning to think the other sibling only existed in her mind.

Two kept pulling at her pinky. "She had nappy red hair. Could hardly get a comb through it."

I closed my eyes. Two was clearly insane. She needed to be in a loony receptacle instead of there. Either way, I was stuck with her until they offed me. I wasn't sure which was worse.

"They took her as soon as they found out and tossed her out of the window."

I reopened my eyes and sighed.

She rocked hard, causing the springs of my mattress to squeak. "Mother jumped right after her. I stabbed the watchman in the neck with a shank I made." She stabbed at the air with an imaginary weapon. Reliving the moment. "I was angry. But I didn't mean to."

I wasn't the compassionate type, so the best I could do was allow her to rock without interruption, even if it bothered the hell out of me.

Suddenly, alarms sounded, and each cell door unlocked. I stopped at the opening and looked through the gaps in the white railing that prevented detainees from falling to the bottom. I could see into all the emptied cubes. Inmates exited their holes and moved in one direction down the levels and past watchtowers. Armed watchmen were stationed at every turn. Just like on the outside.

"Mess time!" Two snapped her fingers. "Come on, slowpoke."

I followed the masses of female inmates dressed in dull browns. Most of them traveled with bowed heads and bends in their backs. Demure, just as the Union wanted. Three healthy-looking inmates cut the lines. One was large with a smooth bald head, and the other two were identical twins, sturdy and slender with half of their faces covered in gang ink. I was shocked with the one-kid rule that the Union hadn't aborted one of them.

"Don't look at them," Two instructed.

I grunted.

The mess hall was a massive arena with rows upon rows of hundreds, if not thousands, of seats and long metal tables fixed to the ground. The lines were ridiculously long as inmates shoved to move one space closer to the tasteless-looking grub. According to Two, very bad punishments were issued when rules were broken.

She handed me a dingy tray. The inmate behind kept bumping her tray into my lower back. Testing me. But there was nothing I could do—eyes were everywhere, and I didn't want to risk earning further punishment. Not with Head Gardner breathing down my neck.

Food monitors were stationed behind shields. They methodically placed soft packs and freeze-dried bricks onto our dishes. Two led us to a table in the middle of the arena next to watchmen stationed above.

"Safer here," she said under her breath, her eyes shifting.

I couldn't help but compare the similarities of the imprisoned workers to the so-called free ones. Either way you went, you were being examined and policed. The only difference was that death was inevitable in the detention facility. It hung over us, hugging us like a thick smog. And they reminded you of it. Head Gardner announced the names of the inmates scheduled for execution that evening. Wincing, Two said they did it every day during evening mess time. It wasn't enough to incarcerate and torture.

How fitting.

I thought about asking Two about escape attempts, if anyone had ever gotten away, but I had to wait for the right time. She could be a mole. I put nothing past the Union.

She crunched into the stale block, then gasped. "How rude of me."

I untwisted the cork of my protein pack. "What?"

"2901. That's what they call me."

I grumbled as if it were the first time she'd told me.

"What are you in for?" Two asked.

"What's it matter?"

Two hunched her shoulders. "I dunno. Just makin' conversation." She didn't speak for a long time after that.

"Look, they disinfected me." I admitted, "I'm still getting over that."

She picked at her nails. "Yeah. Yeah. It's okay."

The bald woman and the tatted twins approached our table with empty trays. Two took a chunk of her hair and stuffed it into her mouth.

"Two, you haven't introduced us to your new buddy," the bald one said casually, patting Two a bit too hard on the shoulder for my taste. "Name's Lox. And these two"—she motioned toward the twins—"are Rock 'n' Rye."

"You're not allowed. You're not allowed. You're not allowed," Two repeated at record speed.

I glanced at the watchmen. They looked back at us but didn't move a centimeter. The twins spoke inaudibly to one another, but their eyes were fixed on me. Two's chants became louder, more forceful than before.

Lox slammed her tray down. "Would you shut it!"

Two flinched.

I crunched on a piece of edible brick. Unbothered by her theatrics and mediocre attempt at dominance.

"Why you hangin' around mutts anyway?" she asked Two but kept her sights on me.

But Two was in a trance.

"Thanks for the warm welcome, Lox," I said, putting emphasis on her name.

She shot me a half grin. A few of her teeth were missing. "I don't take well to newcomers, and I definitely don't take well to mixed breeds. I think me and you are gonna have some problems."

I hated the slur so much. I wasn't a ratchin' dog. I crunched the brick a little bit harder.

Rock 'n' Rye gave each other an exploding fist bump. Then they all scattered.

It took a while for Two to meet me back in reality. When she did, she told me the three had murdered inmates before just for fun.

Nothing surprised me, outraged me anymore. I had seen things, done things. These people had nothing else to live for, nothing to look forward to. This was the end of the line. Living life as a bottom-tier human brought out the worst in people. As long as they didn't bother me, we'd all be good.

"Everybody's killed somebody before," I replied and took another bite.

After mess, it was time for mandatory entertainment. The Union was such an ass-backward place to be. I'd rather have sulked in my cell and wasn't in the mood for socializing or forced fun. Two told me that everyone had to watch Marco Grant videos. It was the highlight of the inmates' day as they fought to get into seats closest to the screen. I'd seen Marco Grant before, but I'd never been forced to watch her perform. She stood for everything fake about the Upper Residents' world. An influencer with a mass following of sheep and lambs. They saw a mega pop star, but to me, she was just another illusion created to hide the cruelty of our society. Pretty things were meant to distract.

Two and I sat in the farthest row in the back. The lights were dimmed like we were in a real cinema. Marco popped on the screen. She had on a two-tone wig with a fat bang; one side was baby blue and the other pink. There was so much hair on it. She wore a sea captain's hat and an orange leopard-print leotard with a green tutu and knee-high boots. Her makeup was too perfect. Her dark-brown skin looked like a baby's, clear and untouched.

"Greetings," she said, holding up a peace sign. "I'm going to share with you my newest album. Hope you like."

Inmates burst into cheers, grabbing one another as if they'd been set free. Two and I remained unmoved. The video began, and eyes were glued to the screen as inmates swayed back and forth to the rhythm.

Two nudged me and pointed to a girl beside me. She was too deep into the electronic beats. Just swaying. Two whispered with her eyes closed, "I don't watch. She turns people into zombies. The government hypnotizes the masses with her music. She's a demon from outer space."

I watched one of the videos. It was mesmerizing. When I felt myself drifting, I closed my eyes just as Two had instructed.

On the third song, the gang decided to act.

A twin brought a chair down over my head. I fell backward. Two wailed. Inmates jolted from their dazes and swarmed around us like hyenas waiting for a fresh kill. The other prisoners lifted me into a standing position. I put my fists up, still unable to identify the attacker in a circle of screaming inmates. Where the hell were the watchmen? From the circle emerged the twins. They came at me simultaneously, one from the front as the other whipped around and brought her forearm around my neck. She punched me in the ribs as I attempted to keep the other from choking me. I lurched forward, lifting her off her feet, and tossed her over my shoulder.

The crowd groaned as if they were in the actual fight, feeling their own bodies smash against the ground.

The other twin tackled, then pinned me. She sat on my chest and pounded away. I thrust my hips forward and slipped my body from underneath hers. I got her in a headlock. She clawed at my arm, but I wasn't letting up. The others shouted and cheered, but it became soundless as I was in tune with the life draining from her.

She fell limp, her chin resting on my bicep.

"Get off!" Another crack to the skull.

Several inmates began kicking me, digging their boots into my back and sides. I curled into a heap and silently prayed for a quick end.

Alarms blared, lights sprang on, and laser shots were fired. A laser went through Lox's chest, blowing a hole through her ribs. Inmates scattered in different directions like roaches when the lights came on. Cloudy mists sprayed from the ceilings. Inmates coughed. Eyes rolled back, and the inmates all dropped just like Lox.

My brain pulsed against my temples. After the fight, I'd been injected, dragged somewhere, and plopped into an uncomfortable chair. A camera zoomed in. My swollen face was unrecognizable in the monitor. The inmates had banged me up pretty good. Equipment hissed, and thin wires trailed along my chest. A soft cuff tightened around my upper arm, then beeped before loosening.

What were they going to do to me?

Chapter Ten
AVI

The slumber pod hissed open. It felt like an anvil had taken refuge on my spine. Pea was waiting for me with an array of fresh fruits, toasted croissants, wild-berry jam, citrus tea, and a pleasant smile. The sun was barely up. I stepped out, took a painful stretch, and consumed a grape. That single piece made my stomach churn. I pushed the platter away.

"You must eat, madam. Today is your first day of General-preparation training. It is intensive. If you don't eat, you won't have enough energy. Then you'll faint. You'll just faint, madam."

I peered out the window. "I just haven't had much of an appetite as of late."

"I keep telling the kitchen staff that presentation is important." She rearranged the orange slices in a perfect layered row. She had a thing for symmetry. "Are you nervous about the matrimony?"

I almost heaved up the solo grape and whatever remained from the evening before when she mentioned matrimony. Elites believed in arranged marriages to keep the bloodline pure and the power centralized, but the choice of Phoenix was unexpected. Father and Mother had been arranged, but usually it didn't happen until twenty-one. I didn't even want to think about why I was getting the early treatment. Did they want to just pawn me off on someone else because they were tired of my rebellious antics?

"I was trying to forget about that." I disappeared into my wardrobe. "I can't seem to find anything in here. Who's been putting things in the wrong place?"

When I emerged, Pea held my training bodysuit.

I could only manage a huff.

"Everything will be fine. Phoenix is a fine man. A very fine young man, indeed." She handed the bodysuit to me. "You'll have a fancy dress and a fancy wedding. With lots of gifts. You'll live together in a beautiful dwelling and make beautiful offspring. For sure, your offspring will be the top of the litter. The best of the best."

I grabbed her to keep balance; I'd gotten light headed just thinking about a future with him. She rubbed my shoulders. "Oh, madam, I didn't mean to make you feel—please forgive me. Sometimes I get a little excited, and I can't control myself and—"

"Pea." I stopped her. "This is worse than any nightmare I've ever experienced. But this—this is real life, and I can't escape it."

She placed my head on her flat chest. Pea was such a tiny little thing.

"All you have to do is follow your heart." She guided me into a plush chair.

My heart. The words pranced through my mind as she laid out an array of combs and creams.

That boy, Liyo, and the electrical currents that transmitted from his body to mine helped force the dreaded thoughts of Phoenix to the outer edges. It could've been just a simple shock, or perhaps it was something more and the tides he emitted were some sort of scientific breakthrough. It was all a mystery, but there had to be an explanation. Everything could be proven with science. I thought about our encounters more times than I thought was appropriate. I chalked it up to a mere coping mechanism or a form of silent revolt against Father. He was a worker, for galaxy's sake.

"Who taught you that?" I asked. "Follow your heart?"

With a wide-tooth comb, she parted my hair in small sections. "I heard it in a Marco Grant video."

I gushed. "I love her." Marco was my idol. She was the Union's darling and a multifaceted artist. A performer. A style icon. An actress.

"How would you like your hair styled today, madam?"

I fluffed it up. "Something that says that I'm ready to be a General."

Pea was the best at braiding intricate designs, which I found peculiar because her bone-straight hair could never hold the same patterns that ours could.

"Seems like at the dinner you had a lot to say about Liyo. What else do you know about him?" I asked.

The teeth of the comb literally tore roots from my scalp.

"Ahh!"

"Apologies, madam." She bowed her head.

I massaged the middle of my head. "What has gotten into you?"

She clutched the comb to her chest.

"Explain, Pea!"

Her eyes stayed upturned to the ceiling. "I can't tell you. I just can't."

"Your loyalty is to me," I said. "Now talk."

She exhaled. "Liyo is very, very bad."

I leaned in. "Tell me more."

"Rumor has it that he's a lazy drunkard. Downright sloppy. The farm workers usually find him napping in the hay, right next to the horses. It's just disgusting, don't you think?"

"The nastiest thing I've ever heard," I replied, except I was very intrigued.

"And let me tell you another thing." She got quiet. "He's a seducer."

I huffed. "How so?"

"Let me put it to you this way: all the girls that go into his sleeping quarters howl like wolves in the night."

"Oh, dear." I allowed my mind to wander.

She finished my hair, then zipped me into the bodysuit. "Just forget about him."

"Already long forgotten," I fibbed.

❖   ❖   ❖

Pea delivered me to the Arena, where Instructor Skylar and Jade waited inside the ring. The floor was blackened and glossy, outlined by white lasers stacked on each side. Blank screens lined the walls. Jade already wore her sparring mask and held a neon fighting staff in hand.

"Glad you could join us," Instructor Skylar said as I ducked into the ring. "Welcome to your first day of pretraining. And congrats on your ceremony last night."

If Jade was able to roll her eyes any farther, any harsher . . .

"Over the next few years, you'll have many additional trainings to prepare you not only mentally but physically to rule as our next General," he said. "My advice would be to pace yourself, because you will be challenged in ways that you never expected."

Instructor Skylar placed a mask like Jade's on my face and handed me a weapon. He activated my bodysuit. The breastplates and panels glowed in an effulgent green. He positioned himself outside the ropes. Jade spun the staff over her head so fast that it became a streak of lightning.

"Two points for the torso and head. The rest of the body is one. Whoever gets to five points wins. Keep it clean, ladies."

The countdown started.

Jade came at me like a beast who had been deprived of meat. All her animosity from last night had reached its peak. She inflicted blow after blow and backed me into a corner. All I could do was block, but the force was so heavy that even blocking hurt. In the process of shielding my head, I left my side open. She jammed the tip of the stick right into my rib. I wheezed. She pulled back, fulfilled.

Two points floated across the screens.

I leaned on the laser ropes, clutching the staff. I wasn't sure how much more of it I could take. Day one had begun, and I was already failing miserably.

"Let's go!" Skylar called out. "A real attacker won't give you a chance to catch your breath. Push."

When he nodded, Jade attacked again. I thought about just coiling into a pile. She could get a few more hits in and win. All she wanted was to beat me anyway. Demonstrate in front of whoever was watching how pathetic I was.

I had some level of pride, though, and I couldn't just give Jade anything. I was at least going to make her work for it. I fought my way to the middle of the ring. I used a three-hit combo, and one landed on the side of her face.

Two additional points appeared, but this time for me.

Jade watched the numbers with fury. She tore off her mask, jumped in the air, and beat down on the top of my staff. When she saw me wearing down, she spun around and brought the staff across the side of my ear. The stick flew out of my hand. Two points added. She looked down at me and howled.

Instructor Skylar yelled, but I couldn't hear him over the incessant ringing. Jade had ruptured my eardrum.

"No competition whatsoever. You're weak. Fragile. Only fit for breeding. That's why Father is in such a hurry to marry you off," Jade spat.

As I lay in agony, she leaned over the side of the rope and changed the middle screen to the feed from the detention facility. Upper Residents were able to tune in to live executions. It had been the Union's form of entertainment for as long as I could recall.

Head Gardner's eyes shone on the monitor as she casually gave commentary on the current inmates on Death Mile. There were several, but one caught my complete attention. Inmate number 7612 had been charged with the assassination of an Elite.

A black hood covered their head so the audience wouldn't know who it was until the grand reveal.

I had a horrid feeling that it was Saige.

A physician placed stickers on her chest that were attached to monitors. She was confined to a metal chair, surrounded by lab machinery, pumps, and refrigerators packed with vials. The killing serum. The cameraman circled her and cut to several more physicians scurrying about. Such a frenzy just to execute one person. I wondered when they'd begin popping the confetti. The Union loved a show. An accumulation of anticipation and suspense. Sometimes the commentary of each case could last hours before the actual execution took place.

I got to my feet, sore, hemorrhaging. And put my fists up.

Jade clapped. "One thing I admire about you, Princess, is your heart. You've got a lot of it. But heart isn't enough when you wander into a lion's den."

She rushed me. We exchanged punches and elbows. She deliberately struck me outside the panels. She slammed me, and we wrestled. She managed to trap my arm and bent it slowly in the wrong direction.

"You've won," I screamed. "You win."

There was more pressure on my elbow as she pressed farther. I braced myself for the bone to snap.

"You don't tell me when I win. The points do."

"That's enough, Jade—finish her," the Instructor said. "An honest warrior doesn't toy with their opponents."

Jade grunted as she slowly dislocated my limb. To take my mind off the pain, I observed the screen. My stomach churned the way it always did when I watched such spectacles unfold. But the pain in my arm was unbearable. My face contorted, but I kept it directed at the screen. The

119

pain I felt was nothing compared to what workers went through on the daily. Somehow, I justified it all.

A physician seized the hood as if exposing a magic trick. I found myself winded. Saige's face. Swollen. Her bottom lip had a fleshy gash in it, and she was clearly heavily drugged.

Just when I thought my arm would crack, Instructor Skylar interceded.

Two points were added to her score.

JADE WINS flashed on the screens.

Saige's head wobbled as if her neck couldn't bear its weight. The camera was very close to her face. Her words came out in low moans.

"Isn't that your little mutt?" Jade said from outside the ring, dousing her face with cold water.

I lay still, protecting my damaged arm. Instructor Skylar summoned a physician.

Jade was the epitome of the ugliness in the Union. The Union should've been proud of what they had created. I was as much of a product of our society as she was, but a human life was a human life. Saige was being punished for being in the wrong place at the wrong time. If the Union was as fair and just as they claimed, Saige should've been allowed a second chance.

❖ ❖ ❖

A physician lasered the torn cartilage in my elbow and the inside of my ear. Instructor Skylar stood over Jade with his arms folded and disappointment on his face. I couldn't hear what he said to her, but she stormed out not too long after.

He approached me in clear frustration.

"She should be happy that she won," I told him.

He breathed hard through his nose. "Jade doesn't know how to follow the rules, so I docked her win."

"Oh," I said.

"Avi, you've got to pay more attention to your opponent while you're in the ring. The General has given me a strenuous circuit for you." He hesitated.

"What else did he tell you?"

He waited awhile before saying, "He told me I've gone too soft on you. That you need to be pushed."

"Ah." I massaged my ear. "I'll do better next time."

"No, Avi, there may not be a next time," he said. "You need to toughen up. You're supposed to be the next General. There are hundreds, thousands of Jades out there waiting to strike as soon as you take the post. If you can't protect yourself, how will you protect a nation?"

He was absolutely correct. I'd been reminded of how fragile I was when I hadn't even been able to protect myself from that crazed worker in the Academy. I'd been taught time and time again how to disarm someone with a weapon. But instead, I'd frozen. I'd allowed her to take control of the situation. What kind of General allowed fear to lead them? What was wrong with me? Was I the weakest link in the bloodline? Perhaps Mother would have been better off aborting me.

"I know that you and Father and everyone have high expectations of me, but the fact is that I can't even protect myself." I began to tear up, as I usually did when life got overwhelming. "I feel like I'm floating about with no direction."

Instructor Skylar knelt, gently taking my hand in his. "No one said that growth was a comfortable process. You've got it in you. You've just got to dig deeper. Deeper than you've ever had to before."

"How? Just tell me how, and I will do it."

"I wish it were as easy as a simple formula." He grinned. "But you can start by believing in yourself. Believe in the decisions you make. And never doubt them, no matter what the outcome is. Okay?"

I nodded.

Every part of my body was still tender because I had refused the pain-relief treatments. I needed to feel it. I was tired of numbing myself, cutting corners to ease my discomfort. The Instructor was right. Growth wasn't meant to be comfortable.

The change began with me standing my ground, no matter the opposition.

Saige didn't have much time before her execution commenced. No matter what the outcome was, the least I could do was try. Even if that meant risking Father's disapproval.

Now that I had entered a new level of training, one of the privileges was access to the military databases. I took a detour to Father's archive and logged in to the comprehensive system. The first few terms I submitted yielded no helpful results.

"Search all documents regarding a worker saving an Elite's life."

Numbers, signs, and letters computed in multiple ranks as the system searched. Pictures of rebel wars surfaced.

"Scroll down."

The next row contained an old photo of a woman and a man—one Black, one Europe—arm in arm. Almost as if they were equal. Like they were smitten. I'd never seen a picture like it in any of the Academy's archives.

"Open." Beneath the photo was a small caption: EQUALITY DOCTRINE.

There were pages upon pages of text. It explained that during the Revolt, many workers had assisted us. They'd been granted immunity and given the chance to be sent over the Border by Lieutenant Kofi Jore. My grandmother of over forty generations ago.

"Search why workers were given immunity." The system scanned through several pages. "Stop. Read."

The mechanical woman's voice read, "Dr. Kofi Jore started out as a neuroscientist and head of the special research department at Emory University. During an unprecedented pandemic, an illness that the

CDC couldn't contain, Dr. Jore dove deep into her research of how it affected the brain. This mysterious illness caused strokes, epilepsy, and ultimately death for over ninety-seven percent of the patients. But there were select patients that exhibited special attributes after being diagnosed: ESP and psychokinesis, electrical currents. All of the Europe race.

"She continued to experiment on and test the subjects. Measuring brain waves and abilities. From the small pool of patients, several could not withstand the rigorous assessments and expired. But one survived. This one Europe male was the supplement the doctor needed to wage the war she'd desperately wanted against the powers that be."

I almost couldn't believe what I was hearing. How could it be true? There was no recent scientific data behind clairvoyance or telekinesis, and now this information was stating otherwise. I hungrily listened on.

"During the formative years of the rebel wars, Dr. Jore went into battle with her soldiers to conquer the rest of Mississippi, which had camps of rebels sprouting up despite the Union's attempts at complete control. Dr. Jore and the Europe subject decided to strike within the enemy territory. Unfortunately, the rebels disabled the subject and held them both captive.

"For forty days, they tortured the doctor as well as the subject to gain crucial information on Union defense tactics. Through journal entries, we learned about the horrors she faced."

There was footage. Live journal entries from the doctor herself.

"Play."

"How'd you escape, Dr. Jore?" the interviewer asked.

She smiled wearily before she began her account. "I'd never seen anything like it. And no one believes me. They are trying to chalk it up to delirium from being starved, tortured, but I know what I saw. They dragged us both into the middle of that road. Europe men all with guns. I told him that there was no way we were getting out alive. Just no way. Before this, I never saw them as humans or even animals. We treat animals with more dignity. A cancerous race that needed to be wiped off the face of this planet. But this one, he—he showed me something different. He made me realize that we are no better than they were, and that with too much power, we all fail." Her hand started to shake as she wiped tears from her chin. "They forced us to our knees. Our hands bound. He looked through me, at me with those blue eyes. Like he knew something big and grand. I'll never forget. They cocked their guns. There had to be dozens of bullets. He just—his body was engulfed by light like some human torch. All the bullets just stopped. Floated. He shrieked so sharp that my ears rang. The bullets just reversed. I wouldn't believe it if you told me either, but I know he did it. I don't know how, but he did it."

"What happened to the Europe male whom you were captured with?" The interviewer asked.

The lieutenant exhaled a hard breath. "He just dropped. He was dead. I think that using all of that energy drained the life right from him, because not one bullet touched us that day."

The recording ended with Dr. Jore creating the Life for a Life clause despite backlash from the novice Union members. What this meant was that in a time of war, if a non–Upper Resident directly saved the life of an Upper Resident, that person could use an indemnification to spare the Lower Resident's life.

Father's voice rang in my head. If I were to bring this information to his attention, I'd need all the facts. Saige was a repeat offender, and it was going to be hard convincing him otherwise.

"Search inmate number 7612."

A younger version of Saige stared back at me. Her first work-as-signment photo.

"Scroll down."

All her crimes ranged from drug trafficking to murder. It also said that Saige's mother had been a worker and her father an unnamed watchman who had gone rogue. Her mother had been executed and her father exiled. I'd never heard of a watchman being exiled before. He was still one of us regardless of his crime, and the Union could've easily made the whole situation disappear.

I had all the information I needed to take to Father.

❖ ❖ ❖

I held the reader tightly to my side as I stood on the sidelines watching Father and Commander Chi exchanging solid blows on a checkered grid. Father paused, and Chi took advantage and struck him with sparring gloves in the chest. Father stumbled. The simulator shut down, and the floor turned white. Father wiped the sweat from his cheek, groaning.

"Gratitude, Avi." Commander Chi took a slug of hydration. "I was losing."

He treated me like I was his own. He was older than Father, light skinned with deep lines across his forehead. He had a fat nose with a hearty laugh you could hear from zones away.

"My apologies," I said, too low for either of them to have heard.

"This had better be life threatening." Father poked Chi in the back, like he was a young boy instead of a grown man. "I hate losing. Especially to this crusted old fool."

Chi chuckled.

"Well, it is, actually, life threatening." I handed the reader to him.

Upon reading the title, Father raised his brow and motioned for his friend. I knew how Chi felt about worker regulations; together, they had come up with the stricter regulations. They scanned the document as one.

Finally, Father asked, "What is the meaning of this?"

I wanted to speak, but their joined hardened expressions kept me silent.

"Spit it out, girl." The lines on Chi's forehead became more prominent.

I closed my eyes, picturing Saige's face: the busted lip and the purple bruises. I uttered, "I want to use the Life for a Life clause to stop Saige's execution."

Chi stepped back like I had struck him. Father looked at me like he couldn't understand the language I was speaking.

"Does she speak of that Impure girl, General?"

Father nodded. "What are you trying to accomplish, Avi?"

Before I could answer, Chi chimed in. "I'll tell you what she's trying to do. She's trying to question the system."

Father pretended not to have heard him. "Answer me."

"I just don't think it's fair that anyone should risk their life for someone else only for the act to be ignored."

He smiled a sorrowful one. "I understand you want to be fair, do what's right, but you don't know a fraction about that inmate."

Chi huffed in between words. "That Impure is filth. A criminal. A murderer. She has killed us. Our own. Do you even care?"

My fists balled. "Saige is her proper name, and she is not a murderer. The murderer has been killed. These claims against her cannot be substantiated."

"Commander," Father said, holding up his palm. "Breathe."

"Yes, yes, breathe," Chi spat, sauntering away.

Father asked, "Is she your friend? Is that why you've brought this to me?"

"We are not friends." I lowered my head. "I know the rules."

"I'm thankful she did that for you—for us. I don't know what I would've done if anything had happened to you. But for some reason, I think there's more to this story than you're divulging."

He looked into my eyes as if he were trying to decipher my innermost thoughts. I wondered if his lab had created a type of mechanism that allowed him to do just that, read a prisoner's thoughts. And I was one of his many test subjects.

Neither of us blinked.

"You can tell me anything—you know that," he said.

I took the reader from him. "Are you going to do the right thing?"

Chi yelled from afar, "For the love of all the galaxies!"

"Before I dignify this situation with an answer, I want you to ask yourself"—he pointed to my chest, then to my head—"not here, but there, whether you're making a sound decision. Will she cause more trouble if released? Will she go on to plan and commit more assassinations? Have you considered the lives that you are putting in danger? Their blood will be on your hands."

I checked the clock. Saige's execution was set to begin at any moment.

"I have considered it all, Father, and I'm using the clause."

Chapter Eleven
SAIGE

Head Gardner told me my rights, rights that I had never known existed, rights that I could barely recollect in my drugged haze. A physician pinched the skin on my neck and stuck me. Just like old times. Like mother, like daughter. Head Gardner must've felt victorious. She finally had me. I curled my fingers into a weak fist but then just let go. I wasn't going anywhere. There was no fight left to fight.

The next thing I knew, my body began to jerk.

The muscles jumped and ticced. My heart pounded as the region watched on, betting on which breath would be my last. Some sicko lottery. A physician turned her face away. Did the daunting process of an inhumane execution disgust her? Didn't she execute people for a living? Maybe she was new.

The poisons worked their magic through my system. The lines of the room were beginning to blend like a fading rainbow but without all the pretty colors. The vitals monitor went crazy as my heart rate sped, then plummeted. The world became grayer and grayer.

There was static over the holomonitor.

"Head Gardner." The General's voice boomed. The same one I heard every day at the Academy during clock-in. "Release her."

I spat up blood as the poisons filled my lungs. Why didn't anyone help? Hadn't they heard what the man said?

"Why are you doing this?" Head Gardner's voice seemed distant. "Do you know how weak this makes the Union look?"

What sounded like an argument ensued, but I couldn't make anything else out.

It seemed like an eternity before someone stuck another needle in my neck. Immediate relief came as if I had been filled with cool water. I would have loved to have seen the look on Head Gardner's face, but I couldn't focus. I slumped over in the chair, and then everything went black.

❖   ❖   ❖

Air horns bellowed. The cell's lights flickered.

I was baby Saige again. I was back in the nightmare from before. A continuation of one terrifying scene to the next.

"Security breach in Sector E. Armed watchmen, report to cells in Sector E. Shoot to kill any escapees."

The entry to the cell unlocked, and a flashlight shone. I squinted, shielding my face. Someone grabbed me. I tugged back, kicked. Another watchman. He threw me over his shoulder and carried me down a long passageway. Red lights blared. The whiteness was replaced by concrete-slabbed walls. The man's chest heaved beneath me as his long legs advanced, one after the other. He was on a mission.

A pair of watchmen caught him turning the corner. "Halt!"

He paused. They drew their weapons and called for backup. He placed me on my feet, then shoved me aside. He pulled two guns from the folds of his bodysuit. It seemed like many shots were fired. One just flying over the next. I shielded my ears against the loud bangs and stayed crouched in the corner. What was happening? He scooped me up once again and limped toward the exit. Although he'd managed to shoot both watchmen, one of the beams had hit him.

We made it to the edge of an empty square. I wasn't sure what time it was. He pulled me into an alley and knelt to my level. He had purplish dark skin and black eyes surrounded by a gray outer film. Tears rolled from them.

"Don't believe anything the Union says. The rebellion is coming, and it's so much larger than your mother and me." He wiped my face. "Go to apartment three B in Subdivision Seven. Find Mama Seeya. Don't stop for anything or anyone. You run as fast as your legs can take you. Do you hear me?"

I nodded. "A-are you my father?" Ma didn't have to say it, but I knew my father was an Upper. I just wasn't sure who. She would never divulge it. She seemed scared to talk about it. I'd always dreamed about what it'd be like to have a real family like the ones on the broadcasts. I'd never had a man be nice to me. Help me the way he had. In my little head I thought that maybe I didn't have to run, that I could stay with him since Ma was gone. It was the only good thing I had left. Looking back, that idea was so stupid, so juvenile. There were no happy endings in the Union. Especially not for people like me.

"I wish." He kept glancing over his shoulder. "I have only one son. Sky."

"But . . ."

He pushed me. "Go. Now!"

I ran. The sun felt weird on my skin after I'd been in the dark for so long inside. My legs were wobbly, but I knew if the watchmen caught me, they'd take me back to that dungeon. Back into the darkness.

Shots rebounded off the sides of buildings and dumpsters. I slowed, flinching with each shot. Men yelled. People screamed. Startled birds flapped their wings, flying high, past the horizon. Innocence drifted. I turned back for only a moment. The man who'd saved me—whose name I never got—was swarmed by watchmen.

They forced him to his knees. And shot him in the head.

❖ ❖ ❖

Gunshots woke me from my flashback. I was panting, wet. My body rigid. It didn't feel like mine anymore. Where was the room with the cameras and the wires and the beeps?

Two popped up with a wry grin.

"Where am I?" I asked.

"Back inside the cell." She tucked in the corners of an aluminum blanket around my feet. "You made it."

"Made what?"

"I've never seen anything like it." She scooted away. "We all cheered when the General exonerated you."

"Exonerated?" I repeated slowly.

Before I could even fathom what any of that meant, Head Gardner entered the cell with a pack of watchmen.

"Step away from the inmate." The watchman advanced.

Two hopped off my bunk and stood between them and me. "You will not touch my sister."

"Will you look at this?" Head Gardner chuckled, advancing. "A honk defending a mutt. How quaint."

I wanted to tell Two to move, to get out of the way, but Head Gardner had already forcefully thrown her body toward the commode. Two's head struck the edge. Blood seeped down the side of her face. That vacant stare. I jumped up from underneath the blanket, caught one of the watchmen in the face, and kicked another. Head Gardner punched me in the spine, then one of her henchmen restrained me by my neck against the bed.

She smacked her lips and began reading from her wristcom. "Inmate number 7612, you are hereby released from the custody of Detention Facility Liaison. Your sentence was vetoed by the General with the Life for a Life clause rendered by the late and great Lieutenant

Kofi. It is my duty to"—she mumbled some words in between—"to deliver you, unharmed, to the Citadel. Do you understand?"

No, I hadn't understood. Nothing fair happened in the Union. Why bring me back just to give me false hope? Just so they could make me a slave again. I wasn't truly going to be exonerated. There had to be a catch. I wished they'd just offed me, because there was no way I was going back to my old life.

Either way, Ma's murderer stood firmly planted in front of me.

"I *will* kill you," I said calmly.

"Get her up," she told the men. And then to me, "I'd like to see you try."

I tried to wrestle from the watchmen's grips. Head Gardner backhanded me. It felt like she had rocks in her glove instead of a hand. Stars swirled in my vision.

I flexed my jaw. "Get all your hits in now while your men hold me back."

Her mouth bent into a sneer. "I thought I had you. And just like that"—she snapped her fingers—"you get away. But you will end up here again, right back with me. In my domain. I'll wait for you to slip, and I promise when you do, you will beg for my mercy. You'll beg for death just like your mother did."

I gathered as much saliva as I could and heaved the wad in her face. The gob hit her in the eye.

"Ratch you," I sneered.

She shrieked and fumbled to find a handkerchief in her pockets. She screeched, "Get this filth away from me before I do something that will cause me more trouble!"

As they dragged me back, I couldn't remember ever smiling as hard as I did that day.

Chapter Twelve
AVI

Saige was exonerated. I should've felt ecstatic that I had held my own, was on the correct side of justice, but when Father called an emergency assembly with Saige present, I knew the excitement would be short lived. I wasn't sure what he was going to do, but I should've known that he would have the last say.

I was embarrassed that our meeting had to be under such circumstances and that the exoneration would be proven a sham. There I was, sitting with the very people who had condemned her.

She hadn't even arrived yet, but I just knew that she'd believe that I was no different from them, without a doubt.

We waited in a long rectangular space lined with linear light fixtures illuminating the extended path. Crossed columns supported a sunken ceiling with diagonal panels. Each square was encrusted with the Union's flag. The mood was somber, and I on the utter edge.

The doors flew open. I held my breath as watchmen yanked a hooded Saige forward.

My body rose from the chair without thought. "Why is she wearing a hood? Remove it."

The watchmen slipped the hood off. Curls fell haphazardly around her face. She scanned the table of members staring back at her and then stopped at me in particular. My cheeks burned. I couldn't read her emotions, because she showed none, but I felt like retreating under the table for the duration of the hearing.

Head Gardner appeared from whatever crawl space she resided in. "It's a precaution that we take during every inmate transport."

"She's no longer an inmate," I said.

Head Gardner rolled her neck in defiance.

A watchman released Saige's shackles and pushed her onto a glowing riveted platform. She tried readjusting her legs, but her soles adhered to the surface. She gazed at her stationary feet, then to the General.

"A provision," he said as he typed. "Before we begin proceedings, I'd like to take a moment to address Head Gardner."

She stepped forward with that same conceit.

Father focused on her with intensity. "I'm awaiting an explanation for the insubordination that occurred yesterday. You questioned me when I gave you a direct order."

She licked her lips to moisten the lies that were about to flow from her mouth. "Inmate number 7612 was scheduled for execution, and we weren't able to—"

Father threw his hand up. "Weren't able to or just did not do?"

"There are no excuses for my behavior." She bowed. "But I was only thinking about the region. How we'd appear to the masses. If I may speak freely and without inhibition, I hardly think some archaic rule mustered from some teenager is grounds for an exoneration."

Father's voice became stern. "If I were you, I'd watch what I say very, very carefully, Head Gardner. That teen happens to be my daughter, and that rule happened to be from the pioneer who built this union and is of the Jore line."

She glided over his underlying threat as if it were never uttered. "I momentarily lost control, General. You of all people should understand that. I am seeking your forgiveness."

"What should I do about your momentary inability to process direct orders?"

She paused, then looked at him with hopeful eyes. "I believe in second opportunities, General."

"Oh, you do, now?" He chuckled. "If I recall, you were the one who tried to veto the Second Strike rule for Lower Residents. You proposed that they needed to be executed on the first offense in order for the others to fall in line."

"Affirmative," she admitted.

"Now you believe in second opportunities?"

"I still stand by my veto. *I'm* not like them. *We* are not like them," she said firmly. "That's why they're called Lower Residents, if I'm not mistaken, General."

He began typing a little harder than before. "Your reprimand for insubordination will be thirty days' work without salary. Do you accept those terms, Head Gardner?"

"Affirmative."

"I am the General here. I don't answer to anyone and especially not to you. I don't need soldiers questioning my directives. I say, and you act. My word is stone. Do not let it happen again."

She nodded, then returned to her post.

Saige was next.

"You may be confused as to your current position as an exonerated worker. I will do my best to thoroughly explain, but you must also answer our questions truthfully and wholly. It will be better for you during this hearing. Understood?"

"Affirmative, General." Her mouth barely moved.

"Let's begin with something uncomplicated. Age?"

"Nineteen."

"Current work location?"

"The Academy."

"It appears that you sustained massive head trauma in a group altercation at the detention facility," he said, watching his reader. "Yet you have suffered no memory loss or lapse in speech."

"Everything is fine."

"Some years ago, your birth mother was detained under Union law for breaking the purity clause. Is this accurate?"

"Yeah."

"Your birth mother was executed for her crimes, and you broke free with the help of a rogue watchman. You managed to elude the government for some time before you were recaptured in the Outskirts. How?" His attention broke away from the screen.

"I don't understand." She blinked as if she were counting how many times was a normal rate.

"What's not to understand? I want to know how you survived."

"I took refuge wherever I could, sir. I was a drifter. I was young, but I had to survive. I lived off whatever scraps I found."

He leaned back. "Do you have any connection to Mama Seeya?"

"No." She didn't display one reaction out of the ordinary. She was too calm. I was a sphere of tension waiting to implode on itself. Saige was either a skilled liar or the sincerest person in the room.

"Are you being truthful in your responses?"

"Yes, General."

"Hmm." He tapped his temple. "An Impure child surviving off the grid. The dates in front of me don't align. You can see why I am concerned. We are fighting a war with Impures, who are running about creating chaos and giving workers hope to overthrow us. Did you plot to murder Elite Oya and the archivist?"

"No."

"I know a killer when I see one," Commander Chi intruded.

"We are a merciful people who follow proven science, who follow rules and law," Father said. "My daughter has found a law that works in your favor. And against my better judgment and the strong opposition of my confidants, we have to uphold the law, no matter how much we may disagree. You are hereby granted exoneration based on the Life for a Life clause."

"Because the clause is outdated, we have added additional provisions," Commander Chi said. "You will work in the fields effective immediately."

"And if I decline?" she asked.

Father chortled. "If you decline, you will return to Detention Facility Liaison."

Head Gardner flashed a sideways grin.

"Then I accept," she called. "I accept."

"Wise girl," the General said.

Cabinet members filed out of the room. Father rose, but as I followed, he stopped at the platform and caressed his beard with a gloved hand. "Don't make me regret sparing you. My wrath is far worse than anything Head Gardner could ever inflict. Remember that we are always watching."

Saige kept her face forward. Expressionless.

A watchman came from behind and snapped a collar around her neck.

"What's this?" she asked, finally showing emotion. Anger.

"Precaution," Father added. "It'll ensure that you don't harm yourself or others during your stay."

She stared down at me with fire that I'd never seen before, as if I were the one who'd collared her, but I couldn't place any blame on her. I was a part of the system that was responsible for her mistreatment. Watchmen ushered me forward. The only thing I was able to do was mouth, "I'm sorry."

Chapter Thirteen
SAIGE

After the so-called exoneration, my new animal collar and I were off to the Citadel's Farmlands. It all just sucked, and I was running on low.

Again, I was left floating with nowhere to go. Caged just like the government had always planned. I don't know why I expected this to end any different. Who was I kidding? In this world, in order for the Elite to flourish, I had to suffer. *We* had to suffer so Elites like Avi could prance around in fine garments and fill their bellies until they burst.

I couldn't stop thinking about what Avi had mouthed as I was lugged away like junk. Why would she need to apologize? She wasn't obligated to feel anything for me. I was the one who was sorry. Sorry that I'd ever thought I could escape, that I could be free. Mama Seeya said that I'd never be alone. That I was destined for something greater. Something better than this. She was nothing but a liar. Just like the rest of them.

Apologies were foreign coming from an Elite. Upper Residents rarely acknowledged us, and fighting for us was even rarer. We were fixtures in their world. Her sincerity caused discomfort. I was used to disloyalty from both sides.

So I defaulted to what I trusted most: distrust.

Dust mushroomed around the watchmen and me as we descended into the empty field. Sunburned workers surrounded the craft as if they'd never seen one before, their mouths wide open. I noted every ashen face, every long gray beard, and every rotten tooth.

Welcome to yet another level of hell. My new home.

I squinted against the sun that beamed down on us through the hatch. The heat wrapped around me like a thick blanket.

A watchman flung me into the middle of the worker's circle. "Got a fresh one."

Silence came from the crowd as I lay in the hot dirt.

"Saige!" Eve ran through the circle with her hands outstretched and her hair flapping behind her. Although my expression remained still, I couldn't help but feel an itch of tenderness knowing that she had made it out alive. It was short lived when a woman snatched her back by the collar.

"What's an Impure doing here?" one yelled.

"We don't want any problems!" The sphere of shouting workers began to close in on me.

A few picked up rocks. I lunged forward, clawing. A couple jumped back. Someone threw a rock. It missed. That one led to another and then another. I was hit in the cheek. I couldn't fight the horde, so I shielded myself the best I could and waited for the stoning to be over.

"Go back to where you came from," a woman shouted.

The next thing I knew, Liyo slid into me, guarding my body with his. "She's got our blood. One of our own! What's wrong with you people?"

He'd made it out of the vents of the Vixen alive. He'd survived. I wanted to throw my arms around him, tell him that I was relieved, happy even, but I couldn't be who he wanted me to be. I couldn't give him hope. I couldn't allow myself the weakness of acting on emotion. I'd lost too many people I cared about, and it was just easier to disconnect. That way if something happened, then it'd be easier to get over.

Move on. Survive. I didn't have time, the luxury for love or anything close to it. Deep down, I was jealous of Liyo, his heart. His belief. No matter how many times I'd let him down, he'd always be there. Accept me for whatever I'd become, in hopes that he'd finally break through to the old me. What he didn't understand was that the old Saige was dead, long gone, and there was not an ounce of belief left in me.

"She's not one of us," a man said. "Look at her hair, her skin. Looks more like one of 'em Uppers to me."

Another added, "She's gotta be a plant."

"I said leave her alone," Liyo growled. Electricity crackled around us. They scattered like rats.

"Everyone get back to work." An old man held out his hand. "Name's Tate, lead worker here."

I reluctantly took his hand, and he pulled me off my ass.

"I thought you were . . ." Liyo swept a ringlet from my eye.

Something foreign happened, something other than the pain of the rock pelts against my skin or the tender bruises from the detention facility. I flinched.

"I'm sorry—I didn't mean to—I won't do that again, if you don't want—" He scratched the back of his head. "You're bleeding."

"Welcome to the Farmlands," Tate said. "Liyo's gonna get ya situated. Then meet me in the fields for your assignment. We ain't like in the city. We work hard 'round here."

I followed Liyo to a barn.

"Sit here." He pointed to a stack of hay. "Let me see." He doused cotton with antiseptic. "It'll sting."

When it touched my flesh, it burned, but I didn't cringe. I just peered into the fields where I'd been ordered into slave labor.

I caught Liyo staring at me more than once, but when I'd look up at him, he'd quickly focus on the many wounds on my face. "I'm glad you're here. You're among family now."

"Does this family welcome all members with a stoning?"

140

He pulled back a little. "They don't know any better. They are afraid. We are all just afraid of the things we don't know. Just give them a chance."

I felt myself getting choked up. I wasn't sure why. "I can't live like this anymore."

"Oh, Saige." He brought his palm to my cheek.

I turned away. I felt the inside of my nose burning and my throat doing something weird. Tears weren't too far away.

I hopped from the bale and dusted the loose straw from my thighs. "I should get to work now."

He called my name again, but I had already disappeared into the field, taking the shame of being too vulnerable with me.

❖ ❖ ❖

Tate situated me in an abandoned row. I wasn't used to the constant heat. I was a domestic worker. The sun had snuck into my basket and hid among the husks. My hair was drenched and lips cracked. I had filled my basket to the rim and lugged the harvest onto the cart as instructed. Workers drank at a watering post where watchmen were stationed. I stood in line, and when my turn came, a watchman with a wandering eye stepped into my path.

"What do you think you're doing?" Lazy Eye asked.

"Water, sir."

He snorted. "You don't get anything until you've asked permission. My permission."

I got it. I was the newbie. He wanted to toss around his weight, show me who was in charge. "May I have water, sir?"

Workers slowed their pace to peek through the stalks and catch the commotion the new girl was causing.

"Get back to work, mutt." He turned his back.

"But what about—"

"I said, back to work." He revealed a metallic stick with two electrical prongs at the end. "Move!"

I returned to my post. With every drip of perspiration, a little piece of me died to hydrate the soil. The circle of life. Something had to suffer for the other to thrive. My basket was a quarter full, and the next thing I knew, I was laid out, blinded by the squiggly rays, with corn spread all over the soil.

Rustling leaves called to me. A breeze. One of those summer breezes that you wished was constant. The voice was a hallucination, but then I heard it again.

"Saige?" Eve hovered over my body with a dripping pouch. She lifted my head and guided my mouth to the spout. I gulped eagerly.

"Slow down," she said when I choked on the water.

"What are you doing?" Lazy Eye emerged from the vegetation. "This is not your row."

Eve held her hands out. "N-nothing, sir."

Workers nearby rushed to the disturbance. Liyo was last, there in time to see Lazy Eye shoot Eve in the chest with the electrical baton as she backed away. The line of voltage attached to her. She convulsed. Just like how Ma had. The memory triggered me, causing my entire body to shudder. Liyo yelped, his face red and twisted as his people held him down. The watchman released the trigger, retracting the line. Workers rushed to Eve's body. Liyo's eyes—full of pain. I'd seen it before, that hurt. The same look when he'd watched his parents die.

I turned away. My eyes burning with sweat and tears.

❖ ❖ ❖

Days passed. I avoided Liyo like an outbreak. I also didn't see Eve either.

I owed her.

I was the reason she'd gotten punished, and I couldn't help but feel bad and wonder how she was. I just couldn't bring myself to ask.

Not that anyone would tell me anyway. No one spoke to me. I was the troublesome Impure bringing havoc to their peaceful lives.

It was yet another end of a monotonous shift; my hands were calloused, and the bottoms of my feet throbbed. Bits of straw were tangled in my hair. I had carried bales of hay from the field to the carts until sundown. I just wanted to get in my clumpy cot and sleep away the ache.

Tate joined me on the trail. "How ya holdin' up?"

I hadn't spoken to another human since the incident. "What do you want?"

"Just wanted to let ya know that Eve's healing."

"How do you know?" I stopped walking.

"I'm her papa."

"Oh," I said.

He came in closer, looking around. "I—uh, heard what ya did for her out there before with the watchmen. She's alive because of you, because of Joe—God rest his soul. I owe ya."

"Consider it a clean slate." I continued on the trail.

"She wants to see ya."

I wasn't sure what to say. I wanted to see her too. See if she was okay. Not dead. I'd dealt with enough death. Eve didn't deserve that, especially not for helping the likes of me.

"Are ya hungry? We got extra," he offered.

I was always hungry. Even though we farmed fresh produce, the rations were the same as they were on the outside. "Yeah. Fine."

Tate's home smelled like pine needles after a heavy rainfall. The pantry was simple. There were no pictures on the walls or figurines on the shelves. There was an old table with a few mismatched chairs and a creaky floor. He scooped stew into a wooden cup.

"Take a seat," he offered.

I stayed upright. "I'm not staying long."

He laid the stew and a piece of bread in front of me.

143

I wolfed it down and then stuck my hand inside the cup and licked the remnants from my fingers.

"Ready?" he asked.

I wiped my mouth with my sleeve.

He led me to a room at the end of the hall, where Liyo sat next to Eve's pod. I stepped inside, and as soon as she saw me, she called out with big eyes.

"Calm down." Liyo swept her hair behind her ear.

She stuck her hand out, urging me forward.

I took two tiny steps.

She giggled. "Closer."

When I was close enough, she grabbed my fingers and swung my arm to and fro. "I can't believe you came. I thought that maybe you were angry because I made the other workers not like you. They've been calling you bad names like mu—"

Liyo cleared his throat. Eve nodded. "Liyo says that those names are hurtful and that I must never repeat them." She squeezed tighter.

Liyo uncrossed his legs. "You're the last person I expected to see here."

I slowly slipped my hand away from Eve's, returning it to my side. "I just came to see how the girl—Eve—was." I cleared my throat.

"How kind," he said.

I ignored his sarcasm. "I have to get going. Glad you're okay."

Before I reached the door, Eve called my name. Her face was the only thing visible outside the waves of sheets. "Well, uh, I just wanted to know if—well, when I feel better, could I maybe braid your hair?"

I didn't like being touched, and I especially didn't like anyone in my hair. But I owed her one.

"Mm-hmm."

Her face lit.

I scrambled along the hall, only making it halfway before Liyo swooped from behind and blocked me in. "You're avoiding me."

"Is that a question?"

"Who are you?"

"No one. That's who I am," I said. "Nobody."

"What happened to the girl I knew in the Outskirts?" His eyes watered. "We saw the same thing, Saige. And that same thing is happening right now. How can you sit still?"

"Get out of my way." I shoved him.

He barely budged. "She's in there. I know it. You know it. Stop fighting this. Stop fighting who you are, who you're meant to be." His eyebrows almost touched. "You are *good*."

I wasn't good. I was an opportunist. An escapist. I was the one who ran away from my issues so I didn't have to deal with them. What did I have to do to get him to stop trying to save me?

"Poor, poor Liyo," I said. "You have no clue who I've become. I've beaten. Tortured. I've killed. I've stolen and cheated to get what I wanted. I am not the girl you remember. She is dead."

"You *are* good." He tried to touch my face.

I turned my head quickly. "If I had the opportunity to slit your throat right now to gain my freedom, I wouldn't hesitate. Goodness doesn't exist here anymore. Only survival."

He looked like he'd lost someone, something important to him at that moment. I had done it. Hurt him so bad that maybe he'd just stop with the delusions. I wasn't good. I wasn't good at all.

I backed away without another word and headed back to my quarters.

Chapter Fourteen
AVI

It'd been weeks since Father and Commander Chi had banished Saige to the Farmlands. There was an inkling of hope that I held on to that they'd do the just thing. I shouldn't have been shocked that they'd stoop to such a level. I found myself embarrassed. She probably thought I was just like them, that stereotypical Elite, dishonest. Inhumane. I wanted to see her, explain to her the situation, but a watchman was assigned to accompany me whenever I left the Citadel's grounds. Per Father's request, of course.

Since I was a prisoner in my own dwelling, the alternative was to escape through Marco Grant, living vicariously through her jaunts. She had an entire network dedicated to her greatness. A continuous livestream of Marco entertainment. A holoscreen filled the entire partition of my quarters. Life-size dancers began to materialize, emerging with exact dimensions and form. Marco Grant was hailed as the Queen of Pop. Her followers mimicked her every fashion choice, her outrageous hairstyles, and even the way she conversed.

As I mirrored her choreography, Jade burst into my quarters, dressed in a black bodysuit. "Father awaits."

I gave an exaggerated sigh instead of screaming at the top of my lungs. My afternoon with Marco was ruined.

❖　❖　❖

I followed Jade through the winding halls of the Citadel and through the double doors that led to the hangar. An official hovervehicle awaited to whisk us away to advanced Elite weekend training. Phoenix, unfortunately, was present along with dozens of other Elite pupils.

Father was stationed in front of the craft. "In order to prepare the Elite generation to successfully lead, you must know the internal and external components of our systems. Today, we will spend time on the Farmlands: monitoring, observing, drawing conclusions based on what we see and what we know. An important part of running an efficient system is being able to assess a situation and either eliminate it, modify it, or keep it constant. The Farmlands are an integral part of the Union's ecosystem. So keep a close eye on the workers' processes."

Father made frequent trips to the Farmlands, but he'd never run an advanced session before. Nothing he ever did was without motive. I quietly strapped myself in next to the Instructor. I leaned my head against the windowpane as the craft ascended through the clouds and over miles of plain.

"Avi, there was nothing I could do about the sentencing," Instructor Skylar confessed.

I tilted my head and gave him a deadly glare.

He sank farther into his seat. "You know your father. And you also know that when he has his mind set on something, it's hard to persuade him otherwise."

"You and I both know that she won't last out there," I told him. "She's a domestic worker."

He chuckled. "Well, she's tougher than you think."

"None of this feels fair." I kept my eyes turned toward the clouds suspended beneath us. "It's as if she's still being punished."

Worker structures appeared in the distance. We descended onto a concrete strip and saw hundreds upon hundreds of workers in the fields. Father led the group into one of the storage facilities and then pulled out his reader. "We must complete an inspection of this season's harvest."

The facility was gigantic and divided into groups of grains and vegetables. Workers handled machinery as others carried crates of vegetation from one place to another. Our objective was to pair off and observe worker procedures. Phoenix and I were instructed to follow Father as he met with lead workers. Phoenix scribbled away on his reader and asked all the right questions while I remained in the background, blending in.

Father caught on to my antics and placed me on log detailing. Time passed slowly as I checked records dating months back. The work was endless and the kind I'd have to look forward to when I was in charge.

Afterward, Instructor Skylar gathered pupils, and we trailed Father into the fields. By that time, the clouds had dissipated, and the sun tinged the back of my neck. Workers carried bales of hay while others stripped the husks from corn. They didn't speak; they only worked, each in their own sphere, behaving like equipment.

Father instructed pupils to explore, make observations again, and report back with their findings. Phoenix pointed to a watchman near a watering post. He began questioning him about ways to better manage the workers' productivity. I was delighted that he had someone to keep his attention, so I took the opportunity to get away. I stepped into a pasture of tall straw and spotted a pregnant worker and a little girl tossing corn into baskets attached to their backs. I noted on my reader that workers who were with child should be placed on light duty. A white-haired girl had her basket on the ground and carried an armful of husks. When her basket was full, she struggled to get the straps around her shoulders. She couldn't even lift the basket, which probably weighed the same amount she did. I stood, partially hidden, going back and forth with myself about whether to assist.

Liyo trudged through the row with a full load strapped to his back.

"I can't carry it all," the girl admitted.

"Here, Eve, you get one side, and I'll get the other."

I found myself holding my breath just observing him, his gentleness with the girl.

"Avi?" Phoenix startled me. Reminding me of my bleak reality.

Liyo and the girl peered through the stalks.

"What are you doing over here all alone?" Phoenix grabbed my upper arm.

"Observing," I said, pulling away from him. "As instructed."

"We haven't really gotten a chance to converse since the matrimony news." His face softened. "I know this is all new. It's different for me, too, but I want to try to be a good husband to you. Just tell me what to do, and I'll do it. I swear it."

The word *husband* made me want to retch. "Phoenix, I am sure you are a lovely fellow, but I—I'm just not ready for any of this."

"You can try to resist this, resist us, but I will be your lifelong companion. We will create pure offspring. It is set. And you will learn to respect me as a man." His voice deepened. "I know all you women care about is love, but matrimony is a business, a transaction. We are Elites. That is our duty to the Union."

"I don't need you to help me rule," I said.

"That's not what is being said. And it's not what I believe either. You need a strong partner to keep you on track, to keep you in line. One weak link could cause this whole system to crumble."

I hadn't thought I could dislike him any more than I did already. I scoffed at his newfound audacity. "So you see me as a weak link, then?"

His attention went from me to over my shoulder. He tore through the stems toward the workers. The girl dropped her side of the basket and buried her face into Liyo's waist.

"What's the meaning of this?" Phoenix pointed to a pile of spilled corn.

"It's nothing, sir," Liyo replied, dropping to his knees to gather the vegetation that Eve had dropped by mistake.

"It's nothing?" Phoenix scowled. "Every piece is important. Needs to be accounted for. The food that goes into every Upper Resident's mouth needs to be plucked and cared for to its highest standard. And you tell me that it's 'nothing'?"

Liyo shot me a look. It wasn't a pleading one but one that told me that I needed to diffuse the situation for Phoenix's sake. Phoenix sensed the borderline defiance. Liyo raised himself up and grabbed Eve's hand, preparing for whatever happened next.

Phoenix chuckled. I wasn't sure what he was going to do, but I grabbed his wrist.

Liyo murmured something to Eve. She quickly grabbed the other side of her basket, and together they dragged it away.

"I'm docking their weekly rations," Phoenix spat. "Stupid honks."

"Don't call them that," I said, making my way back.

He sped up. "I beg your pardon?"

"I said, you aren't docking their rations, and don't call them that." My voice shook with adrenaline.

He stared me down as if I were his mortal enemy. I knew at that moment that he'd report this incident back to his father and possibly mine too.

Jade emerged from the group, eyeing me with her usual displeasure of my existence. "Father's waiting for us."

A horn blared.

Workers immediately stopped, dropping baskets into adjacent carts. Watchmen materialized from every part of the field to wrangle and shove workers into straight lines and began ushering them to the Dome.

We were able to observe the workers from a private chamber. We witnessed them thrown forward, some of the resistant ones being strapped into seats. Terror filled their faces. Liyo kept Eve close, protecting her from the aggression of the surrounding watchmen. Her eyes darted from the people in line to the people being force-fed supplements.

They'd soon be next.

I placed my palm on the two-way display. "What is this? What are they being made to swallow?" I asked, taking my sights off the workers and putting them on Father and Instructor Skylar.

Jade paraded over. "If you must know, they're supplements to keep whatever viruses they have from infecting others."

If what Jade said was true, why did the workers look like death was upon them? Like they were being punished?

"From my observation, there has to be a more humane approach to administering supplements. If it were me, I'd be noncompliant, too, if watchmen tied me down. If workers are in distress, surely that would affect their efficiency and output," I explained to the room. To Father.

The system was flawed. How was no one else in the room able to see it but me?

"A good observation," Father said. "Make sure you add that to your efficiency list. We will make note of it."

An older worker with a hunched back was torn from a woman. He already looked sickly. They tried shoving him into the chair, but he resisted. The woman scrambled over to help, pulling the watchman's arms. "Stop filling us with those poisons!"

The watchman pulled out an electric baton and stuck her. Electricity jumped around her body. Workers cried as watchmen pushed them against the wall. I covered my mouth. Father had no expression. Instructor Skylar lowered his gaze. Everyone else stood by and watched as if it were a normal occurrence.

They placed the old man in restraints and forced a single pill into his mouth. A watchman held his nose and lips closed so that the only way to breathe was to swallow. Comply. Once released from his shackles, the man ran at high speed until he slammed his head into the display. Pupils jumped back, gasping at the impact. The old man looked through it as if he were studying each and every one of us. He breathed heavy, labored breaths that caused fog to form on the glass. Foam spilled from his mouth, and he slid down the window. I saw Liyo cover Eve's face. Pupils rushed back to watch the physician's attempts to resuscitate him. The physician placed two fingers on the man's neck and then shook her head.

I dropped to my knees and vomited.

Instructor Skylar escorted me outside. I placed my head between my knees, embarrassed that I had gotten sick in front of everyone. "I'm going to ask once more, and do not lie to me. What is in those supplements?"

"A combination of antitoxins. Harmless. Workers have been getting supplements since the beginning."

I stood. "Then why do they call them poisons?"

"Some people have adverse reactions to certain ingredients. Perhaps he was allergic to something in the previous one."

"So why wasn't he taken to the Health Department?" I demanded. "Why did he just die in front of all of us?"

"I'm not sure why he didn't get the care he needed. The Farmlands aren't my jurisdiction," he said matter-of-factly.

I couldn't believe what I was hearing. How could I not have known what was going on in my region? I had been sheltered for much too long. I knew about the supplements but never imagined them to have adverse effects such as death. What else didn't I know?

My head was starting to spin again.

I rubbed slumber from my eyes; I must've fallen asleep on the return transport, because I awoke on Instructor Skylar's divan.

"How are you feeling?" he asked, handing me a cup of odd-smelling liquid.

"Slightly better." I sipped, then grimaced. "What is this?"

"A little of this and a little of that," he said. "I've been studying different herbs and their healing properties."

"Is the worker in the greenhouse teaching you?" I took another unpleasant gulp.

He sat up straighter than before. "What worker?"

I lowered the cup. "The one with the white hair." I didn't dare let him know that I knew his name.

"Ah, yes." He sat his cup on the tray a little too hard. "There's some construction going on in the greenhouse, and I think it's best if you waited to visit again until the assembly work is done. Also, I think it's time we got you back to the Citadel."

Something was off. "Can I use the lavatory first?"

He nodded.

I wondered why Instructor Skylar had become bothered at the mere mention of Liyo.

Instead of the lavatory, I made a detour to the greenhouse. I wanted to see if there really was construction. I needed answers. I rushed along the trail; there wasn't much time before Skylar would come in search of me. I whipped around the curve but stopped when I noticed Pea and Liyo. They spoke in harsh whispers. Was the greenhouse some type of meeting quarters? Perhaps they were a pair. Was that why she was so bent on me not pursuing him?

As I waited for Pea to leave, I noticed that there was no construction at all.

I heard the door close, and with Pea gone, that was my cue. "What are you doing here?"

Liyo pulled an African violet from its pot and laid it on the counter. "You're following me."

"I'm not following—"

"Who else is with you?" He looked behind me.

I thought that was an odd question, but before I could think of something clever, I admitted, "No one."

Despite my uncertainty, I moved in closer. He scooped fresh soil into pots, then suddenly paused as if he'd just remembered that I was still present. "You shouldn't be here alone."

I pulled my shoulders back. "Nothing will happen to me. I'm an Elite and the next succeeding—"

"Cute." He grinned. "Pass me those plates."

I couldn't figure him out. He had been born and raised a worker, taught to respect and obey me, but he acted like I was his equal. As I retrieved them, his finger grazed the back of my hand. A jolt passed through me and stiffened every muscle in my arm. Electricity. Just like before. I pulled my hand back and examined it.

Liyo snipped the ends of the roots.

"Stealing more herbs," I said.

"If you must know, I work in the fields during the day and in the greenhouse in the evenings."

"Still doesn't mean you aren't a thief."

"Do you think the Instructor got this place like this all by himself? I mean, he's good but not that good."

I felt comfortable enough to return the witticism with a smile. "Do you and the Instructor get along?"

"I'd like to think so."

"Then why would he tell me to stay away from here? Away from you?"

Liyo burst into laughter.

"Are you a criminal? Part of the rebellion? What is it?"

"You seem to know all my deepest secrets," he said mildly.

I stopped talking, not sure what to make of him. Surely if he were a criminal, the Instructor wouldn't have allowed him in his greenhouse unattended. So what didn't he want me to know?

"Fact or gamble?" he asked.

"Pardon?" He'd caught me off guard.

"Come on. Someone like you can't be that royal to not know the game."

"I know the game very well."

"Then, fact or gamble?"

"Fact."

"What do you do for fun?"

"It's very juvenile," I warned.

"Try me."

I clasped my hands. "I thoroughly enjoy replicating Marco Grant dance choreography."

He sniffed. "Typical."

"That is not fair!"

We both laughed, forgetting everything that was at stake by mingling even on the most platonic level.

"Fact or gamble?" It was his turn now.

"Fact."

"Do you know what's inside the supplements they force-fed the workers in the Dome?"

He moved a little faster than before. "Why would you think I would know anything about that? Your people would know more about it than me, yeah?"

"I didn't mean to—"

Liyo's eyes narrowed. They were intense and mesmerizing like a waterfall. I found myself lost in them as he focused on me. They transported me across time, dimensions. We weren't inside the greenhouse anymore; we were inside a world that was possibly his, and I was a mere guest. I wanted to stay, explore, but I couldn't. Reality awaited.

I snapped back when my name was called.

Instructor Skylar.

"Here, this way." Liyo held the back door open for me to escape. "You were never here."

"Right," I said as I exited. "Gratitude."

Chapter Fifteen
SAIGE

Music played in the distance. Swing. An outdated form of music rehashed by workers way before I was even born. Farmland workers were allowed a celebration if they exceeded output goals. I knew that I didn't belong, but I needed a drink, badly. I moved closer along uneven cobblestone to the blares of saxophones and trumpets. I missed music. Dancing.

The Dome was a huge, glass-paneled auditorium, a one-stop shop for workers: all their needs were met there. They enjoyed the small spoils that the Union allowed and seemed content with it all. It was an interesting switch from the mayhem earlier. Like night and day. The way they were acting, it was as if we'd been given mood enhancers along with the supplements. Something about me was off too. I felt begrudgingly happy when there was absolutely nothing to be happy about.

I wished that that were good enough for me. To be fake happy as the government killed us off slowly.

A husky worker with a smooth head and a long red beard braided into two parts pulled me into the center of the celebration. His breath reeked of fermented barley as he twirled me around and around. He let go, and when the room stopped spinning, I watched workers do the jitterbug. They kicked, flipped, and fell into half splits and bounced back up. Those on the sidelines clapped and clinked overfilled glasses.

The air was humid, sticky, but the dancers didn't seem to mind. I squeezed through wet, packed bodies. Over the crowd, I saw Tate on top of the bar, downing a mug. His Adam's apple bobbed.

I ordered a shot of Fire. Put it up to my nose. Allowed my other senses to taste first. Smelled like hot cinnamon. And burned so good going down. I slammed the little glass like it had done something wrong. "Another!"

At some point, I lost count. The sensation of being sloshed had become addictive. Liyo snatched the umpteenth glass from my hand and downed it. He'd been hovering around, watching me, pretending to mingle with workers. I knew it was only a matter of time before he ruined my fun.

"Can I drink in peace?" I shifted my eyes in his direction and mumbled to the bartender. "Another one."

I drank the shot, intending it to wash away whatever emotions I had left for Liyo. It worked to some extent. I tipped over trying to get up. "Time's up."

"I'll walk you back," Liyo offered.

I said, "I'm *so* good, sir."

Tate knocked into dancers and spilled his drink all over the dance floor.

"I'm walking you back." Liyo stared into my soul. He had that effect when he looked at someone. "Wait for me, please?"

I swiped an entire bottle when the bartender wasn't looking and left. My cheeks tingled as the fresh air hit me. I took another swig and stumbled into the cornfield.

Maybe I should've waited for him, but I was tired of him following me around like some damned puppy.

I wasn't sure how far away I was from the party. I was hyperfocused on placing one foot in front of the other. I drank some more and watched fireflies float about. I chased a fat one. It was fast, or maybe I was just slow.

Finally, I caught it between my palms. "Oh, galaxy."

Without even noticing, I'd made it to the outer edge of the Farmlands. There it was: a hazy outline of the Border, which separated us from the Northern Region.

Grass crunched behind me.

Liyo emerged. "Didn't I tell you to wait up?"

I pointed to the wall. "I'm going right over that."

"Lower your voice." He came closer.

I placed my pointer finger to my lips.

He spoke quietly. "I think I finally figured out a way to infiltrate the Citadel."

I was so enamored with the Border that nothing he said stuck. I was near the thing that I'd been in search of for so long. There it was right in front of me. All was not lost after all.

"This could really work," he explained. "Avi's the closest we can—"

I spun around. "What did you just say?"

"I've been building rapport. I think she's the link. It's a risky move, but I have to try."

I shoved him in the chest.

"What the hell's that for?"

"Are those supplements messing with your head?" He was killing my buzz. "Getting involved with an Elite? That's your big plan?"

"Hear me out," he pleaded. "We have a shot at doing something. I can't just sit around."

I took another swig of the drink and massaged the stress forming in my temples.

"'We'? There is no 'we.'" I pointed the bottle at the Border. "The only thing that I need to be worried about is getting out of here. Right over that."

"Watchmen and drones protect it," he told me.

"Is that supposed to deter me?"

He bumped my shoulder with his. "You really want to leave?"

I stared at him. He just didn't get it.

"Look, if you help me do this, then I'll make sure—"

A branch snapped. I put my finger to his lips and clutched the bottle of liquor underneath my arm. In the next second, a swarm of watchmen surrounded us. One swooped behind Liyo. I smashed the bottle in half and sliced two of them. The third disarmed me, and we fought. I flipped him. The collar I wore beeped slow and then incessantly. A shock went through me. My muscles locked.

I fell facedown in the dirt. More electricity crackled around my body.

❖   ❖   ❖

Commands from watchmen and a bucket of freezing water to the face woke me. Through the cell door stood the General, Head Gardner, and another man they called Instructor Skylar.

Droplets trickled from the ends of my curls.

Watchmen pulled me to my feet while another adjusted the settings on my collar.

"Is it programmed correctly this time, you imbeciles?" Head Gardner asked in exasperation. "Restrain her wrists and ankles."

The General walked away. The others followed like sheep. I was shoved forward. Instructor Skylar spoke over the General's shoulder and then glanced back at me. We went through a thin gray tunnel, then entered an arena. Monitors were displayed on the walls, and there was a ring in the middle. Watchmen guarded each side. The General motioned for his panel to take a seat.

"We meet again." His gloved hands remained clasped. "What were you and that worker doing near the perimeter?"

"I—I don't know," I replied, trying to recall what had happened.

Head Gardner scoffed, uncrossing and recrossing her legs. "How convenient."

Instructor Skylar remained composed; he hadn't moved an inch. The General nodded once. A watchman pulled out an electrical stick.

"I'm a fair leader." He tried to convince me. "We are a fair people. I'd appreciate that you didn't take my fairness for weakness. If you don't comply, there will be grave punishments in store for you because this is a grave matter. Now, I will ask again: Why were you and the other worker near the perimeter?"

I wondered if he had questioned Liyo already. Had he pinned the blame on me? I came to the conclusion that if he had, the General would've killed me already. Out of the corner of my eye, I noticed the watchman about to stab me with his stick.

"I was drunk and wanted air. I got lost. It was dark. Liyo was trying to help me get back."

"Lies," Head Gardner spat. "Obviously she and the boy were plotting escape."

The General gestured for Head Gardner to stop talking. She sat back and crossed her arms like a child close to a tantrum.

He looked to the bruised watchman. One of the two I had sliced with the bottle. "You were there. What did you observe?"

His voice sounded like pebbles were lodged in his throat. "Both workers were at the edge of the Farmland's boundary. It is unclear if their intentions were to escape, sir."

Head Gardner looked more agitated.

Instructor Skylar finally spoke. "Where did you learn your combat skills?"

"Skills?"

"You're fast. The training collar was barely able to catch you before you disabled three of my men. That, Saige, is not normal worker accuracy."

"What we need to do is stop wasting time and execute her." Head Gardner leaped from her seat.

Instructor Skylar moved swiftly, placing his arm out to stop her from coming any closer to me.

"Head Gardner," the General's voice echoed.

The panel spoke quietly, and when finished, the Instructor ordered the watchmen to release me from the restraints.

"Bring her to the center."

That was it. They were done with my tricks. Head Gardner was finally going to get what she wanted.

They pushed me into a squared fighting ring bordered by lasers. I stood in one corner, and Instructor Skylar made the watchman who'd testified stand in the other.

"What are we doing?" I asked.

"What does it look like?" He placed a sparring plate over my chest and a face guard over my head.

"Two points for the head and torso. One point anywhere else," he told the watchman. "Do not go easy on her."

"Affirmative," he replied with surety.

A banner exploded into digital confetti. *Fight* raced across the screen. The watchman was big, built like a sleep pod. Thick and unmovable. Power wasn't my advantage, but speed and strategy were. He rushed me like a bull, but I swiftly dodged him, spinning out of the way. He beat on his chest. The next thing I knew, I was being lifted by my waist while he crushed my ribs against his broad chest. Fair wasn't his objective; he was trying to kill me.

I headbutted him. He stumbled and dropped me. Two points sailed across the screen.

Predictably, he charged again, and I used his momentum against him. I flipped him, and he landed with a pound that shook the ring. Another two points flashed.

I climbed the laser ropes like a monkey. "Is that what you wanted to see? Huh? A show?"

The General stroked his beard.

I pointed to Head Gardner. "You want next?"

"Don't tempt me, Impure filth."

The General's wristcom chimed. "I'll deal with this at another time."

Instructor Skylar stopped him before he could exit. "With your permission, General, I'd like to train her."

"Train her?" His face scrunched. "She's much too feral."

"Sir, with all due respect, we are fighting clever Impures. Perhaps it's time to switch up the strategy. She could be an asset."

"To whom?"

"The Union, sir."

The General glared at Head Gardner, whose face was twisted. He raised his palm. "Very well. Take her out of the fields, and train her with the others. But understand that she's your responsibility. If she fails again, I will shoot her in the head myself."

Chapter Sixteen
AVI

The dead worker plagued me whenever I drifted into a slumber. The thick foam spilling from his mouth. His body contracting. The screams from the children ringing. The way Father sat motionless as it unfolded. My own compliance sickened me. All I had managed to do was expel that morning's nutrients. When I became General, that needless death would never happen again. I vowed to put a stop to it. Whatever it was. But until then, I needed to find out what was inside of those supplements. Were they really making the workers sick? Or was I just trying to unearth evidence to discredit Father out of spite for not being who I thought he was, for forcing marriage on me to a man I'd never love? Either way, I needed to know.

With much persuasion and a forged document from the General, I had a driver take me directly to the main branch of the Health Department. Physicians knew all about the drugs, and it was where I'd get answers. I'd done some research on my own in between sessions, finding the deceased worker's medical chart and death record, but it didn't yield the information that I needed. One odd finding that I had stumbled upon was an uptick in Lower Resident mortalities over the last two years. Many of them were undetermined. All ages. From different sectors. None of the data made sense.

I told Pea to stall, but there wasn't much time before someone figured out I was no longer on the Citadel grounds. My foot tapped until we landed right next to the connected colossal silvery buildings.

My assigned watchman stayed on my heels as I scurried along the walkway; he kept pace until we both stood right in front. A holoscreen played a commercial that began with a robotic blinking eye. The next scene was a muscular man with thin white cords attached to his head and chest while he jogged in slow motion on a treadway. A physician entered through a door and paused in front of the monitor. "Greetings. My name is Physician Pike. I'm the director at the Southern Region Health Department Headquarters."

The camera switched angles. Physician Pike turned his face to meet it. "Here at the Health Department, we take pride in the care we give and guarantee to prevent illness, promote healthy living, and protect our patients."

His overly toothy smile and sleepy eyes caused an odd unease to build in me.

Inside, physicians hurried every which way. Workers with yellowed skin coughed behind white face masks. The second holoscreen showed Physician Pike once again. "Attention Lower Residents: if you or anyone you know has flulike symptoms or any other related ailments, please contact Health Department officials immediately. We must all work together to keep the Southern Region safe and germ-free."

When the commercial ended, I grabbed a face mask and stepped inside the lobby. It smelled of iodine and deodorizer. Everything was vividly bleached: the riveted walls and ceilings, the polished floorboards. To the left was the emergency section, where more ill-looking workers funneled through. At an elevator, a physician scanned her irises. She was lifted to the second level and crossed over a curved passage, then disappeared through a set of doors. Behind a decorative water fountain was a receptionist wearing a clear visor. She moved patients' names around on a holoscreen, placing them in their correct time slots. Her hair was as white as everything else in the vicinity. I waited there as she pretended not to notice me.

She finally glared through the screen. "Do you have an appointment?" Her voice was nasally.

"No, but I've come to see Physician Pike," I said, adjusting the uncomfortable mask higher on the bridge of my nose.

She snorted and glanced at the watchman hovering over my shoulder.

I took a deep breath. "Please, I need to see Physician Pike. Now, if possible."

She leaned back and tilted her head. "He's a very busy man with lives to save. You need an appointment. Have a nice day."

I faced the watchman, infuriated. He only blinked. I was running out of time.

I pulled down my mask. "My name is Avi Jore, daughter of General Jore, and if you don't tell Physician Pike that I'm in the lobby, I'll have this watchman arrest you for contempt of a political leader."

As I spoke, she flinched at every word after the General's name. By the time I finished, her hand shook as she tapped the digits in.

Shortly after, Physician Pike appeared. He spoke into his wristcom, then made his way over to meet me.

"Greetings, Elite Jore." He stuck his hand out and shook mine briefly. "Welcome to the Health Department. Please follow me."

The watchman and I were escorted into his office chamber on the highest level of the building, overlooking the expansive grounds. He interlaced his manicured fingers as he took a seat behind his desk. "How can I be of service?"

A knob swelled in my throat. "I won't take much of your time, but I witnessed something very disturbing."

His fingers squeezed tighter. "Go on."

"I very well understand that workers have been getting supplements for quite some time now, that they are preventative measures." I pulled the worker's medical records up on my reader and expanded his profile. "I recently witnessed a Chattel worker who'd been receiving routine medications have an adverse reaction after a particular dose was given."

His face remained blank, impassive.

"He died." I lowered my eyes, reliving the experience.

"I understand," Pike said.

"This prompted me to do a bit of investigating." The next slide exhibited statistics. "There was a new supplement trial that was introduced to the market not long ago. I've also noticed that worker illness and mortality rate have increased by fifty-two percent despite this new trial, which is supposed to be causing less sickness."

"So why are you here exactly?"

His grin made prickles run along my neck. I took a sip of a breath. "I want to know what side effects this new supplement has on workers."

The watchman's wristcom sounded. A screen appeared between the physician and me.

Father.

"You are dismissed, Physician Pike," he said.

He bowed his head and exited.

Father turned to me. "What in the galaxy do you think you are doing?"

I wasn't able to choose my words properly because I was dismayed. The physician had obviously alerted Father of my visit.

"Trying to get answers," I said, readjusting in the chair. "Ones that are concrete and aren't encrypted."

"Bring her back to the Citadel at once," Father commanded the watchman.

The call ended.

Chapter Seventeen
SAIGE

The Instructor didn't say another word to me after he had made the pact with the General. He just left me there. I stayed inside the ring with no training collar or shackles until a worker came forward clutching a reader. She typed quickly, and then the laser ropes disappeared.

"You can come down now."

My soles became unstuck, and I climbed down. She didn't wait for me to follow. She rushed about, pointing things out, where to go and where not to go, and what would happen if I happened to go where I shouldn't go. Her tiny frame carried a loose bodysuit, and she had a wiry brown bob that flew backward as she sped through the corridors.

She stopped abruptly and pointed to an open cylindrical kitchen space with stations placed around an island. There was an actual stove like the ones we used in the Outskirts, with real fire, not that artificial blue flame. Domestic elder workers with calloused hands operated each post side by side, washing vegetables, seasoning meat, and mashing potatoes. No one spoke or looked at one another. Their faces remained intent on their purpose, preparing a grand meal fit for the General and his family every day of the week.

Wrinkled fingers opened an industrial oven, clouds of steam escaped, and the fragrance of fresh bread took over. I could almost taste it on the back of my tongue.

My guide cleared her throat. I turned away, my stomach mumbling, as she zoomed to the next part.

"Does everyone in the Citadel eat fresh?" I asked.

She spun around and eyed me. "My name is Pea."

"Pea?"

"Yes. Pea. Like the little green ball."

"Saige."

"Nice to meet you, Saige. Now, what was your question?"

"Do they always eat fresh?"

"Oh, yes, yes, yes," she said quickly and began jog-walking again. "Most people eat freeze-dried or packaged food because the cost of fresh food has inflated due to the increase in the worker population."

Pea seemed quite knowledgeable, more so than a regular worker should've been.

"That's probably why they tried to replace us with those droids," she said thoughtfully. "Lucky for us, Uppers thought they were creepy. Gives us a little more time."

"Great," I said in my most sarcastic tone.

"Well, back to your original question. While there's nothing wrong with freeze-dried food, it's still only infused with the necessary nutritional values the human body needs. We are grateful to the General that he allows us to have a fresh meal once a week. That's if no one messes up. We look forward to that meal, Saige. So no one messes up. Keep that in mind. You look like the kind that doesn't take well to authority."

I rolled my eyes.

Pea suddenly lowered her head and fell into a bow. "Good afternoon, Elite Jade."

Jade came close to my face yet spoke to Pea. "Why is this monstrosity wandering my halls?"

"Her name is Saige, an Impure. She will be training with the Instructor. I was just showing her around." She kept her eyes down. "General's orders."

Jade ignored Pea. "You look—oh, you're the one that should've been executed. My poor sister always had a soft spot for orphans."

Pea grabbed my wrist, tight, when she saw my mouth opening.

Jade cupped her ear. "I cannot hear you. Speak if you wish to."

I kept quiet against every urge.

"That's what I thought. Father may have allowed you to come here, but this is my Citadel, no matter what strays my dear sister brings in from the gutters."

Jade snatched Pea forward, then threw her. Pea sat on the ground, cupping her injured elbow. Jade pinned me against the wall. My fingers spread, then balled into a fist. I saw red dots.

"Jade?" a mature voice called.

She quickly removed her hand from my chest. "Mother?"

"What's going on down here?" Her mother rushed along the hall. I knelt down and lifted Pea to her feet. She was so light.

"Nothing," Jade answered. "I was just getting acquainted with our new guest."

Her mother's scowl lingered. "Pea?"

"I'm fine, Madam Vivienne. I fell. I can be very clumsy at times."

"Yes, yes. I suppose." Vivienne's face softened. She turned to me. "And you are?"

I sniffed. "Saige."

"Well, I don't know much about you, but welcome, Saige."

Jade tried to stay behind for another round of torment, but her mother hurried her along. "Come, evening nourishment will soon be served. You know how your father is about tardiness."

"Yes, Mother."

When they were completely out of sight, I asked Pea, "Why'd you let her get away with that?"

Tears rolled down her face. "What can I do?"

"I don't know. Stick up for yourself."

"And then?" She forced a smile. "I am nobody. I will die a nobody. I've accepted that. Why don't you?"

❖ ❖ ❖

Pea led me to the final destination. She scanned her eyes, and the door clicked, revealing a bathing room. The area was open with skylights that allowed the rays inside and wide bay windows that faced lush trees and open fields. An aboveground tub bubbled with transparent green liquid. I'd never seen a washing unit with bubbly water.

Two workers stood near the large tub. Both held clear supply boxes filled with disinfecting items.

"This is Lanah and Bres. They'll be assisting," Pea said.

"With what?" I glowered.

A bot floated to the center of the room and scanned my body. It silently calculated results. The report declared that I was dehydrated and malnourished but otherwise clear of anything transmittable.

"The Instructor has ordered a proper disinfection and grooming."

I shook my head. "I won't be disinfected again."

"It's nothing like Head Gardner's process," Pea assured me, but her word meant nothing.

I backed away.

Her eyes were still swollen from earlier. "You're going to have to trust someone while you're here. We work together to survive. Right, girls?"

Bres and Lanah bowed.

Steam danced along the top of the water, and I wondered if they planned on boiling me alive. Flashbacks of the endless burning of the last process took over. I knocked a container out of Bres's arms and rushed toward the exit. I blinked into the door's scanner. It didn't register my irises, denying my exit.

"I will end all of you," I told her. "Open it."

Lanah's eyes watered as she stepped back. Pea held her hand out. "Every worker must have a hygienic decontamination upon arrival. These are the rules."

The box trembled in Lanah's arms; bottles clanked. Pea remained unmoved.

"Open the door," I enunciated every syllable.

"No," Pea said firmly. "I have direct orders from—"

"Screw orders!"

Lanah's box slid from her arms like the sides were greased. The contents rolled. Lanah hid behind the tub; her sobs echoed.

Bres picked up the container and tossed it at my feet. "We actually rooted for you when you were exonerated. Now I think the General should've just executed you."

Pea said, "Bres, she's still one of us."

"Well, someone else can take her. She—she's going to ruin everything. Just look at her."

Pea hung her head. "You're excused from duty. Lanah and I will finish." Bres opened the door and stormed out.

That was what I'd been waiting for. An exit.

"Go on," Pea said, every word precise. "Let me know when you get past the watchmen stationed along the corridors and, of course, by the front door and outside. With skills like yours, you may be able to take two, maybe three of them. But what about the swarm of others?"

I stood in the doorway. Considering my options. She was right, and I was mad about it. "You think you've won, huh?"

"This has nothing to do with winning or losing." She approached me. "There's only one way. Making them believe you're one of them. I can tell you right now that you're not even close."

It was clear Pea was an informant. For which side, I wasn't sure.

Chapter Eighteen
AVI

The watchman escorted me back to the hovervehicle. We both sat silent, awaiting our fates back at the Citadel. I'd known that taking the trip to the Health Department was pushing the boundaries set by Father to the precipice, but it hadn't been enough to stop me. Now that I had been caught, I almost regretted the decision.

Father had observers everywhere.

Just as I had expected, he was waiting for us as we disembarked. I knew he was irritated—disobedience was his pet peeve—but he hid it well for the time being. He ordered me to wait inside his private quarters as he dismissed the watchman indefinitely from his post. Such a harsh sentence, especially when it really was all my fault.

My punishment was next.

Father entered his quarters and leaned against the top of the polished oak bureau. "You forged documents?"

I couldn't meet his eyes. I knew there'd be disappointment in them.

"We are under constant attack. You are a target. Having a watchman with you doesn't make you invincible."

"I don't recall ever saying that it did." I allowed arrogance to slip from my mouth.

Father held his chin high. "What were you doing there?"

"Conducting an investigation," I said simply.

His eyes bulged as I noticed his irritation moving to borderline fury. "Investigation?"

"Affirmative."

"With fake documents at the Health Department?" he yelled.

His anger caused the small amount of arrogance I had left to turn into panic. I whispered, "I needed to know."

"Everyone had already told you about those supplements!" He grabbed my shoulders and pulled me forward. "Why are you obsessed with challenging this? Me?"

The truth was, deep down, I didn't believe any of them.

His shoulders drooped in frustration. "Focus on your studies. Focus on learning the basics of becoming a well-rounded leader. It's not all about uncovering some grand scheme. It's about maintaining what you have and sometimes choosing the lesser of two vices. Do you understand?"

I remained quiet, still in complete opposition. I understood that the next time, I'd have to be cleverer, more covert. I wasn't going to stop seeking the truth.

It appeared as though his emotions were all over the place, and now he wanted to cry. "You are not to leave the Citadel. Anywhere you go from now on has to be cleared by me. You are dismissed."

When I exited the room, the double doors slid shut, locking behind me. I let the tips of my fingers glide against the corridor's walls like I used to when I was a young girl. When everything Father said had been like a symphony to my ears, when it had held weight and truth. I used to envy him, wanted to be just like him, but as the days passed and my eyes opened more, that desire was surely shifting.

Someone hummed loudly, and water splashed from the workers' bathing quarters. The entry unlocked once my eyes were scanned. I peeked through the crack; Saige sat in a tub. Her hair was wet and curly like springs. I knew I wasn't allowed to fraternize, but she had saved my life, and I'd never had the chance to give her my gratitude. All we'd managed to do was take her from one cruel situation and place her directly into another.

I slipped inside. Pea noticed me as she grabbed towels from the shelves. I put a finger to my lips and tiptoed to the side of the tub, where Lanah massaged lather into Saige's scalp. I sat on Pea's work stool. Saige was lying back, eyes closed, with her moistened arms propped on the sides of the tub. I dipped my fingers into the water. She caught my wrist with precision. Her eyes snapped open.

"What do you want?"

"I—I was just . . ."

Pea grabbed Saige's hand and sighed. "Madam, you shouldn't be in here."

"Yeah, maybe you should go, madam." Saige chortled.

"I will." I nodded. "After I do what I came here to do."

"And what's that, Princess?" Saige's brows furrowed.

"I wanted to give you my gratitude," I told her, observing the bubbles as they floated on the water's surface. "I'd also like to apologize for the way you've been handled. I tried to speak on your behalf, but that didn't go as I had planned."

"That was heartfelt and all, but do you know what you could do to make things between us good?" She leaned forward; her nose almost touched mine. "Set me free."

I chuckled, but Saige didn't. She was serious. I opened my mouth, but the words I intended to say came out as tense breaths.

Pea stepped in between us. "Madam, you should return to your quarters. I can meet you there with some fresh strawberries. Or perhaps lemon custard—"

"If I had the power to set you free, I would," I said, ignoring Pea. I exhaled. "If I had that kind of power, I'd set myself free. Maybe then I wouldn't have to marry someone I deplore."

175

Saige lay back, the water gently swishing against her skin. "Your life is *so* difficult."

Caught between my own thoughts, I couldn't find the energy to respond to her cynicism. I was born with status, status that was supposed to make me superior. I was born free, unlike Saige. So if that was true, why did I feel like I was stuck inside a space with no exit? Saige was so relaxed and confident and strong despite her circumstances. The life she lived was, of course, perilous, but she didn't seem as trapped. Not her mind, at least.

"How can I be strong?" It was an inappropriate question, but I felt comfortable enough to ask it.

She studied my face for a long time before grinning. Her smile was appealing. "Are you serious?"

I nodded quickly.

She cupped her hands and splashed water into her face. "A wise woman once told me you have two choices in this life: be strong or be killed. This world serves weak women on platters."

If that was true, I was in for a rude awakening.

Chapter Nineteen
SAIGE

"Dress quickly. I must deliver you to nourishment." Pea tossed me a bodysuit and sped down the hall. As we turned the corner, I hopped into my boots.

In the back of the kitchen was a cafeteria with cubed tables and workers serving other workers behind shields. They each held trays, standing in the straightest lines I had ever seen. Everyone wore nude bodysuits—but me.

Pea handed Lanah and me trays. "Today is fresh meal day."

When I got to the front, an iridescent beam scanned my eyes. My face and information registered on the screen. The worker knew how much nutrition I was to receive and consume for optimal caloric burn. She placed two vanilla-flavored nutritional packs on my tray and a bowl of thick oatmeal.

"You have eleven minutes to consume," Pea announced. She glanced at the clock every so often.

The clump of oatmeal felt strange inside my mouth. I was used to a liquid diet. The light drizzle of honey made my taste buds throw a parade. A euphoric feeling that I hadn't had in a while. It had been so long. I shoved more spoonfuls into my mouth and swallowed without chewing. I washed it down with the nutritional drink. My stomach churned; I wasn't used to so much in one sitting.

Pea took a bite of her peach. "Finish the other."

I patted my stomach. "Nothing else is going to fit in there. Here, give it to Lanah."

Lanah reached out but withdrew her hand when Pea gave her a death stare. Pea turned back to me. "Drink it."

"I told you I'm done."

Pea picked at the peach skin, visibly annoyed. Then she got up and snatched the nutritional pack off the table and returned it to the cafeteria worker. She was by the book.

I took the opportunity to interrogate Lanah. "How well do you know the area?"

She looked around to see if anyone was nearby. "Why?"

"That large silhouette—"

"The Border." Lanah poked at the oatmeal. She didn't make eye contact with me again.

Pea took Lanah's tray from the table. "Morning nourishment is over. We must deliver Saige to the combat grounds."

❖　❖　❖

Outside was muggy, hot. My skin stuck to the interior of my bodysuit. Pea was on a mission to deliver me on time; she walked with double-length strides as Lanah and I lagged behind.

"Beyond the Border is the Northern Region. We aren't supposed to speak about it, so I'll only tell you this once." The whites of Lanah's eyes were yellow in the sun. I hadn't noticed before. "The wall is made of a mixture of moon uranium and titanium. It's thousands of miles long and dozens of feet high. You can see the massive shiny structure from orbit. No one passes through without the authorization of the General. The Border was made to keep them out and us in."

"Them?"

Lanah nodded. "The savages."

I had heard about them before, but I'd thought they were a myth. The Union would say anything to keep us from trying to escape. "Has anyone tried to get through?"

Lanah began to cough. She spat out thick phlegm onto the sunburned grass and then wiped a streak of blood from her lips.

Pea retraced her steps. "What're you two chattering away about?"

Neither of us answered.

"You told her about the Border, didn't you?" Pea squinted at Lanah.

Lanah cringed and began stuttering, afraid of little Pea. I stepped between them.

"Why don't you tell me what your real duties are around here?"

Pea's sapphire eyes narrowed. "Why do you ask after all this time? You didn't seem to care before."

I smirked. "You seem to be the one in charge, the one who knows everything about everything."

"You wouldn't believe me if I told you anyway." She snorted and turned her back.

"Try me."

She glared at me over her shoulder. "I'm one of the head workers. I keep all the other workers in line. I'm the communication link between them and us."

"A rat, huh?"

"A rat?" She stomped her foot like a child having a fit. "If I was a rat, you'd be dead already. The meals we get, I earned them. Those perks, I earned. I help make life easier for the rest of them."

"For them?" I questioned. "Or you?"

Lanah broke into a coughing fit. Pea brought her close, then motioned at a clearing. "Go."

I watched the two head back to the Citadel. Their bodies became smaller and smaller until the specks turned into nothing but a clear horizon.

That was my cue to join the class.

Men ranging from medium brown to dark purple were grouped at the base of a hill. The sun beamed on them, no shade or cloud or breeze in sight. Rays rippled in the distance. Buff trainees with protruding chests and squared chins stood motionless in rows facing the Instructor. Each had a name tag in red letters on the lapels of their bodysuit, but I identified them by their features. Madison: Long Face, James: Big Lips, Jemison: Droopy Eyes, Peters: Flat Nose . . .

My footsteps seemed loud as they crunched on the scorched grass. Eyes grew large as I neared, while others grinned like vermin who had found crumbs in a trash receptacle.

Instructor Skylar held an engraved staff as tall as he was. He pointed it to an empty space in the front of the group. "State your name."

"Saige Wilde," I said. It felt strange using my full name and not just my worker barcode number. Being seen as an almost human being was odd, especially coming from an Upper.

"Saige Wilde, sir," he corrected.

I set my jaw.

"Saige Wilde, sir."

He stepped forward. "Louder!"

Rage crept along the back of my neck as I studied the face of the Instructor. I had seen him before at the hearing but had been too preoccupied to give it a second thought. Something about his eyes triggered déjà vu, but I couldn't make the connection.

I shouted; spittle flew. "Saige Wilde, sir."

"Hmm," he said and moved on.

Flat Nose and Long Face hooted in the front. They looked familiar, too, like they had been patrons of the Vixen at some point. Instructor Skylar twirled the staff above his head and slammed it down on Long Face like lightning. Long Face hunched over, moaning. The Instructor swooped the staff low, striking the side of Flat Nose's calf. His knee buckled. Both men lay on their backs. Their hooting had been replaced by groans.

"Like Peters and Madison here, some of you are here to be retrained because you've failed to meet the standard requirements out in the Subdivisions. Some of you have forgotten the basics of being a watchman. Some of you are here for the first time and have no idea what to expect. Here we have a saying: never expect anything." He paced back and forth, like a cougar sizing up its prey. "They call me Instructor Skylar. Do not test me, or you'll end up like these men here. In pain. Or worse. Your sole job is to obey any and all of my directives. Is that clear?"

"Affirmative, Instructor, sir," the men said in unison.

Instructor Skylar stood in front of me again. I didn't know if I should look at him directly or not.

"Do you have an eye ailment, girl?" he asked.

"Negative, Instructor Skylar, sir."

He hit me in the shoulder with the tip of the staff. "Then look at me."

My nostrils flared. I had to get a grip on my attitude, or I'd never survive.

His face was unexpectedly calm. "You're the second female that I've ever trained. Head Gardner was the first."

Her name made my toes curl.

"You're the first Impure, though."

"Well, you wanted me," I said, "so now you've got me."

❖ ❖ ❖

We trained every day from dawn until Instructor Skylar deemed it was time to stop. He'd burst into our sleeping quarters and make us complete obstacle courses of death. Neither rain nor heat stopped our trainings. At the end of each session, I was soaked in sweat and covered in dirt or blood and bruises. Trainees fainted, vomited. Many of them were weak without the bulky armor and weapons. I had expected them to be a lot more impressive.

We learned different holds and strikes. I knew most of them already, but I pretended that I didn't and then mastered the moves on the second or third try. I knew I was being watched closely.

Weeks passed, and the end was near.

"Take a knee." Instructor Skylar rubbed his chin. His demeanor was off that day. "I've gotten orders from Head Gardner to expedite the training."

Now I understood his annoyance. Anytime that piece of tripe was mentioned, it was never with good news.

"The Union needs more bodies, said that disturbances and rebel activity are on the rise. I must give you your final test tomorrow." He paused. "So I'll start with the benefits. The winner—the first one across the finish line—will enjoy a feast fit for an Elite. He—or she—will receive an honorable mention from the region and an accelerated promotion to admiral status."

The men high-fived and fist-bumped. I resisted the urge to scoff. I didn't want accolades—I wanted freedom.

"The contest is by process of elimination, and some of you will die trying to make it through." The Instructor clutched his staff. "Rest well and good luck."

And by some, I knew what that meant. He meant me. I was being sent in to die. The perfect plan set by the cunning Head Gardner. She thought she was so smart, giving him the bull setup story. They were all in on it. Had to be. They'd off me in the fairest way possible. No one would bat an eye at the Impure who died during the contest.

But I was never really good at resting well anyway, and I didn't intend to rest now. I'd accepted my fate, but I wouldn't stop fighting until the very end.

Chapter Twenty
AVI

Saige's words invaded my dreamscape night after night for weeks. *This world serves weak women on platters.* And I happened to be the main course.

During the public speaking session that day, I remained preoccupied with them, with her. Multitasking wasn't my strong suit, so I kept stumbling over the words of my lesson and forgetting certain hand gestures and appropriate pauses. The tutor scribbled on her reader, noticeably irate.

She snatched mine out of my grasp. "You are inattentive today."

"But we have—"

The tutor put her hand up to stop further appeals. "You are dismissed until you learn focus. And I will be adding this incident to your record."

Father would find out about the episode and have yet another stern conversation with me. What new punishment was he to wreak for this offense?

I was excited to have a moment of unassigned time, but then I was quickly reminded that I wasn't allowed to leave the grounds.

The only logical action was to visit Saige. I could finally talk to her alone. I was able to get Pea to tell me in which worker quarter she resided.

I knocked first, but she didn't answer. I knocked a little harder, then listened for a response. I scanned my eyes on her access plate, and the door slid open. Her quarters were dark. The only slivers of light came from breaks in the window plates.

"Saige?" I entered with caution, on the tips of my boots. "Are you there?"

There was not one sound until she rose from the shadows.

"What do you want?"

I lingered. "I knocked."

"I know."

"Then why didn't you answer?"

She sighed. "What do you want?"

I made my way toward the windows. "Just wanted to see how you were adjusting."

"Swell." Saige sounded like she hadn't slept in days. "Now beat it."

I waved the window plates open. "You are probably one of the most hospitable people I've ever met."

When I turned around, Saige was right behind me. I stumbled into the ledge. The setting sun illuminated the gash above her brow and the green specks in her eyes. Juxtaposed with beauty was fatigue. Worry.

"We aren't friends," she said.

"I—I know that."

"Then why are you here?"

I didn't know why I was there, actually.

She coughed once.

"Are you ill?"

Saige backed away, chuckling. "You think I got the sickness or something?"

"This is not humorous." I followed her. "You've been taking those supplements."

"Getting them all my life," she said. "You make me."

I swallowed. She wasn't lying. "On the Farmlands, I saw someone have a reaction to them. I've been trying to figure out if these supplements are dangerous or not. The government says they're harmless, that it was only an allergic reaction, but he looked very ill before. A lot of them do."

"Why don't you ask your daddy?" Saige leaned against the wall.

"He keeps saying they're harmless and to stop—" It was shameful to admit.

"Do you really believe they're harmless?"

I put my hands behind my back. "No, but I don't have the proof."

"Oh yeah?" She chortled. "And just for fun, what is this proof going to accomplish?"

"I'm not sure. I haven't thought that far in advance," I said.

"He's right."

"About what?"

"To mind your business. Whatever's going on, it's already begun, and neither me nor you are gonna stop it." Saige slumped into a chair and rested her face in her palm. "None of it matters anyway. I probably won't be coming back after tomorrow. Dead people don't care about politics or illnesses or princesses trying to feel better about themselves."

"What do you mean?"

Saige shook her head. "You really don't know anything, do you? Aren't you like the next General?"

I crossed my arms.

"The final test. The Instructor is expediting our training. We're going into the Cube."

"That's great," I told her. I didn't know the specifics of the Cube, but I knew that in order to become official, a watchman had to complete the tests. "It'll probably be easy for you to pass."

Saige looked at me like she didn't understand the language I spoke. "Let me break it to you, Princess. Head Gardner doesn't want me here. Your father doesn't either. They'll do whatever they can to make sure that I don't make it out. It's a setup."

"A setup?" I wanted to understand where the paranoia was rooted. I knew Head Gardner wasn't the most trustworthy person in the Citadel, and Father had his moments, but I trusted Instructor Skylar, and he'd never set her up to be killed. "Explain."

"There's nothing to explain," she said. "I'm an Impure who survived. I was never meant to make it this far."

I racked my brains for a solution. The first idea that arose was speaking to Father again, but I quickly came to my senses on that one. He had already made his stance clear. He wasn't going to listen, especially to me. I'd caused enough trouble. There must've been something I could do to ease Saige's worry.

We both sat quietly as the sun inched past the horizon.

Chapter Twenty-One
SAIGE

The day of the Cube came in the twinkle of an eye. Trainees assembled in tight rows. They high-fived while I remained still. Physicians started at the front row and began giving each participant a shot in their necks.

I was next.

Instructor Skylar appeared beside me, facing the men being injected. He spoke so only I could hear. "A hallucinogenic. It'll kick in during the last leg. Don't give in." He walked away just as fast as he'd come. Why had he told me? I'd thought he was in on it too. But maybe not. I didn't have time to go over the evidence because the physician shot me with a needle gun.

We followed Instructor Skylar down a hill and then stopped at the base of an enormous block with silver plates that projected images of its surroundings. Big Lips gasped. Droopy Eyes repeated under his breath, "I can do this," one too many times.

Instructor Skylar announced, "The Cube was built as a training tool for soldiers. We desired well-rounded human weaponry. Strength and speed are integral parts of being a watchman, but not the main components. We are looking for courage, brains, tact."

And that was it. He didn't ask if anyone had questions. There was no *good luck* or *Godspeed*. None of it felt right. My instincts shouted that it was a trap. Trainees had probably already been briefed about disposing of me and once inside were to do whatever they had to in order to take me out of the game. I was outnumbered.

I imagined an arena where we'd be thrown into the center and forced to fight to the death. I had lasted as long as I could—more days than I'd expected, anyway. I'd made it further than any Impure, but somehow that still wasn't good enough.

Grayish clouds gathered close to the ground. Birds tweeting usually was a sound that was muffled by all the other sounds, but this time I really listened. It'd be the last time I'd have the pleasure of hearing them. The wind blew firm, and in it, I smelled a brewing rainfall. How ironic: rain to replenish life as the Union prepared to take it away.

At the foot of the Cube, our reflections gazed back at us. I balled my fists and blew out a shaky exhale. I needed all fear to exit. The only thing I wanted to remain inside of me was strength. I was going to survive this or at least try. I was going to show the government that I was not what they believed I was. I was so much more. I just had to believe it myself.

The lower panes opened gradually.

"Begin," the Instructor said.

❖ ❖ ❖

The inside was a sweeping showroom with processors, weaponry, and bodysuits that lined stockades.

The panes sealed shut behind us. No way out until the end.

A holograph appeared from static. She wore a gray bodysuit with a low bun and had a neck like an ostrich. "My name is Khadijah. I am the mainframe inside the Cube. Instructor Skylar has programmed twenty participants." Her transparent finger pointed to the weaponry.

The Union

A light illuminated the glossed metal: chrome guns, serrated stars, and rapiers. "You will have access to any weapon you believe will aid you successfully."

She motioned to the wall with different-colored bodysuits. "Participants have several bodysuits to choose from, ranging from fireproof to poison repellent. You may choose only one."

Her palm opened, and from it emerged a map. "A level must be completed before you move on to the next. And there is one rule: you must only move forward. This is not only a test of strength, endurance, and speed but also a test of your mental capabilities, reasoning, and teamwork." Khadijah paused, then said, "After you have chosen your weapons and suits of armor, please make your way to your individual podiums."

Khadijah pointed to a timer, then dissolved. The countdown began. Men elbowed and shoved toward the weapons. They grabbed the biggest guns their arms could handle. I tried squeezing through buff bodies, but it was no use. I hurried to the bodysuit cage. The blue one was fire repellent, the red was poison repellent, the purple had a built-in temperature regulator, and the yellow was covered in scales and gave the wearer the ability to stay underwater longer. Swimming wasn't my strong suit. Something told me that the game makers planned on preying upon my weaknesses.

Once the arms rack had been ravaged, the men scrambled to the bodysuits. Doubling back, I discovered that all the high-powered weapons were gone. All that remained were a thick rope with hooks, a small laser gun, and a dagger. I took all three.

I stepped onto one of the circular pedestals.

Khadijah's voice counted down. I snapped the gun and knife into holsters and looped the rope loosely around my body. Droopy Eyes bounced on the balls of his feet as if he were about to enter a match. Long Face blew me a kiss. Still on his bullshit. I hoped he'd get taken out first.

189

I breathed. In and out. In and out. Because once this race started, I wouldn't be able to breathe again until it was over.

"Begin," a voice boomed.

Big Lips grunted, then disappeared. The podiums swallowed the men whole. One by one. Mine opened, and I was falling quickly down a tube. My screams ricocheted as I scraped the smooth walls, trying to grab ahold of anything that would slow me down.

When I hit the ground, a sharp pain radiated up my spine.

Other trainees came down with thuds. The underground sweltered. It was hard to breathe in the thick air. *Welcome to hell*—if one even existed. Paths were set up to get across a pit of spewing orange-and-reddish flames. There were several stops that had to be made before the level was completed, a question at each.

I put one foot on the bridge, hanging on to the sides, testing to see its weight-bearing ability. Sweat from my temples and my palms dripped onto the planks and sizzled. I stepped on a glowing circle, and a slender mask appeared over my eyes. It showed me the first question. Statistics.

The creators of the Cube knew workers hadn't been allowed to learn mathematics. Most of us only knew basic arithmetic, depending on our work positions. But on the Outskirts, Mama Seeya had taught us many things. She said that knowledge was power, and that was why the Upper Residents wouldn't allow us to read, to learn like they had.

She was preparing me for more than I'd ever thought I'd encounter, and she might've just saved my life.

I wiped the moisture from my face, calculating the problem on my fingers, toes. I had to find the mean difference and then figure out the standard deviation of the difference. Finally, the Z-score.

The system somehow understood my thoughts. It computed, then blinked green.

I was allowed to pass.

Big Lips's face was covered in streams of his own excretions. His system blinked red. From the three planks, one disintegrated. We were neck and neck, but he only had one plank left. He tightroped to the last marker. I answered correctly and leaped onto the platform that led to the second level. A gust of cool air hit me.

I pivoted to watch the last man. His lips moved as he stuttered different sets of numbers. Red. Red. Red. The last plank vanished. He pummeled into fiery rock and slid into the glowing substance. Burned alive.

❖ ❖ ❖

Khadijah appeared at the foundation of a large rock structure. It went vertically into the ceiling as far as the eye could see. Artificial cloud mists covered the peak.

"Level two will involve teamwork," she said. "Your partners have been selected at random."

Khadijah opened her palm, and the faces of each team appeared.

I got Jemison, Droopy Eyes.

He shook his head and grabbed a handful of the mountain. "Stay out of my way, Impure."

A laser rope between our waists connected us together. If one of us fell, then both of us fell. Jemison swore at the rock.

We climbed to the first marker. The translucent goggles appeared, just like level one. A chemistry-based question.

Jemison's eyes darted as he read his own. I knew basic chemistry but not as well as I did numbers. Two possible answers came to mind, but I wasn't sure.

His screen turned green. Above him were a few other teams already at the second marker. "Come on," he shouted, looking down at me.

"Hold it," I said, trying to eliminate the false answer.

"We're running out of time."

I barked, "Let me think."

"Answer the damned question!"

"Reactants," I shouted.

It blinked red. Incorrect.

Jemison threw his head back and began climbing.

I pulled the gun from my holster, anticipating something bad. Jemison tugged on the attachment, motioning for me to keep hiking, but we weren't going anywhere. The rock rumbled from the inside, and from the foot of the construction burst a boulder.

Another team had also gotten a question wrong. Red. Red. Red. Another boulder detached and stuck to the side of the foundation.

"Move your ass," Jemison scolded.

The boulders popped open like heated kernels, sprouting pebbly limbs. On their backs were spikes and crooked toothless mouths. The twin creatures crawled along the sides, digging their sharp claws into the structure like they were on horizontal planes. The opposing team shot beams at the creatures. The lasers of the larger guns didn't faze them. I climbed faster while Jemison stood his ground, shooting back.

"It's not working." I yanked the rope. "Just move."

I stretched my hand to the next fissure but was pulled down. Jemison wouldn't budge, and I couldn't carry his weight. Beside us, the boulder creature chomped one of the trainees' legs and shook him around, his partner still attached, until the man's leg broke and dangled from its mouth like a noodle. The men tumbled along the formation, each bone, limb crushed on the stony folds. They came to their final resting place, smashed and mangled, at the foundation's base.

The boulder creature rolled into a rock again and returned to an unsuspecting bulge in the mountainside.

Jemison finally got the hint that the lasers were ineffective against the monsters. He secured the gun and began the ascent. The second creature pursued us. I unwound the rope and threw it. The hook latched on to a split in the formation.

There was no outrunning the beast, but we could outsmart it.

"On three, jump!" I yelled.

Jemison's face was packed with apprehension. "Are you insane?"

"You know it's the only way." I tugged at the rope to test its strength. It'd have to hold the both of us.

"Ratch!" His eyes tightened as sweat drizzled along his temples.

"One." The creature's stony mouth opened wide as it galloped. "Two."

It came hurtling at us.

"Three!"

The hook held as we propelled ourselves sideways. The creature lost its footing and took a nosedive. Just as its previous victims had tumbled and smashed against the body of the mountain, the creature did the same dance and shattered into rigid stones on impact. A huge cloud of dust mushroomed around it.

Finally, we made it to the top, panting with our tongues hanging out like canines as we lay flat on our backs. The restraints that had held us together dissolved.

Level two was over.

And I was still alive.

❖ ❖ ❖

We stood in a staggered row inside a creepy water dome. Droplets fell from above and trickled along algae-covered walls. Khadijah appeared, hovering over the soft ripples. "This level will test your ability to work under pressure." She left once again, leaving us to figure out how not to die.

The men dove in with splashes and thunks. I searched for a command source that would allow my bodysuit to activate. The last person jumped in as the rest swam deeper and deeper. My suit wasn't coming alive fast enough, so I jumped too. On impact, it began to change: a partial layer materialized over my eyes and nose, allowing me to breathe. I had oxygen but no clue how much.

The farther I dove, the harder my muscles worked and the more oxygen I required. The first question appeared. Despite my fatigue, I answered correctly. Whenever the men got a correct answer, they were allowed to take breaths of air from a tube. Long Face's and Jemison's questions blinked red. So they got no air. Jemison darted to the next marker while Long Face's arms thrashed through the undercurrents. His head switched forward and back. Each second without a decision was a second of air gone.

His arms finally reached forward as if he were diving again, and he kicked upward, heading back to the top.

But he only made it halfway.

From the darkness emerged a slim silhouette, its limbs close to its sides as its long tail swished, gliding with graceful speed. When it reached him, webbed hands emerged, and it latched itself on to Long Face's torso. The mercreature dragged him downward. He elbowed the creature and attempted to pry its fingers from around his chest, but the thing was too strong. Long Face kicked and wiggled and squirmed, but the mercreature held him steady. A parade of tiny bubbles escaped the trainee's mouth. His face turned gray like the surrounding waters as he breathed in. It didn't take long for him to freeze completely. His arms floated at his sides as if he were about to take one final bow. The mercreature kept its grip on the corpse and zoomed past.

It had diagonal slits instead of a nose; gills started at its temple and went down the sides of its neck. The mouth was a closed slot, no lips. And the eyes. Human eyes.

I swam for my life. Harder. Faster. What the hell had the Union created?

Khadijah appeared, unbothered by the lack of oxygen. "You must finish the course. There is only forward movement."

At the second marker, Jemison held his neck, thrashing in the same way. Those tiny bubbles got away from him just like they had from Long Face. More trainees floated to the surface. The mercreature swam in to sweep their lifeless bodies into the murkiness.

I had two choices. Play the game or die. The Elites were watching.

I propelled myself over to Jemison. His eyes were squeezed shut as he choked on bubbles. I took a deep breath and unlatched my breathing tube. He fought me as I guided his head to the apparatus. He hyperventilated for a moment, then took slow, controlled breaths. Once he had gotten enough air, he handed it back. His eyes were low; maybe he was embarrassed that an Impure had saved him. He looked back at me one last time, then swam away.

The mercreature hovered above, just waiting for me to answer incorrectly so it could strike.

I answered the next marker correctly and thought I was in the clear.

The mercreature swam past at an unnatural speed. Then whizzed by again, stinging my upper thigh. From the slice in my bodysuit came ribbons of red. I descended as fast as I could to the final marker. But it trailed me. Its fluorescent green eyes gleamed, and claws protruded from its webbed hands. I thrust myself back as it swiped at me, and I whirled toward the previous marker, but I was only supposed to go forward. The mercreature grabbed my ankle and hauled me down like a chunk of cargo. Clouds of mini fizz pockets brushed my face as it swam through the course. Its claws dug deeper into the skin. As we touched the dark edge, I grabbed hold of the opening of its underwater dungeon. It pulled, yanked, the burning intensified, but I wouldn't let go. If it got me inside, I was never coming out.

Adrenaline allowed me one last power hit. I kicked it dead in the face. It released me. I propelled myself out of the opening.

I hadn't gotten very far when it tore into my back. I let out an inaudible howl. My blood colored the water around me.

The slit of its mouth curved in eagerness.

The mercreature rammed me, and I plummeted back to the last marker. I had already read it, so I answered it in passing. Green. Green. Green. The creature should've returned to its hole and waited for the next group of trainees to torture, but like its creators, it had a vendetta. Doing what it was programmed to do: finish me.

Me making it this far hadn't been in their plans. I had proven all their calculations and formulas wrong too many times, and their patience was worn. I had been sent into the Cube to die. So why was I still surprised that they wouldn't play a fair game?

As I drifted off the path and away from the last level, the creature tore the air supply from my face. I was trapped in the same unforgiving world that it was trapped in.

But my journey wasn't about to end there.

The dagger. I hugged the mercreature's body and drove the knife through its chest. Its mouth opened very wide.

I took in water. It stung, like the blue water had during decontamination. As liquid filled me, I soared past the point of no return and into a blur.

❖   ❖   ❖

I was stuck in the middle of being dead and alive, that odd limbo of the in-between realm. A gray area. It felt like a long time, but also not really. Finally, a feeling came back into my chest. My lungs were ablaze, and my back was ripped open as I lay in a lake of my own blood. Khadijah's voice broke up around me, in and out, and in and out.

"I can't stop the bleeding!" Jemison panicked.

"I can't believe you went back in," someone said.

"I've got to seal these wounds."

"I'm not using my only kit on her!"

I shot up like a child's toy, spewing water and whatever supplements I'd had before across the room. The mixture felt like an active flare inside my throat, but relief followed. Everyone watched. Jemison was closest. He held a bloody hand out to help me from the floor.

Flat Nose shoulder checked me. "You owe me a kit, mutt."

As we approached a wide metal door, I looked around and took note of how many of us were left. A little bit over half the trainees. How many more of us would die brutally before the end of the game?

"Listen up," Jemison said. "We've lost men. We sure as hell aren't losing any more. Inside this thing, we're all equal. We're all watchmen with one goal. We'll help one another to finish this. Is that clear?"

A few murmurs. Flat Nose gave a weak agreement.

Jemison shoved him in the chest. "Is that clear, watchman?"

"Affirmative!" The men exuded a new kind of intensity.

"Affirmative," I said and pulled my gun from its holster, ready for the next monstrosity.

"Shoot anything that moves," Jemison said as we entered.

The doors slid closed behind us, and it was pitch black until the lights above lit in sync. With guns drawn, we noticed our own reflections, just like outside of the Cube. There were only two paths, right and left. We were in some kind of reflective maze. Jemison led the way forward to the path on the left.

"I'm getting dizzy," Flat Nose complained.

"Keep your eyes open." Jemison stopped at a dead end and doubled back.

I was starting to feel disoriented too. From the blood loss, maybe? I jerked my head from side to side, trying to shake it off, but it got stronger as we dove farther. That was when I started to hear the voices. There was something inside one of the mirrors. I lagged behind.

There was Avi, suspended, right inside. Like she was sleeping. Or maybe dead.

"What have they done to you?" My voice sounded far away.

Her body glided closer and closer, until it was upright. Then her eyes opened, like a doll, and she punched through the glass. I stumbled.

Jemison stood over me. "What part of 'stay together' didn't you understand?"

"Affirmative" was all I could muster.

The path led us right back to the same door that we'd initially come from.

Jemison's brows crinkled. He slammed his fist into the door and then placed both hands on top of his head. "Everybody, pair up. Something weird is going on. Wilde, you're with me."

I kept my head down, my eyes closed at times to make the voices stop, but staring into the mirrors made the voices clearer. The once-solid reflections began to morph into fluid realms. Ma swam inside one of them. "I'm trapped," she whimpered.

"Ma? Mama?"

I got closer to her. And then her face mutated into Head Gardner's. "There is no escape!"

I crashed into Jemison's back.

"Hey, what's—" He pointed.

We had staggered into a room very different from the glass maze.

"We made it," I said, exploring the area. A screen held circles and letters and differently shaded quadrants. A geometrical equation.

On the other side of the glass barriers, figures moved. I drew my weapon. Jemison investigated and discovered watchmen inside a similar room on the opposite side. I tapped on the glass to get their attention, but it only rippled.

"We have to find—" Jemison was in a trance. His pupils vibrated.

When I looked inside the mirror to see what had caught Jemison's attention, I saw Liyo. A part of his skull and face was missing. "You betrayed us."

"Leave me alone." I swatted the air. "You're not real."

"I am real!" he yelled. "And you let them kill us."

He was trapped inside the maze like the others.

"Get me out." Liyo kept looking over his shoulder as if someone were coming for him.

I covered my eyes, but his voice grew more urgent. His hand reached out through the ripples. "Save me before they come."

As I reached to touch his hand, the glass burst. Sharp debris rained on us.

Jemison awoke from his stupor. Men ran in every direction. All the adjoining rooms connected to the one, and we'd been in the center. Flat Nose was halfway inside one of the mirrors, being hauled in. Big Lips hung on to his legs. A silver cyborg beetle was fixed onto his neck, its teeth like razors sawing through him. Blood squirted on the walls, on the ceiling. More mechanical bugs swarmed from the reflections. Jemison shot into the flock, blowing several into metal smithereens. Lasers flew like rockets.

"Wilde, you're up." Jemison motioned toward the screen. The correct answer was the only way to stop the carnage. "We'll cover you."

I holstered my gun and began working on the problem. The timer had begun. I rearranged the shapes. It was hard not to pay attention to the clock or to the pain shooting up my back or the shouts or streams of lasers.

A beetle lowered from the ceiling and attached itself to my shoulder. Before its razors dug too far into me, Jemison shot it. I made myself concentrate through the sound of saws shredding tissue and the yelps. I moved lines over, expanded them, and placed them into adjoining spots. I counted in my head and multiplied numbers as screams reverberated around me. Jemison fell by my side. I helped him to his feet, but he just collapsed again, covered in fresh blood.

"Focus," Jemison said. He applied pressure to a bite in his side with one hand and shot into the herd with the other, covering me as I placed smaller circles into larger ones.

"The square root of twenty-one and x to the second power . . . ," I mumbled as my unsteady fingers moved along the screen. "The solutions are three and seven. Three and seven!" There was nothing else left. I hit the screen and slid down to meet Jemison. My hands began to tremble uncontrollably.

The room turned an ugly shade of green. Beetles released the dead and the dying, ending their butchery.

A pane lifted at the end of the now tunnel-like room, flooding battered bodies with sunlight. Clean air filled the space, carrying the scent of blood and death out into the open. I turned my head to Jemison; he wasn't moving anymore.

My goal this whole time had been to stay alive, and I had almost done my job.

On my stomach, I pulled myself across the floor. My own blood, everyone's blood made it difficult for my hands to grip the surface. My fingers just kept slipping. I used my knees and elbows to scoot toward the light.

Instructor Skylar stood near the pane, at the finish line, holding his staff with both hands. He squinted. The question of why he had given me a heads-up about the hallucinogenic was quickly placed on the back burner as I slowly got to my knees, but the pain in my back, my shoulder stopped further movement. I just dangled. But I had to get up. I had to. It was like tearing off a bandage: the quicker, the better. Pain was pain. I stood jerkily, shrieking, as I held on to the side of the wall.

"Wilde," Butler called from behind me.

He was alive. I looked at him, noticed how he and another trainee were helping Droopy Eyes, who was badly wounded.

"Wilde," he said again, sterner this time. "Jemison needs help."

He called on me like he couldn't do it without me.

I looked at the Instructor, who watched us like this was the climactic end to a broadcast. I could almost hear him and the others wondering what the Impure would do. Would she cross the finish line, win? Or would she risk losing her victory to help the team?

What would a loyal watchman do?

Chapter Twenty-Two
AVI

It had been dreary earlier that day, almost like the earth was troubled by the brutality that had taken place inside the Cube. I had made the decision to see Saige, even if it was just her corpse. I pretended to be ill on the way to our sessions. Just before Jade and I left for the Academy, I filled my mouth with dry oats. In the back seat, the oats began to soften along my tongue, and when they were slimy enough, I spewed them all over her lap. She was furious. After she called me a few choice names, she forced the driver to return to the Citadel.

I dry heaved and told the watchman that I would no longer be well enough to return to the Academy. He suggested I go to the physician's quarters, but I had other plans. I told him that fresh air always helped with my nausea. He took the bait. I led him close to the plain where watchmen trained. It was empty at first as I searched for Saige, but in the distance was a group of physicians and watchmen huddled around the outside of the Cube. I bolted before the watchman could grab me. He pursued, but I ran as hard as I could. Arms and legs pumping with pure adrenaline. I cut through bodies, then stopped directly beside Instructor Skylar.

He didn't notice my presence; his eyes were trained on the brutal chaos that had been Saige. I didn't even recognize her at first; she was covered in flesh wounds, barely able to stand, staring back at the people ogling her. I tried to get to her, but the watchman had caught up to me and held me back. Words were stuck in between whimpers. My mind tried to wrap itself around what had caused this and why everyone was just standing and watching her like an animal in a trap.

Saige looked down at a thick yellow line. Why hadn't she gone over it? Why the hesitation?

Saige had been right all along, and I hadn't fully believed her until then.

The Union—my father—was trying to kill her.

Chapter Twenty-Three
SAIGE

My eyes darted from the finish line to the spectators. Blood trickled along my forehead and rested on my eyelashes. I squeezed an eye shut, which made it worse.

Avi. She looked horrified. Had she really thought that they wouldn't torture me as they had always done?

Everything was eerily quiet, except for intermittent soft moans. There was a beeping sound that I hadn't noticed before coming from the corner of the ceiling. An obscured camera lens with a red light at the bottom zoomed in. Confirmation that they'd been monitoring us being sliced and diced. The people on the other side of that screen were sick, entertained. I aimed my gun at the group of physicians standing outside. They gasped and huddled together, fear smeared across their smooth faces. The barrel of my gun swept over them as I reveled in their fear. It wasn't a game anymore when someone else had the upper hand. I wanted them to know that we all bled from the same gunshot wound at the end of the day.

Avi's guard jumped in front of her. Every watchman aimed their weapons at me. Red dots covered my body.

Instructor Skylar held his hand out. "Everybody relax."

"I *am* relaxed," I said from behind the finish line.

"Stand down," he said.

"Put the gun down, Impure," a watchman ordered, finger almost hugging the trigger.

I didn't put it down. Instead, I shot every camera out that I could find, then tossed the weapon aside.

I made my way back to Butler and helped him scoop up Jemison. Butler and I limped forward as we held Jemison between us. His body shook. Life spilled from the gaping holes in his leg. The three of us stepped over the finish line together. Other survivors crawled out behind us and collapsed in heaps.

Instructor Skylar nodded, and physicians rushed over to rinse, disinfect, and laser wounds. One approached me apprehensively, a watchman at her side. I waved her away and told her to help Jemison instead. We let go of him. He sat on the ground, dazed and calm like the Cube that had stolen his spirit. Stumbling away from the smells of flesh being burned back together, I closed my eyes and raised my head to the sky and breathed in a deep inhale. Wooziness took over, my knees buckled, and I crumpled in the brown grass. My palms were caked in blood and granules of dirt.

A physician saw how nasty my back was and lifted me onto a hovercot. I lay on my stomach, unable to protest, as he lasered me back together. I squeezed my fists and clenched my teeth as I smelled my own burning skin.

At that moment, I should've felt proud, victorious even, that I had done it. That I had managed to outsmart them. I had survived another one of the Union's plots to rid themselves of me.

So why didn't I feel either? The only thing I felt other than the searing pain near my spine was the heaviness of the revenge that would follow. All I'd done was buy myself more time to be in their twisted world. They'd never allow me to live this so-called win down. They'd come for me even harder.

Chapter Twenty-Four
AVI

I was forced away. From Saige. From the others. Tears swelled in my eyes as I stumbled aimlessly along the galleries of our grand Citadel. It was the weakest I'd ever felt. My stomach churned. My head was filled with so much disgust that I could barely keep it upright. I just wanted to lay it on something soft and weep. Something monstrous had occurred inside that wicked contraption. A contraption sanctioned by Father and his minions. There had been blood everywhere. So much of it that I would never be able to forget it. The blood of those men, Saige, and all the people hurt by our government would never be cleaned from our hands.

Before I rounded the tenth curve, I heard low voices. "Is she official?" It was Pea.

"With complications, of course," Instructor Skylar replied.

"Oh dear." She blew out a breath. "This isn't good."

The conversation was odd. Why was Pea talking to Instructor Skylar about Saige? Yes, she was a lead worker, but she managed the workers inside the Citadel. There wasn't any reason for workers to know anything other than their assigned work duties.

Tiptoeing away, I had almost disappeared when Pea called out. She caught up quickly. "Madam, I've been looking all over for you."

I faced her, forcing a surprised expression. "Really?"

She nodded. Instructor Skylar approached us, glaring. "Evening greetings," he said coldly as he passed us.

Pea turned me in the other direction. "Is something wrong, madam?"

"Nothing," I said. "Nothing at all."

Chapter Twenty-Five
SAIGE

We were given injections for pain, injections for infection. And injections of adrenaline. Wouldn't want any of us to faint from exhaustion and ruin the party. We were sent to Pea's team, who wasted no time throwing our stained bodysuits into an incinerator and scrubbing away the remnants of the Cube from every part of our bodies. Blood was caked in my nails, in my mouth and dyed my hair. But even after the fabric was burned and shea butter massaged into my skin, sweet almond oil in my scalp, I still smelled it.

Death's aroma would always cover me.

But there was no time to mourn what had been lost inside of that hole. The feast was ahead.

Instructor Skylar hadn't announced which one of us had won yet. But I knew that I had a slim chance at receiving any recognition. Dead people weren't supposed to win races.

The majestic doors parted. "Welcome to the Citadel's ballroom," Bres said.

The men and I entered single file. The room itself was impressive. Large archways were attached to cathedral ceilings, and golden accents were stenciled on the off-white decor. Each spacious table had bouquets of white calla lilies in tall, slender vases. Along with the soft floral scents was the fragrance of fresh food—real food. Workers stood idly behind stations with their hands clasped behind them, fixed expressions on their faces. When an Upper showed interest in an item, the nearest worker snapped back to life and asked if they needed assistance in choosing the perfect hors d'oeuvre, an item the worker could smell and serve but never consume.

Bres guided us through a mass of Elites dressed in multihued bodysuits with lace and feather detailing, high stiff collars, and pricey cuff links. Hairstyles varied from very big and colorful to bald and demure. On my way to the stage, an Upper yanked a loc of my hair right from my scalp. The partygoer dangled it from her hand, showing it as a souvenir to a circle of others. I rubbed the tiny bald spot and headed straight for her. Jemison took my shoulder and turned me back to the stage. Bres presented us to the Instructor.

He rose. "Everyone, please take your seats."

The three of us stood in the center of the high platform. I was closest to Commander Chi, with his hand under his chin and eyes on me. I faced the crowd, but I didn't look at them. I looked over them, past them, as I had done at the Vixen.

Instructor Skylar began, "The cabinet noticed there were glitches in watchmen training that caused inefficiency in the Subdivisions. What we needed were strong forces to protect Elites and Upper Residents and keep order among workers. Our team proposed an obstacle course that challenged the mind, heart, and body. The Cube consists of levels that weed out trainees who are unable to meet the physical, mental, and intellectual requirements."

He explained it as if it were a standardized test and not a booby-trapped killing course. Elites nodded their heads in agreement. Did they know that the men who didn't make it had died terrible deaths? Would they have cared if they had known?

"Standing before you are official watchmen. Give them a round of applause." Instructor Skylar clapped. The rest followed suit.

"In the last leg, three watchmen crossed the finish line as one. Ladies and gentlemen, this is our first multiway tie in history."

The crowd made a round of cheers and clapped.

Instructor Skylar took a seat, and Commander Chi stood, his attention fixed on me like a fishhook. He tapped on his reader, and a massive holoscreen appeared over the gathering. It played clips of the moments inside the Cube.

"Watchman Butler, please step forward."

Butler waved, and they applauded generously for him. The clips showed flashes of his journey. Clapping broke out again at the end. Butler smiled and bowed his head in appreciation.

"Watchman Jemison, please step forward."

Whistles were mixed in with his applause, mostly from the women and ambiguously dressed men. A few of them even waved refined laced fingers. Jemison straightened his bodysuit. He had a lot of clips that made him look like a leader. They even showed him diving back into the water and pulling my limp body out. The people had jumbled expressions over his act of heroism. They probably couldn't fathom why he would save an Impure. Still, when the video ended, they applauded.

Commander Chi cut his eyes away from the reader in disgust. My name wasn't announced, but I took a deep breath and stepped forward anyway as they played my clips. They showed the moment when I got an answer wrong and almost caused Jemison to be chomped by the boulder creature. They showed when I watched Madison being drowned by the mercreature. They zoomed in on my face. I looked satisfied. Short and incriminating. The audience gasped, grimaced.

Instructor Skylar cut in from behind. "Let's give all of these watchmen a round of applause."

The applause was weak, hesitant.

The last clip was the three of us going over the finish line. The Instructor said, "Admiral Jemison, Admiral Butler, and Admiral Wilde are our champions."

A live band played the official Union anthem while white confetti and golden balloons sailed from the ceiling. Our faces were digitally placed on banners above for all to see. WINNER blinked at the top of each snapshot. Tears welled from Butler's eyes; it was what he must've dreamed it would be like to be seen as an accomplished watchman. Jemison stood proudly and saluted the flag that had been raised. I just stood there. Pretending to be patriotic was more difficult than I'd expected. I was out of place but most importantly, starving.

We were ushered to our seats when the anthem ended. I sat next to Jemison. Instructor Skylar migrated to the empty space beside me. He must've been following me, but the food was about to be served, so I couldn't have cared less. Before the worker could even place the tray on the table, I took it from his hands and held it as if someone were about to steal it from me. The worker lifted the lid. I savored the meat, the rich sauces, and the hot bread with melting butter. Gravy and rice dripped off the sides. My slashed back and blood loss felt almost worth it.

Food was everywhere. I ate without chewing, choking at times, but it didn't deter me from diving in farther with both hands. My stomach swelled painfully with each dish they brought. I didn't even have to ask; they just kept them coming. And dessert, all those desserts.

The whole time, the Instructor watched.

With a mouth crammed with food, I stared back at him and swallowed. "What do you want?"

"That stunt you pulled was idiotic. You put not only yourself in jeopardy but me as well. I'm the one who vouched for you. Remember?"

I chuckled. "Did you ever think that maybe you shouldn't have?"

"I gave the General my word that I'd keep you in line, and you pointed a weapon at his daughter."

I washed food down with wine and held the empty glass up for more. "I did not point it at his daughter. I pointed it in the near vicinity of his daughter."

He stabbed the table right near my hand. I leaned back. He withdrew the blade. "Your complete lack of common sense is disheartening. The General will be notified, and I'll be the one to blame." He peered into the audience. "I trusted you."

I wiped my face. "And why would someone like you trust someone like me?"

"Because I know you better than you know yourself." He stared me down with those black eyes. "And if you ever try something like that again, I'll kill you myself. Do you comprehend?"

I nodded, allowing that to sink in. I was already messing everything up. That would be my last hiccup until I figured out an escape plan.

"Why'd you give me a heads-up?" I asked.

"Did I?"

"Don't play stupid."

"I have no idea what you're talking about." He took a sip from a fancy glass. "I'm part of the certified defense personnel. Why would I give an advantage to a trainee? Preposterous."

My eyes shifted.

"Are you trying to figure me out?" He was almost too handsome as he spoke, but his looks weren't going to sway me. I'd seen his kind in the Underground. "In this life, to get what you want, you must build trust and allies. Play the role. Take it as far to the end as you can go. Commit any act. But when you get there, there's no turning back." He drank the wine until the last sip rolled onto his tongue.

Another trick. The Union seemed to be sharper than ever. They needed me to get comfortable, but it wasn't going to happen.

My stomach began to knot, and my upper lip was moist. I ran to the kitchen, holding my mouth because everything I'd eaten was on its way out. Workers moved out of my way as I knocked into pots and trays. Utensils clanked as I searched for something to explode in.

There was an elaborate urn in the corner. I leaned over and emptied myself. And it was such a pretty urn.

Suddenly, Pea was beside me, trying to help, but I didn't want any. Especially not from her.

"Bring a warm towel," she ordered one of the girls. Lumps dripped down my chin. I slid down a cool wall, exhausted.

"You're reckless," she scolded. "I heard about what happened. You'll blow everything we've worked so hard for."

Word traveled fast around the Citadel. "So what?"

Someone handed her a towel. She tried to place it on my cheek, but I snatched it. Pea sat on her knees. Her face wasn't that of an adolescent but of a person plagued with many burdens.

"I know you don't trust me," she said. "But you should. I watch out for you."

I wiped my chin as Instructor Skylar paraded in to check on me. Pea quietly slipped away into the bustle of the other workers.

Chapter Twenty-Six
AVI

I had been barred from the officiating ceremony where Saige became an official watchman.

"Your father's orders," Pea said as she steered me inside my quarters. Just when I thought the evening couldn't get any worse, there were clear-framed mannequins in outrageous bodysuits positioned throughout the room. One had a feather boa, while another had an enormous fur stole hanging from the shoulder. Pea stood proudly next to her creations.

"Wh—what is the meaning of this?" I tossed my body over the divan.

"I looked over all of the bodysuits and different accessories to find the perfect combinations." She grabbed my arm, pulling me forward. "He also ordered me to clear my schedule for your special evening."

"Special evening?" I ran my fingers through the soft fur.

"Oh dear."

I shook my head.

"You're supposed to meet Phoenix." Pea perked back up. "Which would you like to try first?"

"Is this some kind of punishment?" I stepped away from the mannequins, raging to no one in particular. I knew Pea had no clue as to what games Father was playing, but I knew exactly what he was doing. Trying to control me. "Every time I do something against his wishes, he forces me to be with Phoenix? This is complete madness."

"Madam?" Pea looked worried.

"Avi!" Father's voice bellowed from a holoscreen. "Who authorized you to skip sessions this morning?"

I glanced at the edge of the monitor.

"Look at me." The heaviness in his tone was frightening.

Words came out like little splutters. "I apologize."

"I'm afraid that an apology is not enough." His head hung low. "You put yourself in danger by breaking protocols. Again."

"I had to see what was happening for myself," I said.

"There was nothing to see."

"There was!"

He shot me a fleeting look.

"I'm supposed to be taking over one day, and yet you keep secrets from me. How's that just? I should know what's occurring in *my* region."

His lips twisted through his thick beard. "This is *not* your region until I am dead and gone. And galaxy forbid that you rule as recklessly as you live."

I sucked in tears.

"You've given me no choice but to expedite your union. You are out of control, Avi Anais." He always added my middle name when he was disappointed in me. "Perhaps as a wife, you will learn that not everything is about you. You will marry in the winter."

My heart sank to its lowest depths. I shook my head. "I won't."

"You'll do as I say," he said simply. "And if you keep pushing, keep disobeying, I'll make sure you marry Phoenix before you can even blink. Do I make myself clear?"

If only my stare were a laser. Father would've been full of holes. "Affirmative."

He motioned to Pea, who had hidden herself in a nook. "Escort her to the hovervehicle." His eyes returned to me. "A watchman will be assigned to you. I look forward to hearing about your meeting."

"Wait." I stepped forward. "Saige is an official watchman. Is she not?"

He nodded. "With complications."

"Then I shall have her accompany me this evening as my personal guard."

"Absolutely not."

I remained poised. "Saige is an official watchman. Complicated or not. It doesn't state in any bylaw that I don't have the choice of which watchman can accompany me. If there's a protocol that prevents my choice in the matter, then please bring it to my attention. I have an evening to prepare for."

He sat back and thought hard, or perhaps he wasn't thinking at all but trying to conceal his irritation. He granted the request and, without another word, ended the communication.

My victory was small, but it had been a victory, nonetheless. But knowing Father, he wasn't going to give up.

❖ ❖ ❖

I scanned the countless bodysuits I hadn't even known I owned. Pea had chosen the gaudiest ones: a bright-pink bodysuit with an orange zipper down the front and a flannel one with leather paneling along the sides. I groaned inwardly.

Saige finally arrived and stood by the door with her arms crossed snugly over her chest, wearing the blandest expression I'd ever seen.

I grabbed random bodysuits and laid them out. "Father has requested that I meet with someone this evening," I explained.

"Go on."

The lump in my throat was hard to swallow. "I need you to accompany me as my personal watchman."

"You've got to be kidding." She scoffed.

"I can assure you that—"

"You can't assure anything," she said. "I didn't survive that death trap to be a glorified princess sitter."

I decided to change the tone of the conversation. We'd gotten off to a bad start. I put a red bodysuit up to my neck, admiring it in the mirror. I usually stuck with neutrals, but I contemplated how I'd come off dressed in bright cherry red. Too seductive. I switched over to the purple one with gold chains dangling over squared shoulders.

Saige snatched the bodysuit. Pea rushed to my side in defense.

"I'm not in the mood for this," Saige said.

"Pea," I said, still watching Saige. "You're dismissed for the evening."

I needed to establish trust with her. It was the only way to chip away at the fortress she'd built.

"But—" Pea protested.

"I'll see you at dawn."

"Yes, madam." Pea bowed and exited, leaving Saige and me alone.

I grabbed another bodysuit from the pile and examined the embroidered stitching. "It's the General's orders that a watchman accompany me whenever I go off Citadel grounds. If something were to happen to me while I'm gone, and you're not there . . ."

The veins in her neck were prominent. I was treading too close to her nerves with my demands. She plopped down on a footrest, semi-accepting her fate.

Every time I presented a bodysuit for approval, she'd mutter under her breath and wave me away. I showed her a paisley one. "Does this say 'evening out in the Square'?"

She rested her face in her palms, growing weary of my indecisiveness. She then flew from the seat and into my closet, disappearing into an assortment of fabrics.

"You have an incoming call from Reba," the bot announced.

"Answer."

My friend Reba appeared on the holoscreen.

"Avi." She waved with an exaggerated bounce.

"Greetings."

"You will never guess who's throwing the hugest, most dreg launch party tonight." Her eyes went googly.

I shrugged my shoulders.

A worker stood behind Reba, taking parts of her green hair and curling it. "You have to guess!"

I took a ridiculous guess. "Roblé?"

"Eeewww," she shrieked. "Roblé was soooo last epoch. Guess again."

I huffed. "Reba!"

"Fine." She paused for dramatic effect. "Marco. The Marco Grant."

I almost sobbed. "I love her so much."

"I even had my worker paint my hair green just like hers. It's only semipermanent, though. My parents would pass out. Do you think she'll notice me? Do you think she'll pull me onstage?" Reba was hyperventilating.

"Possibly," I replied.

She pouted. "You don't seem like yourself."

"I suppose the impeding heaviness of the future of the Union weighing down on me is too much to bear at the moment."

"Soooooo." She elongated the word. "You definitely need to come to the Square and live it up before you become an even stuffier Elite."

Reba could always make me smile. "I'm supposed to be meeting Phoenix at Galactica."

"Great. That's where the concert is. Just ditch him."

"Reba, it's not that simple. Father wants a full report by morning of our grand time together."

"A total comedown." Suddenly, she jumped from the chair. The worker dropped the curling mechanism on the carpet. Reba patted the top of her head, searching for the burn. "You freakin' honk. Can't you do anything right?"

The female worker shook as Reba continued to berate her.

"Reba?" I said. "Reba!"

"What?" she snapped.

"She made a mistake."

Reba returned to her seat with half a head of silky curls. "Get out, and send me someone competent."

The worker scurried away.

Saige reappeared from the wardrobe with an armful of bodysuits. Reba came closer to the monitor. "What. Is. That?"

"My escort for the evening," I announced.

Reba giggled. "Looks like some kind of space mutt."

"Enough, Reba."

She was now in a full-fledged laughing fit. "Wait, she's coming with you? If she comes, you've got to make sure you tie her to a pole outside."

"I've got to go." I clicked out of the call, embarrassed by her sentiments. Like most Upper Residents, they were ignorant to the fact that taunts like that were not acceptable.

Saige pretended to inspect the items.

"I apologize for—"

"Don't," she said, without making eye contact.

An uncomfortable smile was all I could manage. I looked over the bodysuits. "These are good choices."

She hurled them at me. "Here."

"Can you at least unzip me?"

She spun me around aggressively and unzipped the zipper down to the curve of my lower back. I shimmied the material from my arm. Over my shoulder, I noticed her watching and cleared my throat. I'd never changed in front of anyone before, except Pea; there was really nothing to see anyway. My body wasn't spectacular like Saige's. I was composed of bones and a bit of muscle.

I slipped on the bodysuit, which had been created with a tribal print mixed with bold earth tones. Different hues of blues and whites were blended at the top and on my arms, leafy greens with snippets of black were painted on my torso, and brown and ivory prints lined the legs. I admired it in the mirror. A worker had probably hand painted it in a crowded factory, forced to create something impressive just for me.

When I took over, I would have to exploit the workers the same way Father, his grandfather, and our ancestors had. The system had been set. A fragile organism, one that would shut down if disturbed.

I wiped a tear that had escaped at the idea of how simultaneously beautiful and ruined everything was.

"It's lovely," I told Saige.

I opened a chest and scattered hair paint, stencils, and a cosmetic compact on the vanity's counter. "Would you mind?"

She blew out an annoyed huff of air. "If it makes this process go by any faster." She started unwrapping my thick bun, roughly combed out the hair, and sprayed the ends with auburn dye. When she finished the style, she dipped a pencillike brush into henna and drew twisty lines around my forehead and eyes. I kept them closed. She was quiet as she worked. Her hands sketched and flicked upon my skin. I imagined the same techniques used by the worker who had created the art on the bodysuit.

After she hadn't touched my face for a while, I opened my eyes to find what she'd left. She had already started on her own makeup when I viewed myself closely. My eyebrows had been colored auburn, just like the tips of my hair, and half of my face was covered in thin intricate vines and tiny dot-like freckles. She'd added blue lipstick and placed a thick orange line down the middle of my lips.

"Where'd you learn how to apply cosmetics so well?"

"Being a stripper has its perks." She hunched her shoulders.

Saige was in the middle of painting a deep purple mask around her eyes. I sat in admiration watching her work. I could've sat there forever, especially because tonight was going to be my last bout of freedom before everything changed.

❖ ❖ ❖

A watchman outside the Citadel's entrance ushered Saige and me to a waiting hovervehicle.

"Where are the government-issued hovercycles kept?" Saige asked.

The driver tried to inform us that his orders were to drive us, but Saige kept badgering me about seeing the hovercycles. I gave the authorization for him to escort us into the hangar. I'd never been inside before, but there were massive hovercrafts along the walls and armored tanks with huge wheels. Saige darted to the hovercycles, which gleamed inside transparent cases. She placed her palms on the glass.

The watchman scanned his eyes, and the container unfastened with a hiss. The hovercycle was low to the ground with a massive but sleek body. She hopped on and ducked low, pretending to cruise. She powered it on. The whir was minimal; I barely knew it was working until it began to hover evenly above the ground.

"Hop on," she said.

"Certainly not." I clasped my hands behind my back.

She shot a half grin. "If you want me to trust you, Princess, then you'll have to start by trusting me."

I groaned. "If I get on, you have to make me a promise."

"Yeah, sure. What?"

"It's just that I have a bad feeling in the bottom of my stomach," I told her. "Perhaps it's just misplaced anxiety, but promise that you'll protect me."

Saige's brows gathered.

"Just agree."

After biting her lip, she agreed. "Okay then."

I leaped on the back and draped myself around her body. She raised the hovercycle like she'd ridden before and zoomed out into the open.

Chapter Twenty-Seven
SAIGE

The hovercycle took to me as nicely as I took to it. A fine piece of upgraded machinery. Citadel living, I thought, all the perks of having fresh food, security, and nice rides to prance around on.

We flew over my old subdivision. While I was not where I wanted to be, at least I wasn't down there with the other workers being robbed, watching people suffer, and being roughed up by watchmen. Now, I just witnessed the suffering from afar.

I couldn't allow myself to get comfortable, though. Like Pea. Like Butler or Jemison. Like any of them. Everything I'd done was for one reason. And that was to escape for good. I thought it wasn't possible, but now I was closer than I had ever gotten, and I couldn't let it go.

I'd forgotten that Avi was bent over my back like a huge tumor as I pushed the speed of the hovercycle over the limit. She shouted directions, but I knew exactly where the Square was. I had been a slave worker there for as long as I could remember but had never been allowed the experience of it without restraints. I was disgusted to admit that I was eager to see it from the other side.

We landed in a busy lot. Hoversport vehicles with drop-tops and trucks with customized graffiti were already parked. I removed the helmet and shook my hair out, scrunching the curls on the sides. A young Upper jumped off his hovercycle, then carried his girlfriend off the back. He had a high-top fade, a chain-link choker around his neck, and fingerless gloves. Her hair was teased into a huge sun-yellow 'fro, and she wore a pair of rectangular shades with teardrop diamonds hanging from the bottom of the frames. She glanced at Avi, then at me, and tossed her head back with laughter.

Avi took my elbow. "Follow me."

My eardrums became captive to the music carried from every opening within the Square. Avi spun around, soaking in the flashing lights and loose bubbles and smoke vape clouds. Partiers hung from balconies and shot firework streamers. The pellets blew into a million bright sparkles. Avi pointed to an illuminated billboard of Marco Grant. She had bright-blue box braids and was wearing a crown covered in emeralds and rubies. Her smile was big and too white, like an animation.

Galactica glowed in red cursive letters. Beneath that was a lengthy line of what seemed like every adolescent in the region. Avi led the way. Chilled air nibbled at my skin, but it didn't bother the crowd as they swayed to the entrance in groups. Outside of the rope, wildly adorned patrons stood near the wall, wearing platform shoes and glow-in-the-dark lipstick. Naked spliced felines, fluffy birds, and neon lizards were held in people's arms like live accessories.

"The line starts back there," I said as Avi led us to the front.

She waved me off. "Elites don't do queues."

No matter how hard she tried to be modest, deep down she was an Elite and carried the ingrained privilege that came with it.

A girl who wore a snakeskin bodysuit tugged at her friend's sleeve. "What's that?"

I was the "that."

He had several nose rings on both sides and a long cigarette holder perched between his fingers. "An Impure, darling. Very rare. Must be a new Elite statement piece."

Her eyes widened. "I've gotta cop one."

They saw me as some expensive bag perched on Avi's shoulder. An accessory. The least human form. All of these people were the same.

As soon as the bouncer saw Avi, he bowed and allowed us to pass.

The inside roared. Sounds of chattering people were interlaced with deafening beats. There were too many levels of the club to count, but the lower floor was the most packed. The terraces filled with patrons tossing confetti onto the partiers below. Interactive screens set high above showed Marco Grant's music videos. There was a multilayered stage occupied by a DJ and dancers. Skimpily dressed performers covered in sparkles and feathers hung from long strips coming down from the ceilings and performed aerial stunts. A girl at the very top of the strip spun.

Attendees held on to their hats and chests as she unraveled like a spool of thread. I thought she would smash into the floor, but she stopped only inches from the ground and posed with perfectly pointed toes. They cheered, popping corks off bottles. Fizz erupted, spilling onto knuckles and leaving puddles on the blackened floor.

As workers turned tricks for drug lords, Uppers played games and lived in a fantasy.

Together we pressed through bodies. Nearby a famous person was surrounded by readers and cameras that were shoved into her dewy bronzed face. Giant officers stood on either side with their hands held out for space. Her sleeveless bodysuit was gold, probably the real stuff mined by child workers. Her headpiece had dangling rows of diamonds. She blinked, flaunting thick lashes and vivid gray contacts.

Reba burst through the crowd and hugged Avi. "Let's go up. The ground floor is for the normies."

The bouncer stepped aside and allowed us onto a clear elevator that jetted upward to a penthouse suite, revealing a much grander, private party. The space was dim. Clusters of silhouettes packed the floor, moving slowly to sultry rhythms. Patrons fell playfully over friends and took shot after shot. Colored orbs floated around like oil in a lamp. I caught a sapphire-colored orb. It was weightless, transparent. I threw it back in the rotation. A celebration for the young and privileged who yearned to let completely loose of their rigid schedules and parents.

A few bouncers guarded a discreet raised alcove at the back, but again we were allowed entry. The walls of the VIP section were covered in iridescent sequins. Above the tables were hovering ice sculptures, and there was a centerpiece waterfall with fat black fish that swam in circles.

Avi shrieked. I'd never seen her so excited. "How do I look?" She smoothed her hair.

Reba threw a thumbs-up. I trailed behind the duo.

Marco Grant wasn't as tall as the billboard had depicted. She blinked like a human. I counted. She moved like one, but that could've been a characteristic perfected by physicians. After seeing the Union's underwater experiment, I'd put nothing past them. Her eyes widened as she embraced Avi as if they were longtime friends. I moved in closer. It was odd that her skin had no flaws. No creases or discoloration. It was like colored porcelain against waves of green tresses that fell perfectly at her hips. Her waist was the tiniest circumference I'd ever seen, yet her breasts poked out, and her thighs were round and full. She had shiny pink nails that were long and pointed like claws.

She grabbed my hand unexpectedly. Her touch was cold, her grip firm as she shook, then released. "Nice to meet you," she said as if she'd rehearsed beforehand.

Was she real or not? I couldn't tell anymore.

After a few moments of chatting, Marco's publicist whisked her away to speak to the next person in the long line of people waiting to ogle over her, so Avi and Reba decided to catch up. They talked and talked, one small story leading to another larger one. Avi and I weren't that far apart in age, yet her upbringing, her experiences were so different, so much purer than mine. While she reminisced about stories of rich-people problems, I stewed in memories of loss. Unable to take any more of their chatter, I leaned over the bar and massaged my temples. How much longer was I going to have to babysit?

"Be with you," the bartender said from the other side.

I sat there hoping that her boy toy would take her off my hands; then I could call it a night. Being cramped up with a bunch of advantaged teens wasn't my idea of a stimulating evening.

A couple across the room wore matching crystal masquerade masks. At first, I thought they wanted me to be their unicorn. The crowd seemed to be the freaky type, but they seemed out of place as I observed them. A glass was perched near the woman's chin. Neither spoke to the other. Must've been Citadel cronies keeping an eye on me, but I'd been monitored all my life. Nothing new.

A partygoer in a blue bodysuit approached their table. The woman sipped from her drink.

"Can I get some service?" I asked, irritated by the long wait.

The bartender twirled around with an empty glass. "I apologize, miss . . ."

I couldn't believe it. I hadn't seen her since I'd been arrested at the Vixen. "Drake?"

Her eyes lit brighter than the strobes. "It's so good to see you. We thought you were done for."

"I'm tougher than a bag of titanium chips." I winked.

She squirted Fire into a shot glass and slid it over.

"Why are you dressed in Upper gear?" She gawked at me.

"I'm, uh, in the Citadel now," I explained. "An Elite's guard."

She filled the glass again. "Hmm."

"What?" I wanted to know what was on her mind.

She bent over the counter. "Don't you think it's weird for them to be treating you like one of them?"

"After the detention facility, I had to take what I could get. Besides, this gig isn't permanent."

Her eyes shifted as she wiped the rim of the glass. "What do you mean?"

I spoke low. "The Border isn't far from the Citadel. I saw it with my own eyes."

"The Citadel?" Drake tossed the towel over her shoulder. "Sounds like a death mission to me."

I checked for Avi, but she was gone.

"My entire life has been a death mission." I took the last shot and began to scan the area. Where the hell had the girl gone?

Halfway through the search, I found Avi being led away by a man in shades. I rushed through the bodies until I reached them and cut in front of him.

"Why are you dragging me?" Avi yelled.

"Let her go." I grabbed his arm. He ripped himself away.

"Do you know who I am?" His lenses were so dark that I saw only my reflection in them. He wore an arrogant smirk that I wanted to rid the world of.

I tilted my head. "Don't know and couldn't give an ass less."

"I'm Phoenix Chi, son of Commander Lex Chi." He shoved me. "Move along before I have you imprisoned."

Avi squeezed my wrist in passing. "Stay close," she whispered.

Suddenly, Marco Grant's concert started. The music was louder, and fans pushed to get closer to the stage, taking me with them. I'd lost Avi in the rush. White exhaust from Marco Grant's boots jetted her above the mob. She glided, landing right onto the hexagonal stage. She stood under a halo centerpiece that shone with blue and white beams. She touched the tips of outstretched fans' fingers. The horde erupted in cheers and whistles, and more hands reached for her as if she were a deity. Marco glowed.

"I just want to give you my gratitude. My new single hit the number one spot in the entire region!" Marco pumped her fist and took in the adoration from her fans, looking down at them the way the General looked at his watchmen. Lights flashed, and the crowd chanted her name.

Her dancers wore metallic bodysuits and silver face guards. Sparks spurted from jets, and a cool fog permeated from below. The crowd thrust forward, trying to get closer and closer. She was making them lose their minds—just like Two had said.

I spotted the creep in the blue bodysuit from earlier, staring me down. I flowed with the crowd and pumped my fists, hoping to put distance between us. The next thing I knew, he'd tackled me. People screamed, blending in with the sounds of cheers for Marco. He pinned my arms to the ground. He made the mistake of bringing his head to mine.

I headbutted him and then twisted his arm into his shoulder blade. "Who are you?"

"A watcher," he spat.

People were scrambling away, and it was only a matter of time before security showed. I let him go.

He slid his pointy tongue over his teeth. I chopped him in the throat. He seized his neck and stumbled into a group of girls.

It was time to go.

I'd completely lost Avi in the madness, so I moved across the busy space, frantically trying to find her. I was failing miserably at being a watchman.

In a hidden VIP alcove, I spotted pairs of reflective eyes, like light glinting off a mirror, exactly like the girls in the Underground. I was surprised that the group included Reba and Jade, high out of their minds.

Security piled out of the elevator. They scanned the vicinity. Looking for me.

"Where's Avi?" I shook Reba.

She burst into a frenzied laugh. Her head fell into Jade's lap. Then Jade started sniggering. When I realized that they were going to be no help, I started down one of the back halls, which was lined with doors. It had a bluish tint to it, and white lantern garlands draped the ceiling. Even this far from the stage, the pulse of the instruments still coursed through the walls.

I put my ear to each door and listened. There were thumps and shouts, but none of the sounds belonged to Avi, until I finally heard a man's voice behind one. Then Avi's. I banged over and over. No answer. Then I heard her yell. I kicked until the door busted open.

"What the—" Phoenix's shades were off, and so was half his bodysuit. His eyes swirled with sparkles. Past his shoulder, Avi was curled up in a bed, clutching shredded pieces of her bodysuit. Makeup ran down her face.

Phoenix drew back his fist, but before he could strike, I bobbed and kicked him in the stomach. He flew back into a trendy nightstand. It shattered. He lay there, his back impaled by shards of glass. I picked up a piece and held it so tight that my hand bled. I stood over him. He was the personification of everything evil in the world. The region had originated from people like him. In his face, I saw everything that I hated and wanted to rid myself of. I imagined jamming the glass into his throat. Watching him bleed out.

The kill would count as a favor.

As I knelt, I placed the shard to his neck. It pierced the skin, and there the blade just hovered as his chest heaved with his own demise. He looked deeply into my face, my eyes as I looked way past his. He was nothing to me.

Avi gently placed her hand on mine.

I twitched at the warmth. I was so deep into my own thoughts of revenge that I forgot that she was even there. Why I was even there in the first place. I expected her to say something. Anything. How messed up I was. How I was nothing but a savage. A killer. But she didn't. She kept her palm on my skin.

Slowly, I lowered my hand. Watchmen shouted from outside the door. I stood, tossing the fragment to the side.

I hurried to the picture window.

It was time to jet.

Chapter Twenty-Eight
AVI

Saige had already pried open the window. Frosty gusts of wind whipped through the tattered parts of my bodysuit. All I could do was shiver. I racked my brain trying to make sense of it all, but I just couldn't comprehend. It all happened so fast. Phoenix lay on the ground in a bloody mess, moaning. I heard the weighty boots of watchmen clamoring along the hall.

They were coming after Saige. They wouldn't hold back this time; I just knew it.

Saige stuck her leg out and straddled the ledge.

"I'm coming with you," I said.

She shoved me back. "You can't. Stay here."

Tears streamed along my face as I pulled her arm, stopping her from going any farther. "If I don't go with you, they will kill you this time."

Saige weighed her options.

"Avi!" Phoenix had rolled onto his stomach and took hold of my ankle.

I pulled, but he was too strong. A watchman rushed in. Then Head Gardner right behind.

"Stand down," I screamed.

More watchmen skidded inside. "Release the Elite!"

Without hesitation, Head Gardner aimed and pulled the trigger. The laser hit Saige in the shoulder. She hugged my waist, and we tumbled back through the window.

We fell backward out of the window, tumbling down rusty metal stairs. She groaned and quickly got her bearings. Laser pings ricocheted off the fire escape. We jetted farther down the stairwell and then climbed onto a balcony. Saige clutched my hand as we wove through bodies. My legs became a blur as they pumped faster.

We exploded out into the alleyway, startling a girl smoking. We looped around the building and ran to the hovercycle. I slowed as we approached.

People were starting to rush out of the club. They cheered as if the escape were a scene from the cinema. Saige told me to hurry, but my chest was too tight. She had already started the engine, and the hovercycle began to soar. Security officers mixed with watchmen toppled from the entrance, shoving partiers out of the way.

"Stop them!" Head Gardner ordered.

I thought it was over, for me anyway, but Saige parked the hovercycle above me and gripped the back of my bodysuit like a lioness carrying a cub. A security officer tried to grab my dangling feet. I pulled myself onto the back seat. From overhead, I saw Jade and Reba standing among the crowd. Their eyes swirled, just as Phoenix's had. I wanted to vomit, but that feeling soon subsided as Saige pushed the speed. I clung to her, digging my head into her uninjured shoulder. Watchmen were on our tails, hovering in a triangular formation. Saige bobbed through traffic and made sharp turns. Over time, one by one, she managed to lose them.

Her body released its tension, but she was still bleeding. My grip loosened. We thought we were in the clear.

"Get your helmet," she said as she quickly placed hers on.

We weren't far from the Citadel when Head Gardner and her cronies appeared in the rearview mirror. Every time we switched lanes or made turns, they imitated us. Saige increased speed, and so did the team of riders. They managed to wedge us in with their hovercycles.

"Why won't they stand down?" I said over the wind.

In the next moment, a flash banged. The laser was like a mini explosive as it zipped from the barrel. Saige yanked the steering panel. We spun. Their hovercycles floated as we struggled to regain control. We sideswiped a building; sparks flew in my face as the engines ground. Saige took us higher. They began shooting a barrage of lasers. Our engine was hit. A crackling sound, lights on the control panel beeped, and the voice command alerted us that all systems had failed. As we descended, Saige got us as close as she could to the forest's edge. The bulky hunk of metal rattled the tops of the trees; leaves rustled, and branches cracked and split as we zoomed lower and lower.

We were going to die. I hadn't expected that Head Gardner would be the cause of it.

The hovercycle nose-dived. I flew off.

❖ ❖ ❖

I awoke facedown, suspended in a body of water. Alive but paralyzed. My breath was the only thing I could control. Arms lifted my soaking body. I was then carried up a foothill. My eyes burned. All I could see were shadows.

"Saige?" I mumbled.

Not too far away, a watchman shouted, "Hands where I can see them!"

Saige's body was sprawled out near the base of a splintered tree trunk. The mangled steel of the hovercycle rested feet away.

"Put me down." I struck the watchman in the chest, and he released me.

231

I mustered enough energy to stand on my own, holding my ribs as if they would slip out of place. Watchmen held position on the immobile Saige while a physician lingered over her with a bot.

"Get away from her!" I shoved through their guns.

Twigs were twisted in the waves of her locs, and a bone in her leg protruded through the skin. I dropped beside her.

Her eyes stayed stuck in one spot. "Mmmmm."

"What?" I put my ear to her mouth.

"Mmmmmove," she said.

I argued. "I'm not leaving you."

She moaned, lifted her head a little, and made eye contact with each watchman. She dumped her head back down. She was a watchman, yet they still treated her like a worker. Disgust tossed within me; I could only describe it as hatred. Hatred for the way things were and how they had become. I was supposed to rule it. How was that power? I was to become a pawn, as others before me, a face of a movement that was true and pure for the Upper Residents to never question, a vessel for the real thinkers to make decisions through so the people would stay exactly as they were: blinded.

"Put your weapons down," I said as I rose. "That is an order."

The watchmen hesitantly placed their guns to their sides.

The head watchman stepped forward. "Elite Jore, this woman has been accused of assaulting an Elite. By the orders of Head Gardner, we have authorization—"

"Head Gardner?" I laughed.

Why hadn't she finished the job herself? Was she really nothing more than a coward?

"She is not the General and has no jurisdiction here," I told them all.

"But—"

"Stand down."

He backed away, taking all his goons with him.

I returned to Saige's side as the bot scanned. I put my hand on her. She was cold.

"Data shows no major organs were hit," the physician said. "A laser wound to the left shoulder and a broken leg. A temporary fuse should do. It'll be sore, but at least she'll be able to walk."

She didn't flinch when he shot her in the thigh to numb the pain. She never looked at me, just into the shimmering evening sky. The bone cracked when he reset it. When he finished lasering her wounds, he packed his tools, and the bot trailed him back through the bushes.

Then it was very quiet.

I watched her watch nothing. The silence led to thoughts, and thoughts always led to unfavorable conclusions. Each ending always concluded with Father's tyranny. Our people's tyranny. The inoculations. The drugs. Phoenix had attacked me because he was under the influence of Glitter. I didn't want to believe that he would've behaved the same under different circumstances.

The strip he'd torn from my bodysuit flapped in the gusts.

"That boy, the one you—I'm betrothed to him." I tried to paste the strip to my skin, make the bodysuit whole and beautiful again, but it just kept sliding. "Father's doing."

Saige still stared upward.

"Do you know where they get the Glitter? Jade was on it. Reba. Phoenix." I asked, "How is it being distributed under the Union's jurisdiction?"

"You can't trust Phoenix." Saige broke out of her trance. "Or Jade. None of them."

"I asked you a question. How are they getting it?"

Jade had problems, but we were still bonded by blood, and I wouldn't want her to die over drugs that the rebels manufactured. Saige propped herself up. "She isn't worth it."

"I don't understand why she would want to—"

Saige glanced at me. "If I were you, I'd cut her loose."

233

"Kin is important, Saige. I'm sorry that you've never experienced that, but I don't think it's possible for me to just 'cut her loose.'"

"You really do live in a fantasy world." She grabbed the trunk, putting weight on her newly fused leg. "You sit here and ask me how Glitter is distributed, when it's been on the market for decades. It's older than the both of us combined. Why don't you tell me why the Union doesn't know about it? Ask your father why these things happen, why his watchmen are probably the ones who smuggle it."

"The Union has thrived for centuries. Loyalty from his officials is the foundation of our civilization, our culture."

"Are those your words or your father's?" She squinted.

Blood rushed to my head.

Saige began, "All Uppers are opportunists and couldn't care less about morals or loyalty. They're like—"

"Like you?"

Guilt, sorrow perhaps, washed over her. She shrank a little. "I never told you I was a good person." Her cheeks became redder. "You people have the nerve. Your father was the one who put me in this. The grand General Jore. You think he's a great man, don't you? Full of integrity? Your father's just like me. Scum." She heaved a wad of spit into the dirt.

"Stop."

"Or what?" She pulled back. "What are you going to do? What do you do about anything? You're so pathetic that your family is forcing you to marry a crazed drug addict, and all you've done is accept it. You don't know anything about suffering. Have you ever seen someone you loved shot in the head? Raped? Been so hungry that your stomach curved inward and touched your spine? Answer me, Princess."

My bottom lip jiggled. I pursed my lips together to resist the urge of becoming too emotional, irrational. Words became tangled. Fragmented. She was right. I had never been hungry. I had never wanted for anything. But my ancestors had. She had no right to disgrace my family. I was my father's daughter, and an insult to him was an insult to me.

"This is the last time you will be warned. Do not demean my family's name."

She staggered near me. Her expression set just like the mug shot. I traced the lines of her face; her pain was etched in the faint contours around her mouth and between her brows.

"You want to think that you're good, that you're morally better than the Union," she said. "You've never even been inside the Subdivisions. Never seen the sickly workers still forced to work. Children begging. The beatings and the executions by the very watchmen who protect you." She shoved me. "Have you ever seen your mother beg, beg for her life? Your father pulls the strings on who thrives and who dies. How is that just?"

I'd never wanted to consider those horrific things, but lately I'd toggled back and forth between our comfortable system and the future of equality. Currently, Father just lived by the structure of the bylaws. Father—the Union—had maintained a system so that we were able to live. That was what was pounded into our heads. It was what I hung on to. Their word. The Union had prided itself on justice. Our way of life. Workers were well maintained, he said. They had adequate shelter and food, he said. When my people had been enslaved, they'd never given us anything but deep gashes in our backs, disease, burning crosses, and brutality. They'd ruined our economy, our atmosphere. How many of us lay at the bottom of the sea during human trafficking? Had she forgotten the struggle of her other half?

"I never asked you to save me." She poked my chest with each word. "Why did you stop them? You should've just let me die."

I shook my head.

She shoved me. "Why?"

"I don't know."

"You know."

She kept badgering and badgering, and I couldn't cope any longer, so I pushed her as hard as I could. She groaned, clutching her sore leg. I took off. An adrenaline-fueled race ensued. I was running from—toward—anything. Before I knew it, I'd be the one in charge of the scheme that was the Union. I'd have to marry a man I'd never love, in a world that I had never chosen to be in.

My eyes were swollen, cloudy. My weeping echoed off the trees. Although I was alone, I was embarrassed. My father had raised strong, independent girls who were prepared to solve any task at hand. So what was wrong with me?

In my haste, I'd run all the way to the greenhouse. It was the only place to go. The light from the window flooded through the darkness. I knocked. When Liyo opened the door, I collapsed. He caught me inside the entryway and slowly lowered me to the ground.

"Are you hurt?" he asked, checking over my body.

"Everywhere hurts." I sighed.

"What happened?" He shouldn't have cared. I was the enemy. His enemy.

I tried to answer, but only sniffles surfaced.

"Breathe," he said in my ear. "Just breathe."

His compassion, compassion I didn't deserve, made me even more of an emotional wreck. That he even had any left after what we'd done to him—his people.

"I want to know everything, Liyo."

He pulled me to my feet, dusted his knees, and then moved over to the workstation. I limped toward him and watched as he began pruning stems.

"Please," I said. "I beg you."

"Why?"

"Something's happening. Something catastrophic. I know it."

He placed his palms on the counter. His shoulders tensed closer to his ears.

"I no longer trust my own family," I cried. "I need to know. This is my region. I have a right to know."

His jaw flexed. "How can I trust an Elite?"

"I don't have anything to offer other than my word."

"That's not enough where I come from," he said. "You've got to prove it."

I thought harder. "What do you need?"

He scratched his chin. "A reader. From an official."

"Instructor Skylar?"

Within no time at all, I had smuggled the reader from the main living quarters and placed it on the counter in front of Liyo. It hadn't been as hard as I'd thought to steal it. I had all access to his home. And the Instructor hadn't returned yet.

Liyo examined it like a piece of treasure. "It's secured. We can't crack it from here. We've got to take it to the Farmlands."

"Farmlands?" I exclaimed.

"There's something on here that can get us some answers. Do you want to figure out what's going on or not?"

I frowned, thinking about Father and the punishments I'd have awaiting when I returned. It was too late; I'd already begun piecing together the puzzle.

❖ ❖ ❖

Liyo took me to a modest-looking dwelling, where he disappeared inside. When he returned, he ushered me inside, shutting the door very slowly behind us. He dug into a wooden chest and withdrew bits of tangled wire and damaged devices. He stuck an ancient data card into the side of the Instructor's reader. The card scrambled the screen.

"It'll take a second," he told me.

"Where did you get all of this old hardware?"

"Scavenging," he said. "You'd be surprised what Uppers toss."

The screen turned black. Was it broken? Did the Instructor know we'd stolen it and had overridden the system? After consecutive blinking, the screen powered on. The main page. Liyo tried opening files, but they were locked. Classified.

A message icon appeared. From Head Gardner. We looked at each other, and immediately, I felt sick.

"Greetings, Instructor Skylar. Since you were absent. Here's the ruling. Enjoy."

I tapped play.

The meeting began. My father and the cabinet were seated in the library.

"All Elites and most Upper Residents have been given the serum. We plan to have the rest administered very soon," Commander Chi said.

"So there's no chance of these poisons affecting us, our families?" a man asked.

"It's been tested and tested again on laboratory-birthed Impures and Europe subjects," Father said. "The virus won't attack our system; it won't even attack an Impure's system. The serums are just an added precaution. No need to worry, my friend."

Head Gardner spoke. "General, can you explain the recent threats so we all can get a clear understanding of how grave the situation is?"

"We have come to a time where our very existence is at risk, yet again." He sighed. "Lower Residents are populating faster, living longer, and taking more space and resources than initially forecasted. They're also creating health issues within the Subdivisions. Illnesses are spreading into surrounding localities and into our backyards. Too many cases of unidentified viruses have arisen, which physicians have traced back to them. We are being driven into an ineffective system. It cannot continue."

"How exactly will we spread this epidemic?" a woman asked.

"The final capsules will be brought from below and delivered to the Health Department to be given as routine supplemental doses per usual. For the stragglers, the zones will be misted with another formula with similar qualities."

Chi added, "Workers will be replaced with the updated droids. We have worked diligently to solidify the droid's human mannerisms and functions. These modifications will not cause any major shocks to our community. As each worker falls ill, physicians will bring them to the Health Department. Families will be notified that the workers are no longer active, and that they will be replaced promptly. No wrinkles, ladies and gentlemen."

"Won't they want to fight back?" the same woman asked. "When they take notice of their people leaving sick and not returning?"

"They already have," Head Gardner spoke up. "But their attempts are meaningless. They will fail. I'm confident that the environment's hierarchy will always prevail."

My stomach twisted, and I fought the urge to retch.

"Head Gardner is correct," said Chi. "They can't stop this. The virus is fast but not too fast. A quiet kill. We couldn't maintain all of them dropping at once."

I pictured Liyo having vials of yellow mists spewed over him, over the Subdivisions. Workers' corpses littering the grounds, strewn about with oozing bubbles over their skin.

When the meeting was adjourned, the fate of the Southern Region was set.

Liyo rubbed his temples. "Beasts."

"Is there a cure?"

"I don't know," he replied. "We knew that they were planning mass genocide but didn't know where the vials would be distributed. I've got to tell the others."

I blinked rapidly. "You knew this all along?"

"Of course."

"So I'm the only one who had no knowledge?"

He placed his palm on my cheek. A shock went through me. "You needed to see for yourself."

A man burst into the room. Liyo's hand dropped away as if my skin were made of searing coal.

"Come quick." For a moment, the man's eyes held shock as he scanned my face and figured out who I was. His voice trembled. "It's Lilith."

A woman with stringy hair and pale-gray skin lay on the wooden floor. That same little girl, Eve, rested her head on the deceased woman's stomach.

"She's gone," the man said. "It didn't work. The antidote didn't work."

Eve burst into a fit of coughs. Her father pried her from the corpse and eyed me like I had no right to be present. I knew that I didn't belong. Liyo's face turned red, and his fists remained tight at his sides. The floor trembled. Like an earthquake, the disturbance came from everywhere. Items clashed and tumbled from shelves. The window fractured, and shards came at me like horizontal rainfall. I shielded my face.

The whites of Liyo's eyes had gone pink. "I am so sorry. I didn't mean to—"

Eve's father glared at me with unnaturally gray eyes. "What's she doin' here?"

"I'm so sorry for your loss," I said. He looked like he wanted to end my life right there. "I should be getting back now."

"She's helping," Liyo told him.

"An Elite is helping us?" He chuckled once, his eyes watery. "Liyo, stop this nonsense. It's over. Look at Lilith. She's dead. Dead! We'll all be dead soon. It's over. Now take her back to the Citadel. Just halfway. If they see you with her . . ."

Liyo nodded.

I returned to Liyo's room to remove the card from the port of the reader. Floorboards creaked.

"Who's there?" I said quietly.

"Me." Eve came into full view.

"Greetings." I smiled.

She wiped her face.

"Come." I placed the reader down and patted my lap.

She dragged her feet. I shot her a reassuring smile, and then she flew into my arms full speed, almost knocking me over. She wrapped herself around me. I nestled my cheek into the top of her head; her hair smelled like warm lemons. Her neck became limp so soon. I placed my palm in front of her nose and mouth. I thought she'd succumbed to the same demise as her mother. Although her little breaths were faint, she was only asleep.

I nestled her closer. It was the least I could do. Lend some type of comfort. I couldn't imagine seeing Mother pass away at this age. Or any age really. What were we doing to them?

She began stirring and then coughing violently. The child's lungs sounded full of phlegm. Blood colored her lips. I wiped it away. Red residue was left on my thumb. Liyo entered and swept her from my arms.

❖   ❖   ❖

In the forest, Liyo walked ahead of me. The return route he took wasn't familiar.

"Mind slowing down?" I huffed.

He stopped. "No." Then he walked faster than before.

"Which way are we going?"

"The back way," he grumbled.

He tore through grass and then led me along a creek. Crickets chirped near hollowed logs, and the cicadas' song flooded the forest. The temperature had dropped, and I quivered, still damp from the hovercycle crash. He leaped onto the uneven trunk, balancing his way across. He stopped halfway. "Are you coming or not?"

"No," I mimicked his tone.

He stomped, jumped off the end of the log, and stared at me coldly.

"Eve has it, doesn't she?"

He knelt and peeled bark from the log. "Hmm."

I climbed carefully and balanced across. "How can we stop this? I want to help."

"Her mom was sick for a long time. We tried everything." He tossed bark into the water. "Physicians will come in the morning, take her body. Burn it."

I became light headed. My legs couldn't bear weight. I fell forward. Liyo caught me by the wrist. I wasn't sure how deep the creek was or if my limbs would even work if he decided to let go. I wanted him to release me, allow me to float. Far away from the truth, the lies that were my life. I imagined that letting go crossed his mind too.

He pulled me back to safety.

"Can you really help us?"

"What if I got you meds from the Citadel?" I told him. "Maybe that will help until . . ."

He studied me for what seemed like forever. I became self-conscious and focused on the moon's reflection off the currents. I wished he could've seen me earlier when I wasn't tarnished and my hair didn't have twigs stuck in it. He lifted my chin. Our eyes met, but his attention stayed on my lips. A familiar tingle went through my soles, the tips of my fingers. Something about him enticed me.

"You're different," he said in one breath.

His face remained open, relaxed, almost as if he had forgotten who I was and who he was.

I turned away. "What will your family say when they notice that you haven't returned?"

"What will the General think of your absence?" he countered.

I hadn't wanted to think about that yet. The looming consequences. The words tumbled out. "What are you?"

"You really wanna know?"

"You move things without touching them. I saw it—I saw you."

"I know," he admitted.

"You're not human, and you're not a droid."

He turned my hands palms side up and traced the lines. The crooked shapes glowed. As logical as I was, there was no explanation. Energy coursed through my hands and radiated outward into every cell. It felt light. Airy.

"A long time ago, cultures believed in a divine being," he said. "Higher and more powerful than anything science or technology could make. He had different names: Yahweh, Jehovah, Allah. People called upon it for guidance, and it gave people hope. It created the entire universe, and when humans are born, it breathes into us its spirit, the soul." He patted his chest. "It breathes something more into some of us. A gift, they say."

The glowing stopped. He tucked a loc of hair behind his ear. "I don't know if I believe it, though."

"God?"

"No," he said. "The gift."

As his energy leaked from my body, the pain of before crept back.

He fixated on my lips again. Perhaps he found the fullness of them alien. Possibly he wanted to taste.

I knew it was wrong, but I could no longer resist the urge. I leaned in.

I kissed him. I'd never initiated one before, and I wasn't sure if I was doing it right. His eyes were closed, so I shut mine, too, and draped my arms around him, pushing my body into his. His lips varied from opened to closed, from loose to tight as he wrapped his hands around my back and snaked them up my waist. The electrical currents weren't coming from him this time; they emerged from me. The prickly, warm feeling radiated throughout my entire being. I could've stayed in it for eternity.

And then we heard sounds beyond the bushes.

Chapter Twenty-Nine
SAIGE

They kissed.

They heard me creeping in the blackness, but I didn't let them see me. As I limped away, I stumbled over a root that stuck out of the soil. Pain shot up my leg as I fought to keep my cries quiet. As I lay on the solid ground, I thought about all the things that had led me to that very moment. Liyo must hate me. I had said the nastiest things I could muster so that he could just stop caring about me. Stop saving me. I'd pushed him away and into the arms of Avi. He'd said he was just using her, but I knew Liyo. Maybe there were feelings there. Either way, it was none of my business. I didn't own Liyo. But, for some reason, it still kept picking away at me. What if he did? It bothered me that it bothered me.

I'd chosen my route. Why did I now find it becoming harder to accept?

Had my wanting to escape clouded reality, judgment? I didn't even have a clue what I'd do once I was over that wall. What I'd find. I fixated on running away so much that I pushed everyone away instead. Tears welled as I thought about Mama Seeya. The promise she'd made me make. The one that I continually broke.

After each training, when I was missing Ma something bad, laid flat in the dirt, defeated, Mama Seeya would lift me and squeeze my cheeks with one big hand so taut that my lips would purse. "You are more than what they say you are. You are more than your traumas. Promise me that you will repeat this when you are tired, lost, when you feel like you can't go on. Remember these words. I won't always be here, picking you back up." She squeezed tighter. "Promise me that you will not survive, Saige, but that you will thrive. You and Liyo are our hope."

She was also born of two races. Like me. She'd seen things. Like me. She knew I could, but I didn't know that I could. I'd lost hope.

This whole time I was existing when she'd drilled in me to thrive. What would thriving even look like? I had trained myself to bury and bury. Now it had become a nasty habit. How could I come back from something like that?

Someone approached. I ducked in the shrubbery.

Pea walked in short fast strides on a dirt trail. Her face was concealed by a hood, and a large cloak floated behind her. To my surprise, Drake wasn't too far behind. I followed. She looked around, then entered a clearing surrounded by huge oaks. Workers sat inside with light orbs in their laps. An old man stood in the center, holding the brightest one. He wore large glasses that made his dull brown eyes appear enlarged. Wisps of hair surrounded a bare, freckled scalp.

"We have been notified that Lilith has passed on," he said.

A woman cried out. An orb rolled from her lap.

"We must use this and every murder as ammunition."

The people murmured.

"We've gotten word from the Subdivisions. Slowly but surely, they are trusting that this—this way of life . . . they are killing us . . . !" he said in a broken voice. "They have kept us in captivity, dictated our every move."

It was the first time in a long time I'd witnessed workers break free from their mechanical conditioning. They squeezed their fists and threw them in the air. Hope and anger, attributes the Union had successfully snuffed out.

"They call themselves civilized." The man wagged his finger. "They believe that science will save them. Ha! Pure foolishness created to satisfy what they want to make real. And what do we do? We have become what they've always wanted: extinct. I have looked to the heavens and prayed, prayed hard, despite their freethinker beliefs." His mouth spread in a grin. "He has finally sent us a sign, and Mama Seeya has said it's time."

The meeting carried on, but I felt his presence before I knew he was actually there.

Liyo stood in the shadows. He'd discovered my hiding spot. "What do you think?"

I was thinking a lot of things, but nothing came out.

He came forward, the rest of his face and body revealed in the moonlight. "We all have a duty, Saige."

"Look what happened to our parents," I said. "That is the fate of duty."

He appeared pained. I looked away, unable to witness the hurt I'd caused him yet again.

"You are playing a dangerous game, Liyo. The girl. Your plan. It won't work."

The long piece of whitish hair that had been behind his ear fell in front of his eye. "And if I say no?"

"Under the law, the crime of integration is punishable by execution."

"You sound like one of them."

"I'm trying to save you," I said harshly under my breath.

"It was you near the creek. Wasn't it?"

I pinched the stress that formed between my brows. "If the Union finds out, they will torture you. Make an example out of you. You haven't seen the things that I saw."

Liyo opened his palm. A stone from the ground flew above his hand like a magnet attracting metal. I'd heard rumors a long time ago about people being able to move things with their minds, but I'd thought it was an old tale that parents told their children before bed.

He took a deep breath. "Do you ever wonder how many out there are exactly like you? I do. A lot. I always wonder what I am. I mean, sometimes, I know, and then there're times I don't." He allowed the rock to fall. "The rebels say I'm their weapon."

"But you don't have to be a martyr. You could just go."

He stepped in closer. "Stop the games. You want something. I know you."

"Are you a mind reader too?"

An invisible barrier had been placed all around me. I pushed, but it didn't budge. Liyo's palm faced me, glowing lines churning on it. I resisted the foreign presence that overtook me, but his energy willed my body back to him. I felt breaks in the force as I fought. He was strong but not strong enough. I skated forward, at times taking tiny steps back. Liyo's face contorted. His forehead glistened as he tugged harder.

He was hurting himself to stop me from leaving, so I stopped resisting. "You can't keep me in here forever."

He let go. "I have a proposition."

What could he possibly have that I wanted?

Liyo leaned against the tree with a curve in his back. "I'm so very tired, Saige, but there's nothing left to do but fight. I told the rebels about you. About your position in the Citadel."

"Flattered," I said. "Spit it out."

"At one point, I thought that it was possible to coexist with the Uppers, but we are no longer necessary. We die, or we die trying." His eyes narrowed. "We only get bits of information, sometimes reliable and sometimes not. The workers in the Citadel don't have access to military information, but you do . . ."

"What makes you think that they'd just let me go roaming around the General's quarters?"

"If we strike, it's got to be on accurate information. From the inside."

"So what's the proposition?"

Liyo became serious. "Information on the Border, the Northern Region. An escort. You want to leave? I can make that happen."

"You mean to tell me that you were sitting on information that I needed this whole time?"

"That's because I didn't want you to leave," he admitted.

"That is not your choice to make." I poked him in the chest. "Now you want to dangle freedom over my head in order to get information?"

He stood taller. "We are in a war, Saige. It is bigger than me and you."

I had been backed into a corner once again. I just hadn't expected it from Liyo. But at the end of the day, we were all just pawns in a one-sided game. "How can I trust you?"

"How can I trust that you won't go back and expose us?" he answered.

Drake appeared, slicing through the stiffness that Liyo and I had caused. She placed her elbow on top of Liyo's shoulder.

"Hey, friend." She eyed me. "You on board or what?"

I scoffed. Shaking my head in disbelief. I couldn't believe what I was about to agree to do.

"Shit."

He took that as an agreement.

"Let's get started," he said.

I had until nightfall the following day to get an access card and infiltrate the Citadel's internal underground lab. I would retrieve any tactical information that would help the rebels. I would meet him in the forest with the info, and in return, I'd get a first-class ticket to the Border.

Chapter Thirty
AVI

After the creek, Liyo and I had escaped in different directions, creating as much distance as we could between ourselves. I wasn't sure who had been lurking, but there was a strong possibility that it could've been one of Father's associates.

For now, it was just an anxiety-ridden waiting game.

Too much had occurred for Father to stay in the dark. Our confrontation was inevitable. I had to strategize. If he believed that I had switched sides, he'd lock me inside my dwelling indefinitely. I'd be of no use imprisoned. The ability to get in touch with Liyo had become much more valuable. I had work to do now, a purpose. What I planned was punishable to the fullest extent of the law. Treason. Not even I was safe from that.

Just as Father had said, there was no gray area. I'd have to finish it.

Something in the back of my mind, fear perhaps, told me to stop. To choose the easy path of ignorance. Because this wasn't my war to fight. I should marry Phoenix and rule over the Southern Region as planned. Disregard Liyo. Ignore what had happened between us.

I was still unsure about what exactly had happened between us. But one thing was for certain: I was an Elite and he a worker. Whatever *it* was would never, could never work.

I banged on Instructor Skylar's door.

"Avi?" He rubbed the sleep from his eyes. "What are you doing out at this time? Where is Sai—your watchman?"

I shoved the reader into his chest.

"How'd you get this?" he asked, surprised.

"You lied. About everything. About the supplements!"

"Avi. Stop." He grabbed my wrist.

I snatched it away. "I trusted you."

His expression went from hardened to apologetic, but it didn't matter. "I wasn't permitted to divulge that information. Those were orders from the General, and I abided by them."

Nothing he said was going to change how I felt about him. The sight of him made my stomach boil. "Evening greetings, Instructor Skylar."

He held his hand out. "Avi, don't leave like this."

How could I have been so naive?

❖ ❖ ❖

A hovercycle had been demolished, Saige was missing, and I looked like I had been through warfare. Pea greeted me at the entrance of the Citadel. "Where's Father?" I asked.

"He's in the fields," she answered.

I waved her away without another word. She could tell that I wasn't in the mood and scurried away without question.

I disrobed inside my quarters and tossed the bodysuit into the incinerator. I sat inside the bathing unit, allowing the jets to cleanse the grime from my skin. I anxiously waited for some profound plan to arise as the water massaged my aching muscles. To my dismay, no grand scheme surfaced.

It was only a matter of time before Father would figure it out. He'd be pushed to the extreme once again. He'd have his reason to drive Saige back to Head Gardner. Avi the Helpless. Avi the Weak. Just like Saige had said. And the others.

The jets stopped. My time was up. I came to a slow realization that I was no longer in my own element. The Citadel had become enemy territory.

Damp hair dangled in my face. I brushed it back, mentally preparing to speak with Father. I would confess, but first I was going to have Pea deliver medications to Eve. I would steal them.

The corridors were eerily vacant, the bustle of day workers gone. The door to the physician's ward was locked. My eyes were scanned. Once inside, I quickly shoveled shelves of glass bottles and vials into a slimpack.

Every light turned on. I froze and tucked the sack under my arm. Jade stood in the doorway. Her eyes were back to normal, Glitter flushed from her system.

"Jade?"

"The one and only." She stepped forward.

"I was just—"

"—stealing meds, property of the Citadel."

She waited for a reply, but nothing surfaced. She analyzed me; her eyes narrowed to the cut on my face from the crash. "What happened?"

I straightened myself, releasing strain.

Jade clicked her tongue, then spoke in a high-pitched voice: "Dear Princess, what have you gotten yourself into?"

She showed me her reader. The photo I'd taken of Liyo. The first time I'd seen him in the greenhouse.

"I hack into things in my spare time," she said matter-of-factly.

I choked on acid.

"I take that your silence means that you wouldn't mind me showing Father this?" She headed toward the exit.

I blocked the entry. "Jade. Please. No."

Her face twisted. "Blair was right. You are a honk lover."

I no longer needed to confirm what information she knew or what she meant. I didn't need to grovel or argue. I had been an idiot. Jade had waited for an opportunity that would lead to my demise. Now she had more than she could have ever hoped for. I'd given her exactly what she wanted and wrapped it with a flimsy bow.

Who knew how much she knew about Liyo, but she knew enough to take me down. Tears fell, not because she had won but because now she had the power to destroy him, and it was entirely my fault.

Jade remained impassive, her chin held high.

"You have only one choice. You leave this place for good. Never to return. You don't tell a soul." She spoke in a monotone. "We have made arrangements for you on a cargo load that will ship you to the Outskirts."

"We?" I said.

She blew out. "None of that matters at this point. You will never return to this place again. If you ever decide to show your face again, interfering with my position as succeeding General, I will make sure that Liyo and anyone he's associated with are strung by their necks."

"So this is about power?" I said, "You want me exiled so that you can become General?"

"I can't believe I am dignifying this with an explanation." She laughed. "It has never been about power, sister. It's about survival, and you, your ideas, threaten our survival."

"Have you gone mad? You will not get away with this. Father will see right through your lies. He will never stop searching for me."

"You always were the favorite daughter. The one who could do no wrong." She grinned. "They will learn to love me, respect me, and they will learn to live without you."

She paused to allow her words to sink deeper in my psyche.

"Do not leave the Citadel until I give you the word, and don't fret—it shall be soon."

I wanted to bow my head in defeat, but instead I held it high. "You can't do this."

"I am," she said. "I'm making sure this region stays unsullied."

She hugged me like she had never done before. Nausea hit me, and I dropped the sack of medicines. Jade patted me on the shoulder, then sent me on my way.

The Citadel didn't feel like mine anymore; the majestic halls that had once been my safe haven had become distant, uncomfortable. I had been gutted like an animal, my innards dragging, leaving an outer crust of what appeared to be a frail human. I had been degraded, stripped of my rights as an Elite by my own. Father had never prepared me for this kind of treachery.

When I returned to my dim quarters, I noticed someone in the shadows. "How did you get in here?" I asked.

"I have my ways," Saige replied.

I turned my back on her.

"Where'd you go?" she asked.

"Instructor Skylar's."

"This late?"

I nodded, then unclasped my hands. "It's good to know that you take pride in your position."

Saige looked at me as if I had told a lie. "Right."

"Where were you?"

"Around."

"So you've been sneaking around, watching me," I accused.

No reply.

She was the only one I had at the moment, and I took all my frustrations out on her.

"Do you have something that you want to tell me?" She stepped forward.

Chapter Thirty-One
SAIGE

I wasn't the kind to allow people to touch, let alone hug, me. When Avi fell into my arms, I wanted to push her away, but I was supposed to be playing the role of a devoted watchman, and no matter how much it killed me to be affectionate, I placed an arm over her. I may have even patted her on the back once.

"Saige," she said, "something awful is happening."

I didn't have to ask. She'd found out about her family's plans, which included Liyo. Those plans included me as well, but I wouldn't be there long enough to care, change anything. My job was to retrieve that information.

Alarms went off. Avi covered her ears. From the wristcom, a screen appeared with Commander Chi. Worry hit. Did he know about the chase with Head Gardner?

"Avi is to stay in her quarters, and you are to immediately report to the landing." Then he disappeared.

"What's going on ?" Avi asked.

I could only shake my head and follow orders. Truth was, I had no clue.

The ground vibrated in the halls. Wind hit me from the horde of watchmen that spilled from the exit. I joined the crowd, funneling outside. Maybe off the hook, for now.

On an elevated stage stood the General, facing what seemed like every watchman on duty. They were clad in bulky armored plates and boots laced to the knee. Gun straps lay across their broad chests. Lightning streaked beyond the gray skies like dying orbs. Electricity crashed furiously in the background. I tasted moisture and metal in the atmosphere. Watchmen faced forward, feet hip-width apart, shoulders linked to the next man's like a human fence along each row. Lungs rose and fell like past civilizations. They hung on every command like monkeys from vines. I wondered what he could've said that they wouldn't have obeyed. The life of a watchman: to protect and to serve. Their existence started to make sense. They were engineered to lay down their lives, enforce the supposed betterment of society. No questions asked. No hesitation.

I was not. Yet I still stood with the chosen, with the men of a government responsible for sticking me inside the Cube, executing the ones closest to me. A fetid taste filled the back of my throat. What was I doing there, trying to blend in with monsters that prided themselves on false morality? Loyalty and phony patriotism. I had been taught to understand that the Union was a strong and unified force. At one time, I had thought it couldn't be destroyed and that its systems were impenetrable. Assigned work was put in by its members, and the machine did the rest. The Union had thrived for nearly a thousand years on the same system.

But I had never looked at the bigger picture; my vision was always clouded by one idea. I failed to notice the signs of their weaknesses and my own strengths. It only took a small piece to rip a larger design. I was more integral than I had once believed, but for some reason, I was still torn between running toward destiny or away from it.

"Never repeat the past's mistakes," the General said.

He was right about that.

"You must be ready to go all the way for the greater cause of mankind."

There were those of us who were ready to die for the cause, whichever cause it was. Casualties were inevitable.

"Aerial techdrones have spotted increased thermal activity in the southeast quadrants of the Outskirts. We found rebel disturbances. We need to contain the situation before it sprouts any further," he said. "Commander Chi sent a team to eliminate the targets, but the tour failed. Less than half returned alive. The rebels have stolen sophisticated weaponry from one of the off-site warehouses." He smashed his gloved hands together. "We must hit them quick, hard. Show them that we are united and we don't sympathize with the enemy."

Bellows burst from the testosterone-saturated crowd.

"We will eradicate all targets." He looked in my direction. "Noble watchmen, soldiers of the Union, I stand before you in flesh, blood, and honor." He pounded his fist into his diaphragm. "I, the General of the Southern Region, protector of the sectors, have fought beside you for the freedom of our people, the safety of our existence, and the longevity of our offspring. I ask each and every one of you to trust your leader and fight to the death with your leader, as well as with the men beside you, your brethren, for the sake of the Union of Civilization. Will you sacrifice now for a better tomorrow? Will you fight, or will you allow these beings to destroy the mighty Union?"

The men chanted, pumping their guns over their heads. "Union of Civiliza—tion. Union of Civiliza—tion."

I mouthed the words. Who would've thought something so slight would be so painful. Never in a million eons would I have fathomed being in that moment in time, saying what I said and feeling what I felt. But since I was there, the choice was simple. I'd do whatever they ordered me to do, and in return, I would remain on the victorious side, thus not becoming prey again. I had to play the part of loyal watchman. I had a much bigger goal, but I kept asking myself, at what cost?

The thunder receded. Men loaded into the open mouths of hovercopters. Soldiers sported sleek angular helmets with dark visors so that their eyes were no longer visible. My face was reflected in a wider, distorted fashion. I was handed a laser gun on the ramp that led to the loading deck.

Commander Chi placed his arm out, prohibiting me from walking any farther. Did he know what I had done to his son?

"I don't trust you, Impure," he said at last. His top lip almost touched the bottom of his nose, as if I reeked. "I'm waiting for you to make the wrong move." He cocked his gun, then pulled mucus from the depths of his throat and spat near my boot. "I won't hesitate."

Watchmen strapped themselves into crisscrossed seatbelts, sniggering at me. Jemison tapped his microchip plate, and a helmet covered his head. He elbowed one of the giggling men in the chest, then patted the empty seat next to him. I secured myself and sat back. Jemison spoke into the transmitter located inside our helmets. "It'll get better."

His encouragement seemed more like a joke.

He said conversationally, "They just need to see you in action. They need time to get used to . . ."

I interrupted. "An Impure?"

He didn't respond for a while. The hovercopter lifted into scattered clouds and zoomed into an early dawn.

"What if I said that I accepted you?"

"Don't." I groaned. "Wouldn't want the higher-ups to hear."

His helmet shook from side to side. "They can't hear us. I have the channel set between only you and me."

"Romantic."

I couldn't tell if the sound he made was a snort or a chuckle. "I'm not so sure what will happen to either of us when we get down there, but—"

"Save the dramatics, Jemison."

"I guess I just want to say that I appreciate your bravery, Wilde. You saved my life, and I owe you."

The hovercraft quivered. The fleet ascended past the speckled clouds. I looked through the thick-plated glass at the squared buildings that stuck out of the Subdivisions; they became insignificant in size as we got higher. The details of the foliage, the water, the places that I once knew, were like spatters on brick. The people didn't exist from this high up.

I was only one person, one thing less than a speck, an Impure who couldn't make up her damned mind or apologize or save anyone. Whether I got the information for Liyo or not, I wasn't sure if it'd help the rebels overtake the government like they believed it would. Either way, freedom was my salvation. And it was so close. I tasted it.

I didn't want their land or their riches; the rebels could have it all. Maybe they should've wanted escape, like me. It was easier to just leave it all behind. Instead, they wanted to take back something that belonged to no one.

While everyone plotted and slaughtered, I'd be far away. Even if the rebels did take over, I was still half-Upper. Where would that leave me once everything was said and done? Would they scorn me as an Impure too?

It seemed like we had been floating endlessly. Structures had been long left behind, replaced by open fields. The sun rose past the horizon, spilling from the inside out like melted honey. The hovership descended. Dark puffs of smoke slithered past the pane. We were suspended in a V shape. Thick ropes were flung from underneath the crafts. Watchmen rappelled, one after the other, like spiders on webs. Their soles landed on leveled ground. The men disengaged from their connections, weapons drawn.

A harness was placed between my thighs with swift fingers. I was guided to an opening where thin-foliaged terrain lay beneath, occupied by camouflaged watchmen. They slithered on their knees and elbows in tall auburn grass.

I wasn't briefed before being shoved and left dangling. I steadied myself and held the line. In my other hand, my gun pressed against my stomach. The stench of war permeated the crevices of my helmet. The scents took turns burning my nostrils: charred wood and grass, the musk of sweat, blood, and scorched tar.

I got a panoramic view of the demolished metropolis. The wood still smoldered. Everything was an ashy gray. The wind pushed dust, swirling mini tornadoes. The houses were in rows, like a real city. Roofs were caved in and windows busted, and electricity crackled from downed power lines. Watchmen kept the inferno going by igniting the remainder of the homes, the wounded rebels, and piles of pills. Glitter.

I was dropped into the bleeding clot of a battle.

Bodies. Everywhere. Twisted, sitting hunched over against homes, in mounds with others. They were even floating in shallow waters. Part of a woman's body was submerged in a nasty pond. She clawed, trying to crawl to dry land. Both of her legs were missing. A watchman blasted a stream of fire in her face as if he were watering a dry flower.

The noise she made as she was cooked alive . . . I spiraled further into the chaos. The tips of my boots finally touched the straw. I detached the latch as the others had and crouched. The rope returned inside the ship, and another man was attached. A human conveyor belt.

Watchmen stood in front of me, fingers set loosely on triggers, and crouching as they were trained as we delved farther into the city. They scanned the perimeter, made hand gestures, moved forward a few feet. I took small wobbly steps, my eyes to the ground, searching for any disturbances in the clay. I was afraid I'd step on an active bomb and lose my limbs too. Limbs that I needed in order to escape. My gun became too heavy for my arms, my usual weight was too much for my knees, and I couldn't remember any of the training I'd received.

I couldn't understand how these people had built homes aboveground without Union detection. When we'd been in the Outskirts, we stuck to bunkers. This city being out in the open meant the Union had known about it and even known about the Glitter being produced there.

Watchmen kicked in the doors. More bodies inside were littered like trash. Limbs, fragments of bones, and blasted stone covered the floors. The men seemed to have no problem stepping on faces or kicking detached arms from their paths. I walked on the tips of my toes. Any crunch would've killed me. Those were people.

A rebel with tattered clothes and a gaping chest wound struggled for oxygen. His eyes fixed on nothing. His gasps quickened as if the angel of death had arrived. He grabbed my leg. I tried to yank him off, but he just began shaking like a malfunctioning droid. I lost my balance and fell into a pile of muck. No matter how hard I pulled, he wouldn't let go. He was able to crane his neck, and his eyes bulged out of his head.

Jemison shot him in the head with a loud crack. He took my arm and pulled me to my feet. "Stay tight." He motioned for us to keep moving forward.

The action was happening in the distance. Rebels shot from a fortress built out of scraps of metal and chunks of rock. Their protective wall was too short, and parts of it were unfinished as if they hadn't had enough time to prepare for the Union's arrival.

They'd gotten their hands on the Union's weaponry. How? There were holes in the system that I hadn't even imagined.

Commander Chi spoke over my internal speaker. "Penetrate the fortress, and eliminate all targets." Our tactic was to collect watchmen in the red zone and rush the fortress full force. Getting to the red zone was the problem. It was too open, and rebels were waiting to shoot us down.

"Two at a time," Butler announced.

Two men darted across the bare plain in a zigzag pattern. Rebels sent a barrage of lasers, which took both of them down before they'd even made it halfway. It seemed like no pair had made it to the other side. Dead watchmen lay in the dirt in the same positions in which they'd fallen when they'd been hit. One was missing part of his skull; his brain oozed down his forehead.

I twisted my neck, looking back over my shoulder as they shouted for me to move my ass. I could've left, I thought, but there was nowhere to go. I'd have to steal a hovercraft, all of which were filled with watchmen already prepared for my betrayal. I'd be deemed a traitor and thrown back into the detention facility with Head Gardner. Forget that.

I ran across the plain, eyes darting from the rebel fortress to the group of men safely behind an advanced shielding system. Lasers flew, hitting the earth near my boots and flying over my head. I leaped forward and crashed into the line of men.

Commander Chi appeared on the shield's screen. "Go! *Go!*"

Watchmen multiplied, swarming from each direction. Shells of blue flames erupted. Lasers dashed like missiles from above, and war cries became a continuous melody. A man in front of me stepped on a hidden plate. It detonated into a massive wave of indigo. Orange flames hit my helmet and blew out the shield. I flew and landed hard. I lay on my back, winded. A loud buzzing rang in my head, my ears. The last scenes played out like a hazy memory as boots trampled over my arms and legs. Then everything went mute.

I was on fire.

I rolled from side to side, smothering the flames. A watchman grabbed the nape of my suit and dragged me away from the chaos.

❖ ❖ ❖

I wasn't sure how long I had been out, but I awoke inside a ruined house. My eyes shot open, and I sucked in a shaky breath. I wasn't able to hold my own head up. For a while, I just remained a prisoner in my own body.

A baby's voice. The coo faded in and out as I wavered on the edge of consciousness. Finally, I found the strength to raise my head. I thought I had imagined it, but as my hearing returned, I knew that it was as real as the war unfolding outside those decayed walls.

I was in a rebel's kitchen. From where I lay, I could see a gas stove and cast-iron pans that dangled above an island. I lifted myself. The paint had peeled; the wood on the floor was discolored, rotted; and the ceiling had an abnormal curvature in it as if something heavy would fall right through.

Watchmen had already been inside: scattered toys, broken dishes, and overturned tables. There was a pool of blood and a trail of it smeared on the wall.

I pressed the microchip panel to retract the busted helmet.

The coos started again. I pulled off a glove and dug into my damp scalp, checking for fractures and wondering if auditory hallucinations were an effect of the blast.

I dabbed my fingers in the shiny red drops on the counter: still moist. More droplets led into the corridor. I slowly drew my gun and crept over creaky floorboards. Soft gurgles came from behind a cracked door, where the blood trail stopped. I thrust the door forward. It slammed against the wall with a *snap*. I panned the gun from corner to corner. Ragged clothes covered the ground, overturned drawers and desks were strewn about, and a makeshift mattress had been torn. Fluffy material protruded from its wounds.

I pressed my head against the shedding plaster. It was cool on my skin and soothed the ache.

Gurgling came from a nook where a huge pile of chairs and broken wood planks had been fashioned into a cage. Strips of sheets and cloths covered the top. At first, it hadn't looked deliberate.

I tore away the material.

Inside was a baby on a dirty blanket.

The infant had its fat fingers in its mouth, sucking, drooling. Its limbs kicked like a rabbit's, and the eyes wandered around the dilapidated room and then stopped at me. The irises were blue but darker than Liyo's, and the skin had a tinge of yellow. A curly, jet-black 'fro.

An Impure baby.

Blood dribbled from my ear. The gun dropped to my hip.

Whoever left her there should've killed her.

Had they thought that allowing her to live would give her a decent life? If she didn't die of starvation, she would grow to become an orphan, a product of bias. At least I had memories of Ma. She would never have that chance. Her tiny brain would soon forget about her parents, what they even looked like.

Killing the baby before any of those misfortunes were able to touch her would have been a mercy. Better to die free than live a life of the dead.

A sharp force cracked the back of my skull. I grabbed the base of my head, wincing.

Before I could turn around, another blow came across my side. My gun fell as I staggered into a table leg. A worker held a plank above his shoulder and came in for a third blow. I shielded my face.

He suddenly dropped the weapon. The man had a soiled bandage around his neck and a black eye.

"Why are you in their uniform?" His voice shook.

My gun was in full view beside him. He glared at it before picking it up and examining it. "Why are you in their uniform?" he repeated.

"I'm a watchman," I said.

He revealed rotten teeth. "You're an Impure. One of us. You can't be a watchman."

I repositioned myself on the floor. "I'm a watchman of the Union."

"No, no." He shook his head quickly, coming closer. "You work with the group. Don't you? You've come to protect me and the girl. Right?"

I stood slowly with my hands outstretched. "I'm an official watchman with no rebel affiliations."

"No, no, no. Not the rebels," he said. "Th-the other group. The one with the woman who orders the Glitter, the distributor."

I wondered if the man was delirious. "I'm not her or a part of her group. I *am* with the Union."

He pointed the gun at me with both trembling hands. "You don't understand. The distributor *is* the Union; we made a deal. She said that she would keep us safe as long as we manufactured Glitter. She said that she would send for us—send relief before the watchmen came." He wept as he picked up the baby; the gun was planted under her head like a pillow.

He pushed her into my arms, but I resisted.

"Please have mercy," he cried. "I'm all she has now. Her mother has been executed in the streets, burned with the rest. Her name is Basi. She's just like you, an Impure. Have mercy."

"I can't help you."

He slobbered, clutching the baby to his torn shirt.

"Never trust them. Never, ever trust them," he said into her ear. "God help us. God help this sweet, sweet child."

The soft buzz of powered laser guns approached. Watchmen saw my hands raised and a rebel with a gun. They fired without question. The laser hit his thigh, obliterating his leg. The baby went flying. A pause, then a piercing cry followed as she hit the floor. More watchmen packed into the room. One grabbed the infant by the ankle and dropped her into a sack. He tied the bag, tossed it over his shoulder, removing her like waste. The rebel lay on the floor in agony, his leg torn apart so badly that it was unrecognizable.

The General was the last to enter. Watchmen parted for him like oil from water. He raised his fist. "We have successfully subdued the enemy!"

They shouted. Patted one another on the backs. Another slaughter well done.

The Union

The General looked down at the sniffling man and withdrew his gun. He held it out to me. I considered using it to kill the General, but I wouldn't have made it out of the room alive.

I carefully slid the gun from his grip.

"I hereby order the execution of this rebel for treason against the Union." He ordered, "Kill him."

A test of loyalty.

A real watchman would never hesitate to accept an order. And that day, I was a real watchman and would do exactly as told. Kill my own. A part of myself.

The rebel's eyes were pinched as he clutched the upper part of his bleeding thigh—or what was left of it. Blood drained from the severed veins and pooled around him. With all the blood loss, he would die anyway. His pain seemed to subside as I towered over him.

No hesitation, I repeated internally.

He tried to speak, to plead some more, but I had already pulled the trigger.

It didn't feel the way I'd expected it to, the way I'd imagined it, the way a normal person killing another person would react. He was just another to add to the list of people I'd ruined. Was my freedom worth killing the innocent? Had my freedom meant more than his?

The General placed his hand on top of the gun, lowering it. I stared at him as he stared at me. For some sick reason, I wanted to know what he was thinking at that moment, but his facade showed no hint of what was going on inside.

From the General's wristcom, a box unfolded into a large screen. It was Commander Chi.

"General, there are rebel disturbances happening in the Subdivisions."

He grunted like a horse. "Lock down the Citadel. We're on our way."

Chapter Thirty-Two
AVI

When Saige left for battle, I was on my own. I melted into a puddle next to my slumber pod. The lights were too bright, burning my eyes every time I dared to open them. I was a void, an old star that had sizzled and imploded. I'd failed Liyo—and Eve too. They'd die quicker if I stayed and tried to contest Jade. But either way, the Union was going to get them.

I was aware of Jade's looming presence before she even spoke. She was a cobra slithering across my shoulders, flicking a split tongue.

"Your ride awaits." Her voice carried over from the arch of the doorway.

I wiped the tears from my face. "Will you grant me one request and allow me to give the meds to a worker—"

"Not possible." She cut me off. "You must leave now. I've gotten word that Father plans on shutting down the Citadel soon."

I stood, woozy as Jade became impatient. "I should grab a few things, then—"

"No," she said sharply. "We've already taken care of everything."

She kept saying *we*. At first, I suspected she was only using it to take the blame off herself in the event that she was caught, but I knew Jade couldn't have masterminded my expulsion alone. Not when it included the Border. That took a different kind of government pull. But who was she working with?

Jade towed me along the corridors by the hand. "Why is Father shutting the Citadel down?" I demanded to know.

"The rebels are creating organized disturbances in the Subdivisions. Father wants to make sure none of them can penetrate us. Just a few empowered honks." She sighed. "This is the best time for you to leave."

"Jade—"

"You will sneak out of the front while I cause a distraction. Climb into the back of the hovertruck, and hide among the shipments. Once you arrive at the Border, await further instruction."

"But how—" I stammered.

She pushed me near the front door, next to a large helix-shaped statue, and vanished. I waited. Anxiety cramped my fingers, my toes.

I expected Jade to reappear, but it was Head Gardner who strolled by instead. The last time I'd seen her, she'd shot me out of the sky.

It was all starting to make sense.

"I know it was you," I said.

My teeth ground as she flounced toward the opposite hall, ignoring me.

"Head Gardner!" My voice had never been so loud. "Attention."

She stopped and offered a salute.

I got closer. "You won't get away with this. That I can promise you."

"Such strong threats for such a weak princess." She tossed her head back. "Have a wonderful trip."

Anger swelled within me, and I was on the verge of bursting. I wanted to snatch every strand from her scalp. Throw her off the highest mountain and watch her smash into atoms. She was evil, just like Jade, and they had linked up with a common goal in mind: to rid themselves of me. When I was gone, would Mother be their next target?

But I allowed Head Gardner to leave. What other choice did I have?

I had to let her go.

Abruptly, Jade cried out. Watchmen rushed inside toward the disturbance. The entrance was wide open. I stepped over the threshold. A hovertruck waited, just as she'd said. I strode down the stairs and hurried to the hovertruck's platform. I grabbed the rack and slipped inside the dim trunk. The driver seemed to know when I was inside. The engine shuddered, and we lifted into the sky.

I scooted back against the immense containers and pulled my knees tightly into my chin. A lumpy slimpack lay on the other side of the cargo hold. All the things I would need, she'd said.

We'd reach the Border soon, and no one would even notice that I was missing until it was too late. I'd be long gone before Father deployed a search team. Father would disintegrate each subdivision to find me. He had taken so many precautions to protect us from the outside world that he hadn't noticed the real enemies were right inside the Citadel's walls.

Burying my face deeper between my knees, I began to weep just thinking about how it would all play out if by a small chance I managed to survive. The only information that I knew about the Northern Region was that those who inhabited it were considered unrefined, savages. The Border had been built as part of a treaty. The savages wanted nothing to do with any technological advancements the Union had to offer. They wanted nothing to do with us. They hadn't seen anyone who looked like me in centuries. I wouldn't be welcomed with hospitality, because I would be breaking the treaty.

I went over all possible outcomes, and each led to me being dead in a matter of hours.

I lay down on the metal bed using the bulky pack as a cushion and pictured Liyo. From the beginning, I'd understood that the connection we shared would be brief and unforgiving. It was dangerous. Illegal. In no land would we be accepted as allies. Lovers. It was stupid to even be thinking of him at all, but somehow those short interactions brought me comfort.

The craft came to a jerking stop. The driver shouted from the other side of the divider. I pressed my ear against the metal.

"Over, over, control tower. Come in, control tower. It's an emergency."

Seconds felt like days as we waited for someone to return the distress call. There was heavy static, then a voice. "This is control tower. What is the emergency? Over."

"Rebels. They're everywhere," the driver said. "They're in makeshift hovercrafts."

Before the voice could respond, we were hit with a heavy object. I was tossed to the other side of the trunk. Containers toppled over as the hovertruck swerved and spun out of control. I scrambled, trying to find something to grip. Cargo clunked and bounced off the sides. We plummeted. I flew to the other side of the hold, slamming into a container. The driver revved the engines and accelerated forward, and I was thrown against the back door.

We were hit again. I wasn't sure with what, but it was strong enough to have penetrated the craft this time. A whistling sound came from a hole in the exterior. We were going down. Fast. I braced myself. The air hit me hard, and I hung on, waiting for impact.

Crash. Metal scraped concrete, and sparks flicked. We skidded until the craft couldn't skid anymore. Then, just like that, it stopped. The back door popped open and smashed into the asphalt.

I was banged up, disoriented, but alive. My arm wasn't so lucky. In search of supplies, I grabbed the pack that Jade had left. I dumped it. Empty vials rolled out. I dug deeper into the bag, checking every compartment, ripping the cloth in the process.

Nothing. She had left me nothing.

She had never intended for me to survive beyond the Border.

I hobbled around the side of the hovertruck. Blood ran down my arm, ran down my fingers, and landed in dots. The driver was tipped over in the front seat. His chest belt held him in place.

"Are you injured?"

He didn't respond, and I couldn't tell if he was breathing. I scooted closer and tilted his head back. He was dead. I retched, turning away.

Full darkness was approaching, and I was nowhere close to being rescued. I searched for a distress signal on the console. There were so many buttons, some glowing, some dim. I pushed random ones. The big green button made the engines start. It buzzed like before, but then something popped and sparked. The control panel sizzled. I opened the cover. The processor was fried. I exhaled, then checked the talk box, but there was only heavy static.

"Come in. Over," I said. "Control tower, do you read me? Over."

Static.

I found a medical box, disinfected my arm, and lasered my wound. We had crashed in one of the farthest subdivisions, but I wasn't sure which. I stepped onto an unoccupied street as the sun moved downward.

The environment was nothing that I'd ever experienced. It was as if an acidic mist lingered over the entire block, turning everything into the same dull color. The buildings were tall, connected, and intimidating, like they had trapped any soul that had tried to escape. It was like being in a parallel universe, eons away from home.

Windows were either boarded or smashed. Graffiti littered the brick exteriors: *War, Rebellion, and Freedom* were smeared in charcoal. How could a place like this exist in the region?

Before we'd crashed, the driver had notified the control tower of trouble. Help had to be on the way. So I returned to the back door and waited and watched. No one had come out of their cubes yet to investigate the crash, which seemed peculiar. I knew they had heard the screeches. They must've even seen the injured Elite hobbling about.

As I examined the area, searching for hidden onlookers from the ground level, I felt it—them examining me from within the privacy of their dwellings. I just had a feeling they were all there. Waiting.

The temperature dropped when the sun disappeared, and I kept catching myself dozing. I heard a door open. I stood with anxiety and looked around. No one showed their face.

Sitting idle had become too dangerous. Threatened by sensations, noises I thought I heard, and an invisible audience, I knew that I couldn't stay.

Fear would drive me to the brink of insanity if I didn't get moving.

Chapter Thirty-Three
SAIGE

We returned to the Citadel. On our way inside, Jemison caught up with me and held his hand out. I took it after staring at his dry knuckles for a good moment, a show for the rest of the men watching. I shook. Firmly. Jemison looked pleased. I thought I'd add a compliment to seal the deal—that way, he could go around telling everybody what a team player I was.

Jemison bowed his head and then stood at ease like the other men as the General made a postvictory announcement.

He paced, stroking his beard, clearly troubled. "This is a small triumph for the Union, but we still have much more to do." He made it a point to meet every man's eyes. "We've got information that rebel groups are plotting to overtake the Subdivisions, then hit the Square. We must be ready when the time comes."

Watchmen remained in their ranks, unmoved.

"We have deployed thousands of watchmen in order to restore the peace. We estimate that things will be back to normal soon, and the rebels and all who assisted them will be punished for their crimes."

The meeting ended.

Commander Chi told us to rest. Then gear up for the second shift. We were going back out into the field. I hadn't planned on resting—while everyone else was occupied, I'd have to get to work. The information that Liyo needed wasn't going to fall into my lap.

The panel on my wristcom emitted a screen. "Meet me in the study," the General directed. The video flickered out.

Either he'd figured out what I'd done earlier in the Square, or this was a job well done, but if he'd already figured that out, I'd have been dead by now. I must still be in the clear. For now. So I was a little bit less tense standing at his royal door. I put my face to the eye scanner. The beam calculated. The light turned green. The entrance unlocked.

Displayed on the study's ceiling was a glowing rendition of the solar system. A mixture of fiery asteroids, white comets, and moons shone a bluish tint on the gray walls and the shiny floor. There was a black painting with thick white squares that started off big but then got smaller in the middle, creating an optical illusion of a never-ending tunnel. I stepped in front of his massive bureau, at attention.

Without a word, he lifted himself from his throne and circled me like a panther waiting to pounce. I kept calm as his warm breath prickled at the back of my neck. I was used to this. I wouldn't let him see me crack. Intimidation was always their tactic.

"How were you able to comprehend those equations in the Cube?" he asked.

Ratch. Whatever was left in my intestines wanted out. I clenched my cheeks together in anticipation. I had expected him to talk about the rebel I had killed and express his pride that I had come to my senses and joined the right side to fight against the unruly Impures. Mama Seeya. Why had he waited so long to interrogate me about equations?

I hadn't prepared myself for this move. He was playing an advanced level of chess, while I was still a rookie. My mind tumbled over believable answers and their possible outcomes. I couldn't stay silent for too long because that was hesitation.

"Don't do that." He clicked his tongue. "No need to think. The truth would be greatly appreciated."

He already knew me, my game. I sensed that he had something on me. A new lead maybe. I couldn't outright lie. The best lies were ones mixed with the truth. Give some, gain some. I needed his trust. "I learned how, sir, in the Outskirts."

The General returned to the front again with his gloved hands clasped. "What if I told you that during the Administrator's investigation, she witnessed you on surveillance footage sneaking into the Archives, reading texts? What would you say to that?"

My jaw locked. My nails dug into my palms as they stayed positioned behind my back.

"Did you know that it's against the law for a worker to read unauthorized materials?"

"Yes, sir."

"Did you honestly think we wouldn't find out?" he kept on. "I mean, did you really believe that you could outsavvy the Union. Me?"

"No, sir."

"So why did you do it? Why take such risks?" His voice was almost lyrical in my ear.

"I don't know, sir."

"You don't know," he mocked. "I think you do." His lips spread thin through a silky beard. "You enjoy keeping secrets. You're a liar, a deceiver."

My insides boiled. "Can you blame me?"

That slipped out.

He chuckled before answering. "You're unlike any worker I've met before. All of them would have urinated themselves by now. I admire that fire, but your absence of respect for authority troubles me."

He stepped in closer and caressed my temple. "Did you know that we're working on a method? It would just extract information right out of the base of your cranium. Science is potent, Saige. It has the ability to transform the world. It is power."

The General returned behind his bureau and propped his feet on the surface, crossing one leg over the other. "That is why you risked everything to read, to learn. You want power, just like everyone else, but you don't want to admit it. Not to me at least." He placed emphasis on the *me* part. "You fascinate me. Your mind fascinates me. And I must tell you that I'm rarely ever fascinated."

He sat up once more, his shoulders squared and leveled. "What do you think of the fact that in spite of all of your caution, we were still able to figure you out?"

I lowered my head a little. Wordless. No way to respond to his assaults.

He pulled off a glove and took a gun from his holster. Laid it on the table. The barrel faced me. That same gun he'd made me kill with.

I saw a mark.

On the lower part of his thumb. A mark I had never noticed before since he'd always had it covered. A puzzle-piece-shaped birthmark. Like mine. Exactly like mine. To the sharp curved piece at the bottom. Ma's face flickered like a broken recording. I felt her wet lips kissing my thumb. My fingers. My little hand. *Your father has the same one.* It echoed until her voice was gone completely. Before they took her life in front of me. Like the demons they were.

Impossible. The General? My father. How could that be? Was that why she hadn't wanted to tell me? Because she was afraid that he'd kill me if anyone knew?

The great General dipping into slave girls in his spare time. Had he raped her? Was she a sex worker like the girls underground?

My head spun as I willed my knees not to knock against each other. It was by the grace of the universe that I didn't thaw into a watery puddle.

Tears flowed. I couldn't help it. I wasn't any closer to knowing anything or avenging Ma's death than I had been before. All I knew was that I was half-monster. I had his cruel DNA swaying inside of me.

My eyes darted from his thumb to his face, again and again. He must've assumed it was fear, but I wasn't afraid of death. Not anymore. At the same time, it was the weakest I'd ever felt. The unbreakable Saige had deserted me, and the child had returned. That hopeful child, that naive child who didn't know anything about anything except the world Ma had created. I hated it. I hated the weakness so much. Inside I was dying, falling, tumbling around, and clawing to escape. I wanted to leave myself behind and float away. The person I had believed I was had never existed. I had his pure Elite blood coursing through me. The same as Jade and Avi. They were my—my sisters. I wanted to throw up.

"I should kill you right now. End this attachment my daughter has formed. She'll understand someday."

"That wouldn't fix anything." I wiped my face. "Killing me."

He snorted. "Enlighten me."

I wanted to beat that arrogance right off him, but I had to play his games. "You can eliminate the vessel, but its essence will always live on." I thought of Ma. "If you kill me, I'll become a martyr for the Impures, for the workers."

"A martyr." I sensed his annoyance. "I find it difficult to trust a word that comes out of your mouth. You led me to almost believe you were a worthy soldier, an ally. I was prepared to integrate you into what we've built, but I no longer see you in the same light as I did when I saw you execute one of your own. Although that was a spectacular show."

Of course it had been spectacular. Like father, like daughter. Killing was in our genes.

He returned the gun to his holster. "You remind me a lot of myself." The whites of his eyes were rosy and glazed. "There are things I'd like to share." He hesitated with every word. "But you—you're not ready for them yet. You have to prove to me that you are worthy. And that will take time."

A heavy fist pounded at the door.

"I have proven myself!" I yelled. My desperation was starting to show. I had managed to save my own life, but he hadn't given me anything useful.

He grinned. "Have you?"

I glared at the grand bookcase as a watchman entered to relay an urgent message. He rushed the General away, leaving me alone. Just like that, it was over. I pulled my hands from behind my back and laid them flat on his desk. The sight of my own birthmark enraged me further. My fingers curled into fists. The government was in the process of shutting the Citadel down. The General hadn't given me anything. I was back to square one.

Maybe he should've just shot me, because that was what it felt like. I was a dead girl anyway.

The General had taken away Ma, and now he'd taken away my chance of freedom.

"Saige?" Pea's mousy voice called.

She stood behind me, her catlike eyes wide. I hadn't even heard her slip in.

"What?" I spat.

She looked concerned. "I heard you"—she paused and looked both ways before continuing—"joined us."

I sniggered.

Her face remained serious. "I can help you get the information," she murmured. "I know what the General was talking about. I know what Liyo needs too. You're supposed to be meeting him soon. Right?"

Pea's eyes darted left and right again as she dug into her pocket. Then she held out a holographic access card. I reached for it, but she snatched it away.

"Does it lead to—"

"The Union's salvation."

"What's in it for you?" I asked, suspicious.

"Protection."

"For you?"

She shook her head. "For Liyo."

"What?" I grimaced.

"Don't talk." Pea placed her finger up. "I probably won't live to see the day the Union falls. They're watching. They know everything. It's only a matter of time before they find out I've been helping the rebels. I know it, and I'm prepared. But I know I won't die in vain. Liyo's the only way. But he isn't strong enough, Saige. He needs you. I can't—we can't afford to lose him, not now. We've come too far. You have to promise that you will protect him." She spoke in a harsh whisper. "If you promise to protect him, I'll give you what you need."

I eyed the girl.

Pea's neck was cocked forward. "What do you say?"

I didn't know what to say exactly. I'd never trusted her, and I wasn't sure if I trusted her right then either. The entire display could be a ploy, a setup. What if the General had put her up to it to test my loyalty again?

"No," I said.

She took my elbow, so I pinned her to the desk. My hand wrapped around her dainty neck. She swung with her left, but I grabbed it and held it at her side. With the other, she tried to peel my fingers off.

"Don't try that again," I said.

As I tried to leave, she attacked again. The girl never learned. I shoved her, and she stumbled. Her stringy hair flew into her face. I approached the door, and Pea gripped my ankle. She was on her stomach with both hands clamped on my shin.

"Let go."

"Never," she said. "Not until you agree."

278

She would rather be beaten to a pulp before allowing me to leave. She had never been so aggressive before. The girl had heart. Even though she was scrawny, she was a fighter. I could respect that. Plus, I really had no other choice.

I grabbed her by the back of her bodysuit until she was in a standing position, then seized the access card. "If this is a trick, I'll kill you. After today, I've got nothing else to lose."

Pea had a triumphant look on her face. "Come on. I'll show you where the lab is."

❖ ❖ ❖

We stood at a wide titanium door. On the other side was the underground lab.

"This is it," Pea said.

"I can't believe I'm doing this." I tried rubbing the migraine from my eyes.

"Believe it," she said somberly. "And be quick. Once the physician finds out his card is missing . . ."

She took my hand and made me wave the card across the scanner. The dead bolts cranked, whirred, unlocked, and then opened. Pea had already skittered away.

I entered a narrow channel with a concrete floor. Thick tubes lined the metal walls, and the lights above led to an elevator platform. Double doors slid open again, and physicians stepped on. I froze.

One of the men typed in the destination while the other eyed me. "Coming?" he asked impatiently.

I snapped out of my stupor and positioned myself between them. We rode many floors to the bottom. My ears popped as the air became denser. When the physicians exited, I casually followed. They entered one of the labs. I waited until they went farther inside before I grabbed a random lab jacket off a hook. The nameplate above the front pocket read Physician Octavia.

The lab spanned in every direction. It was like a small city, bustling with physicians in white uniforms with foot covers and hoods enveloping their heads. Clear visors were over their faces. There were holoscreens everywhere, small and large. Sets of data were being processed and charts produced. Words and figures overlapped each screen so much so that I didn't even know where to start.

Metal barrels were positioned against frosty walls, machines hummed, and windows separated the bays inside the underground lab. Bright fluorescent lighting gleamed off silver goggles, illuminated brown faces, and hit the marbled countertops. There was an unspoken rhythm, a working pace that couldn't be broken, not even by the awkwardness of my presence. And the smell. I couldn't get over the scent of chlorine and ammonia; it was like being blasted back to my former work detail.

One particular partition was the central focus of the lab. It held a detailed map of the Southern Region and spanned the space of an entire wall. The Subdivisions, the Farmlands, and the Outskirts were shaded in red and numbered, while the inner zones, where the Elites and Upper Residents lived, were in blue. Red must've been where the virus was going to hit. According to the data, they were going to release the remaining toxins that day.

I kept walking. And found yet another tunnel. An underwater aquarium that looked freakishly like the Cube's simulated one.

I placed my hand on the cool partition.

At first, I couldn't see a thing, but then something moved. A mer-creature rushed forward, slamming into the glass. I lurched back as it held its webbed hands to the translucent barrier. A protruding scar on its chest.

The one I had inflicted.

Suction cups on its palm unpeeled. It turned its head over its slimy shoulder and floated back into the shade.

I ventured farther.

On one side of the glass wall, an Impure was strapped to a chair. He looked like the one who they'd captured, one of Mama Seeya's men. His mouth and eyes were pried open by metal instruments. A physician held a reader while the other conducted the tests. The detainee struggled against the restraints, but his struggles were of no use. What were they about to do to him? The physician pulled his head back and forced a liquid substance into his mouth. The Impure's Adam's apple dipped as he yelled. But I couldn't hear him. A soundproof prison.

Adjacent to that room were dozens of fully developed Impure babies inside egg-shaped sacs. Monitor wires attached to their wrinkly skins. In the center, a physician placed a baby on a silver platter. She punched something into the keypad, and laser confinements appeared around its limbs. Its head thrashed and bottom lip quivered. Pointy metallic limbs materialized from beneath the platter and hovered over the child.

I imagined myself in that child's position. Being poked. Prodded. Tested on. Those supplements they made us ingest were given to those infants first. How many babies had they mutilated? How many more had they planned on testing on?

Because I was triggered. Because I saw myself in that child. I had no idea if anyone was around, nor did I care. There was so much pent up inside of me that it came out, and I had no way of controlling it.

"Stop!" I banged on the barrier with my fists.

The physician paid me no mind. Couldn't hear me.

"Stop!" I pounded. "Stop!"

As the robotic limbs penetrated the subject, I slid down the wall to my knees. I couldn't watch anymore. I couldn't save any of them. The ones above the lab or the ones trapped inside it. Mama Seeya had gotten it wrong. I wasn't strong enough like she'd thought.

The only person I could save was me. So like I always did, I left. I left the test subjects, my people, behind.

The underpass led to another part of the facility, with an assembly line below. On the conveyor belt were workers wearing suits with bubble helmets. From the helmets were breathing pipes connected to oxygen tanks on their backs. They moved methodically. On the lines were tubes traveling down to the first worker, who weighed each one and then placed a distinctive mark on the label. The last worker carefully lifted each tube and put them into red-and-black hazardous crates. A separate worker secured the cargo and wheeled the crates away.

"Saige?"

I nearly leaped from my body when I heard his voice.

Instructor Skylar tugged the lapel of the lab jacket. "Physician Octavia?"

"The temperature down here's different than above," I said conversationally. "I just borrowed it."

By his expression, it seemed as though he wasn't buying any of it. I smiled like maybe in another life, I'd flirt with him casually at some event. Suddenly, he chuckled, then eyed the access card poking out of my pocket. I tucked it away.

"The General decided to let you in, I see."

I played along. "Why wouldn't he?"

"I suppose executing that rebel won him over." He peered down at the workers.

"I suppose."

With his hands tucked behind his back, he returned his attention to me. "Well, I'm glad that he came to his senses about you. I was worried."

Instructor Skylar took a stroll and motioned for me to join him. We went across a bridge while workers labored without interruption. We observed them using machinery to transport sealed crates into categorized sections within a warehouse.

"I wouldn't be doing this if he hadn't trusted you to witness it," Instructor Skylar explained. "Do you know what's happening? What they're manufacturing?"

"A virus."

"The workers have been conditioned to follow orders, never to question. They don't even know that they're stacking the very poisons that will ultimately eradicate their race."

I nodded. "Hmm."

"How does that make you feel, Saige?"

I turned slowly to meet his gaze. "What kind of question is that?"

"They're your people." He pointed. "How can you stand here with no ill feelings toward the Union?"

His questions struck me as odd. I'd felt something kind of off about the Instructor since I'd met him. He seemed too understanding, too helpful. I'd wondered why throughout. I wasn't sure how it hadn't come to me until that instant.

"I know who you are," I said.

"Tell me. I'm curious to know."

"You favor him." I began watching the workers below again. "He saved me once. Your father is the reason I'm here right now. Why would a watchman do that? Go against his own people to save a second-class citizen."

A watchman appeared, patrolling the area. Instructor Skylar cleared his throat, and his eyes wandered everywhere but my face. "My father was a traitor. A disgrace to the Union. We don't speak of him."

I waited until the watchman left. "Why—"

"Do you trust me?" the Instructor asked with intensity.

I nodded, hesitantly though.

"Good." He continued, "We've already started trial versions of the virus on workers." He scratched his chin. "This systematic approach will guarantee their complete removal. We have an inoculation that will be injected into the rest of the populace. It's only a precaution, though. The virus was created to only attack Lower Resident DNA."

"And just like that . . . ," I said, "it's over."

"Just like that." His fingers snapped. After a gap of silence, he said, "I want to show you something else."

We walked along a curved corridor, stopping at a heavily guarded door. It not only needed an access card and an iris scan but a fingerprint too. As the translucent beam scanned him, he said, "No watchmen are allowed beyond this point. Even some physicians weren't cleared. You will be the first outsider to view the improved droids."

"Lucky me."

He held his arm out. "After you."

I stepped into the enclosed silo. Each floor we passed contained rows upon rows of thousands of capsules filled with droids resembling humans.

I followed him to a physician with a wide nose and a soft voice who clutched a reader to her stomach as she studied a droid closely.

"Physician Bailey," Instructor Skylar greeted her.

She pushed her glasses farther along the bridge of her nose and nearly squeezed her reader in half. "Instructor Skylar." She tittered as she backed away and went to observe the next droid.

The Instructor typed into the control panel, then unhooked the latch to the capsule.

The red plate under the droid's forehead turned green and then vanished, blending in with its skin. Wires that were attached to it snapped. Hissed. Its chest never moved, and the muscles in its face remained relaxed. Its lids lifted to expose humanlike eyes. Its fingers flexed open and closed. It grabbed the sides of the capsule and hoisted itself out.

I backed away.

"The Union has been diligently trying to perfect the human characteristics of the N37s." Instructor Skylar demonstrated its different movements. He held his hand out. The droid shook it without applying too much force. "Past physicians began with a basic chrome model: two arms, two legs, a head, and a body. They were called the D16s. They weren't an ideal prototype. A few were tested in the field, but glitches occurred, and statistics showed that the robotic look was less appealing than even the actual workers.

"So the Union's scientists went back to the drawing board. Smoothed out the technical issues, utilized a stronger grade of moon titanium, and gave the droid a face. The N37s are efficient. One can lift as much as ten men. They move faster than a human. They're gentle enough to care for an infant yet durable enough to battle in a war. They don't eat or need to sleep, really. During inactivity, they recharge themselves inside their capsules. An N37 could survive for some time without even being charged."

I couldn't help but to reach out to touch its papery skin.

"This one hasn't been completely programmed yet, so he doesn't react to human stimuli, but he will be ready soon to take the place of a Chattel worker."

We stepped back onto the platform. He typed in another coordinate. We zoomed past more levels, higher and higher until we came to a smooth halt. We were at the highest point of the dome, looking down over an android that was as big as a building. At every nook of the robotic monster, physicians tended to its polished parts. The head was the size of a hovership, and its face was a glossy black screen. Thick valves were attached to its insides. The arms and legs had gigantic bolts attaching the mechanical limbs in place. The hands held only three squared fingers, and a black hole covered each palm.

"This is the Transmega," Instructor Skylar asserted.

"Why are they building this?"

He craned his neck. "The war, Saige. I would have deduced that someone as intellectual as you would have realized that by now."

"It's overkill."

He cackled. "How so?"

"Because the workers won't . . ."

"Stand a chance?" he inquired. "There's more to the world than the Southern Region. An entire universe is right outside the bubble we live in. A universe that is waiting to strike. The Union doesn't care about rebels. They don't pose a big enough threat. We know them inside and out: their strengths, their weaknesses, and their psyche. That's what a thousand years of psychological reconditioning will do. Make them believe they are less than human so that they continue to obey."

"And you want me to trust you after telling me all this?" I asked.

He held his head low, then began talking as if I hadn't even asked anything. "The Union wants to be prepared for the entities that we don't know or understand. Those unforeseen forces that will threaten everything we've worked so hard to sustain. Look back into history. Every great nation has fallen. It's only a matter of time, Saige. The General knows it, the cabinet knows it, and I know it. But the Union will not go down without a fight."

"Why are you telling me all of this?"

He briefly flashed those perfect teeth. "Because you will be the piece to bring it all crashing down."

His wristcom buzzed. A screen emerged. An urgent message from Commander Chi. "You must return to the Citadel at once. The General has ordered a full search for Avi. She's not on the grounds."

"We must go." Instructor Skylar's nostrils flared. "Now."

An opportunity had arrived.

"I can find her," I told him. "Let me help."

His expression was uneasy. "If you know something, then tell me."

"I need access off Citadel grounds, first," I said. "I'm here for the long run. I trust you; you trust me. Right?"

"Come on. We don't have time to waste. Report back to me in two hours. I'll assemble a search team in the meantime."

And just like that, I was cleared to leave the Citadel's grounds.

❖ ❖ ❖

I had everything Liyo needed. I dove into the forest, weaving through branches and vines, faster and faster, pure adrenaline driving me.

I considered Avi. My little sister. I couldn't believe I even called her that. She was an Elite, and I was a nobody. I still couldn't wrap my head around it. Nor did I have the time to. All I knew was that she was brainless for leaving her quarters. I'd told her to stay put. She was so hardheaded, like—well, like me. I knew her absence had something to do with Liyo. She must've been with him. I'd make sure she got back to the Citadel before I left. That was all I owed her.

I arrived at the clearing in the forest. I looked around for anything out of the ordinary. I knew that watchmen were going to be scouring the grounds double time. Wherever Liyo was, he needed to hurry because watchmen were scouring the area, and sooner rather than later they would appear.

I waited and waited some more. What if Liyo didn't show? A full-on battle would have already broken out by then, and I'd be trapped. Once again. But this time, I wasn't going to get the watchman treatment. They'd find out about me attacking Phoenix. Working with the rebels. Stealing the access card. There were no loopholes that were going to save me. There was no returning to the Citadel. I'd be wanted. If the General ever saw me again, he'd have me mutilated, my remains carried down the streets of every subdivision like a parade for each to witness what happened to Impures who messed up a second chance. He hadn't hesitated to execute Ma, the woman who'd carried his child. Who was I to receive any kind of mercy?

But before he could ever hurt me, I'd make his men kill me. I'd attack the watchmen first. Shower them with lasers. That much I owed myself. They'd have no choice but to return fire. I could leave the planet as some sort of martyr. Maybe it'd be the push workers needed to fight harder.

287

"It's better to die free than live the life of the dead," I whispered to myself.

Bushes rustled. I aimed.

Liyo placed his hands in the air.

In one of them, he clutched a piece of rolled parchment. I lowered the gun.

"Surprise," he said.

I snorted. "I hate surprises."

"Did you get the information?"

"Yeah."

"What is it?"

"Show me the map first."

He gripped it tighter. "We had a deal."

"And I'm making sure the deal is kept."

Liyo tossed me the map. I spread it over the dirt. There was an outline of the Border, bodies of water shaded gray, and thin black lines that meandered all over the place. The words were curvy, squiggly lines connected to each other. Cursive, an old style of writing that I wasn't familiar with.

"What is this?" I asked.

"The map."

"I don't have time for games!"

"And neither do I," he said. "Now give me the information, and I will gladly decode it for you."

I scowled. "The Union is planning on releasing the remaining vials of supplements into the Subdivisions. Tonight."

"Antivirus serums?"

"Not for anyone who has worker DNA."

His spine bowed painfully with each word. "But there is a serum. If we can just get our hands on one, then maybe we can figure out a way to manipulate it before it's too late."

I sighed. "They've already begun. They have an entire warehouse of crates stacked up to the ceiling with viruses. They plan on shipping them to the Health Department. If you can destroy those vials, it'll at least slow them down."

He spread the map out over a stump and pointed out the different markings and symbols. His directions were swift, precise.

"The Border was built by workers. It was supposed to be perfect, but a few of them had other plans in mind. So they made an undetectable hole. The Union has yet to find out about it. You must be careful not to be seen. If they see you, they'll kill you and patch it."

"Have you ever been . . . to the Northern Region?"

Liyo blinked a few times. "It's quiet." He rolled the parchment and stuck it inside his bodysuit. He turned to leave.

"Have you seen Avi?"

"No." He jerked back. "I thought Avi was in the Citadel."

Suddenly, Drake burst through the brush, out of breath. "We've got a problem. Our sources say an Upper is running loose in the Subdivisions. What's going on?"

Avi couldn't have been so stupid as to have wandered off into rebel territory, could she?

"Alone?" I asked Drake.

Liyo shook his head. "I promise you that I had no idea."

"I swear, if she's hurt . . ." I couldn't get it out. "This is your fault. She's probably out there because of you. You should've never—I told you to just leave her be."

"We've gotta bring her back," Liyo said. "She's more valuable alive."

"She isn't an object." I couldn't believe what I was saying.

"Why do you all of a sudden care so much?" he questioned.

Drake grabbed him, argued, telling him that he wasn't going anywhere, and that it was too dangerous, and the elders wouldn't approve. While they went back and forth, I considered my options. The Border was in the opposite direction of the Subdivisions, so going after Avi would take me out of the way. I knew that the longer I stayed in the region, the greater the odds of my capture.

I was an official outlaw.

"Tell the rebels to deliver her unharmed to the Citadel, and there will be—"

"No harm done?" Liyo said coldly. "You really do think you're one of them. Don't let the armor you wear fool you. You're beneath them. You're one of us and always will be. They'll never accept you. You can eat with them, fight beside them, but they'll always see you as nothing but a worker."

"And your brothers have welcomed me with such open arms."

"We stick together—"

"I don't have a side!"

"Then you're a coward," he retorted.

I pressed the barrel of the gun to his head. I wasn't a coward; I was a survivalist, and he had no right to call me that.

"Is this supposed to intimidate me?" he scoffed. "And even if I did speak to the rebels, it wouldn't make a difference."

"You don't want to do this." Drake wedged herself in between us. "We need him. And so do you. You just don't know it yet."

I withdrew the gun.

"Are you still leaving?" she asked me.

I hunched my shoulders. "I am. I just need to make sure she gets back okay."

"You can't go on your own." Drake stepped forward. "I'll go."

I nodded.

"So will I," Liyo said.

"That isn't in the plan, Liyo," Drake protested.

"I don't care." He pushed her hand out of the way. "The quicker we get there, the faster we can get back to our plans. Let's go."

Chapter Thirty-Four
AVI

I trudged along streets that were barely lit; malfunctioning streetlamps cast eerie glows. The sheet of night had engulfed the subdivision, and I was stuck completely out of my element. Every time an object hit the ground or a rickety hinge squeaked, I ran without hesitation, only to stop, breathless, and find no one chasing me after all. It happened over and over again. My fatigue grew, and sharp pains stabbed my chest.

Sooner or later, someone would come after me.

I stumbled upon a hovertram platform. I hobbled faster toward it. Maybe, just maybe, there was help there. As I got closer, I saw that it was deserted. No one was there, nor was there a hovertram present. Father must've halted all public transport. I collapsed. Then crawled forward. I bumped into a pair of wobbly legs. An old man stood there with an outstretched hand that resembled pigskin. He helped me up but then grabbed the chest part of my bodysuit. His pupils were cloudy.

"Spare nutrition?" His breath reeked of vinegar.

I tried to strip his bony fingers from my fabric.

"Spare nutrition," he said. His eyes wandered above my head. He was blind.

"I—I don't have anything. I—I apologize."

He became insistent, shoving me backward until he slammed me into the side of a brick fence. I held my hands out, pushing at his forehead, his cheeks. He started chomping the airspace around my face, snarling. Saliva shot like darts, and I wanted to turn into a bird and fly away.

"Let go!"

I turned my head to the side and thrust my palm forward. I felt the cartilage of his nose smash against my hand. He stumbled.

"You. Upper. Bitch."

He spat a blob on the concrete, then charged forward with a notable hop. Once again, I was running for my life.

After a while, I couldn't go any farther, so I hid in an alleyway and settled behind a receptacle on top of a heap of trash. The soles of my feet burned like fiery logs, and my legs were raw. I couldn't even bend them without wincing. I wasn't going anywhere else; my body had finally quit, and at the worst time possible. I leaned over into the mess that the workers had discarded from their cubes and took solace in the cushion it provided. The scent of rotted excrement didn't bother me as much as it would've before.

The General's daughter had been reduced to this. Who would have thought it? If someone had told me that I would be cast out of my home like common filth shaken from an old rug, I'd have called them mad.

Worry was quickly replaced by fear when I was seized from behind. A man pinned me and, with his other hand, held my neck. Deep craters resembling the moon's surface covered his cheeks. He had a crooked nose, and his eyes sparkled and swirled white and silver. Another man with the same eyes hovered over my head, upside down.

His voice was guttural. "What d'ya got?"

Warm tears rolled along the sides of my face, hitting the trash beneath us. When I didn't respond, his grip only tightened.

"Check her," he barked at his accomplice.

He began digging into my bodysuit, yanking cloth and burrowing his fingers into the slips. He found nothing and raised his hands. The other man leaned forward. More of his weight crushed my lungs. He sniffed my hair, then licked my ear.

"No money. No escape," he murmured.

My eyes closed, squeezed tight until it hurt.

I heard his accomplice gurgle. Then fall. I opened my eyes. The man on top of me searched the perimeter, just as confused as I was, and in the next moment a blade was sticking out between his crossed eyes. Blood dripped down the base of the wooden handle, then all his mass collapsed on me. His chest covered my mouth and nose, trying to murder me even in death.

Saige rolled his body off mine. I turned to my side, gasping. I didn't know how she had found me, but I couldn't contain my gratitude. I hugged her, burying my face in her shoulder.

"Is Liyo safe?" I asked, pulling back.

Saige looked at me like I'd offended her. "What are you doing out here, Avi? Everyone is looking for you."

A girl with red hair placed her foot on the man's chest and removed the knife from his forehead. She wiped both of its sides on his bodysuit. She stuck her hand out. "Name's Drake. Nice to meet ya."

I shook it.

Liyo jogged into full view. Drake groaned. "I told him to stay put."

I had meant to say his name, but it disappeared on my tongue. I wanted to jump into his arms, embrace him, but the whirs of government hovercopters approached. At first, I assumed they were there to save us, but I should've known better. Yellowish mists spewed from the bottom of the crafts.

"The poisons!" Drake yelled.

Liyo pulled out a handkerchief and tied it around the back of my head, covering my nose and mouth.

"They won't affect her," Saige said.

He put his on last. "I know, but just in case."

From the other end, a makeshift hovervehicle very different from the government one began shooting lasers. The rebels were fighting back. Missiles from the official one traveled from the pods beneath the craft. One stray struck the street, crumbling the concrete as if it were toasted bread, and the other annihilated the building near the alleyway. Pieces of misshapen blocks flew, sparks bounced, and we took cover behind the receptacle.

Saige choked on the dust. "Get her out of here!"

Lasers whizzed past our heads as we dodged. Explosions were scattered. Liyo never let go of my hand. We crouched behind a hedge while Drake and Saige advanced forward.

Armed watchmen marched through the smoke. He led me around the bend. Dozens of shots bounced off concrete and metal. Liyo pulled me into a gutted cube.

We sat on the dusty floor. Time became motionless. He spun around, crouched down, and peered over the other side of the barrier.

"Someone's coming," he whispered.

We heard footsteps. Liyo motioned for me to stay still and then pulled out a gun. Saige and Drake leaped behind the barrier with their guns aimed too. When everyone saw that no one was the enemy, they withdrew their weapons.

Drake wasted no time and started trying to get a signal on a wristcom.

"Got any fluids?" Saige stood over Liyo.

He had been staring at her just as intently as I was. He dug into his slimpack.

Fluids rolled down the edges of her mouth as she gulped eagerly. Everything about Saige was attractive, and Liyo couldn't seem to take his eyes off her. They had a connection of some sort—I just couldn't figure out what it was.

Drake finally got a signal and sprinted outside the cube. A corroded hovercraft lowered itself. They guided me inside. Its engine rattled as we soared.

"I tried to get the meds, but Jade, she . . ." It felt odd to expose my sister to Liyo. I had been conditioned to never befriend workers, to never let them know personal matters. I knew better now, but it was still difficult.

He took my hand, sending a jolt of pleasant electricity through me. "It's okay. You tried. That's all that matters."

"I want to help."

Saige interrupted. "You're going back to the Citadel."

"I can no longer sit idle. This is my region too. Let me save it."

"There's no saving the region," Saige yelled. "Have you taken a look around?"

Drake stepped forward. "The girl's right. We need someone from the inside to help us break into the Health Department. We need to get our hands on that serum. It's the only chance we've got to create one for us."

Liyo eyed Saige first, then me. "She's right. Drake and I can't go inside, get access like you two can. We've got to try."

"Oh, I get it now." Saige chuckled. "This was all a ruse to get us to go to the Health Department? The deal was we get Avi and get out. No damned detours."

"We can do this," I said softly.

"Avi, no." Saige shook her head. "This is crazy."

"I have to," I told her. "You can stay here if you'd like, but I'm going to retrieve those vials. With or without you."

"It's settled." Drake turned to the driver. "Dee, take us to the Health Department."

Chapter Thirty-Five
SAIGE

I was shocked Avi had survived in the hardest-hit subdivision. She was a lot tougher than I had thought, but when it came to Liyo, she was weak. I wasn't sure if she was motivated by her patriotism or a blind crush. Either way, she was about to risk her life and everyone else's.

Somehow, I couldn't stop comparing her erratic behavior to my own. What was my motivation for making that U-turn from freedom? Was it purely obligation because I'd just found out that she was kin? Up until now it'd only been me that I had to worry about. The General being my father had set off a chain of events. Up until this point, I'd been alone. No blood bonds. The thought of being attached to another human being—other than Ma—bothered me. A lot. Emotional attachment meant disadvantages in my eyes.

Whatever the reason, I couldn't turn my back on her. I might have been selfish, but I was a woman of my word. When she was safe, I'd leave. That was it.

I approached Drake near the cockpit as she sharpened her blade.

I stooped to her level. "So much for that grand escape, huh?"

Drake sighed. "You know I wouldn't be holding you up if there was any other way. We have the girl, and we've got you too."

"I never asked to be part of any of this."

"Well, you are now." She sniffed. "Look, you made a pact with Pea."

"He's alive, isn't he?"

She looked me square in the eyes. "Liyo's our savior. If he dies, so does all of this. Everything dies, Saige. I put my life on the line for his, for the cause, for the future. But I'm afraid Miss Missy over there might be getting in the way."

"And how exactly do you expect me to break the lovebirds up?"

"I dunno, take him with you."

I frowned. "What?"

"Keep it down," she grumbled.

"If you think that—"

"Listen, what we're about to do is risky. If there wasn't a war before, there's definitely gonna be one now. I need you to promise me that you will do whatever you can to protect him. Just get him out when the time's right. I'll do anything you want. Look, I'll even protect Avi. Make sure she gets back to the Citadel safe." She held up four fingers, tucking her thumb in. "Honor."

Drake was right. Plus, she was the only one I trusted enough to get Avi back. The safest place for Avi was inside the Citadel, whether she believed that for herself or not.

Avi snuck up on us from behind. "Saige?"

It was as good a time as any to break the news. "I'm leaving."

"Where to?"

"North."

She giggled for a bit, then stopped as she realized I was serious. "How?"

I shrugged. "I found a way."

She sat quietly, perplexed, probably a million more questions swirling around in her little head.

There was no easy way to tell her. We were all running out of time. "You and Liyo, whatever team thing you've got going on, isn't real. You know that, right?"

297

She opened her mouth to say something but then pressed her lips together.

"This whole idea you've got to join the rebels isn't going to work."

Her expression hardened.

"You're an Elite, not a fighter."

She said, "I can help them. I can help us. I can change the system from the inside out."

"Avi, listen to me. This isn't some fairy tale—it's real life. People will die. They are dying right now."

"You think I don't know that?" She started to tear up. "I'm tired of watching from the Citadel as this world goes awry at the hands of my own. I want freedom just as much as they do, as you do. I've sat on a throne, unable to breathe, unable to feel or live. I've made my decision already, and I'm not backing down. If you want to help, that's fine, but if you need to leave, then go."

The girl was truly working my nerves. I rubbed my temples. "I didn't want to have to do this."

It was a last-ditch effort. "Either you tell her, or I will," I said to Liyo.

He knew very well what I was going to divulge. "Saige" was the only thing he could get out.

I took Avi by the shoulders. "He told me that he planned on using you to get intel. As leverage for the rebels. Whatever you think you feel for him, it's not real. Okay?"

"And how could you possibly know what I feel?" Avi pulled away, taking a step back and creating distance between herself and me.

Liyo tried to take her hand, but she jerked back.

"Don't," she said.

"In the beginning, the plan was to get—"

She put her hand up, stopping Liyo from explaining any further. "I would've helped you if you'd asked. You didn't need to—to use me." Her eyes were watery, but she still maintained that Elite composure.

His shoulders slumped.

"And you thought by telling me this, you'd seem better than him." She looked at me. Through me. "I know you think I'm weak, disposable perhaps, but right now, I feel stronger than ever before. You can do as you wish, say as you wish—I couldn't care less about your quarrels, your deceptions—but I still choose to help the rebels. I won't punish the whole for a few individuals' stupidity."

❖   ❖   ❖

They'd used tech blockers to shield the craft from detection as the driver landed in the city's forest edge near the Square. The rebels were more prepared than I had known, but was it enough to outsmart the Union?

Dee slid the earphone down. "No alerts have been made on the broadcasts."

"Impossible," I said to myself. "They're toying with us. They know. This is a trap."

"We don't have any other choice," Dee explained. "Avi's supposed to have a personal watchman accompany her. We've gotta pretend that everything's normal."

"That's easy for you to say—you get to hide in here while I dive into the deep end."

Drake hooked up Avi's earpiece and tested its frequency. "We've used this equipment many times. It literally scans all their channels."

"What about a secret one they may have? Like maybe some internal system that the rebels haven't figured out?"

"Saige, trust us." Liyo stepped in.

"That's super reassuring."

"Stop!" Drake yelled. "I reprogrammed this reader with the General's signatures for Avi to gain access to the lab's storage facility. See that case over there? You will take it, leave it somewhere in the room.

Grab as many vials as you can. Then get out of there. You won't have much time after it detonates."

"What do we do if we're exposed?" Avi asked.

Drake tried her hardest to hide her apprehension. "Think positive thoughts. Okay? We've gone over this plan hundreds of times. It's gonna work. In and out."

❖   ❖   ❖

I kept going over how the hell I'd gotten myself in this situation. I should've left when I had the chance. But Avi. She didn't deserve to be hurt. None of us did. Those goons would've raped and killed her without a doubt had we not shown up. I couldn't have that on my conscience.

The watchman suit I wore became much tighter around the neck, constricting underneath my pits. I found myself sweating in places that I hadn't noticed before. I'd be drenched in no time from my own sweat. I couldn't remember a time when I was that afraid of everything going wrong.

As we walked along the path, people slowed to stare. The Impure girl in the watchman's suit.

"What are you staring at?" Avi said to one of the gawkers.

The woman clutched her chest and hurried away.

I stepped in front of Avi. "What the hell are you doing? Trying to blow our cover?"

"Of course not."

"I know you're still upset, but you'll never have to see me again after today. Does that make it better?"

"Much," she said and shoved me aside.

I didn't care much for this version of Avi.

Avi approached the receptionist's desk as I waited close by. The receptionist eyed me over Avi's shoulder and crossed her arms over her chest. What had Avi said to piss her off? The girl was ruining it already as she fumbled with the reader, then handed it to the woman. The receptionist put on her glasses and scanned the fake documents. She handed the reader back and tapped the screen. A male's face popped up.

"Please escort Elite Jore to Storage Room Delta," the receptionist said in a nasally tone.

A physician emerged from a secured door and led Avi inside. I eyed every person who walked past. Detailing every movement, every ear tug and sneeze and dig into a slimpack. Making myself look even more guilty. I had forgotten how to be discreet, or maybe I was overthinking everything because this could be the place I died. I felt every curly strand of hair on the nape of my wet neck. Where was the nearest exit? Should I abandon ship? Leave now while I still had a chance? Let Avi deal with it. She thought she was so grown and experienced anyhow. Did she really even need me?

I checked the time as the minutes wore on. What was she doing in there, having tea?

Finally, she emerged with a hard-shell case. My body sighed internally with relief.

"We're on our way out," Avi said into the earpiece, wearing a grin of triumph.

The energy shifted. People around us moved slower, more deliberate. The receptionist's eyes shifted toward the entrance. My throat went dry. I weighed my options. Pulling my weapon. Running. Telling Avi to run. But by that time, we were already surrounded. I knew that sound from anywhere. The boots of watchmen came from the revolving door. They swarmed from all the orifices of the lobby. A physician appeared with another gang of watchmen at his side from the door Avi had just exited from.

"ETA?" Drake asked through the channel.

"Put the case down, and put your hands where I can see them!" a watchman shouted. Avi and I looked at each other.

I placed my hands up, but Avi refused. "I am Elite Jore. Put away your weapons—and that is an order."

The men didn't budge.

"I will relieve each and every one of you." She commanded, "Step away from the door, and allow my watchman and me to pass."

Avi tested the waters and moved forward. The watchmen stayed in place.

"Elite Jore, put the case down and raise your hands."

"Anytime now," I whispered to Drake.

"Damn it," she replied, and then there was static.

That was the end of that. They'd be long gone after they'd set off the explosives, killing whoever was in the way of the blast. I had the urge to kick myself for going along with this cockamamie plan, knowing the risks. Two things were for sure. We'd be crushed to death with the vials, or we'd make it out, and I'd be put to death for defying the Union.

"Come on," I told her. "It's over."

Avi refused to accept defeat and clutched the case. "You won't shoot me," she said.

"No, but we will shoot her." Dozens of weapons migrated toward my head and torso. Kill shots.

"Avi," I said, backing away slowly.

She rubbed the stress from her forehead. "There's a bomb located in this building, and if you shoot her, I will discharge it."

The stakes just got higher.

"You're bluffing!" the physician announced.

"It's voice activated," she lied. "I won't hesitate. Move out of our way."

A watchman behind him spoke calmly into his wristcom, probably calling for an evacuation and alerting the hidden guards to scour the place for bombs.

"You would kill your own for this Impure filth?" He baited her. "What would your father say, your mother?"

Avi fought the shame that I knew she was feeling. Having to choose a side wasn't all it was cracked up to be.

There was a thump on the roof. Watchmen pointed their guns toward the disturbance. The physician covered his head. "One of you idiots go see what that is."

Drake's voice came over the channel. "You might want to stand back."

An explosion. Rubble collapsed around us. Avi tumbled back. A gaping hole was right above the main desk; a ray of light shone through it. As the dust settled, Drake and Liyo rappelled down. They were absolutely mad, but I wasn't complaining.

"Come on!" Drake stuck her arm out.

Avi and I bolted and latched on to the pair. The ropes recoiled quickly as we jetted toward the craft. Just as we hit the top of the ceiling, watchmen unloaded ammo.

"Take us up, Dee." Drake slammed the cargo hold shut.

The hovervehicle's engines cranked as Dee lifted us into the dull atmosphere. Drake pressed a button, and from the small circular window, we watched the second explosion unfold. They blew up that branch. I couldn't believe the havoc they'd wreaked on the oppressors. I'd be lying if I didn't feel satisfaction seeing them burn. Seeing them run from the flames, terrified. They'd get only a piece of what they'd done to me. A gaping hole filled with smoke and fire bloomed into the sky.

Liyo was too enthralled with the case to care about the spectacular show we'd sparked. He opened the lid and basked in the glow of the substance that floated inside the delicate vials.

"You really did it," he said to Avi, hugging her.

Our celebration was brief, and the Union was officially pissed. Drake yelled from the deck, "We've got company."

"Everyone to their seats!" Dee ordered.

I snapped the chest straps across my body and watched Liyo take hold of Avi's hand. Why was he still playing this role? If it was even a role at all.

There was a faint whistling sound. Dee had managed to maneuver the craft, and we saw the missile explode midair. Another whirring, then another. They were relentless. Dee jerked the joystick control as we wove in and out of the clouds, but it wasn't enough. We were struck. With each hit, the craft would bounce and jerk. The last missile tore into the back end of the craft, blowing it off completely. The lights flickered, and the wind hit me so hard that I could barely breathe or think of the next move. Equipment got sucked through the hole. My slimpack flew out too. Dee tried his best to hang on, but he was swept out with everything else after yet another hit took out the front cabin. With the case of vials.

The last thing I saw was the ground hurtling toward us.

❖   ❖   ❖

I woke up to pure mayhem. I was upside down, still attached by the hovercraft's seat straps. Fires were scattered like seeds on top of splintered wood and chunks of the wreckage. I was in and out of consciousness. Every time I awakened, I heard an incessant ringing. Real-life time was chopped into portions, some short, others long. Liyo was on the ground. His hair covered in gray fragments. I knew Avi was screaming because her mouth was the widest I'd ever seen it. Her tonsils bobbed, and her eyes pinched shut.

I blacked out again.

When I woke, Drake met my eyes. Somehow, she knew what I wanted. She crawled over and pulled Avi off Liyo's body. Avi tried to fight Drake but was quickly overpowered and dragged away.

It was just Liyo and me left.

I unfastened myself and fell to the ground, hard. The sloppy landing caused instant pain. I clawed my way to him, with each movement a throb that I couldn't ignore. I flipped him over and laid him in my lap. I nudged his face. He wouldn't respond. Ratch! His head just flopped around. I called his name so many times as if that were the magic needed to wake him. I breathed air into him. Every second waiting felt like years had passed. I laid him on his back and breathed again, more forcefully, emptying out my lungs, and then I pumped on his chest until he finally gasped.

Lights from their weapons flashed before they arrived.

Watchmen and bots trained lasers on us; our bodies were coated in red dots. I pulled the gun from my ankle.

It was time.

I fired lasers into the herd. A last-ditch effort before the road terminated.

Liyo sat up as if a cord from the skies had pulled him. Lasers had already come from each gun. He held out his hand. The illumination started slight, then overtook his arm and grew up his shoulder like a plant. The barrels' openings flashed with yellow and red. The lasers took on a cherry color as they whizzed in slow motion, angled over one another. Liyo's chest sank. His energy drained as he used his power to protect us from being as full of holes as a lotus root. I laid my hand inside the light radiating from his arm. It entered my body and filled me. His eyes drifted and rolled back. He wasn't going to make it.

I whispered something in his ear.

His arm dropped. The radiance subsided. The frozen laser beams fell, but it gave us enough time to escape into the woods. My hearing had come back in one ear; the other was still foggy. The good one picked up on how close the watchmen were. Shouts filled the vicinity as fumes that reeked of burnt grass and metal almost smoked us out of hiding. Liyo was heavy on my shoulder and barely able to walk straight. His head flopped around like a newborn's.

We both tumbled into a duct filled with shallow water. Liyo was facedown in it, so weak that he couldn't even lift his face to keep from drowning. I flipped him over and dragged him to the fine wet gravel. He spat up, drooled water dribbling down the sides of his mouth.

"Leave"—he was barely able to say—"me."

Watchmen were right above us, shuffling in the undergrowth. "I've thought of that."

"Go." He closed his eyes.

Every moment that I sat idle thinking about leaving him or not was another moment wasted. I couldn't get to the Border, with or without him. They'd find me trekking through the brush.

Once it was quiet again, we wandered with no destination. The wind had picked up. Damp leaves brushed past my skin while thistles pricked at my calves.

Liyo collapsed. I tried lifting him again, but he wouldn't budge. "I can't go any farther. My leg."

I propped him against a trunk and tore the fabric of his bodysuit. His ankle was swollen, purple. His face was caked with perspiration and soot. Every time he closed his eyes, he resembled a lump of coal.

"Stay here." I dragged him backward into the undergrowth. "I'm going to find help."

I tore branches covered in leaves down and placed them over the exposed areas. "Stay quiet, and don't move until I come back."

"That won't be an issue," he said with a smile that I remembered too well.

I thought about going to the Farmlands, seeking help from his people, but that was too obvious. The watchmen would check there first for us. Pea had probably already been detained and questioned. Still, I kept going, hiding behind trees and dipping into bushes, when a twig snapped.

A light was flashed in my direction.

Had I been caught?

"Stop where you are," Instructor Skylar said, his gun pointed at me. I held my hands up but cowered lower in the brush.

He scowled. "What happened to you meeting me back at the Citadel?"

I was going to have to end him right there. There were no other options. He'd alert the others. I had to protect Liyo, myself. And if that meant removing an obstacle, then so be it. Unfortunately, killing him wouldn't be as easy as pulling the trigger. If any weapons discharged, the rest would hear them. I had to play it cool for now.

"Please," I managed to say.

"Please?" Lines riddled his forehead.

I didn't want to hurt him. He was decent.

"I need your help," I said. "Please."

"Have you found anything, Instructor?" a watchman yelled from afar.

As his attention went to the voice, my hand hovered over my gun.

"No, nothing here!" He finally lowered his weapon. "Keep searching that way. I think I heard something."

I was able to breathe again.

"Where's Avi?" He stepped closer.

"Safe," I said. "Can you help me?"

He trailed me back to Liyo, who had already passed out. I was surprised that Instructor Skylar didn't ask any questions. He scooped Liyo up.

❖ ❖ ❖

Once we were inside his dwellings, the Instructor told me to shut all the windows and lock every entrance. He placed Liyo on a steel table and began mending his ankle.

"Is everything secure?" Instructor Skylar asked when I returned.

"Yes." I stood beside him and watched him laser Liyo's bones. "What do we do now?"

"Wait it out."

"Wait it out?" I exclaimed. "We've got to get out now. We aren't safe here."

Liyo woke up in the middle of the procedure.

"Hold him down," Instructor Skylar ordered.

"Where are—ahhhh!" Liyo yelled.

"Shhh." I placed my hand over his mouth. "You have to be quiet."

When he finished repairing Liyo, the Instructor snapped off his gloves and tossed bloody towels into the incinerator.

I flung Liyo's arm around my shoulder and hoisted him to a standing position. "Don't put any weight on it just yet."

We limped into the Instructor's quarters, where he intently watched the broadcasts. A crisis announcement. Red banners ran across the top and bottom of the screen.

"This is an emergency broadcast from Union of Civilization Frequency Modulation." A correspondent with two-strand twists announced, "This afternoon armed subjects entered the Health Department."

They paused the surveillance tape and zoomed in on our faces. "Elite Avi Jore, daughter of General Jore, and a newly appointed Impure watchman gone rogue, Saige Wilde, who has a long list of pardoned criminal offenses ranging from conspiracy to harming a political leader, were caught on camera. At this time, we're not sure whether Elite Jore was under duress during this heist, but what we do know is that the rebels are behind this heinous crime."

The next clip showed the explosion and then Drake and Liyo rappelling into the Health Department. The footage zoomed in again. They placed both of their worker numbers and names on the screen.

"And now to Correspondent James, who is on-site at this horrific scene," she said. "Can you tell us what's happening on the ground level?"

Workers and Uppers covered in soot from the blast ran in zigzags behind the journalist. "Yes, we are here. We are speaking to a woman who was in the building when the blast happened. She explained that she was nearly crushed by a piece of the ceiling and barely made it out with her life intact."

An Upper Resident woman snatched the mic from James. "The region would like to know—I would like to know—why an Impure, a criminal, was even appointed to a position as high as a watchman. It just doesn't seem stable of the General, the cabinet, to make such a frivolous move, placing not only us but the region in harm's way."

This was really, really bad. "Ratch," I said under my breath.

"You are right, Saige." Instructor Skylar began pulling weapons from covert spots in the floorboards and strapping them to holsters on his body. "We can't stay here."

Pictures of all four of us filled the screen. "If you have any information on these assailants, please contact your—"

The holoscreen cut the broadcast and was replaced by a strange static.

"Look." Liyo pointed. "Look!"

Mama Seeya was covered by shade. Only a single light hit her brown face in the monitor. She was born Impure like me, but because she wasn't too light, she was able to pass as an Upper for many years before she turned to the rebellion. She could've lived a good life, but she opted to sacrifice herself for the whole. I'd always admired her for that, but I could never find that same courage, that same moral compass she possessed.

She sat there for a good while, just staring down the camera with those warm, dark eyes—one lower than the other. Her hair was dark too. In fat Bantu knots. The edges riddled with gray strands from age, from stress, from war.

"Welcome to hell on earth," she said simply. "For a long time, hell was only distributed to us, the ones on the bottom from the ones at the very top." She illustrated the levels with a flat hand.

"Every great power must fall. We have seen it occur in history. Time after time after time. None of us are invincible, no matter how much we pillage and hoard and misuse and abuse the systems. It only takes one little ripple to cause the blocks to come tumbling down. Only one. And, for the Union, your time is up."

More static.

Her address sent chills through my spine. Mama Seeya was back, and she'd just tipped the scale a little more.

Avi was now on the screen. She had cuts on her face and a busted lip and dried blood near her ear, and her hair had those gray specks stuck in it from the crash.

"How'd she hack into the system?" I asked without taking my eyes off her.

"Drake," Liyo replied. "Computers are her thing."

Instructor Skylar switched channels. Avi was on the next one too. And the one after that.

She smoothed her hair back, but it only popped right back into its untidy position. "My name is Avi Jore, the succeeding General. Daughter of General Jore and Vivienne Jore." Her voice cracked. "I don't have much time. They are breaking in as I speak."

In the background, watchmen banged against whatever barrier she had placed between herself and them.

"Elites, Upper Residents, and workers. We have all been living a sham. The Union has betrayed us. My family has betrayed the Southern Region. The Union has created the rebels by misuse of power and deception. They've created deadly supplements to kill off the entire race." Her body trembled as if she'd been doused with a blast of cold air. "How is it morally right to starve, imprison, allow another human to go through an excruciating illness resulting in death?"

She paused, listening to the watchmen pound away. Her voice rose to drown out the continuous hammers. "I'm not acting under the influence of any rebel or man. I'm only trying to make things right and make this a just society. The society we all deserve—have the opportunity to still be. I will not be run out of my own region. I will take over and lead justly as planned. If you just give me a chance to correct these misdoings. I'm going to reform the Union if it takes my last breath. But I need you, my people, to stand tall and support me, support the new world, and place humanity back in order." She gave a weak smile.

"They're coming for me. If you can hear me out there, if you can see me, don't stop fighting for what you believe. Don't ever stop, because when you do is when you have truly lost the battle."

Watchmen barged in. Placed a dark sack over her head and whisked her away.

Another watchman stepped in front of the camera and shot it.

The screen went dark.

Instructor Skylar strapped a band of weapons across his chest. "We're going to the Border."

We sailed above the trees in a private hovercraft. Liyo stayed quiet, shooting me odd looks, not sure what I had gotten us into. Hell, I didn't even know what I had gotten us into.

Instructor Skylar remained as focused as if neither of us were even there, which made me more nervous. He was usually obnoxiously talkative. Why was he even helping us in the first place?

I unbuckled my chest strap.

Liyo's brows gathered. "Where are you going?"

"To talk to him."

"Let's take him out, take the craft."

"No," I said. "No more."

I stood next to Instructor Skylar as he navigated the controls.

"Avi," he said. "I knew she had it in her."

I admitted, "She's definitely got some balls."

Instructor Skylar pointed as we approached the Border. It was a massive structure, an endless fortress with tall silver watchtowers placed at every mile of wall space. Watchmen were inside, on top, and at the bottom, scanning the grounds.

"Have you decided whether to take me out yet?" Instructor Skylar asked.

"I wasn't—"

"You don't have to explain. If I were you, I'd be suspicious too."

"Why are you doing all of this?"

"The question is, Why wouldn't I?"

I grimaced. "What?"

"I've wanted to expose the General for quite some time now. Ever since he killed my father and made it look like he'd committed treason."

"Don't tell me you're some covert rebel."

"No, I'm more of a double agent," he said. "After my father's death, I couldn't understand why he would defy the Union. He was a man of honor. He'd found out what the General had planned and was repulsed. My father tracked your mother down. They came up with a plan. They knew they were going to die, but they wanted to save you. You'd be proof of the General's infidelity.

"The Union needed someone to pin it on. Everything is a spectacle with them. They would blame your birth on my father to cover for the General. He was furious when my father set you free. My father has been known as a traitor since then, and I vowed to do whatever I could to find and protect you as my father had. The General must be exposed, but sadly, now is not the time. You and Liyo must go to the other side and wait."

Wait. He wanted me to wait. It all sounded so simple. Bulletproof. But I knew that things would only get harder, more complicated from here on out. There were too many things the Instructor had said for me to even process. I had to file it all away, leave it where it was until another time. I was sure I'd have lots of it on the other side. I was fleeing from the unknown into just another version. Escaping was all I'd ever dreamed of, but now faced with the opportunity, I wasn't so sure.

One extreme to the next.

There was nothing more to say. To question. No reassurance. It'd be dumb for me to ask Instructor Skylar if there was another option. Any option. We were shit out of luck and out of picks. If we went back, we died. End of discussion.

I looked back at Liyo. He shot me a weak smile. I looked forward at the gigantic Border. Funny how the universe functioned. It had brought us back together again, just like he'd always wanted, like Mama Seeya had predicted. I was still unsure about what I wanted exactly in the end, but I was sure of one thing. I'd lived because others had sacrificed themselves. For me. They had left me on earth to fulfill a purpose, and it was not to escape but, instead, to take the General down.

He took Ma's life.

And now he needed to pay with his.

Chapter Thirty-Six
AVI

I was imprisoned in my quarters. For how long, unknown. I carved lines underneath the window to keep count, sunrise and sunset. One. Sunrise. Sunset. Two, three, four. But after a certain point, I didn't even have the energy to continue.

During an initial search sanctioned by Father, watchmen had seized every gadget: reader, the bot, and even my wristcom. Objects I had once thought I needed to survive. Nourishment was brought by workers. Even workers that I had grown up with treated me like an inmate, locking me in before and after every removal of trays. They were not allowed to answer any questions either. After the first few days of failed communication attempts, I stopped speaking altogether.

The routine was the same. When I wasn't thinking about Saige or Liyo, I would force myself to read old books that I had collected from the Archives. Most of the time, it didn't work, and my mind would replay every possible scenario of how they had escaped to the other side or died. Was one deceased and the other alive? Both killed? Both alive? One badly hurt? Had Father found them and just hadn't notified me yet as further punishment?

What had he done to them?

I set my slumber pod to the highest amount of sleep time allotted; that was the only way to escape into my dreams and be exactly where I wanted, swathed in Liyo's arms, lying on his chest in some meadow that I had never visited before. The vivid dreams had begun the last night I'd seen him in the ruins. The dreams always continued on from the previous one. I wished he would speak to me in the dreams, but he never said a word. I was starting to forget how he sounded.

One day, watchmen rushed through my door. I dropped an open book that had rested in my lap as they grabbed my arms and launched me into the corridors. They were walking so fast that I couldn't keep up. I was dragged. Their boots echoed with each clomp. Workers covered their mouths in disbelief as their leader was treated like one of them.

They took me to the area of the Citadel where Saige had been sentenced when she'd first arrived. A simple stool sat on a glowing podium. They flung me onto it, and my bare feet became stuck to the base, just as Saige's had. My moist palms lay flat on my thighs as I contemplated what Father was going to say, do to me.

I'd made the government look weak. I'd given workers hope. I had to be penalized for my disloyalties.

Every cabinet member, Father, Head Gardner, Commander Chi, and Instructor Skylar were present.

Mother held a handkerchief to her mouth and could barely make eye contact with me.

Jade was there. Of course. I'd expected her to be shocked that I hadn't died in the Subdivisions like she'd planned and fearful that I'd expose her devious plot, but Jade knew that I had no proof of what she and Head Gardner had done. They'd covered their tracks well. So it was my word against theirs, and Father would never believe me.

"Elite Avi Jore, you have been accused of treason against the Union. What is your plea?" Father asked, typing on a translucent panel.

Mother couldn't bear it any longer; she burst into wails and slid from her seat, falling into a pool of bones and skin. Watchmen rushed to her side and led her away. Her shrieks were full of a mother's pain.

I cringed.

Father frowned but continued. "What is your plea?"

I remained silent. Father had refused to speak with me before that day. Why should I have to speak to him?

He said, "Very well, then."

A monitor materialized. Every picture that I'd taken of Liyo in the greenhouse had been enlarged. Jade settled into her chair, pleased by her discovery. I knew that Father had analyzed the photos beforehand and just wanted to show this to make me unravel. Give him the information he wanted, needed so badly. I didn't care what he had on me, on Liyo, or on Saige. I wasn't going to give in.

"What say you of this evidence?"

I remained like a stone, cold. Still.

He nodded, and a physician made his way to the floor. He began dissecting the photo of the floating objects.

"I'm Physician Odom. I specialize in physics, microgravity, and astronomy. My team and I have investigated the evidence thoroughly. The findings have been peculiar yet amazing to say the least. I would also like to add that the research conducted by Dr. Jore on unlocking the brain waves was phenomenal." His laugh sounded like a snort. "We first looked at the validity of the photos. Due to increasing technological advancements in modern editing software, a picture can be manipulated into, quite frankly, anything."

Father leaned in, holding his beard like it was going to be snatched off.

"The items that are suspended around the subject," he said, pointing to a few with his laser, "are not held by any invisible lines or added to the photo by any software that we could locate. They are suspended by what seems to be the subject."

"How?" Father's torso was almost halfway over the bureau.

"That's where the peculiarity comes in." Physician Odom sniffed. "We do not know exactly."

"How is it that you do not know?" Commander Chi's voice rose. "What kind of dark magic do these workers possess?"

"Magic? Perhaps." The physician rested his chin in his hand. "There is one theory that hasn't been explored since Dr. Jore passed. Current physicians completely disproved the hypothesis at one point."

"Well?" Commander Chi's eyes became prominent.

Physician Odom huffed on his glasses and wiped them on his sleeve. "Telekinesis."

The crowd gasped in unison.

"Telekinesis, or psychokinetic abilities, allows a person to influence physical change without physical interaction. A few examples are the abilities to move objects, levitate, and in some instances, even teleport."

"By the planets and all that exists in between, this type of sorcery can only be categorized as some sort of evil," Commander Chi said.

"Human teleportation?" Father sat back. I could see his mind working out probable outcomes.

"That's why it's imperative that we locate this specimen. Run tests." Physician Odom turned his head and spoke directly to me. "You wouldn't happen to know where he is, would you?"

I felt the urge to spit at him, but I knew better.

"Gratitude, Physician Odom," Father said.

When the members had calmed themselves, Father began to probe me further. Every time I failed to answer, veins protruded from his neck and temples. Soon, one would surely burst.

"This is how you want it to end? You want to protect an Impure and a Chattel worker. They discarded you as soon as you served your purpose. Left you to take the brunt of the punishment. You were manipulated and used. I cannot for the life of me understand what you don't get about that fact," he said. "And you sit in front of the Union, unapologetic for aiding our enemies. This is what you've chosen? This is where your loyalty lies? You have failed me as a daughter and as an Elite. Your actions are deplorable, and frankly, I can't stand the sight of you."

Before, I would've cried—wailed even—at his feet, begging for his forgiveness. The words he uttered were fueled by hate and false pride. No one could deny what I had seen with my own eyes and heard with my own ears. The Union was criminal. What he failed to understand was that I was not the same person I had always been. He just couldn't accept that I wasn't that naive girl anymore.

And Father was no longer a father. He had finally become just the General to me. General Jore.

"Do you love him?" His eyes were wet with anticipation, maybe pain.

Nothing.

"I can see it, that sputter of hope that one day you will be reunited and run away to no-man's-land and create Impures. My pure blood coursing through them." His voice rose to a harsh yell as he raised himself. "I can guarantee that it will never happen, not as long as I breathe. You have embarrassed your people, your family. And for your treachery and your inability to cooperate, others will be punished because of you. They will be killed because of you. But I cannot imprison you with the real criminals because they will rip their little savior to shreds. I have something better in mind. I will hunt both of them down. With or without you. I will find them. And as the universe is my witness, I will have both their skulls as ornaments in my study."

I closed my eyes. I believed he'd act on every one of his threats.

"And as for you, my dear daughter, you will marry Phoenix. You will obey him, tend to his every need. You will gain back the trust of this family. And you will both rule and create pure Elites as planned. You are mine, Avi. Mine! Do you hear me?"

The tears started coming.

"Get her out of my company," Father ordered the watchmen.

I was dragged away.

❖ ❖ ❖

I was bombarded by that same trio of stylists and designers who wanted me to choose and finalize every detail of the expedited matrimonial ceremony. Mother was finally able to talk to me without sobbing. She was always around, smothering me, when all I wanted was to be alone. She seemed excited about the nuptials, though. I tried my best to smile and gesture when appropriate. I still hadn't gotten used to speaking; everything I wanted to say usually remained locked inside.

On one occasion, as Mother and I sifted through fine lace samples, I excused myself to use the lavatory. I didn't really need to use it. I just needed to breathe for a moment, but on the way, I heard workers shushing one another to listen to the broadcasts. I slowly approached the open quarter and concealed myself behind the partition.

The news of the rebellion had taken over every airway. It was how I found out about Liyo and Saige. I was pleased to know that no bodies had been discovered in the wreckage and that they were still at large. Their faces were plastered across the screen: wanted and dangerous. For some reason, I had a feeling that they'd made it out of the region. I hoped so.

Father hadn't figured it out. Yet. But if he ever did, he was going to hit them with every resource he had.

The journalist reported that over the past weeks, workers had been detained for treason and questioned. They showed clips of watchmen swarming cubes. The camera went back to the journalist, who said that new and more restrictive bylaws had been passed to ensure the safety of Upper Residents.

Knowing Father and how angry he was, I already knew that there were going to be harsher rules enacted.

One of the workers turned off the holoscreen. "They only show what they want us to see. Watchmen have come into our homes and pulled people out of their pods and made them get to their knees. I've seen it." Her lip trembled. "They lined them up and shot them in the heads."

She wept. Another worker allowed her to lay her head on her shoulder.

"They weren't questioned. They weren't tried. They just blew their brains out. Oh, God."

"Please, Mary. They'll hear you." The other shushed her. "You have to be quiet."

I felt a small hand on my shoulder. When I turned around, I was relieved. It was little Pea with a sideways smirk. I fell into her with open arms. She wept quietly into my neck, which made me tear up too.

"I missed you, madam," she whispered in my ear. "He wouldn't let me see you. I tried. I really tried."

I smoothed her hair. "You don't have to explain."

Pea wiped her nose with her sleeve. "I have something to tell you."

"Go on."

"We saw you." Checking behind herself, she said, "And we are with you. All of us."

I fiddled with the hem of my sleeve and erupted into a fit of laughter, like some sort of crazy woman. Pea smiled. I didn't need to ask questions. The rebels had seen me. And if they had, I knew Liyo and Saige had too.

Pea and I heard a violent, whooping cough. We spun around and saw a worker stagger and knock a vase from the counter. The glass shattered into large bits. Workers led the sickly man to a chair.

"So. Hot," he got out.

They slipped his arms out of his sanitizing pack and used plates to fan him.

His face was as chalky as if he had never been in the sun. Faint purple blotches circled his eyes. He coughed into the fabric of his bodysuit, and streaks of blood dotted the sleeve.

"Get him fluids," someone ordered.

He began convulsing.

Pea held me, stopping me from going any farther.

"Don't," she said as I looked back at her.

One worker held his head, the other held his arms, and the third pulled out a syringe of pale green liquid. She flicked off the excess. After yanking his sleeve up, she injected it. As it slowly entered his vein, his body calmed.

I couldn't stay hidden for long.

"Is he—?" I knelt at his side and placed my fingers on his pulse. It was weak, but he was still alive.

The worker tried to hide the syringe behind her hip.

"Let me see it," I ordered.

She handed it over. "Yes, madam."

I held the tube to the light. Inside were the remnants of the substance. Somehow, they had done it.

Drake must've found the case from the wreckage.

They had figured out a way to extract a serum for the workers to combat the virus.

There was still hope.

Epilogue
LIYO

It's quiet.

But occasionally, in the distance, I can hear gray wolves howling and caribou snorting. The sun rarely shines here. It's usually hidden behind heavy clouds and mountains covered in snow. There's so much snow, always falling in the night. Even though I know the snowfall is continuous, I still can't bring myself to expect it every single day.

The winter is brutal.

In the morning, I crawl to the mouth of the cave and gather a handful of the fluffy substance. I watch it until it melts and slowly drips between my dry knuckles. This is my only form of entertainment.

Because I'm sick.

And Saige won't allow me outside to hunt, to breathe, until my illness breaks.

She leaves before I wake and returns late with fish, a bag full of shrews, or if she's lucky, a plump hare. She uses a spear that she made from a long piece of wood, twine, and a bit of metal she found in the caverns. I watched as she scraped and shaped the metal along a rock into a sturdy weapon.

She has a corner that she claimed when we first arrived. There she skins and hangs her catch from a makeshift rack. I don't know how she did it, but she once speared two wolves. She couldn't drag them both back, so she returned with a pile of furry gray skins and a lump of meat. Together we pieced the hides into coats, hats, and boot coverings. Other than that task, I feel useless. My strength is limited, and there is only so much I'm able to do.

I built a fire without her knowing. It took all the little energy that I had stored, but it's the least I can do. She nods once in appreciation and lays the meat over the rough cage. While the meat smokes over the flames, I grab a stick with crooked spikes and flip the pieces.

They feel so heavy, but I have to do this.

My arm begins to shake on the last piece. I'm sweating, struggling. Saige turns around and asks if I'm okay. Fine, I say. But I'm not fine at all. On the other slab, she eyes me with intensity. The orange specks in her irises light like a cat's. I get nervous on top of the weakness of my arm. I can't manage to turn over the last piece. Sweat drips down my face and rolls along the edge of my nose. My whole body vibrates, and my breaths are forced. I fall back; Saige catches me before I hit my head on a rock.

I feel like crying. I'm a man. And I can't flip a piece of meat.

"You need to rest," she says, looking down on me.

"Do you remember when we all crashed in the forest, and you whispered in my ear?"

Saige's face shifts. After a pause, she says, "I don't know what you're talking about." Then she says, "The meat is going to burn."

I grab her wrist so she doesn't leave like she always does when things get emotional. "It took some time to remember," I say, "but you said that you needed me. Is it true?"

I have never seen her look so uncomfortable. She's always so sure and confident. For those few moments, I see the old her, the one without all the walls up.

"Pillow talk," she responds and tends to the meat.

I didn't know how much words could hurt. What do I expect from her? A happily ever after?

After that, I don't bother her, and she doesn't bother me. We are left to our own selves. Perhaps I'm only an accessory to her. She is a survivalist, and with or without me, I'm sure she'll make it. Sometimes, I get these thoughts. Maybe they are delusions of the illness, maybe not, but I think that Saige couldn't care less whether I live. I was never in her plans when she thought about escaping. Somehow, being here, outside the barrier, was in everyone else's.

While my people are tortured, I sit inside a dark cave, weak and trapped like an injured animal.

At night, I know she thinks I'm sleeping, but I'm usually wide awake. It's the only time she drifts off. During those hours, I think about leaving, sneaking away, and going back to the Border, returning to my people—to Avi, even, to explain my side of the story. But I know better than that. Plus, the Union isn't going to allow me back in that easy. They'd kill me on sight.

Who am I kidding? I can't even stand for more than a minute. So I'm stuck with her.

Lost.

I think of Avi often.

We kissed. That wasn't part of the plan. Somehow, I can't get her off my mind. Thinking of her spares me the loneliness of the cave.

Saige is here, but then again, she isn't.

I worry about Avi. The Union isn't kind to traitors. She's being punished. I know it. She went against her own for the cause. That meant something. She trusted me. A worker. She risked her life to make the Union's treachery known. I owe it to her to survive and to fight. And I owe it to my people.

I need to return, protect her as she did me. No one—not even her father or the entire Union—is going to keep me away from my family. My people need me. I'm their savior, and I will fight beside them until the end. I'm in hiding now, but believe me, I'm planning. And when I'm stronger, I will go back full force, and the Union won't know what hit them.

The General is first.

AUTHOR'S NOTE

Why I wrote it:

Ah, here we are. A whole book. A published series. *The Union* has been my problem child for well over eight years. My baby has gone through so many transformations as I have watched her grow and morph into a finished multicultural dystopian novel.

She started out when I was in a bad place in life. She was the only thing I could look forward to creating when I was at a dead-end job in Michigan that made my eye twitch involuntarily with every clock-in. I was broke—like selling my plasma for thirty-five bucks broke—in an MFA program. I was married to a high school sweetheart, a marriage that ended up in a nasty divorce almost a decade later. All these things and more occurred while writing and editing this very story. I went from "this is really, really great" to "this is really, really stupid" more times than I can count.

The hope that all my pain turned into art, turned into words, turned into a cohesive story was what got me through the toughest parts of my journey.

To say that *The Union* saved my life is a sore understatement.

The power of a series of individual words being strung together. A story. The power behind seeing oneself in a character is much deeper, much more profound. Everyone deserves to be seen and truly represented.

I wrote this story because the characters spoke to me—as they always do. I wrote it because I was so into seeing Black people, People of Color, in the future. What would it look like, feel like? In our current world, what would it feel like as a Black girl to be on top? To have every privilege that the privileged had?

I would dive into dystopian novels, and too many times, one thing was always missing. Us. In their stories, we hadn't really existed. And if we had, we were one dimensional.

"If there's a book that you want to read, but it hasn't been written yet, then you must write it."

Toni Morrison's quote has stuck with me for a long, long time.

So that's what I did. I wrote it.

ACKNOWLEDGMENTS

It's been almost a decade since I first picked up a pen and started jotting down the characters for *The Union*. How time flies.

Because I'm a Leo, I'd like to start off by thanking myself. *The Union* was rejected and then rejected some more. I put this story on the shelf—multiple shelves and drawers, to be exact—many, many times.

I never thought she'd see a bookstore shelf.

I give thanks to myself because I never gave up on Saige, on Avi, on myself. Because had it not been for my inability to take no for an answer, we would not be celebrating such a momentous occasion.

A shout-out to my agent, Penelope Burns with Gelfman Schneider / ICM Partners, for answering random distress calls during sleep hours and for putting me at ease when I acted like—well, an author. She loves it, though. Melissa Valentine, who acquired my book when everyone else had their head in the clouds. I love an editor who's willing to take risks. Adrienne Procaccini, who took over for the second half. And everyone at the Amazon Publishing team who's had their hand in making this dream become reality. Thank you, a gazillion times.

My former Wilkes University MFA mentor, Taylor Polites, who marked up the mess out of my earlier drafts and caused me to cry because I thought he hated my story. But looking back, I know he just wanted to make it better. When I asked him to tell me how not to make people uncomfortable with my book, he told me that I shouldn't write to make people comfortable—I should just tell the story. It was simple yet so profound.

I initially self-published this book because I had been rejected by dozens of editors and publishing companies. A shout-out to all eighty-nine people who purchased the very early and rougher versions that I had poured all my savings into during a nasty divorce. And my big sister, Tonisha, for coming to the readings with my nieces to support my crazy ideas. Y'all are some real ones.

I want to shout out my dear writer and Gemini friend, Leigh Green, for putting me on track when I wanted to toss the whole manuscript into a dumpster and set it ablaze. You know what you did!

Last but certainly not least, I want to thank the universe for allowing all my manifestations to come true.

And last-last, the readers. Whew! Who would I be without y'all! My readers, my fans, my community: the V-Hive continuously shows up for me. You make it possible for me to do the impossible. I am forever indebted and forever grateful.

ABOUT THE AUTHOR

Photo © 2020 Maryam Saad

Leah Vernon is an author, body-positive activist, and the first interna-
tional plus-size Hijabi model. During her double master's program, she
started a blog about being a fat Black Muslim in Detroit experiencing
everything from eating disorders to anti-Blackness. She's been featured in
ads from Target to Old Navy and even made it to the *New York Times* and
HuffPost. She currently resides in New York City. Connect with her on
Instagram (@lvernon2000) and on her website: www.LeahVernon.com.